I0651389

Sofia Vasilevna Kovalevskaia

Sónya Kovalévsky

Her recollections of childhood

Sofia Vasilevna Kovalevskaia

Sónya Kovalévsky
Her recollections of childhood

ISBN/EAN: 9783337218218

Printed in Europe, USA, Canada, Australia, Japan

Cover: Foto ©Raphael Reischuk / pixelio.de

More available books at **www.hansebooks.com**

SÓNYA KOVALÉVSKY

HER RECOLLECTIONS OF CHILDHOOD

TRANSLATED FROM THE
RUSSIAN BY ISABEL F. HAPGOOD

WITH A BIOGRAPHY BY ANNA
CARLOTTA LEFFLER, DUCHESS OF CAJANELLO

TRANSLATED FROM THE
SWEDISH BY A. M. CLIVE BAYLEY

AND A BIOGRAPHICAL
NOTE BY LILY WOLFFSOHN

NEW YORK
THE CENTURY CO
1895

Sónya Kovalévsky unfortunately dropped the thread of her delightful Recollections at a point just before the direct foundations of her future fame were laid. It is a piece of good fortune for the world that so clever and sympathetic a hand as that of her friend, the Duchess of Cajanello, picked up that thread of mingled strands—pure gold entwined with black.

Sónya's Recollections of her Childhood and the Duchess's memoir of her after career, as combined in this volume, furnish a wonderfully perfect mental and spiritual record of a woman upon whom the union of a masculine mind with a feminine heart imposed the difficult task of solving diametrically opposite problems which all women, gifted or otherwise, must face.

CONTENTS

RECOLLECTIONS OF CHILDHOOD
BY SÓNYA KOVALÉVSKY

TRANSLATED FROM THE RUSSIAN
BY ISABEL F. HAPGOOD

RECOLLECTIONS OF CHILDHOOD

I

I SHOULD like to know whether any one can definitely fix that moment of his existence when, for the first time, a distinct conception of his own personality, his own *ego*, the first glimmer of conscious life, arose within him. I cannot, in the least. When I begin to sort out and classify my earliest recollections, the same thing always happens with me: these recollections disperse before me. At times it seems to me that I have found that first definite impression which has left a distinct trace in my memory; but as soon as I concentrate my thoughts on it for a while, other impressions, of a still more remote period, begin to peep forth and acquire form. And the difficulty of it is that I cannot myself in the least determine which of these impressions I really remember; that is to say, I cannot decide which of them I really lived through, and which of them I only heard about later on,—in my childhood,—and imagine that I recall, when, in reality, I only remember the accounts of them. Worse still, I can never succeed in evoking a single one of these original recollections in all its purity; I involuntarily add to it something foreign during the very process of recalling it.

At any rate, this picture is among the first which

presents itself every time that I begin to recall the
very earliest years of my life.

A chiming of bells. An odor of incense. A throng
of people comes out of the church. Nurse leads me
by the hand from the church porch, carefully shield-
ing me from being jostled. "Don't hurt the child!"
she repeats every moment, in a beseeching tone, to the
people who are crowding about us.

As we emerge from the church, one of nurse's
acquaintances approaches, clad in a long under-cas-
sock (he must have been a deacon or a chanter), and
gives her one of the little sacramental loaves.[1] "Eat,
and may health attend you, madam," he says to her.

"Come, now; tell us your name, my clever child,"
he says to me.

I make no reply, but stare at him with all my eyes.

"'T is shameful, miss, not to know your name!"
says the chanter, jeeringly.

"Tell him, my dear, 'My name is Sónetchka, and
my father is General Krukovsky,'" nurse prompts me.

I try to repeat after her, but it must have been a
failure, for nurse and her friend break out laughing.

Nurse's friend accompanies us home. I dance about
all the way, and repeat nurse's words, mangling them
after my own fashion. Evidently this is a new fact
to me, and I try to engrave it in my memory.

As we approach our house, the chanter points out
the gate to me.

"You see, little *báryshnya* [miss], there is a hook
hanging on the gate," he says. "When you forget

[1] A *prosforá*: the little leavened double loaf, from bits of which
the communion is prepared. When more than one *prosforá* is
used the auxiliary loaves are generally given to persons of distinction who may be present. Such a gift is regarded as a com-
pliment and favor.—*Trans.*

your papa's name, all you have to do is to think, 'A hook [*kriuk*] hangs on Krukovsky's gate,' and you will immediately remember it."

And thus, shameful as it is for me to confess it, this wretched chanter's pun imprinted itself on my memory, and constituted an era in my existence; from it I date my chronology, the first invasion upon me of a distinct idea as to who I was, and what was my position in the world.

As I reflect upon the matter now, I think I must have been two or three years old, and that this scene took place in Moscow, where I was born. My father served in the artillery, and we were often compelled to move about from town to town, accompanying him in accordance with the requirements of his military duties.

After this first scene, which is distinctly preserved in my memory, comes another long gap, against whose gray, misty background divers little wayside scenes detach themselves, only in the shape of bright, scat-tered spots: picking up pebbles on the highway, bivouacs at posting-stations, my sister's doll which I threw out of the carriage window,— a series of de-tached, but tolerably clear pictures.

My coherent recollections begin with me only at the age of five years, and when we lived in Kaluga. There were three of us children then: my sister Aniuta was six years older than I, and my brother Fedya was three years younger.

Our nursery presents itself before my eyes. A spa-cious, but low-ceiled room. We could easily touch the ceiling with our hands, by standing on a chair. All three of us slept in the nursery. There was some talk of sending Aniuta to sleep in the room of her governess, a Frenchwoman; but she did not wish to do it, and preferred to stay with us.

Our childish beds, guarded by railings, stood side by side, so that in the mornings we could, and did, crawl from one to the other without setting foot on the floor. At a little distance stood nurse's large bed, upon which rose a perfect mountain of feather beds and down pillows. Nurse was very proud of it. Sometimes, during the day, when she was in a particularly good humor, she would permit us to tumble about on her bed. We would climb upon it with the aid of a chair, but no sooner did we reach the very summit than the mountain slid out from under us, and away we went into a soft sea of down. This delighted us greatly.

No sooner do I think of our nursery than, by an inevitable association of ideas, I begin to be aware of a peculiar odor—a mixture of incense, olive-oil, May balsam, and the smoke of tallow-candles. It is a very long time since I chanced to encounter anywhere that peculiar odor; indeed, I believe that, not only abroad, but even in St. Petersburg and Moscow, it is now very rarely to be encountered. But two years ago, when I was visiting some of my country acquaintances, I went into their nursery, and that familiar smell immediately surged to meet me, and evoked a whole series of long-forgotten memories and emotions.

The French governess could not enter our nursery without cautiously putting her handkerchief to her nose.

"Do open the window-pane, nurse!" she would entreat, in her broken Russian.

Nurse took the remark in the light of a personal insult.

"What idea has she got into her head now, the Mohammedan heathen! As if I would open the pane and give the master's children their death of cold!" she would mutter as the governess left the room.

The skirmish between nurse and the governess was repeated, point for point, every morning.

The sun has long since peeped into our nursery. We children are beginning, one by one, to open our eyes, but we are in no haste to rise and dress. Between the moment of wakening and the moment of setting about our toilets lies a long interval of nestling about, throwing pillows at one another, seizing one another by the bare feet, and chattering all sorts of nonsense.

An appetizing odor of coffee begins to waft through the room. Nurse herself, only half clad, and having merely changed her night-cap for the silken kerchief which invariably conceals her hair during the day, brings in a tray with a big copper coffee-pot, and begins to regale us — still in bed, still unwashed, uncombed — with coffee and cream, and with rolls prepared with milk, eggs, and butter.

It sometimes happens that, after eating, we are wearied with the process of digestion, and fall asleep again.

But now the door of the nursery flies open noisily, and the angry governess makes her appearance on the threshold.

"Comment! Vous êtes encore au lit, Annette! Il est onze heures. Vous êtes encore en retard pour votre leçon!"[1] she wrathfully exclaims.

"They cannot be allowed to sleep so long. I shall complain to the general!" she says to nurse.

"And the master's child can't even have enough sleep! She's late for your lesson! A great misfortune, truly! Well, just you wait — you 're not such a grand person, after all!"

[1] "What! You are still in bed, Annette! It is eleven o'clock. You are late again for your lessons."

1*

Nevertheless, despite her grumbling, nurse now considers it expedient to set about our toilets in earnest; and it must be confessed that if the preparations have lasted a long time, the toilet itself is very speedily despatched. Nurse wipes our faces and hands with a wet towel, draws the comb a couple of times through our disheveled manes, puts on our clothes (which often lack several buttons), and we are ready!

My sister is sent off to her lesson with the governess, but my brother and I remain in the nursery. Not in the least disturbed by our presence, nurse sweeps the floor a little with a brush, raising a perfect cloud of dust, spreads the coverlets over our beds, shakes up her own down pillows, and the nursery is again considered to be in order for the whole day. My brother and I sit on the divan covered with waxed cloth which is pierced in places with holes through which the horsehair protrudes in huge tufts, and amuse ourselves with our playthings. We are rarely taken to walk, only in the case of exceptionally fine weather, and on great festival days, when nurse takes us to church with her.

As soon as my sister has finished her lesson, she runs back to us. She is bored when she is with the governess, and finds it more amusing with us —the more so because visitors often come to see nurse—other nurses or maids, whom she treats to coffee, and from whom we may hear many interesting things.

Sometimes mama looks into the nursery. When I recall my mother during this first period of my childhood, she always presents herself to me as a very young, very handsome woman. I see her always very merry, and handsomely dressed. I recall her most frequently as in a ball-gown with low-cut corsage and bare arms, with a multitude of bracelets and rings.

She is going somewhere, to some evening party, and has come in to take leave of us.

As soon as she showed herself at the door of the nursery, Aniuta would run to her, begin to kiss her arms and neck, and inspect and handle all her golden trinkets.

"I am going to be just such a beauty as mama when I grow up!" she says, fastening mama's ornaments on herself, and standing on tiptoe to get a look at herself in the little mirror which hangs on the wall. This greatly amuses mama.

Sometimes I feel an inclination to caress mama, to climb upon her knees; but, somehow or other, these attempts always end in my hurting mama through my awkwardness, or tearing her gown, and then I run away and hide myself in the corner with shame. For this reason I began to develop a sort of shyness toward mama, and this shyness was further augmented by the fact that I often heard nurse say that Aniuta and Fedya were mama's favorites, and that mama disliked me.

I do not know whether this was true or not, but nurse often said it, quite regardless of my presence. Perhaps it only seemed so to her, because she herself loved me much more than she loved the other children. Although she had brought up all three of us in exactly the same manner, for some reason or other she considered me her nursling in particular, and therefore took offense, on my account, at every slight which was, in her opinion, shown to me.

Aniuta, as considerably the oldest, naturally enjoyed special privileges over us. She grew up wild as a free kazák, recognizing no authority over her actions. She possessed the right of free entry to the drawing-room, and from her infancy she had won the reputation of being a charming child, and was accustomed to entertain the guests with brilliant and sometimes even impertinent sallies and remarks.

But my brother and I showed ourselves in the state apartments only on extraordinary occasions. We generally breakfasted and dined in the nursery.

Sometimes, when we had guests to dinner, mama's maid, Nastásya, would run into the nursery during the dessert.

"Nursey, put on Fédenka's blue silk blouse, and take him to the dining-room. The mistress wishes to show him to her guests!" she would say.

"And what am I ordered to put on Sónetchka?" asks nurse, in an angry tone, because she already foresees what the answer will be.

"Sónetchka is not wanted. She is to stay in the nursery! She 's our little stay-at-home!" replies the maid, with a laugh, knowing how this answer will enrage nurse.

And, in fact, nurse does regard this wish to exhibit Fédenka only to the guests as a bitter insult to me; and she goes about in a rage for a long time afterward, muttering to herself, gazing at me with compassion, and stroking my hair, as she adds: "My poor child, my bright darling!"

It is night. Nurse has already put me and my brother to bed, but she has not yet taken off her inevitable silk kerchief, the removal of which signifies with her the transition from meditation to repose. She is sitting on the divan, in front of the round table, and drinking tea with Nastásya.

A semi-darkness reigns in the nursery. The rather dirty flame of the tallow candle alone stands out like a yellow spot amid the gloom, because nurse has forgotten this long time to snuff it, and from the opposite corner of the room the quivering little blue flame of the shrine-lamp casts wonderful shadows on the ceiling and brilliantly illuminates the hand of the Savior raised in benediction, which stands out in relief against the silver vestment of the holy picture.

Almost directly beside me I hear the even breathing of my brother, and from the corner beyond the stove-couch comes the heavy, nasal respiration of our nursery serving-maid, snub-nosed Feklusha, nurse's scape-goat. She sleeps in the nursery, on the floor, on a piece of gray felt, which she spreads down at night, and tucks away in a lumber-room during the day.

Nurse and Nastásya are conversing in a low tone, and, imagining that we are asleep, they discuss all the household affairs without reserve. But, in the meantime, I am not asleep; on the contrary, I am listening intently to their conversation. Of course there is much that I do not understand; much is very interesting to me. It sometimes happens that I fall asleep in the middle of a story, and do not hear the end. But the scraps of their conversation which do reach my consciousness form themselves into fantastic figures therein, and leave behind them ineffaceable traces for the rest of my life.

" Well, and how am I to help loving her, my darling, more than the other children ? " I hear the nurse say, and I understand that they are discussing me. " Why, I have reared her almost entirely by myself. When our Aniutka was born, papa, and mama, and grandpa, and the aunts never could get their fill of gazing at her because she was the first-born. I never got a chance to nurse her properly. Every minute they were taking her away from me. Now one, and now another. But with Sónetchka it was quite another matter."

At this point in the oft-repeated tale, nurse always lowered her voice mysteriously, which, of course, made me prick up my ears all the more.

"She was n't born at the right time, my darling, that's what's the matter!" says nurse, in a half whisper. "You know the master lost all his money at cards in the English Club on the eve of her birth, so that they let everything go. They were forced to pawn the mistress's diamonds! Now, and how could they rejoice that God had sent them a daughter? Moreover, master and mistress both wanted a son without fail. The mistress used to say to me: 'You 'll see, nurse, it will be a boy!' They had prepared everything properly for a boy—a cross with the Crucified One, and a little cap with a blue ribbon—but no, go to! another girl-baby was born! The master and mistress were so chagrined, that they would n't look at her, and it was only Fédenka who consoled them afterward."

Nurse repeated this story very frequently, and on every occasion I listened to it with the same curiosity, so that it became firmly engraved on my memory.

Thanks to similar stories, the conviction was early developed in me that I was disliked, and this was reflected in my whole character. I began to grow more and more shy and self-contained.

They would take me into the drawing-room, and there I would stand with down-cast eyes, clutching nurse's gown with both my hands. Not a word was to be got out of me. No matter how much nurse coaxed me, I maintained an obstinate silence, and merely gazed askance at every one with fear and malice, like a hunted beast, until mama said, at last, in vexation: "Well, nurse, take your savage back to the nursery! Nothing but shame is to be had from her in the presence of guests. She certainly must have swallowed her naughty little tongue!"

I held aloof, also, from strange children, and, indeed, I rarely saw them. I remember, however, that when I was walking with nurse, and sometimes met little street boys and girls playing at some noisy game, I felt envious, and wished to join them. But nurse never permitted me. "What's the matter with you, my dear?[1] How is it possible for you, miss, to play with common children?" she said in a voice of such reproach and conviction that, as I now recall the matter, I immediately became ashamed of my own wish. Soon even the desire and capability of playing with other children abandoned me. I remember that when some little girl or other of my own age was brought to visit me, I never knew what to talk to her about, and all I could do was to stand stock-still and say to myself: "Will she go away soon?"

I was happiest of all when I was left alone with nurse. In the evening, when Fedya had been put to bed, and Aniuta had run off to the drawing-room, to the grown-up people, I would sit down beside nurse on the divan, nestle up very close to her, and she would begin to tell me fairy tales. I judge as to the depth of the trace which these fairy tales left on my imagination by the fact that, although now I can recall only snatches of them when I am awake, yet in my sleep, down to the present day, I suddenly begin

[1] *Mátotchka,*— literally, "My dear little mother."

to dream of "black death," or of the "wer-wolf," or "the twelve-headed dragon"; and this dream always produces in me the same unaccountable, soul-oppressing fear which I experienced at the age of five years as I listened to nurse's tales.

About this period of my life, something strange began to take place in me: a feeling of involuntary distress, of anguish, began to come over me at times. I have a vivid recollection of this feeling. It generally fell upon me if I were left alone in the room at the approach of twilight. I would be playing with my toys, thinking of nothing. All at once I would look up and see behind me a sharp, black strip of shadow, creeping out from under the bed, or from the corner. A sensation would seize upon me as if some strange presence had crept into the room; and this new, unfamiliar presence would suddenly clutch my heart so painfully, that I flew headlong in search of nurse, whose proximity usually had the power to soothe me. It sometimes happened, however, that this torturing sensation did not pass off for a long while, for the space of several hours.

I believe that many nervous children experience something similar. In such cases, it is usually asserted that the child is afraid of darkness, but this expression is entirely inaccurate. In the first place, the sensation experienced in these circumstances is very complicated, and much more nearly resembles anguish than fear; in the second place, it is not evoked by the darkness itself, or by any fancies therewith connected, but precisely by the feeling of the oncoming darkness. I remember, also, that a very similar feeling came over me in my childhood, under entirely different circumstances; for example, if, during my walks, I suddenly espied before me a big, half-built house, with bare brick walls, and empty openings instead of windows. I experienced it, also, in summer, if I lay on my back on the ground, and gazed up into the cloudless sky.

Other symptoms of great nervousness also began to make their appearance in me: my disgust, which approached fear in its intensity, for all sorts of physical monstrosities. If a two-headed chicken or a three-legged calf was mentioned in my presence, I began to tremble all over, and then, the following night, I inevitably saw the monster in my dreams, and woke nurse with a piercing scream. Even now I remember the three-legged man who persecuted me in my dreams during the whole of my childhood.

Even the sight of a broken doll inspired me with terror: when I chanced to drop my doll, nurse had to pick her up and tell me whether or no her head was broken; if it was, she had to take her away without showing her to me. I still remember how, one day, Aniuta caught me alone, without nurse, and, wishing to tease me, began forcibly to thrust before my eyes a wax doll, from whose head dangled a black eye which had been torn out, and thereby threw me into convulsions.

On the whole, I was on the highway to turn out a nervous, sickly child; but soon all my surroundings changed, and there was an end to all that had gone before.

II

WHEN I was about six years old, my father retired from the service, and settled on his hereditary estate, Palibino, in the Government of Vitebsk. At that time persistent rumors were afloat about the impending "emancipation"; and they spurred on my father more seriously to occupy himself with the management of affairs, which had been hitherto superintended by the overseer.

Soon after our removal to the country, a circumstance occurred in our house which remained very vividly imprinted on my memory. Moreover, this occurrence produced so powerful an impression upon every one in the house, that it was frequently referred to afterward, so that my personal recollections became entangled with later accounts of it to such a degree that I cannot disentangle the former from the latter. Therefore, I narrate the occurrence as it now presents itself to me.

Various articles suddenly began to disappear from our nursery; behold, first one thing would vanish and then another. If nurse forgot anything for a time, it was nowhere to be found when she wanted to get it again, although nurse was ready to take her oath that she had put it away in the cupboard, or the chest of drawers, with her own hands. At first, these losses were accepted with a good deal of indifference;

but when they began to occur with ever-increasing frequency, and to extend to articles of greater and greater value; when things began to disappear in rapid succession — a silver spoon, a gold thimble, a mother-of-pearl pen-knife — an uproar arose in the house. It became apparent that we had a thief in the house. Nurse, who considered herself responsible for the children's belongings, was more alarmed than all the rest, and determined, at any cost, to discover the thief.

Naturally, suspicion must fall, first of all, on poor Feklusha, the maid appointed to our service. It is true that Feklusha had been attached to the nursery for the past three years, and nurse had never noticed anything of the sort about her during all that time. But, in nurse's opinion, this proved nothing at all. "Before, she was young, and did not understand the value of things," nurse argued, "but now she is grown up and become wiser. Moreover, her family live yonder in the village, and she is carrying off the master's property to them."

On the foundation of this reasoning, nurse became so permeated with the inward conviction of Feklusha's guilt that she began to treat her with increasing surliness and disfavor; and poor, frightened, unhappy Feklusha, who instinctively felt that she was suspected, began to exhibit a more and more guilty aspect.

But watch Feklusha as she would, nurse could not for a long while catch her at anything. One fine day Aniuta's money-box, which always stood in nurse's cupboard, and contained forty rubles or more, disappeared. The news of this last loss reached even my father's ears; he ordered nurse to be sent to him, and gave strict orders that the thief must be found without fail. Then every one understood that it was no jesting matter.

Nurse was in despair, but one night she awoke and heard a queer munching proceeding from the corner where Feklusha slept. Already inclined to suspicion, nurse cautiously, noiselessly put out her hand for the matches and suddenly struck a light. What did she see?

Feklusha was squatting on her heels, holding a huge pot of sweetmeats between her knees, and was devouring it like a plowman, and licking out the pot with a crust of bread.

I must state that a few days previously the house-keeper had complained that preserves had begun to disappear from her storeroom.

Of course it was only the work of a second for nurse to spring out of bed and seize the culprit by her braid of hair.

"Ah! I've caught you, you good-for-nothing! Tell me, where did you get those preserves?" she shouted in a thundering voice, shaking the girl unmercifully by the hair.

"Nurse, darling; I'm not guilty, truly I am not!" Feklusha began to entreat. "The seamstress, Marya Vasilievna, gave me this pot of preserves yesterday evening. She only enjoined upon me not to show it to you."

This justification appeared thoroughly improbable to nurse.

"Come, woman; 't is plain that you are not an adept at lying," she said scornfully. "It is a likely thing that it should enter into Marya Vasilievna's head to treat you to sweetmeats."

"Nurse, darling; I'm not lying—aï, aï! it is the truth. Only ask her yourself. I heated her irons for

her yesterday, and she gave me these preserves for doing it. Only she ordered me, 'Don't show them to
nurse, or she will scold, and say that I am spoiling
you,' " Feklusha continued to asseverate.

"Come, that will do; we 'll investigate that to-morrow," said nurse decisively, and she locked Feklusha
up to await the morning in a dark lumber-room,
whence her sobs long continued to resound. The
next morning an investigation was begun.

Marya Vasilievna was a seamstress who had lived
many years in our house. She was not a serf, but a
free peasant, and enjoyed great respect among the
rest of the servants. She had a room to herself,
where she dined on food sent from the master's
table.[1] She bore herself very loftily, and was never
intimate with any of the other servants. We valued
her highly in the house because she was so clever in
her work. "Her hands are simply golden," they said
of her. I think she was about forty years of age.
Her face was thin, sickly, with large, dark eyes. She
was not pretty, but I remember that my elders always
said that she was very distinguished in appearance.
"You would never dream that she was a common
seamstress." She always dressed cleanly and precisely, and kept her room very neat, with even some
pretensions to elegance. Several pots with geraniums
always stood on her window-sill, the walls were hung
with cheap pictures, and on a shelf in the corner
various porcelain trifles were set out — a swan with
a gilded beak, a slipper all covered with little pink
flowers — over which I went into ecstasies in my
childhood.

---

[1] Servants are generally fed on food specially prepared for
them, such as cabbage soup, buckwheat groats, cucumbers,
black bread, etc. — *Trans.*

2

Marya Vasilievna was especially interesting to us children, because the following story was current in regard to her. In her youth she had been a handsome and healthy girl, and had been the serf of a certain woman with a landed estate, who had a grown-up son, an officer. The latter had once come home on leave, and had given Marya Vasilievna several silver coins. Unfortunately, the old lady entered the maids' hall just at that moment, and saw the money in Marya Vasilievna's hands. "Where did you get it?" she asked; but Marya Vasilievna was so frightened that, instead of replying, she took and swallowed the money.

She became ill immediately. She turned quite black, and fell, choking, on the floor. They had great difficulty in saving her, and she lay ill for a long while, and from that time her beauty and freshness vanished. The old lady died soon afterward, and Marya Vasilievna received her freedom from the young master.

The story of the swallowed money was awfully interesting to us children, and we often insisted that Marya Vasilievna should tell us how it all happened.

Marya Vasilievna came to our nursery quite frequently, although she and nurse were not on very good terms. We children were also fond of running to her room, especially at the twilight hour, when she was forced, willingly or unwillingly, to lay aside her work. Then she would sit down at the window, and, supporting her head on her hand, she would begin to sing various touching old romances, "Through the level valleys," or, "Dark flower, gloomy flower." She sang very mournfully, but I was very fond of her singing in my childhood, though it always made me sad. Sometimes her singing was interrupted by a fit of the terrible coughing which had tortured her for many years, and which seemed as if it must burst her flat, dry chest.

When, on the morning following the affair with Feklusha which I have described, nurse addressed herself to Marya Vasilievna with the question: was it true that she had given the girl the preserves? Marya Vasilievna, as was to have been expected, assumed a look of surprise.

"What have you got into your head, my dear nurse? Would I spoil the wretched little girl like that? I have n't any preserves myself!" she said, in an offended voice.

The matter was now clear; but Feklusha's impudence was so immense that, despite this categorical denial, she persisted in her assertion.

"Marya Vasilievna! Christ be with you! Is it possible that you have forgotten? Only yesterday evening you called me to you and gave me the preserves," she said, in a voice that was broken by tears, and she shook as if in a fever.

"You must be ill and raving, Feklusha," replied Marya Vasilievna, calmly, without betraying the slightest excitement in her pale, bloodless face.

No doubt now remained in the mind of nurse, or in the minds of all the rest of the household, as to Feklusha's guilt. The criminal was led away and locked up in a lumber-room, far removed from all the other rooms.

"There you 'll sit, you wretch, without food or drink, until you confess!" said nurse, as she turned the key in the heavy hanging padlock. Of course this affair created an uproar throughout the house. Every one of the servants invented some pretext for running to nurse and talking over the interesting matter with her. All day long our nursery was a regular club room.

Feklusha had no father, and her mother lived in the village, but came to the manor house to help the laundress wash the linen. Naturally, she soon heard of what had happened, and ran to the nursery, uttering loud complaints and asseverations that her daughter was innocent. But nurse soon quieted her down.

"Don't make so much noise, my good woman! Just wait. We 'll soon find out whither your daughter carried her stolen goods!" she said to her, so sternly, and with such a significant look, that the poor woman was frightened, and took herself off to her own place.

The general opinion expressed was decidedly unfavorable to Feklusha. "If she carried off the preserves, of course she stole the other things also," said everybody. Another reason why the general indignation against Feklusha was so strong lay in the fact that the mysterious and repeated thefts had weighed like a heavy burden over the whole household of servants for many weeks. Each one feared that he might be suspected; who knows? Hence, the discovery of the thief was a relief to every one.

But still Feklusha did not confess.

Nurse went several times in the course of the day to see to her prisoner, but the latter only repeated her assertion: "I have stolen nothing. God will punish Marya Vasilievna for injuring the orphan."

Toward evening mama entered the nursery.

"Are n't you too severe with that poor girl, nurse? How could you leave the poor child all day without food?" she said in a troubled voice.

But nurse would not hear of mercy.

"What do you mean, ma'am? Have mercy on such a person! Why, she came near bringing honest folks under suspicion!" she said, with such conviction that mama could hardly make up her mind to insist, and went away without having obtained any alleviation of the fate of the little criminal.

The next day came; still Feklusha had not confessed. Her judges began to feel some uneasiness; but suddenly, about dinner time, nurse came to our mother with a triumphant countenance.

"Our bird has confessed," she cried joyfully.

"Well, and where are the stolen things?" asked mama very naturally.

"The wicked wretch has not yet confessed what she did with them," replied nurse in a troubled tone. "She utters all sort of nonsense. She says she has forgotten. But wait, perhaps she will remember after I have kept her locked up an hour or two longer."

In fact, toward evening Feklusha made full confession, and narrated with great detail that she had stolen all the things with the intention of selling them somewhere later on; but as no convenient opportunity had presented itself, she had hidden them for a long time under her bed-felt in the corner of the lumber-room; but when she perceived that the things were remembered and that serious search was being made for the thief, she became frightened, and began to think of putting them back in their places; but afterward she was afraid to do that, and, instead, tied all the things up in a bundle in her apron, and flung them into the deep pond beyond our farm.

Every one was so anxious for some explanation of this annoying and painful affair that Feklusha's story was not subjected to very severe criticism.
2*

When their grief at the loss of their property was somewhat assuaged, every one was content with this explanation.

The criminal was released from confinement, and a brief but just sentence was pronounced on her. It was decided that she should be well whipped, and then sent back to the village to her mother.

In spite of Feklusha's tears and her mother's protests, this sentence was immediately executed. Then we took another little girl into the nursery in Feklusha's place to run the errands. Several weeks passed. The usual routine of the household was gradually reestablished, and every one had begun to forget what had happened.

But one evening, when the house had become quiet, and nurse, having put us to bed, was preparing to retire herself, the nursery door opened softly, and Alexandra, the laundress, Feklusha's mother, made her appearance. She alone had stood out obstinately against the plain facts, and had continued without ceasing to assert that her daughter had been disgraced without cause. She and nurse had already had several severe quarrels on this point, until nurse at last declined to discuss the matter, and forbade her to enter the nursery, having made up her mind that it was of no use — you could n't reason with a stupid woman.

But to-night Alexandra wore such a strange and significant look that nurse understood, as soon as she looked at her, that she was not come to repeat her customary empty complaints, but that something new and important had taken place.

" Look here, dear nurse; see what sort of a trick I am going to show you," said Alexandra mysteriously, and after casting a scrutinizing glance around the room, and having convinced herself that no stranger was present, she drew forth from beneath her apron and gave to nurse our favorite mother-of-pearl penknife, the very one which had been among the stolen articles supposed to have been thrown into the pond by Feklusha.

At the sight of the penknife, nurse threw up her hands.

"Where did you find it?" she asked with curiosity.

"That's exactly the point—where I found it," replied Alexandra with a drawl. She remained silent several seconds, evidently enjoying nurse's confusion. "Our gardener, Philip Matvyeevitch, gave me his old trousers to mend. I found this knife in the pocket," she said at last in a significant tone.

This Philip Matvyeevitch was a German, and occupied one of the highest positions in the ranks of our house-servants' aristocracy. He received quite a large salary, was unmarried, and although to an impartial eye he seemed merely a fat, middle-aged, rather repulsive German, with reddish, typical square jaws, he was regarded as a beauty by our female servants.

When she heard this strange hint, nurse could not at first understand at all.

"But where could Philip Matvyeevitch have got hold of the children's penknife?" she asked in bewilderment. "Why, he never enters the nursery, you know. Yes, and is it a likely thing that a man like Philip Matvyeevitch would steal the children's knife!"

Alexandra gazed at nurse for several moments in silence, with a long, scornful stare; then she bent down to her ear and uttered a few sentences in which the name of Marya Vasilievna was frequently repeated.

A glimmer of the truth began, little by little, to make its way into nurse's brain.

"Te, te, te, so that 's it!" she exclaimed, throwing
up her hands. "Ah, you meek hypocrite; ah, you
wretch; well, just wait, and we 'll show you up in
your true light," she cried, brimming over with indignation.

It appeared, as we were told later on, that Alexandra had long cherished suspicions of Marya Vasilievna.
She had observed that the latter was carrying on
an intrigue with the gardener. "Well, and you can
judge for yourself," she said to nurse, "whether such
a fine fellow as Philip Matvyeevitch would love such
an old woman for nothing. She certainly won his
good-will with gifts." And in fact she soon convinced
herself that Marya Vasilievna was in the habit of giving him presents and money. Where did she get
them? So she instituted a regular system of espion-
age on the unsuspecting Marya Vasilievna. This penknife was merely the last link in the long chain of
evidence.

This affair turned out interesting and absorbing to
a degree which no one could have foreseen. There
suddenly awoke in nurse that passionate instinct of
the detective which so often lies slumbering in the
souls of old women, and instigates them to fling
themselves with fury into the unraveling of any
tangled affair, even though it does not concern them
in the least. In the present case, nurse was encouraged in her eagerness by the fact that she felt guilty
of a great sin toward Feklusha, and was burning with
the desire to expiate it as speedily as possible. Consequently an offensive and defensive league against
Marya Vasilievna was formed between her and
Alexandra.

As both women were already morally convinced to
the last degree of the woman's guilt, they decided on

extreme measures—to get possession of her keys, and to open her trunk at a favorable opportunity, when she was absent from the house.

No sooner thought than done. Alas, it appeared that they were perfectly correct in their assumptions. The contents of the trunk fully confirmed their suspicions, and proved in the most undoubted manner that the unhappy Marya Vasilievna was guilty of all the petty thefts which had created such an uproar in the immediate past.

" What a wretch! Of course she gave the preserves to poor Feklusha in order to divert attention, and cast all the suspicion on her. Ugh! the impious creature! She even did not spare a little child," said nurse with horror and disgust, quite forgetting the part which she herself had played in the whole affair, and how by her cruelty she had forced poor Feklusha to testify falsely against herself.

It is easy to imagine the wrath of all the servants, and of the household in general, when the terrible truth was brought to light and made known to every one.

At first, in the heat of his wrath, my father threatened to send for the police and put Marya Vasilievna in prison; but in view of the fact that she was already advanced in age, and a sickly woman, and had lived so long in our house, he soon became pacified, and decided merely to deprive her of her place and send her back to Petersburg.

It would seem as if Marya Vasilievna ought to have been satisfied with this sentence. She was such a clever seamstress that there was no danger of her being left without bread in Petersburg. And what sort of a position awaited her in our household after such a scandal? All the other servants had previously envied her, and hated her for her pride and arrogance. She knew it, and knew also how bitterly she would now be compelled to expiate her former grandeur. Nevertheless, strange as it may seem, she not only did not rejoice at my father's decision, but on the contrary began to pray for forgiveness. Some cat-like attachment to our house, to the place among us which she had won for herself, made its voice heard in her.

"I have not long to live; I feel that I shall die soon. How am I to drag myself around with strangers just before my death?" she said.

"But that had nothing to do with it," nurse explained to me, as we recalled the story many years afterward, when I was grown up. "She simply could n't leave us as long as Philip Matvyeevitch remained, and she knew that if she once went away she would never see him again. In any case, as it was difficult to find such a good gardener, and the garden and farm could not be left at the mercy of fate, it was decided to keep him with us for a time at least."

I do not know whether nurse was right as to the causes which made Marya Vasilievna cling so obstinately to her place in our house; but at any rate, on the day appointed for her departure, she came and threw herself at my father's feet.

"Let me rather stay with you without wages, punish me like a serf, only do not drive me from you," she pleaded, sobbing.

Such attachment to our house touched my father; but, on the other hand, he was afraid that if he forgave Marya Vasilievna it would exert a demoralizing influence on the other servants. He was in a very difficult dilemma as to what he ought to do; but all at once the following expedient occurred to him.

"Listen," he said to her. "Although theft is a

great sin, I might forgive you if your fault consisted only of theft. But an innocent little girl has suffered on your account. Reflect that, because of your sin, Feklusha has been subjected to public disgrace; she has been flogged. On her account I cannot pardon you. If you insist on remaining with us, I can consent to it only on condition that you beg Feklusha's pardon, and kiss her hand in the presence of all the servants. If you will agree to this, then you may remain, and God be with you!"

No one expected that Marya Vasilievna would agree to such a condition. How was she, such a haughty creature, to accuse herself publicly before a little serf girl, and kiss her hand! But, to the universal amazement, Marya Vasilievna did agree to it.

An hour after this decision all the house-servants were assembled in the ante-room of our house to look on at a curious spectacle, Marya Vasilievna kissing Feklusha's hand. My father had stipulated that this should take place in solemn and public fashion.

A large crowd assembled. Every one wished to see. The heads of the household were present also, and we children begged permission to look on.

I shall never forget the scene which followed. Feklusha, confused by the honor which had so unexpectedly fallen to her lot, and also fearing, probably, that Marya Vasilievna would take revenge later on for her enforced humiliation, came to her master and began to entreat that she and Marya Vasilievna might be excused from the handkissing.

"I forgive her without that," she said, almost in tears.

But papa, who had screwed himself up to a lofty pitch, and had convinced himself that he was acting in accordance with the demands of strict justice, only

shouted at her: ''Be off with you, you fool, and don't
meddle with what does not concern you! This is not
being done for your sake. If I, your master, had
sinned against you in this manner, do you understand, it would be my duty to kiss your hand. You
don't understand? Well, then, hold your tongue,
and don't try to dissuade me!''

The terrified Feklusha dared make no further reply, and, all trembling with fear, she went and took
her place, awaiting her fate like a criminal.

Marya Vasilievna, white as a sheet, passed through
the crowd, which made way before her. She walked
mechanically, as if in a dream, but her face was so set
and vicious that she was alarming to look at. Her
lips were convulsively closed, and bloodless. She approached quite close to Feklusha. ''Forgive me!''
burst from her mouth, in a sort of suffering scream.
She grasped Feklusha's hand, and raised it to her
lips so abruptly, and with an expression of such
hatred, that it seemed as if she were on the point of
biting it. But a spasm suddenly swept over her face,
froth made its appearance round her mouth. She
fell to the floor, giving utterance to piercing, unnatural shrieks, her whole body writhing in convulsions.

It was afterward discovered that she had previously been subject to hysterical attacks, but she had
carefully concealed the fact from her employers, fearing that they would not keep her if they knew about
them. Those of the servants who had come to know
of her disease had not betrayed her, out of class
spirit.

I cannot reproduce the impression which her present
attack called forth. Of course we children were hastily led away, and we were so thoroughly frightened
that we ourselves were on the verge of hysterics.

But the point which made the most vivid impression on my mind was the sudden change which took place after this in the frame of mind of all our house-servants. Up to that time they had all borne themselves toward Marya Vasilievna with malice and hatred. Her action had seemed so vile and black, that every one felt a sort of pleasure in showing her how they despised her, inventing some means of vexing her. Now, all this underwent a sudden alteration. She all at once appeared in the light of a sufferer, of a victim, and the general sympathy was transferred to her side. The servants even got up a private protest against my father for the unnecessary severity of his sentence.

" Of course she was guilty," said the other maids in an undertone, when they assembled in our nursery for consultation with nurse, as was customary after every important event which occurred in our house. " Well and good. The general might have scolded her himself, the mistress might have punished her, as is the way in other houses. All that is not so insulting. It can be endured. But lo, and behold! what sort of a thing has he suddenly invented? To make her kiss the hand of such a cricket, such a dirty-nosed person as that Feklusha, in the sight of everybody! Who could endure such disgrace?"

Marya Vasilievna did not come to herself for a long time. One convulsion followed another for the space of several hours. She would look about her, come to herself, then suddenly begin to fling herself about again, and scream. We had to send to town for the doctor.

Pity for the sufferer increased every moment, and discontent with the master and mistress grew in proportion. I remember that mama came to the nursery in the middle of the day, and perceiving that nurse was carefully and anxiously making tea at an entirely unfitting hour, she asked her, in perfect innocence: "For whom is this, nurse?"

"For Marya Vasilievna, of course. Why? Is it proper in your opinion, to leave her without tea in her illness? We servants have Christian souls!" replied nurse, in so harsh and exasperated a tone, that mama was quite confused, and made haste to depart.

And a few hours earlier this very same nurse would have been capable of beating Marya Vasilievna half to death had she been permitted.

A few days later Marya Vasilievna recovered, to the great joy of my parents, and went on living in our house as before. No further mention was made of what had happened. I believe that even among the servants there was not one who reproached her with the past.

So far as I was concerned, from that day forth I began to feel for her a sort of strange pity, mingled with instinctive horror. I did not run to her room as formerly. When I met her in the corridor I involuntarily pressed close to the wall, and tried not to look at her. It always seemed to me as if she were on the point of falling on the floor, and beginning to writhe and shriek.

Marya Vasilievna must have observed my estrangement, and she endeavored in various ways to regain my former liking. I remember that she invented some little surprise for me nearly every day. She would bring me colored scraps, or make a new gown for my doll; but all this did no good. My feeling of secret terror of her did not pass off, and I ran away as soon as I was left alone with her.

However, I soon came under the authority of my

new governess, who put an end to intimacy of all sorts with the servants.

But I vividly recall the following scene. I was seven or eight years old by this time. One evening — it was the vigil of some festival; the Annunciation, I think—I was running along the corridor, past Marya Vasilievna's room. All at once she peered out of her door and called me. "*Báryshnya*—hey, miss! Come in and see what a pretty dough lark I have baked for you!"[1]

A semi-darkness reigned in the long corridor, and there was no one in it except Marya Vasilievna and myself. As I glanced at her pale face, with its enormous black eyes, I was suddenly seized with such terror that, instead of answering, I flew headlong away from her.

"What, little miss, 't is evident that you have entirely ceased to love me; that you despise me!" she called after me.

It was not so much the words as the tone in which she uttered them, which struck me; but I did not halt, and continued to flee. But when I turned into the schoolroom, and recovered from my terror, I could not forget her deep, sorrowful voice. Try as I might, by playfulness and an augmentation of mischief, to dull that unpleasant, gnawing feeling which was stirring in my heart, it would not cease. I could not get Marya Vasilievna out of my head, and, as is always the case with a person whom you have offended, she suddenly began to seem to me extremely charming, and I began to feel drawn to her.

[1] The larks are supposed to fly back for the summer at the beginning of the spring, according to the almanac, and the shops are full of rolls and bread baked in the form of birds.— *Trans.*

I could not make up my mind to relate to my governess what had taken place. Children always become confused when they talk of their feelings.
Moreover, we were forbidden to be intimate with the
servants, and I knew that the governess still praised
me. I also knew by instinct that she praised me
without cause. After evening tea, when bedtime
came, instead of going straight to my bed-room, I determined to run to Marya Vasilievna. This was a sort
of sacrifice on my part, because I had to run through
the long, deserted corridor, which was now entirely
dark, which I always feared and avoided in the evening. But now I developed a desperate courage. I
ran without stopping to take breath, and rushed into
her room like a hurricane, panting.

Marya Vasilievna had already finished her supper.
Because of the festival she was not at work, but was
sitting at a table covered with a clean, white cloth,
and reading a little book on some pious subject. The
shrine lamp flickered in front of the holy images.
After the dark, dreadful corridor, her little chamber
seemed to me unusually light and comfortable, and
she herself very kind and good.

" I have come to say good-night to you, dear, dear
Marya Vasilievna ! " I cried in one breath ; but before I had finished my sentence, she had seized me
and begun to cover me with kisses. She kissed me
so vehemently and so long, that I began to feel em-
barrassed, and to consider how I might get away
from her without offending her again, when a fit of
her terrible coughing forced her to release me from
her embrace.

This terrible cough persecuted her more and more.
" I barked like a dog all last night," she would say of
herself, with a sort of grim irony.

She became paler and more reserved with every passing day, but she persistently refused all my mother's suggestions that she would apply to the doctor for advice; she even exhibited a sort of angry agitation if any one spoke to her about her illness.

Thus she lingered on for two or three years, keeping her feet almost to the very last; she only took to her bed two or three days before her death, and they said that her death agony was very painful.

By my father's orders, a very gorgeous funeral (according to village ideas) was provided for her. Not only all the servants, but all our family, including the master himself, were present at it. Feklusha also walked behind the coffin and sobbed violently. Philip Matvyeevitch was the only one who was not present at her funeral; without waiting for her death he had left us several months previously, and betaken himself to a more lucrative situation somewhere in the vicinity of Dunaburg.

WITH our removal to the country everything in our house underwent a great change, and the existence of my parents, which had been hitherto gay and free from care, suddenly assumed a more serious turn.

Up to that time our father had paid very little attention to us, because he regarded the rearing of children as the business of women, not of men. He took a little more notice of Aniuta than of his other children, because she was older and very amusing. He loved to pet her, on occasion, and in winter he sometimes took her to ride with him in his little sledge, and he was fond of bragging about her to his guests. When her mischievousness transgressed all bounds, and positively drove the whole household out of patience, complaints about her were sometimes made to my father, but he usually turned the whole matter into a jest, and she understood perfectly well that although he sometimes for the sake of appearances assumed an aspect of severity, in reality he was ready to laugh at her pranks.

As for us younger children, our father's relations to us were confined to his asking nurse, when he happened to meet us, whether we were well, pinching our cheeks in a kindly way to convince himself that they were plump, and sometimes taking us in his hands and tossing us up in the air. On days of high festival, when father was going off somewhere for official presentation, and was dressed in his full parade uniform, with his orders and stars, we were summoned to the drawing-room "to admire papa on parade," and this spectacle afforded us remarkable satisfaction; we danced around him, clapping our hands with delight at the sight of his glittering epaulets and orders.

But on our arrival in the country these benign relations which had hitherto existed between father and us suddenly underwent a change. As not unfrequently happens in Russian families, father suddenly made the unexpected discovery that his children were not such models, such beautifully educated children, as he had supposed.

The beginning of it all was apparently that my sister and I ran away from home one day, got lost, and were missing for an entire day, and when they found us toward evening, we had managed to overeat ourselves on *herb-Paris* berries, and were sick for several days afterward.

This occurrence demonstrated that the oversight over us was very bad. This first discovery was followed by others; one revelation followed another. Up to that time every one had stoutly asserted that my sister was a remarkable, almost a phenomenal, child—clever and accomplished beyond her age. But now it suddenly appeared that not only was she dreadfully spoiled, but ignorant to the last degree for a twelve-year old girl, and that she did not even know how to write correctly in Russian.

What was still worse, something was discovered about our French governess, so bad that no one was permitted to speak of it before us children.

I have a confused remembrance of those troubled days, which followed our escapade, as a sort of painful domestic calamity. All day long there were tears, cries, and uproar in the nursery. Everybody quarreled with everybody else, and everybody caught it, whether rightly or wrongly. Papa was in a rage, mama was weeping, nurse roaring, the Frenchwoman wringing her hands and packing up her belongings. My sister and I became meek and quiet, and dared not utter a sound, because every one now vented his or her wrath on us, and the slightest fault was reckoned up against us as a heavy crime. Nevertheless we watched our elders quarreling with curiosity, and even with a certain childish malicious delight, and waited "to see how it would all end."

Father, who did not like half measures, decided upon a radical reform in the system of our education. The Frenchwoman was dismissed, nurse was released from the nursery, and set to look after the linen, and two new persons were taken into the house — a Polish tutor and an English governess.

The tutor was a quiet, learned man, who gave splendid lessons, but who had very little real influence on my education. On the other hand, the governess introduced an entirely new element into our family.

Although she had been brought up in Russia, and spoke Russian, she had retained in full the typical peculiarities of the Anglo-Saxon race — straightforwardness, endurance, and a knowledge how to carry out any undertaking to the end. These qualities gave her a great advantage over the rest of the household, all of whom were distinguished by precisely the opposite traits, and they explain the influence which she acquired in our house.

When she came to us all her efforts were directed

toward arranging out of our children's room a sort
of English *nursery*, in which she could rear exemplary
English misses. But God knows how hard it was to
establish a nursery of English misses in the house of
a Russian landed proprietor, where the ages and gen-
erations had all been imbued with the habits of manor
lords, inaccuracy, and lack of orderliness. Nevertheless, thanks to her remarkable persistence, she attained her object to a certain extent.

It is true that she never succeeded in getting the
better of my sister, who had been accustomed up to
that time to perfect freedom. At last, when Aniuta
had passed her fifteenth birthday, she made her final
escape from authority. The formal act by which her
freedom from the tutelage of the governess was
expressed was the removal of her bed from the nursery to a room next to mama's bedroom. From
that day forth Aniuta began to consider herself a
grown-up young lady, and the governess made haste
to announce, on every convenient occasion, in a
touchy sort of way, that she had nothing to do with
Aniuta's conduct—that she washed her hands of her.

But, on the other hand, she concentrated all her
efforts with great vigor upon me, isolating me from
all the members of the household and hedging me
about, as though guarding me from an epidemic,
against the influence of my older sister. This yearning for separation on her part was favored by the
dimensions and construction of our country house, in
which two or three families could have lived simultaneously and remained entire strangers to each
other.

Almost the whole of the lower story, with the
exception of several rooms for servants and for cas-
ual guests, was given over to the governess and to
3*

me. The upper story, with the state apartments, belonged to mama and Aniuta. Fedya and his tutor were lodged in the wing, and papa's cabinet formed the foundation of a three-story tower, and stood quite apart from the rest of the dwelling. Thus the varied elements of which our family consisted had each their independent domains, and could carry out their separate lines of action without incommoding each other, meeting only for dinner and for evening tea.

IV

THE wall clock in the school-room struck seven. These seven strokes reached my consciousness through my slumber, and begat in me the sad conviction that Dunyásha, the maid, will be coming now at once to wake me; but I am still sleeping so sweetly that I try to convince myself that I have only imagined those seven repulsive strokes. Turning on the other side and drawing the coverlet closer about me, I hasten to enjoy the sweet, brief bliss afforded by the last little moments of sleep which, as I well know, will soon come to an end.

And, in fact, the door creaks, and Dunyásha's heavy tread becomes audible as she enters the room with a load of wood. Then comes a series of familiar sounds, which are repeated every morning: the noise of the armful of wood flung heavily on the floor, the snapping of matches, the crackling of the pitch-knot, the rushing and roaring of the flames—all these customary sounds reach my hearing through my dreams, and augment in me the sensation of agreeable indolence and unwillingness to desert my warm little bed. "Another minute, just another little minute's sleep !" But the crackling of the flame in the stove grows louder and more even, and turns into a measured, regular hum.

" 'T is time to get up, *báryshyna!*" (little mistress),

rings out in my very ear, and Dunyásha, with pitiless hand, drags off the coverlet.

Day is but just breaking out of doors, and the first pale rays of the cold winter morning, mingling with the yellowish light of the stearin candle, impart to everything a sort of dead, unnatural look. Is there anything more disagreeable in the world than getting up by candlelight? I sit up in bed, squatted on my heels, and begin mechanically to dress myself; but my eyes involuntarily close again, and my uplifted hand, which grasps a stocking, becomes rigid in that position.

Behind the screen where the governess sleeps, the sound of splashing water is already audible, accompanied by snorting and vigorous rubbing.

"Don't dawdle, Sónya; if you are not ready in a quarter of an hour, you will bear the ticket 'lazy' on your back during luncheon," rings out the threatening voice of my governess.

This threat is no jest. Corporeal punishment has been banished from our educational system, but my governess has taken it into her head to replace it by other means of intimidation. If I am guilty of anything, she pins upon my back a paper on which my fault is stated in large letters, and with this decoration I must present myself at table. I fear this chastisement like death; hence the governess's threat has the power to banish my sleep instantaneously. I immediately leap from the bed. At the wash-stand the maid is already awaiting me, with an uplifted jug in one hand and with a shaggy towel in the other. Cold water is poured over me every morning, after the English fashion. One second of sharp, breath-destroying cold, then boiling water seems to flow through my veins, and then a wonderfully agreeable sensation of remarkable vitality and elasticity is left behind all over my body.

But now it is quite light. We go to the dining-room. On the table puffs the samovar, the wood in the stove is crackling, and the bright flame is reflected and multiplied in the large frozen windows.

Not a trace of my sleepiness remains. On the contrary I feel very alert, most unaccountably joyful at heart; as if I wanted noise, laughter, merriment. Ah, if I only had a companion, a child of my own age, with whom I could frolic and romp, in whom the superabundance of healthy young life bubbled up like a spring, as it did in me. But I have no such companion, and I drink my tea alone with my governess, as the other members of the family, including my brother and my sister, rise much later. I feel such an uncontrollable desire to make merry and laugh over something or other that I make a feeble attempt at sprightliness with the governess. Unfortunately she is not in a good humor to-day, which is often the case with her in the morning, as she suffers from liver disease; consequently she considers it her duty to repress my ill-timed burst of mirth, with the remark that this is the time for lessons and not for laughter.

My day always begins with a music lesson. The temperature in the big hall up-stairs where the piano stands is very low, so that my fingers become stiff and swollen, and my nails stand out against the background they furnish like blue blotches.

An hour and a half of scales and exercises, accompanied by the monotonous beats of a small stick with which my governess indicates the time, chills to a considerable degree that sensation of joy in mere living with which I began my day. Other lessons follow the music lesson. I had enjoyed my lessons very

much while my sister was studying also; moreover, I
had been such a little thing then that they did not
teach me seriously; but I entreated permission to be
present at my sister's lessons, and listened to them
with so much attention that it often happened that
she, a big fourteen-year-old girl, did not know the
appointed lesson the next time, while I, a chit of seven
years, remembered it, and prompted her in it with
triumph. This was a great delight to me. But now
when my sister had ceased to study, and entered
into the rights of womanhood, the lessons lost half
their charm for me. I studied with considerable
industry it is true, but how I would have studied had
I had a companion!

At twelve o'clock comes breakfast. As soon as she
has swallowed her last morsel, the governess betakes
herself to the window to inspect the state of the
weather. I follow her with a trembling heart, because this is a very important question to me. If the
thermometer indicates anything above 10° below zero[1],
and there is no wind, I must take a tiresome walk of
an hour and a half with my governess, back and forth
on the alley, which has been cleared of snow. But if,
to my happiness, the cold is severe, or it is windy,
the governess takes herself off alone for the walk,—inevitable, in her opinion,—and sends me up-stairs to
play ball in the hall by way of exercise.

I am not particularly fond of playing ball. I am
twelve years old now. I consider myself already
quite grown-up, and it is rather insulting to me that
the governess should think me capable of being
amused by such a childish entertainment as playing
ball; nevertheless, I hear her command with the
greatest satisfaction, because it presages an hour
and a half of freedom for me.

1 Réaumur. 10° above zero, Fahrenheit.—*Trans.*

The upper story is the special domain of mama and Aniuta; but now they are both sitting in their own chambers. There is no one in the large hall. I run several times around the hall, chasing my ball before me. My thoughts wander far afield. Like the majority of children who grow up alone, I have already managed to fabricate for myself a rich world of fancies and dreams, whose existence is not even suspected by my elders. I am passionately fond of poetry. The very form, the very rhythm, of poetry afford me the greatest pleasure. I eagerly devour all the scraps from the Russian poets which fall under my eye, and I must confess that the more stilted the verses, the more they are to my taste. Zhukóvsky's "Ballads" were for a long time the only specimens of the Russian poets which were known to me. No one in our house took any particular interest in this branch of literature, and although we had a fairly large library, it consisted chiefly of foreign books. It did not contain the writings of either Púshkin, Lérmontoff, or Nekrásoff. I could not wait with patience for the day when Filónoff's "Compendium of Russian Literature" should be purchased for us at the instigation of our Russian tutor. This was a real treasure-trove for me. For several days afterward I went about like a mad creature repeating under my breath strophes from "Mtzyri," or from "The Prisoner of the Caucasus"[1] until the governess threatened to take the precious book away from me.

The very rhythm of verse always produced upon me such an effect of fascination, that from the age of five I began to write verses myself. But my governess did not approve of this occupation. She had formed in her own mind a very decided opinion of the healthy, normal child, who was bound to develop into

[1] Both by Lérmontoff.— *Trans.*

an exemplary English miss, and the composition of
verses did not in least enter into this opinion. Therefore she severely persecuted all my poetical attempts.
If, to my misfortune, there fell under her eye a scrap
of paper scribbled over with my rhymes, she immediately pinned it to my shoulder, and then, in the presence of my brother or sister, declaimed my unlucky
composition, distorting and mangling it horribly, as
a matter of course.

But this persecution of my verses did no good. At
the age of twelve I was profoundly convinced that
I was destined to become a poet. Out of fear of my
governess, I decided not to write down my verses,
but I composed them in my head, like the ancient
bards, and confided them to my ball. As I ran
through the hall, chasing it before me, I declaimed
aloud my poetical productions, among which I took
pride in "The Bedouin's Address to his Horse," and
"The Sensations of the Fisherman as he Dives for
Pearls." I composed in my head a long poem entitled, "The Fountain Jet," something half way between "Undine" and "Mtzyri"; but for the present
only ten strophes were ready. I planned to have one
hundred and twenty.

But the muse is capricious, as every one knows,
and poetical inspiration did not always descend upon
me at the exact moment when I was ordered to play
with my ball. If the muse did not appear at my call,
my situation became dangerous, for temptation surrounded me on all sides. The library adjoined the
hall, and beguiling little volumes of foreign novels, or
numbers of Russian magazines, were there strewn
about on all the tables and divans. I was strictly
forbidden to touch them, because the governess was
very particular about the reading which I was al-

lowed. I had not many children's books, and I already knew most of them by heart. The governess never permitted me to read any book, even one designed for children, without having previously perused it herself; and, as she read very slowly, and was always short for time, I found myself, so to speak, in a chronic state of book-hunger; and here, all of a sudden, what riches close at hand! Well, how was it possible not to be beguiled?

I struggle with myself for a few minutes. I approach some little book, and at first I only glance at it. I turn over a few leaves, read a few lines, then run after my ball again as if nothing had happened. But little by little the desire to read attracts me. Perceiving that my first efforts have passed off successfully, I forget the danger, and begin eagerly to devour page after page. It makes no difference that the volume of the novel which I have hit upon is not the first. I read from the middle with quite as much interest, and supply the beginning from my imagination. From time to time, however, I exercise the precaution of making my ball execute a few bounds, in case the governess should return, and come to see what I am doing, that she may hear that I am playing as I have been commanded.

As a rule my trick proves successful. I hear the governess's steps in time, as she ascends the staircase, and manage to throw the book aside before her arrival, so that the governess remains convinced I have been amusing myself all the time by playing ball like a good, sweet-tempered child. Two or three times during my childhood it happened that I was so carried away by my reading that I observed nothing until the governess rose up before me as if through the floor, and caught me in the very act of transgressing.

In such cases, as in general after every especially
important crime on my part, the governess had recourse to the most extreme measures: she sent me to
my father with orders to relate my guilt to him myself. I feared this more than all other punishments.

In reality father was not at all severe with us; but
I saw him rarely—only at dinner. He never permitted himself the slightest familiarity with us except when one of the children was ill. Then he was
completely changed.

The fear of losing any one of us seemed to make
quite a new man of him. Remarkable tenderness
and softness were revealed in his voice and manners;
no one understood so well how to pet us, to jest with
us, as he did. We simply adored him at such times,
and retained the memory of them for a long while.
But on ordinary occasions, when all were well, he
stuck to the rule that "a man must be severe," and
therefore was very sparing of his caresses.

He loved to be alone, and he had a world of his
own, into which no member of the household was
admitted. In the morning he went off on a round of
domestic inspection, either alone or in the company
of the steward; he sat in his study almost the whole
of the rest of the day. This study, which lay quite
apart from the other rooms, constituted a sort of
holy of holies in the house; even our mother never
entered it without knocking first. It would never have
entered the heads of us children to appear there without an invitation.

Hence, when the governess used to say, " Go to your
father; make your boast to him of how you have
been behaving," I felt genuine despair. I cried and
resisted, but the governess was implacable, and taking me by the hand, she led me, or, to speak more

correctly, she dragged me through the long suite of rooms to the door of the study, left me to my fate, and went away.

Crying was no longer of any use; moreover the anteroom adjoined the study, and there I could see the face of some idle, curious lackey watching me with interest.

"Evidently the young mistress has been naughty again," I could hear behind me the half compassionate, half jeering voice of papa's valet Ilya.

I deigned him no reply, and tried to look as if there were nothing the matter—as if I were going to papa by my own wish. I could not make up my mind to go back to the school-room without having complied with the governess's orders. That would have been to intensify my fault by open disobedience; to stand there at the door, a mark for the laughter of the lackey, was intolerable. There was nothing left for me to do but to knock at the door, and bravely enter to meet my fate.

I knock, but very softly. Several moments, which seem to me interminable, elapse.

"Knock harder, *báryshnya;* papa does not hear," remarks that intolerable Ilya, who is evidently much interested in this whole affair.

There is nothing to be done; I knock again.

"Who 's there? Come in," calls father's voice at last from the study.

I enter, but halt in the semi-darkness on the threshold. Father sits at his writing-table with his back to the door, and does not see me.

"Who 's there? What 's wanted?" he cries impatiently.

"It is I, papa. Margarita Frantzovna has sent me," I gulp out in reply.

Then for the first time father divines what is the matter.

"Ah, ah! you have been naughty again, of course," he says, trying to communicate to his voice as stern an intonation as possible. "Come, tell your story. What have you been doing?"

And I, with sobs and breaks, begin my denunciation of myself.

My father listens in an absent-minded way to my confession. His ideas of education are very elementary, and the whole of pedagogy he puts under the rubric of woman's, not man's, business. Naturally he does not even suspect what a complicated inner world has formed within the head of that little girl who now stands before him and awaits his sentence. Occupied with his " man's business," he has not observed that I have gradually grown up from the chubby child that I was five years ago. He evidently finds himself in difficulties as to what he shall say to me; how he ought to act in the case presented to him. My misdemeanor seems to him of small importance, but he is a firm believer in the necessity of sternness in the rearing of children. He is vexed at heart at the governess, because she has not known how to settle so trivial a matter herself, instead of sending me to him; but he is bound to exhibit his authority now that his intervention has been invoked. Therefore, in order not to diminish his authority, he endeavors to assume a look of severity and disapproval.

"What a horrid, naughty little girl you are. I am very much displeased with you," he says, and pauses because he does not know what else to say. "Go, stand in the corner," he pronounces judgment at last, because, out of all his pedagogic wisdom, his memory has retained nothing beyond the fact that naughty children are made to stand in the corner.

And so you may picture to yourself how I, a big girl of twelve—I, who a few minutes previously had been going through the most complicated dramas with the heroine of a romance perused on the sly,—I am obliged to go and stand in the corner like a foolish little child.

My father continues his occupations at his writing-table. Profound silence reigns in the room. I stand motionless, but, good heavens, through what a gamut of thoughts and emotions do I not pass in those few minutes! I understand and recognize so clearly the fact how stupid and awkward this whole situation is; a certain feeling of inward shame in my father's presence makes me obey in silence, and does not permit me to burst out into a roar and make a scene. Nevertheless the feeling of bitter insult, of powerless wrath, rises in my throat and chokes me. "What nonsense! What is it to me that I must stand in the corner?" I console myself inwardly, but I feel hurt that my father is able and willing to humiliate me, and he that very father of whom I am so proud, whom I place above all others.

It would be well enough, too, if we were alone. But some one knocks at the door, and that intolerable Ilya makes his appearance in the room, under some pretext or other. I am perfectly well aware that the pretext is invented, that he has come simply out of curiosity, to see how the young mistress is being punished; but he makes no sign of this, does his business with deliberation, as if he perceived nothing, and merely casts a scoffing glance at me as he leaves the room. Oh, how I hate him at that moment!

I stand so still that my father sometimes forgets me, and makes me stand for quite a long time, because, of course, I am too proud to ask forgiveness on any account. At last father remembers me, and

4

dismisses me with the words: "Well, be off with you, and see that you play no more pranks!" It never enters his head that his poor little daughter has been undergoing great moral torture during that half-hour. He would probably be frightened if he could look into my mind. Naturally, after the expiration of a few minutes, he forgets all about that disagreeable, childish episode. And in the mean time I leave his study with a feeling of such unchildlike pain, of undeserved injury, as I never experienced afterward save in the very hardest moments of my life, and that only twice or thrice.

I return to the school-room, quieted and subdued. The governess is satisfied with the results of her pedagogical process, because I am so quiet and good for many days after this, that she cannot sufficiently praise my conduct; but she would be less satisfied if she knew what traces this process of my subjugation have left in my soul.

In general, there runs through all the memories of my childhood, like a black thread, the conviction that I was not beloved in the family. In addition to the remarks of the servants, which I accidentally overheard, the isolated life which I led with my governess contributed, in a large measure, to the development of this sorrowful conviction.

The governess's lot was not a happy one either. Homely, lonely, no longer young, parted from English society, and never thoroughly acclimated in Russia, she concentrated upon me the whole stock of affection, the whole hunger for moral ownership, of which her strong, energetic, unyielding nature was capable. I really served as the center and goal of all her thoughts and cares, and gave a meaning to her life; but her love for me was oppressive, jealous, exacting, and utterly devoid of tenderness.

My mother and my governess were of such entirely different natures that no sympathy whatever could exist between them. My mother, in character and appearance, belonged to that class of women who never grow old. There was a great difference of age between her and my father, and my father even to old age continued to treat her like a child. He called her Liza or Lizok, while she always addressed him as Vasíly Vasilievitch. He sometimes reproved her even in the presence of us children. "You 're talking nonsense again, Lizotchka!" we heard quite frequently. And mama never took offense at this remark; if she continued to insist on her own way, it was only like a spoiled child, who has a right to desire even what is irrational.

Mama was decidedly afraid of our governess, because the independent Englishwoman frequently spoke the truth to her with cruel boldness — claimed to be the sole and sovereign mistress in the rooms belonging to us children, and received mama there as a mere guest. Consequently mama did not look in on us very often, and did not meddle with my education in the least.

As for me, I was very enthusiastic in my own heart over my mama, who seemed to me more beautiful and charming than all the ladies of our acquaintance; but, at the same time, I constantly felt rather hurt — why did she love me less than the other children?

I am sitting in the school-room of an evening; my lessons for the morrow are all ready; but still the governess, on various pretexts, does not let me go up-stairs. In the mean time sounds of music reach us from the hall up-stairs, which is situated directly over the school-room. Mama is in the habit of playing the piano in the evening. She plays for hours to-

gether without notes, composing, improvising, passing
from one theme to another. She has a great deal of
musical taste, and a marvelously delicate touch, and I
am awfully fond of listening to her play. Under the
influence of the music and of fatigue from my lessons,
a wave of tenderness surges over me, a desire to nestle up to some one, to caress some one. Only a few
minutes remain before the hour for evening tea, and,
at last, the governess lets me go. I run up-stairs and
find the following scene: mama has already ceased
to play and is seated on the divan; Aniuta and
Fedya are sitting there also, one on each side of her,
cuddling up to her. They are laughing and talking
about something in so very lively a manner that they
do not observe my arrival. I stand beside them for
a few minutes, in the hope that they will notice me,
but they continue to talk about their own affairs.
This is enough to chill all my warmth. "They are
happy without me." The bitter, jealous feeling
sweeps across my soul, and instead of running to
mama and beginning to kiss her lovely white hands,
as I had pictured to myself down-stairs in the school-
room, I hide myself somewhere in a corner, far away
from them, and sulk, until we are called to tea; and
soon after that I am sent to bed.

V

THIS conviction — that my family loved me less than the other children — pained me very deeply, the more so as the craving for a strong and exclusive affection was very early developed in me. The result of this was that no sooner did one of my relatives, or one of the friends of the family, show me the slightest attention, for any reason whatever, above the attention shown to my brother or sister, than I, on my side, immediately began to feel for that person a sentiment which bordered on adoration.

I remember two particularly strong attachments of my childhood — for my two uncles. One of them was my father's oldest brother, Piótr Vasilievitch Korvin-Krukovsky. He was an extremely picturesque old man, of lofty stature, with a massive head entirely framed in thick, white curls. His face, with regular, severe profile, with thick, bushy eyebrows, and a deep, vertical furrow cutting through his high forehead, almost from top to bottom, might have seemed stern, almost harsh, in effect, had it not been lighted up by such kind, ingenuous eyes, such as belong only to Newfoundland dogs and to small children.

This uncle of mine was, in the fullest sense of the word, a man who was not of this world. Although he was the elder by birth, and should have repre-

seuted the head of the family, as a matter of fact
every one who took it into his head could order him
about, and that was the way every one in the family
treated him — like an elderly child. He had long enjoyed the reputation of being an eccentric man, and a
dreamer. His wife had died several years earlier.
He had made over the whole of his fairly large estate
to his only son, having stipulated only that he should
receive a very insignificant monthly allowance, and,
being thus left without any fixed occupation, he came
frequently to visit us at Palibino, and remained for
weeks at a time. We always regarded his arrival as
a festival, and the atmosphere of the house became,
somehow, more agreeable, more lively when he was
there.

The library was his favorite nook. He was exces-
sively lazy where any sort of physical exertion was
concerned, and would sit motionless for days together
on a large leather-covered divan, with one leg tucked
up under him, with his left eye, which was weaker
than the right, screwed up, and wholly absorbed in
the perusal of the " Revue des Deux Mondes," his
favorite periodical.

His sole weakness was reading to excess, to the
verge of insanity. He was greatly interested in politics. He devoured with avidity the newspapers,
which reached us once a week, and then he sat and
meditated for a long while: " What new mischief is
that scamp of a Napoleon concocting now ? " During
the last years of his life Bismarck also caused him a
great deal of mental labor. However, uncle was convinced that " Napoleon would gobble up Bismarck,"
and, as he died shortly before 1870, he retained that
conviction to the end.

As soon as it was a question of politics, uncle exhibited remarkable bloodthirstiness. It was nothing to him to annihilate an army of even a hundred thousand men on the spot. He exhibited equal lack of mercy when he chastised evil-doers, in his imagination.

A criminal was to him a fantastic personage, as he considered every one in real life upright.

In spite of our governess's protest he condemned all English officials in India to be hung. "Yes, madam, all, all!" he shouted, pounding the table violently with his fist in the heat of his passion. His aspect, at such times, was so savage and menacing that any one who had chanced to enter the room would certainly have been frightened. But all of a sudden he would calm down, and confusion and repentance would be pictured on his countenance. This was because he had suddenly observed that his unguarded movements had terrified our universal pet, a greyhound, Grisi, which had been on the point of taking a seat beside him on the divan.

But uncle was carried away most of all when he came upon the description of some new scientific discovery, in a newspaper. On days when this happened hot disputes and discussions took place at table, though in uncle's absence dinner usually passed off in sullen silence, as all the members of the household, in the lack of common interests, did not know what to say to each other.

"Did you read, my dear sister, what Paul Behr has invented?" uncle would say, addressing my mother. "He has made some artificial Siamese Twins. He has made the nerves of one rabbit grow fast to the nerves of another rabbit. You strike one and the other feels pain. Well, now, do you know of what that savors?"

And uncle would begin to communicate to those
present the contents of the newspaper article which he
had just read, involuntarily, almost unconsciously,
adorning it, and filling it out, and deducing from it
such hazardous conclusions and results as the inventor
himself had, most assuredly, never dreamed of.

His narration would be followed by a heated discussion.   Mama and Aniuta usually went over immediately to uncle's side, and waxed enthusiastic
over the new discovery.   The governess, in accordance with the spirit of opposition which was peculiar to her, almost as infallibly ranged herself against
him, and began vehemently to demonstrate the incon-
sistency, and, occasionally, even the peccability, of the
theories advanced by uncle.   The tutor sometimes
put in a word when it was a question purely of a
statement of facts, but wisely avoided direct share in
the dispute.   As for papa, he turned himself into a
skeptical, scoffing critic, who sided with neither of
the antagonists, but confined himself to keeping a
sharp eye on both, and emphasizing all the weak
points in both camps.

These discussions sometimes assumed a very warlike character, and by a sort of fatality they always
ended in the opponents suddenly leaping from questions of a purely abstract character into the domain
of petty personal assaults.

The most obdurate opponents were always Margarita Frantzovna and Aniuta, between whom a tacit
"Seven Years' War" was in progress, interrupted only
by periods of temporary armed truce.

If uncle amazed us by the boldness of his generali-
zations, the governess in turn distinguished herself
by no less talented applications.   In the most abstract
scientific theories, which were apparently the furthest

removed from the sphere of every-day life, she would suddenly espy grounds for condemning Aniuta's behavior—grounds so original and unexpected that none of us could do anything but raise our hands in amazement.

Aniuta did not remain in her debt, and retorted in so bold and vicious a way that the governess would jump up from the table, and declare that after such an insult she would not remain in our house.

Every one who was present felt awkward. Mama, who hated disputes and scenes, took upon herself the part of mediator, and the matter ended in the conclusion of a peace after long negotiations.

I can even yet recall what a storm was raised in our house by two articles in the " Revue des Deux Mondes," one on the "Conservation of Energy" (an account of Helmholtz's pamphlet), the other on the experiments of Claude-Bernard on the excision of portions of the brain in the pigeon. Probably Claudet Bernard and Helmholtz would have been greatly astonished if they had known what an apple of discord they had flung into a peaceful Russian family dwelling somewhere in the waste places of the government of Vitebsk.

But it was not alone politics and the accounts of new discoveries which possessed the power of upsetting the temper of my uncle Piótr Vasilievitch. He read romances and travels and historical articles with equal enthusiasm. He was even willing to read our children's books in the absence of anything better. I never met with such a passion for reading as he had in any one, unless in a few half-grown boys. It would seem as if there could not be a more innocent passion, or one which a wealthy landed proprietor could more easily indulge. Nevertheless Uncle Piótr Vasilievitch

had hardly any books of his own, and it was only
during the last years of his life, and that thanks to
our library at Palibino, that he was able to enjoy the
only pleasure which he prized.

Thanks to the remarkable weakness of his character, which formed such a contrast to his harsh, impos-
ing exterior, he had been under somebody's thumb
all his life, and under a thumb so stern and imperious
that there could be no question of his indulging any
whims or personal tastes.

In consequence of this weakness of character, he
had been acknowledged in his childhood to be unfit
for military service, the only occupation which was at
that time regarded as decent for a nobleman of ancient descent; and as he was of a mild temper and
not addicted to pranks, his tender parents decided to
let him remain at home, giving him only so much
education as was required to prevent his becoming a
hobbledehoy among the gentry.[1]

Everything he knew he had arrived at by dint of
thinking it out for himself, or by reading it afterward
in books. But his knowledge really was remarkable;
only, as in the case of all self-taught persons, it was
scattered and unequal in quality. On some subjects
it was very great, on others quite insignificant.

When he grew up he continued to live at home in
the country without exhibiting the slightest selfishness, and contenting himself with a very humble
place in the family. His younger and far more brilliant brothers treated him in a condescending, ami-
ably patronizing manner, as a harmless, queer fellow.
But all at once an unexpected piece of good luck descended upon him as if from heaven: the greatest

[1]An allusion to Von Vizin's famous comedy, "The Hobbledehoy."—*Trans.*

beauty and richest match of the whole government, Nadézhda Andreevna N., turned her attention to him. She was carried away by his handsome person, or simply made up her mind that he was the sort of husband she wanted, that it would be pleasant always to have at her feet this big, submissive creature, entirely devoted to her—God knows what she thought. At any rate she gave it plainly to be understood that she would be glad to marry him if he would ask her.

Piótr Vasilievitch himself would never have dared to dream of anything of the sort, but his numerous aunts and sisters made haste to set forth what a piece of luck had fallen to his lot; and before he had succeeded in recovering himself, he found himself the affianced husband of the beautiful, imperious, spoiled darling, Nadézhda Andreevna.

But no happiness resulted from this match.

Although all we children were thoroughly permeated with the conviction that Uncle Piótr Vasilievitch existed in the world especially for our pleasure, and chattered all sorts of nonsense with him that came into our heads, without the slightest restraint, still we all felt, as if by instinct, that one subject must never be broached: we must never ask uncle about his deceased wife.

The most sinister legends about Aunt Nadézhda Andreevna were current among us. The elders—that is to say, father, mother, and the governess—never mentioned her name in our presence.

But Aunt Anna Vasilievna, my father's youngest unmarried sister, was occasionally seized with a talkative mood, and she would then begin to communicate to us divers horrors about " her late dear sister, Nadézhda Andreevna."

" There was a serpent for you! God preserve us!

She simply worried me and my sister Marfínka to
death! And did n't brother Piótr catch it from her!
She would fly into a passion at one of the servants,
and would run straight into his study, and demand
that he should chastise the offender with his own
hands. He, in his kindheartedness, would object,
and would try to reason with her. Much good that
did! His arguments only made her more furiously
angry. She would fall foul of him, and begin to
abuse him with every bad word possible. And he 's
a regular marmot, not in the least like a man! It
made one feel ashamed to listen. At last she per-
ceives that she will not move him with words, so she
snatches an armful of his papers, books,—whatever
she can lay her hands on upon his table,—and flings
them all into the stove. 'I won't have any of this
rubbish in my house!' she screams. It even happened sometimes that she pulled a slipper from his
feet, and struck him on the cheeks with it. Truly!
And how she would lay on! And he, dear, peaceable
dove, would not defend himself, and would only try
to hold her hands,—and so carefully, lest he should
hurt her,—and reprove her. 'What are you doing,
Nádenka? Come to your senses! Are n't you
ashamed of yourself? And before the servants,
too!' But she had no shame about her."

"How could uncle endure such treatment? Why
did n't he leave his wife?" we exclaimed indignantly.

"Eh, my dears, does a man throw away his wedded
wife as he would a glove!" replied Aunt Anna Vasilievna. "And I ought to add that she was not unhappy with him, and that, nevertheless, he loved her
without bounds."

"Did he really love her? Such a wicked woman!"

"He loved her so, dear children, that he could

not live without her! When they settled her he mourned so that he came near laying violent hands on himself."

"What 's that, aunty? What do you mean by saying 'when they settled her?'"

But aunty, perceiving that she had said more than she intended, suddenly broke her narrative off short, and began energetically to knit at her stocking, in order to show us that there was to be no continuation. But our curiosity was inflamed, and we would not cease.

"Dear aunty, tell us, that 's a darling!" we entreated.

And, evidently, aunty herself cannot stop, since she is in the talkative mood.

" Why, this was the way of it. Her own serf girls strangled her!" she suddenly replied.

"Heavens! How horrible! How did that happen! Aunty, dearest friend, tell us!" we cried.

"Why, very simply!" answered Anna Vasilievna. "She was left alone in the house one night, having sent brother Piótr and the children away somewhere. In the evening her favorite chambermaid, Malánya, undressed her, and had taken off her shoes and stockings, and put her to bed in proper fashion, when, all of a sudden, she clapped her hands! At this signal other maids made their appearance from all the neighboring rooms, and Feódor the coachman, and Yevstignei the gardener. As soon as sister Nadézhda Andreevna had looked at their faces she knew that matters were serious with her; but she did not become terrified; she did not lose her presence of mind. She shouted at them: 'What are you up to, you devils? Have you lost your wits? Begone this moment, every one of you!' They turned cowardly,

out of habit, and were already retreating toward the
doors, when Malánya, who was bolder than the rest,
began to argue with them.

"'What are you about, you vile cowards? Have n't
you any mercy on your own hides? She 'll pack you
all off to Siberia to-morrow!' Then they came to
their senses, and the whole horde rushed up to her
bed, seized my late sister by the hands and feet, flung
a feather-bed on her, and began to smother her. She
begged for mercy, and offered them money and all
sorts of goods! No; they would accept nothing.
For Malánya, her favorite, continued to exhort them:

"'A towel; throw a wet towel over her head so
that no blue marks will be left on her face.' The people themselves, those miserable serfs, confessed it afterward. They told in detail, in court, under the
rods, just how it took place. Well, and they were
not patted on the head for this, their fine piece of
work. Many of them, I think, must still be rotting
in Siberia."

Aunt relapsed into silence, and we also remained
silent with horror.

"See now that you don't tell papa and mama that
I have been so silly as to chatter all this to you,"
were aunt's parting words to us. But we already
knew for ourselves that such things were not to be
mentioned to papa, nor mama, nor to our governess.
Nothing but a row would come of that.

But at night, when bedtime approached, this tale
pursued me, and would not let me sleep.

Once, when I was on uncle's estate, I saw a portrait
of my aunt Nadézhda Andreevna, painted in oil, full
length, in that commonplace, stereotyped manner in
which all portraits of that date were painted. And
then she presented herself vividly to me: small of

stature, elegant as a porcelain doll, clad in a low-necked, scarlet velvet gown, with a garnet necklace on her magnificent white neck, with a brilliant color on her round cheeks, an arrogant expression in her large, black eyes, and a stereotyped smile on her small, rosy mouth. I tried to imagine how those huge eyes must have opened wider yet, what terror must have been depicted in them, when she suddenly saw before her the peaceable slaves who had come to kill her!

Then I began to imagine myself in her place. While Dunyásha was undressing me it suddenly flashed across my mind: what if her kind, round face were to undergo a change all at once, and become malicious; what if she were suddenly to clap her hands, and then Ilya and Stepàn and Sasha were to enter and say: "We have come to kill you, miss!"

All at once I am thoroughly alarmed by this absurd thought, so that I do not detain Dunyásha, as usual, but, on the contrary, am almost glad when she finishes my toilet for the night, and goes off, at last, carrying the candle with her. But still I cannot go to sleep, and I lie for a long time in the dark with eyes wide open, impatiently waiting to see whether the governess will come soon, when she gets through playing cards up-stairs with the grown-up people.

Every time that I am left alone with uncle Piótr Vasilievitch this story involuntarily recurs to my mind, and it seems to me strange and incomprehensible that this man, who has suffered so much in his day, should now play chess with me as calmly as if nothing had happened, make me paper boats, or wax enthusiastic over some project or other of reclaiming the ancient bed of the Syr-Darya, or over some other newspaper article. Children always find it hard to imagine that any one of those nearly connected with them, whom they have been accustomed to see on simple, easy terms, in domestic intercourse, has lived through anything out of the ordinary run, or tragic, in his time.

Sometimes I felt a longing which was simply painful to question uncle in detail as to how it all had happened. I would gaze at him for a long time without taking my eyes off of him, and it seemed to me as if I could imagine that big, powerful, clever man trembling before his little beauty of a wife, and weeping, and kissing her hands, while she was tearing his papers and books, or slapping him on the cheeks with the slipper which she had taken from his foot.

Once, only once, in the whole course of my childhood, I could not restrain myself, and I touched uncle's tender point.

It was in the evening. We were alone in the library. Uncle was sitting as usual on the divan, with his legs tucked up under him, and reading. I had been running about the room playing with my ball, but at last I had got tired, had seated myself beside him on the divan, and, fixing my eyes on him, had given myself over to my customary meditations regarding him.

All at once uncle dropped his book, and, patting me affectionately on the head, inquired: "What are you thinking about, dear child?"

" Uncle, were you very unhappy with your wife?" suddenly burst from my lips, almost involuntarily.

I shall never forget how this unexpected question acted on my poor uncle. His calm, stern face suddenly became furrowed with fine wrinkles, as if from physical pain. He even stretched out his hand in front of him, exactly as if he were warding off a blow; and I felt so sorry for him, so pained and so

ashamed. I fancied that it was I who had taken the
slipper from his foot and struck him with it on the
cheeks.

"Uncle, darling, forgive me! I spoke without
thinking!" I said, cuddling up to him, and hiding
my face, which was crimson with shame, on his
bosom. And my kind uncle had to comfort me for
my indiscretion.

From that day forth I never returned to that prohibited subject. But about everything else I could
question Uncle Piótr Vasilievitch boldly. I was regarded as his favorite, and we used to sit together
for hours at a time, chatting about all sorts of things.
When he was interested in any idea, he could think
and speak of nothing else. Quite forgetful of the
fact that he was addressing a child, he frequently
developed before me the most abstract theories. And
this it was precisely which pleased me, that he conversed with me as with a grown-up person, and I
bent all my efforts to understand him, or at least to
present the appearance of understanding him.

Although he had never studied mathematics, he
cherished the most profound respect for that science.
He had gathered a certain amount of mathematical
knowledge from various books, and loved to philoso-
phize about them, on which occasions it frequently
happened that he thought aloud in my presence. I
heard from him for the first time, for example, about
the quadrature of the circle, about the asymptotes
which the curve always approaches without ever
attaining them, and about many other things of the
same sort—the sense of which I could not of course
understand as yet; but which acted on my inspiration,
imbuing me with a reverence for mathematics, as for
a very lofty and mysterious science, which opened out

5

to those who consecrated themselves to it a new and wonderful world not to be attained by simple mortals.

While referring to these my first encounters with the domain of mathematics, I cannot refrain from mentioning one very curious circumstance which also contributed to excite my interest in that science.

When we transferred our abode to the country the whole house had to be done over afresh, and all the rooms were repapered. But as the rooms were many, there was not paper enough for one of the rooms belonging to us children; it was a great undertaking to order more from St. Petersburg, and to order for a single room was decidedly not worth the while. They kept waiting for an opportunity, and in the interim this ill-treated room stood for many years with nothing but common paper on its walls. But by a happy accident the paper used for this first covering consisted of sheets of Ostrográdsky's lithographed lectures on the differential and integral calculus, bought by my father in his youth.

These sheets, spotted over with strange, incomprehensible formulæ, soon attracted my attention. I remember how, in my childhood, I passed whole hours before that mysterious wall, trying to decipher even a single phrase, and to discover the order in which the sheets ought to follow each other. By dint of prolonged and daily scrutiny, the external aspect of many among these formulæ was fairly engraved on my memory, and even the text left a deep trace on my brain, although at the moment of reading it was incomprehensible to me.

When, many years later, as a girl of fifteen, I took my first lesson in differential calculus from the famous teacher in mathematics in Petersburg, Alexander Nikolaevitch Strannoliúbsky, he was astonished at the quickness with which I grasped and assimilated the conceptions of the terms and derivatives, "just as if I had known them before." I remember that this was precisely the way in which he expressed himself, and in truth the fact was that at the moment when he began to explain to me these conceptions, I immediately and vividly remembered that all this had stood on the pages of Ostrográd-sky, so memorable to me, and the conception of space seemed to have been familiar to me for a long time.[1]

[1] S. K.'s tutor, Mr. Malévitch, says that when he first knew her she exhibited rare understanding, a power of quickly mastering whatever was taught her, and that she always knew her lessons well. During the first lessons in mathematics which he gave her he did not observe in her any special capacity in that direction; she was like all his previous girl pupils in that respect. "One day, after dinner, the General asked his favorite daughter: 'Well, Sófa, have you taken a fancy to arithmetic?' 'No, papa,' she replied. Less than four months later my pupil, in reply to nearly the same question from her father, answered: 'Yes, papa, I love to study arithmetic. It gives me great pleasure.' Three or four years of uniformly successful study passed without any noteworthy episode; but when we got to geometry, to the relations of the circumference of a circle to its diameter, my pupil, in explaining what I had told her in the preceding lesson, to my amazement reached the same goal by an entirely different road, and by special combinations of her own." Mr. Malévitch admits that, when he pointed out to her the somewhat circuitous road which she had taken, the young mathematician flushed up and began to cry. "But," he adds, "those were the first and the last tears which my pupil shed over her lessons in the whole nine years during which I taught her."

—"Recollections of Sophia Kovalévsky," by I. I. Malévitch.

VI

$\mathbf{M}$Y attachment to my other uncle, my mother's brother, Feódor Feodorovitch Schubert, was of an entirely different nature.

This uncle, the only son of my deceased grandfather,[1] was considerably younger than my mother; he lived permanently in Petersburg, and, in his quality of sole male representative of the Schubert family, he enjoyed the unbounded adoration of all his sisters, and of numerous aunts and cousins, all unmarried spinsters.

His arrival to visit us in the country was regarded as a real event. I was nine years old when he came to us for the first time. Uncle's coming had been talked about for many weeks in advance. The best room in the house was assigned to him, and mama herself saw to it that the most comfortable furniture was placed in it. The carriage was sent to meet him at the capital of the government, one hundred and fifty versts distant; and in the carriage were placed a fur coat, a fur lap-robe, and a plaid, that uncle might not take cold, as it was late in the autumn.

[1] Sophia Kovalévsky's grandfather, Feódor Feodorovitch Schubert, general of infantry, was a fine mathematician, and was at the head of the Topographical Corps. His father was still more noted as a mathematician, being an astronomer, at the end of the last century.—"S. V. Kovalévsky," published by the Mathematical Society of the Moscow University.

All of a sudden, on the eve of the day when uncle was expected, we looked out, and behold, driving up to the porch, came a simple peasant cart, harnessed to three post-horses, regular old nags, and out of it leaped a young man in a light city overcoat, with a leather traveling-bag slung over his shoulder.

"Good heavens! Why, it's brother Fedya!" cried mama, as she looked out of the window.

"Uncle, uncle has come!" resounded through the whole house, and we all ran out into the ante-chamber to welcome the guest.

"Fedya, my poor dear! how could you come with relay horses? Did n't you meet the carriage we sent for you? You must be jolted to pieces," said mama, in a voice of compassion, as she embraced her brother.

It appeared that uncle had set out from Petersburg twenty-four hours earlier than he had intended.

"Christ be with thee, Liza!" he said, laughing and wiping the drops of ice from his mustache before he kissed his sister. "I had no idea that you would make such a turmoil over my coming! Why should you send for me? Am I an old woman that I cannot travel one hundred and fifty versts in a post-cart?"

Uncle spoke in a deep, agreeable, tenor voice, with a rather peculiar lisp. Apparently he was still quite a young man. His closely cut chestnut hair framed his head in a thick, velvety mass, like beaver fur; his red cheeks were shining with cold, his brown eyes were warm and merry in their gaze, and a set of large, white teeth peeped out every moment from between his full, brilliantly red lips, surrounded by handsome whiskers.

"What a fine, dashing fellow uncle is! He's a dear!" I said to myself, as I gazed rapturously at him.

5*

"Who is this — Aniuta ?" asked uncle, pointing at me.

"What are you thinking of, Fedya ? Aniuta is quite a grown girl already. That is only Sónya !" mama corrected him, in a hurt voice.

"Goodness, how your daughters have grown! Look out, Liza, if you don't take care you 'll be set down among the old people!" he said, laughingly, as he kissed me. I felt an involuntary shame, and blushed all over at his kiss.

At dinner uncle occupied the place of honor, beside mama, of course. He ate with great appetite, which did not, however, prevent his talking the whole time, without cessation. He narrated divers Petersburg news and bits of gossip, which often amused all, and broke out into hearty, merry, ringing laughter himself. Every one listened to him with great attention; even papa treated him with much respect, without a shadow of that haughty, patronizingly scornful manner which he so frequently used with young relatives who came to visit us, and which the latter disliked extremely.

The more I looked at my new uncle the more he pleased me. He had managed to bathe and change his clothes, and no one, to look at his fresh, healthy face, would have guessed that he was just from a journey. His short coat, of thick English material, opening widely, sat particularly well on him, not at all as on other people. But his hands pleased me most of all — large, white, well-cared-for hands, with shining nails, like large pink almonds. I never took my eyes from him during the whole of dinner, and I even forgot to eat, so absorbed was I in scrutinizing him.

After dinner uncle seated himself on the little corner divan in the drawing-room and took me on his knee.

"Come, let 's get acquainted, mademoiselle, my niece!" said he. Uncle began to question me as to what I was studying, what I was reading. Children know themselves, generally, much better than grown people imagine; they know their own strong points and their weak points. Thus, for example, I knew perfectly that I learned my lessons well, and that every one considered me very "advanced" in my studies for my age. Consequently I was greatly pleased when uncle took it into his head to question me about it, and I answered all his queries willingly and freely. "Here 's a clever girl! She knows all that already!" he kept repeating every moment.

"Uncle, tell me something now!" I entreated him, in my turn.

"Well, here goes; only one can't tell fairy tales to such a clever young lady as you," he said, jestingly. "One must talk to you only of serious things." So he began to tell me about infusoria, about marine algæ, about the formation of coral reefs. Uncle had not been out of the university very long, so that all this information was still fresh in his memory. He narrated very well, and it pleased him that I listened with so much attention, with eyes opened very wide and fixed firmly upon him.

After this first day the same thing came to be repeated every evening. After dinner papa and mama went off to doze for half an hour. Uncle had nothing to do. He would sit down on my beloved little divan, take me on his knees, and begin to talk to me about all sorts of things. He proposed that the other children should listen also, but my sister, who had only just freed herself from the school-room, was afraid of

lowering her dignity as a grown-up young lady, if
she listened to such instructive things, "interesting
only for little children." My brother stood about and
listened once, found that it was not at all jolly, and
ran off to play at horse.

As for me, our "scientific lectures," as uncle jestingly termed them, became inexpressibly dear. Those
half-hours after dinner, when I was left alone with
my uncle, were the best part of the whole day to
me. I actually adored him; to speak frankly, I will
not swear that there was not mingled with this feeling a certain childish falling in love, of which little
girls are much more capable than their elders suspect.
I felt a certain confusion every time that I had to utter uncle's name, even if it were only to inquire, " Is
uncle at home ? " If any one, observing at dinner that
I never took my eyes from him, asked me, " Evidently
you are very fond of your uncle, Sófa ? " I blushed up
to my ears and made no reply.

I hardly saw anything of him all day long, as my
life was almost entirely separated from the life of the
grown-up members of the family. But during the
whole time of my lessons, the whole time of my recreation, my constant thought was, " Won't evening
come soon ? Shall not I soon be with uncle ? "

One day, while he was staying with us, some neighboring landed proprietors came to see us, with their
daughter Olga. This Olya[1] was the only little girl of
my own age whom I had happened to meet. However, they did not bring her to see us very often; but,
on the other hand, they left her for the whole day,
and she sometimes spent the night with us. She was
a very merry and lively little girl, and although our
characters and tastes were very dissimilar, so that no

[1] Diminutive for Olga.—*Trans.*

genuine friendship existed between us, yet I was generally glad to have her come, the more so as, in honor of the occasion, I was freed from my lessons, and given a whole holiday.

But now, when I saw Olya, my first thought was, " How will it be after dinner ? " The greatest charm of my conversation with my uncle consisted precisely in the fact that we were left alone together, that I had him all to myself, and I had a presentiment that the presence of stupid little Olya would spoil everything. Consequently I greeted my friend with much less pleasure than usual. " Won't they take her away earlier to-day ? " flashed across my mind constantly, with secret hope, in the course of the morning. But no ! it appeared that Olya was not to go until late in the evening. What was to be done ? I steeled my heart, and determined to speak frankly to my friend and beg her not to interfere with me.

" Listen, Olya," I said to her, in an insinuating voice, " I will play with you all day, and do everything you like, but, in return, do me the favor to go off somewhere after dinner and leave me in peace. I always talk with my uncle after dinner, and we don't want you at all."

Olya agreed to my proposal, and I honorably fulfilled my part of the agreement all day long. I played all the games that she could invent, assumed all the parts which she assigned to me, turned from a lady into a cook, and from a cook back into a lady, at her first word of command. At last we were called to dinner. At dinner I sat as on needles. " Will Olya keep her word ? " I pondered, and I cast uneasy, furtive glances at my friend, reminding her of our compact by significant looks.

After dinner I kissed papa's and mama's hands as

usual, and then pressed close to uncle, and waited to hear what he would say.

"Well, little girl, are we to have our chat to-day?" asked uncle, pinching my chin affectionately. I fairly leaped for joy, and, merrily grasping his hand, was preparing to set off with him for our wonted place. But all at once I perceived that faithless Olya was following us.

It appeared that my stipulations had had the effect of ruining things. It is very possible that if I had said nothing to her, when she saw me and my uncle preparing to talk seriously, she would have made haste to flee from us, as she cherished a saving terror of everything that smacked of instruction. But seeing that I prized my conversation with my uncle, and that I wished to get rid of her at any price, she took it into her head that we were certainly going to talk about something very interesting, and she wished to listen also. "Can I go with you?" she asked, in a voice of entreaty, raising her lovely blue eyes to my uncle.

"Of course you can, my dear," replied uncle, and looked at her very graciously, evidently admiring her pretty, rosy face.

I cast a glance of wrathful disapproval on Olya, but it did not confuse her in the least.

"But Olya certainly knows nothing about these things. She will not understand anything anyway," I ventured to remark in an angry voice. But this effort to rid myself of my intrusive friend had no result.

"Well, then, to-day we will talk of matters in a more simple way, so that they may be interesting to Olya," said uncle good-naturedly; and taking us both by the hand, he set out with us for the little divan.

I walked along in sullen silence. This conversation of three, in which uncle was going to talk for Olya, taking into consideration her tastes and her understanding, was not in the least what I wished. It seemed to me that something had been taken from me which belonged to me by right, which was inviolable and precious.

"Come, Sófa, climb up on my knee," said uncle, evidently quite unconscious of my evil frame of mind.

But I felt so hurt that this proposal did not soften me in the least.

"I won't!" I answered angrily, and going off to a corner I sulked.

Uncle stared at me with astonished, laughing eyes. I do not know whether he understood what a feeling of jealousy was stirring in my soul, and whether he wished to tease me; but he suddenly turned to Olya and said to her, "Well, if Sónya does n't wish it, do you sit on my knee."

Olya did not force him to repeat this invitation, and before I had recovered myself, before I had succeeded in realizing what was happening, she had taken my place on my uncle's knee. I had not in the least expected this. It had never entered my head that matters would take that dreadful turn. It seemed to me, literally, as if the earth were giving way under my feet.

I was too astounded to give voice to any protest; all I could do was to stare, with widely opened eyes, at my happy friend; and she, a little confused, but much pleased nevertheless, settled herself on uncle's knee as if there were nothing the matter. Setting her little mouth in a droll grimace, she tried to communicate to her childish, chubby face an expression of seriousness and attention. She was blushing all over, even her little neck, and her little bare arms were crimson.

I stared and stared at her, and suddenly—I swear that even now I do not know how it happened— something terrible took place. It was exactly as if some one were urging me on. Without stopping to think what I was doing, I suddenly, quite unexpectedly to myself, fastened my teeth in her bare, plump little arm, somewhat above the elbow, and bit her until I drew blood.

My attack was so sudden, so unforeseen, that for a moment all three of us remained stupefied, and merely stared at each other in silence. Then all at once Olya gave a piercing shriek, and her scream brought us all to ourselves.

Shame, wild, bitter shame, took possession of me. I fled headlong from the room. " Hateful, wicked little girl ! " my uncle's angry voice called after me.

My customary refuge in all the great griefs of my life was the room which had formerly belonged to Marya Vasilievna, and which was now allotted to our former nurse. There I now sought safety. Hiding my face on the good old woman's knees, I sobbed for a long time; and nurse, seeing me in this condition, lavished endearing names upon me without inquiring what was the matter, but only stroking my head.

" God be with thee, my dear bright little one. Calm thyself, my own," she said, and in my excited state of mind it was very soothing to me to be able thus to have a good cry on her knees.

Luckily my governess was not at home that evening. She was gone on a visit to some of our neighbors for a few days. Therefore no one thought of me. I could weep my fill with nurse. When I had become a little calmer she gave me some tea, and put me in the little bed, where I immediately fell into a dull, leaden sleep.

But when I awoke on the following morning, and suddenly remembered what had taken place the night before, I again felt so ashamed that it seemed to me I should never dare to look any one in the face again. However, everything passed off better than I had expected. Olya had been taken home the night before. Evidently she had been magnanimous enough not to complain of me. It was evident from the faces of all the people in the house that they knew nothing about it. No one reproached me with what had happened on the day before; no one teased me. Even uncle pretended that nothing of particular importance had taken place.

Still, it is strange that from that day forth my feelings toward my uncle entirely changed their character. Our after-dinner conversations were not renewed. He returned to Petersburg shortly after this episode, and although we often met afterward, and he was always very kind to me, and I loved him greatly, yet I never more felt for him my former adoration.

VII

BUT incomparably greater than all the other influences which were reflected in my childhood was
the influence upon me of my sister Aniuta.
The feeling which I cherished for her from my very
infancy was extremely complicated. I admired her
beyond measure, I obeyed her implicitly in everything, and felt very much flattered every time that she
permitted me to take part in anything in which she
was concerned. I would have gone through fire and
water for my sister, and at the same time, in spite of
my warm attachment to her, there nested in the
depths of my soul a grain of that particular sort of
envy which we so often, almost unconsciously, feel
toward people who are very near to us, whom we
admire greatly, and whom we would like to imitate in
all things.

Nevertheless it was a sin to envy my sister, for her
lot was far from being a happy one, to tell the truth.

My parents had removed to the country for permanent residence precisely at the time when she began
to emerge from childhood.

Not long after our removal, the Polish insurrection
broke out, and as our estate lay on the very borders
of Lithuania and Russia, the echoes of that upris-
ing concerned us. The majority of the neighboring
landed proprietors, and especially the wealthiest and

most cultivated, were Poles. It appeared that many
of them were more or less seriously compromised.
The estates of some of them were confiscated. Nearly
all of them were subjected to fines. Many voluntarily
abandoned their farms and went abroad. In the
years which followed the Polish insurrection, no
young people at all were to be seen in our parts; for
some reason or other they had all flitted away
somewhere. No one was left but children, old people,
—inoffensive, frightened creatures, afraid of their own
shadows,—and divers new-comers in the shape of officials, merchants, and petty gentry.

Of course, under such conditions, life in the country
was not especially gay for a young girl. Moreover
all Aniuta's previous education had been of such a
sort that no taste for the country could develop in her.
She did not like to walk, or to gather mushrooms, or
to row. Added to this, the leader in all such pleasures
was always the English governess, and the antagonism
which existed between her and Aniuta was so great
that as soon as one of them made any proposition the
other immediately opposed it. One summer, it is true,
Aniuta had a passion for riding on horseback, but this
was, apparently, chiefly an imitation of the heroine in
some romance which interested her at the time. As
no suitable companion could be found, she soon
wearied of these solitary rides in the company of a
tiresome coachman; and her saddle-horse, which she
had christened by the romantic name of "Frida," soon
passed to more humble duties, to carrying the overseer through the fields, and again became known by
its former name of "Little Pigeon."

There could be no question of my sister occupying
herself with the housekeeping; such a suggestion
would have struck her and all around her as in the

highest degree absurd. Her whole education had
been directed to the end of making her a brilliant society woman. She had been accustomed, ever since
the age of seven, to be the queen of all the children's
balls, to which she was often taken when my parents
lived in large towns. Papa was very proud of her
childish triumphs, of which many traditions circu-
lated in our family.

"When our Aniuta grows up she'll be fit to take
straight to the Court! She would turn the head of
any Crown Prince," papa was accustomed to say,
jestingly, of course; but the misfortune was that not
only we younger children, but Aniuta herself, took the
words in earnest.

In her early youth my sister was very handsome —
tall, slender, with a beautiful complexion, and a mass
of light hair, she might almost be called an ideal
beauty, and she possessed, in addition, a great deal of
special charm. She understood extremely well that
she could play the leading part in any society. And
behold, all of a sudden, she was condemned to the
country, to the wilds, to boredom.

She often came to papa and reproached him, with
tears in her eyes, for keeping her in the country. At
first my father got rid of her with jests, but sometimes
he condescended to explanations, and very rationally
demonstrated to her that, in the present troublous
times, it was the duty of every landed proprietor to
live on his estate. To abandon the estate at the present moment was equivalent to ruining the family.
Aniuta did not know how to reply to these arguments.
She only felt that she was no better off for all that,
that her youth would not be repeated. After such
conversations she went off to her own room and wept
bitterly.

But once a year, in the winter, father generally took my mother and sister to Petersburg, for a six weeks' visit at our aunts'. But these trips, which cost a quantity of money, did no real good. They only fired Aniuta's taste for pleasures, and afforded it no gratification. The month in Petersburg always passed so quickly that she had not time to collect herself. She could not meet a man competent to direct her mind to serious matters, in the society to which she was introduced; neither did any suitable offers of marriage present themselves. They fitted her out with toilettes, took her three or four times to the theater, or to a ball at the Club of the Nobility. One of her relatives gave an evening party in her honor. She heard compliments on her beauty. Then, just as she had begun to enter into the real spirit of the thing, she was taken back to Palibino, and again there began for her solitude, idleness, tedium, roaming hour after hour from one corner to another of the huge rooms in our Palibino house, living over again in fancy the recent joys, and passionate, fruitless dreams of new triumphs in the same career.

In order, in some degree, to fill up the void of her life, my sister was constantly inventing artificial diversions, and, as the life of the members of the household was also very poor in inward contents, every one in the house generally flung themselves eagerly into each new scheme of hers, as a pretext for discussions and excitement. Some blamed her, others sympathized with her, but she provided for all an agreeable contrast to the usual monotony of life.

When Aniuta was about fifteen years of age she exhibited her first act of independence by pouncing upon all the novels in our country library, and devouring an incredible number of them. Fortunately

there were no "bad" romances in our house, though
there was no lack of inferior and talentless works.
But the chief wealth of our library consisted in a
mass of old English romances, principally historical,
whose action took place in the middle ages, in the
period of chivalry. These novels were a real treasure
trove for my sister. They introduced her into a world
of wonders hitherto unknown to her, and gave a new
direction to her imagination. The same thing happened with her which had happened many centuries
previously with Don Quixote — she believed in the
knights, and imagined she was a young damsel of the
middle ages.

Unfortunately, also, our country house, a huge and
massive structure, with towers and gothic windows,
was built somewhat in the style of a castle of the
middle ages. During her knightly period, my sister
could not write a letter without placing at the head
of it, Château Palibino. The upper chamber in the
tower, which had long been unused, so that even the
winding stair which led to it had become rotten and
decrepit, she ordered to be cleaned of dust and spiders'
webs, hung it with old rugs and weapons, which she
had unearthed somewhere among the rubbish in the
garret, and converted it into her permanent abiding-
place. I can see her now, with her slender, graceful
figure clad in a closely fitting white gown, with two
heavy braids of light hair hanging below her waist.
In this attire my sister would sit at her embroidery
frame, embroidering the family coat-of-arms on canvas with beads — the arms of King Matthew Corvinus
— and gazing out of the window on the highway to
see whether a knight were not approaching.

"Sister Anne, sister Anne! do you see any one coming?"
"I see only the dust that's blowing and the grass that's
    growing!"

Instead of the knight came the chief of rural police, came the revenue officials, came Jews to buy father's vodka, and oxen, but there was no knight.

At the very moment when she began, unconsciously, to set her teeth on edge with romances of chivalry, the wonderfully exalted romance "Harold" fell into her hands.

After the battle of Hastings, Edith "Swan's Neck" found among the slain the body of her beloved King Harold. Just before the battle he had broken his oath, a mortal sin, and had died unrepentant. His soul was condemned to eternal torment.

After that day Edith vanished from her native land, and none of her kinsmen heard anything more about her. Many years elapsed, and people were beginning to forget Edith.

But on the opposite coast of England, amid wild cliffs and forests, stands a convent, renowned for its severe rules, where has dwelt for many years a nun who has taken upon herself the vow of eternal silence, and who enraptures the whole community with the feats of her piety. She knows no rest, either day or night; in the early morning hours and at dead midnight her kneeling figure is to be seen before the crucifix of Christ in the convent chapel. Wherever there is any duty to be performed, and aid to be rendered, the sufferings of others to be alleviated, she is the first to make her appearance. Not a single person dies in the neighborhood without seeing the tall form of the pale nun bending over his deathbed, without feeling his brow, covered with the death sweat, touched by her bloodless lips, sealed by the terrible vow of eternal silence.

But no one knows who she is, or whence she came. Twenty years before, a woman enveloped in a black cloak had presented herself at the convent gates, and, after a long and mysterious conference with the abbess, had settled there forever.

That abbess had died long since. The pale nun still flitted about there like a shadow, but none of those who now dwelt in the convent had ever heard the sound of her voice.

The young nuns, and all the poor folks of the country round about revered her as a saint. Mothers brought their sick children to her, that she might touch them with her hand, in the hope that they would be healed by her touch. But there were people who maintained that, in her youth, she must have been a great sinner, since she was obliged to expiate the past by such a penance.

At last, after many, many years of self-sacrificing toil, the hour of her death arrives. All the nuns, young and old, are bending over her deathbed. The mother abbess herself, who has long since lost the use of her feet, has ordered them to carry her to the dying woman's cell.

Then the priest enters. By the authority delegated to him by our Lord Jesus Christ, he releases the dying woman from her self-imposed vow of silence, and adjures her to tell him, before she dies, who she is; what sin, what crime, weighs on her conscience.

The dying woman, with great effort, sits up in bed. Her bloodless lips seem to have turned to stone with their long silence, and to have become unused to human speech. For several seconds they move convulsively and mechanically before she can succeed in uttering a single sound. At last, obeying the command of her confessor, the nun begins to speak, but her voice, unused for twenty years, sounds choked and unnatural.

"I am Edith," she utters with difficulty. "I am the wife of the dead King Harold."

At the sound of that name, accursed by all devout servants of the Church, the timid nuns make the sign of the cross in terror. But the priest says:

"My daughter, on earth thou hast loved a great sinner. King Harold is cursed by our holy universal mother, the Catholic Church, and there is no forgiveness for him forever; he must burn forever in the fires of hell. But God has seen thy deeds of piety for many years. He has valued thy repentance and thy tears. Go in peace. In the heavenly habitations another, a deathless bridegroom, awaits thee." The sunken, wax-like cheeks of the dying woman suddenly become crimson. A passionate, feverish light flashes up in her eyes, which seem to have faded out long ago.

"I want no paradise without Harold!" she cries, to the horror of all the nuns who are present. "If Harold is not forgiven, let not God summon me to his habitation!"

The nuns stand silent, rooted to the spot with horror, but Edith, rising from her bed with supernatural strength, throws herself on her knees before the crucifix.

"Great God!" she cries, with her broken, hardly human voice, "for one moment of thy Son's suffering thou hast removed from all mankind the seal of original sin. But I have been dying every day for twenty years, dying every hour a slow death of torture. Thou hast seen, thou knowest my sufferings. If I have deserved anything in thy sight through them, forgive Harold! Show me a sign before I die. When we recite 'Our Father,' let the candle which stands before the crucifix light of itself; then shall I know that Harold is forgiven."

The priest recites the "Our Father." He utters every word solemnly, distinctly. The nuns, both

6*

young and old, repeat the sacred prayer after him.
There is not one among them who is not penetrated
with pity for the unhappy Edith; who would not willingly give her own life to save the soul of Harold.

Edith lies prone upon the floor. Her body is already quivering with the throes of death, and all her
life, which is on the point of extinction, is concentrated in her eyes, which are riveted on the crucifix.

Still the candle does not light.

The priest has recited the prayer. "Amen," he
says, in a sad voice.

The miracle has not taken place; Harold is not forgiven.

A curse bursts from the mouth of the pious Edith,
and her eyes die out forever.

This romance brought about a complete change in
my sister's inner life. For the first time in her life
the questions presented themselves clearly to her
imagination: "Is there another life? Does all end
with death? Do two loving hearts meet and recognize each other in the world beyond?"

With that unrestrained vigor which she put into
everything she did, my sister saturated herself with
these questions as if she were the first person who
had ever encountered them, and she began to think,
in the utmost seriousness, that she could not live if
she did not find answers to them.

As I now recall the facts, it was a splendid summer
evening; the sun was already setting, the heat had
decreased, and everything in the atmosphere was
wonderfully calm and pleasant. The perfume of
roses and new-mown hay was wafted in through the
open windows. From the farm came the lowing of
the cows, the bleating of the sheep, the voice of the
laborers — all the varied sounds of a summer evening

in the country — but so changed and softened by distance that their harmonious blending only heightened the sensation of stillness and repose.

I felt particularly light and cheerful at heart. I managed to escape for a moment from the watchful eye of the governess, and flew up-stairs like an arrow to the tower to see what my sister was doing there. And what did I behold?

My sister was lying on the divan with unbound hair all flooded by the rays of the setting sun, and sobbing as if her heart would break— sobbing so that it seemed as if her bosom must burst.

I was terribly frightened, and rushed up to her. "Aniutotchka, what is the matter with you?" But she did not answer, and only waved her hand to me to signify that I was to go away and leave her in peace. Of course I only began to beseech her the more vigorously. She would not reply for a long time; but at last she rose and said in a weak voice which seemed to me thoroughly exhausted:

"You won't understand anyway. I am not crying over myself, but over all of us. You are still a child you need not think about serious things, and I was the same; but that wonderful, that cruel book"— she pointed to Bulwer's romance — "has made me look more deeply into the mystery of life. Then I understood how visionary is everything for which we strive. The most brilliant happiness, the most fervent love —all end in death. And what awaits us afterward, and whether anything awaits us, we do not know, and never, never shall know. Oh, this is terrible, terrible!"

She fell to sobbing again, and buried her head in the cushions of the divan.

This genuine despair of a sixteen-year-old girl for

the first time introduced to the idea of death by the perusal of a high-flown English novel, these pathetic, bookish words addressed to her ten-year-old sister— all this would probably have made a grown person smile. But my heart literally stopped beating with terror, and I was thoroughly permeated with reverence for the importance and the seriousness of the thoughts which were engrossing Aniuta. All the beauty of the summer evening was suddenly obscured for me, and I even felt ashamed of the causeless happiness which had filled my being to overflowing a moment earlier.

"But we do know that there is a God, and that after death we shall go to him," I made an effort to say nevertheless. My sister looked gently at me, as a grown-up person looks at a child.

"Yes; you still preserve your pure childish faith. We will say no more about this," she said in a voice which was very sad; but which at the same time was filled to overflowing with such a consciousness of superiority to me that I immediately felt ashamed of her words for some reason or other.

After this evening a great change took place in my sister. For several days following she went about with a gently sad demeanor, as if expressing in her whole person renunciation of all earthly bliss. Everything about her said *memento mori*. The knights and the beautiful dames with their tourneys of love were forgotten. What is the use of loving, of wishing, when all is to end in death!

My sister did not touch another English novel; she had conceived a dislike for all of them. On the other hand she eagerly devoured "The Imitation of Christ," and decided in emulation of Saint Thomas à Kempis to stifle dawning doubts by self-castigation and self-renunciation.

With the servants she was unprecedentedly gentle and condescending. If I or my younger brother asked her anything, she did not snarl at us as had been her habit hitherto at times, but immediately yielded to us, but with an air of such soul-crushing resignation that my heart contracted, and I lost all desire for cheerfulness.

Every one in the house was filled with reverence for her pious frame of mind, and treated her tenderly and cautiously, like an invalid or like a person who has suffered a heavy affliction. Only the governess shrugged her shoulders incredulously, and papa jested at dinner over her gloomy aspect—"son air ténébreux." But my sister humbly endured all father's scoffing, and treated the governess with an exquisite courtesy which enraged the latter more than roughness. Seeing my sister in this state, I could take pleasure in nothing. I was even ashamed of not being sufficiently depressed, and in private I envied the strength and depth of my elder sister's feelings.

This mood did not last long, however. The fifth of September was approaching: this was my mother's name-day, and that day was always celebrated in our family with special solemnity. All the neighbors for fifty versts round about came to our house; as many as a hundred people assembled, and something special was always got up by us for this day: fireworks, tableaux-vivants, or private theatricals. The preparations of course were begun long beforehand. My mother was very fond of these private theatricals, and played well and with much enthusiasm herself. That year we had just built a regular stage, quite in proper form, with side-scenes, curtain, and decorations. In the neighborhood there were several old, thoroughbred theater-goers who could always be enlisted as actors. My mother was very fond of private theatricals, but now that she had a grown-up daughter she felt rather ashamed of showing too much zeal in this matter; she wished to have everything arranged as if for Aniuta's pleasure. But here Aniuta had, as if of deliberate purpose, got into a conventual frame of mind.

I remember how cautiously, how timidly my mother approached her, endeavoring to get her into the mood for theatricals. But Aniuta did not yield at once. At first she displayed great disdain for the whole scheme. "What a fuss! And to what end?" At last she consented, with the air of yielding to the wishes of others.

But now the people who are to take part have arrived, and have set about choosing a piece. This, as every one knows, is not an easy matter; the play must be amusing but not too free, nor one requiring too elaborate a setting.

This year they fixed upon a French vaudeville, "Les Œufs de Perette." Aniuta was to take part for the first time in private theatricals in her quality of a grown-up young lady. Of course she had the principal part. The rehearsals began; she displayed wonderful dramatic talent. And lo! the fear of death, the conflict with doubts, the terror of the mysterious beyond—all fled. From morning until night Aniuta's ringing voice resounded through the house, as she sang French couplets.

After mama's name-day she wept bitterly again, but for another reason — because father would not yield to her urgent entreaty that she might be placed in the theatrical school. She felt that her vocation in life was to be an actress.

VIII

A T the time when Aniuta was dreaming of knights, and weeping bitter tears over the fate of Harold and Edith, the majority of the intelligent young people in the rest of Russia had been captured by an entirely different current, by wholly different ideals. Therefore Aniuta's impulses may appear to be strange anachronisms. But the nook where our estate was situated lay so far removed from all centers, such strong and lofty walls guarded Palibino from the outside world, that the wave of new currents could only reach our peaceful inlet a long while after it had arisen in the open sea. On the other hand, when these new currents did reach the shore at last they instantly seized upon Aniuta and bore her along with them.

It would be difficult to say how, when, and in what form the new ideas reached our house. It is well-known that such is the peculiarity of all periods of transition — to leave few traces behind them. For example, a paleontologist studies a layer of a geological section, and finds in it a mass of petrified traces of sharply characterized fauna and flora, from which he can construct in his imagination the whole picture of creation at that epoch; he goes one layer higher, and there, before him, lies a totally different formation, entirely new types; but whence they have come, how

they have been developed from those which preceded
them, he cannot say.

The petrified specimens of fully developed types
are everywhere found in abundance; all museums are
stuffed full of them, but the paleontologist is bliss-
fully happy if he accidentally succeeds in digging up
anywhere a skull, a few teeth, a bit of detached bone,
of some transitional type, by which he is enabled to
reconstruct in his scientific imagination the road by
which the development proceeded. One might suppose that nature herself zealously erases and eradi-
cates all traces of her work. She seems proud of
perfect specimens of her handiwork, in which she
has succeeded in incarnating some fully developed
thought, but she pitilessly annihilates the very memory of her first, uncertain efforts.

The inhabitants of Palibino lived on peacefully and
quietly; they grew up and waxed old; they quarreled
and became reconciled to each other; by way of passing the time they bickered about this or that magazine
article, about this or that scientific discovery, being
all the while thoroughly convinced, nevertheless, that
all these questions pertained to another world, wholly
distinct from theirs, and that they would never have
any direct contact with every-day life. And all of a
sudden, no one could say how, signs were revealed
close beside them of some strange fermentation, which
was indisputably drawing nearer and nearer, and
threatened to culminate directly in a line with their
quiet, patriarchal existence. And the danger threatened not from one quarter only; it seemed to come
from all points at once.

It may be said that, in the period of time included
between the years 1860 and 1870, all the educated
classes of Russian society were occupied exclusively

with one question — the family discord between the old and the young. Ask about whatever noble family you would at that time, you always heard one and the same thing — the parents had quarreled with the children. And the quarrels had not arisen from any substantial, material causes, but simply upon questions of a purely theoretical, abstract character. " They could not agree about their convictions ! " It was only that, but this " only " sufficed to make children abandon their parents and parents disown their children.

An epidemic seemed to seize upon the children,— especially the girls,— an epidemic of fleeing from the parental roof. In our immediate neighborhood, through God's mercy, all was well so far; but rumors reached us from other places: the daughter, now of this, now of that landed proprietor had run away; this one abroad, the other to Petersburg to the "nihilists."

The principal bugaboo of all parents and instructors in the Palibino district was a certain mythical community, which, rumor asserted, had been established somewhere in Petersburg. In it, at least so it was believed, they enlisted all young girls who wished to leave their home. There the young people of both sexes lived in full communism. There were no servants, and nobly born young ladies of the aristocracy washed the floors and cleaned the samovars with their own hands. As a matter of course, none of the people who spread these reports had ever been in this community themselves. Where it was situated, and how it could possibly exist in St. Petersburg, under the very nose of the police, no one knew exactly, yet no one had the slightest doubt that such a community did exist.

Signs of the times soon began to manifest themselves in our immediate vicinity.

The parish priest, Father Philip, had a son who had always hitherto rejoiced the hearts of his parents by his good temper and obedience. Suddenly, just as he had finished his studies in the ecclesiastical seminary, almost at the head of his class, this model youth, without a word of warning, turned into a disobedient son, and flatly refused to become a priest, although he had but to hold out his hand in order to obtain a desirable parish. His Reverence, the Bishop, summoned him to him, and entreated him not to quit the bosom of the church, giving a very plain hint that all he had to do was to express a wish for it and he would be appointed priest in the village of Ivánovo (one of the richest in the government). Of course, to this end he would be obliged, as a preliminary requisite, to marry one of the daughters of the former priest, because it has been the custom from time immemorial, that the parish forms the dowry, so to speak, of one of the daughters of the deceased priest. But even this enticing prospect did not beguile the young man. He preferred to go to Petersburg, enter the university at his own expense, and condemn himself to a diet of tea and dry bread during the four years of his studies.

Poor Father Philip grieved over his son's folly, but he might yet have consoled himself had the latter entered the department of law; of course, because that was the most profitable. But his son entered the department of natural sciences instead, and, on reaching home for his first vacation, uttered such nonsense about man being descended from the ape, and about Professor Syetchenoff having proved that there is no soul, but only reflection, that the poor, embittered father seized his sprinkler and sprinkled his son with holy water.

In former years, when he returned to his father

from the ecclesiastical seminary, the priest's young son had never allowed a single family festival at our house to pass without presenting himself to offer his congratulations, and at the festival dinner he sat at the lower end of the table, as befitted a young man of his rank in life, devouring the festival cake, but not mingling in the conversation.

But this summer, on the occasion of the first name-day which occurred after his arrival, the young man shone by his absence. On the other hand, he presented himself once on a day when we were not receiving, and when the servant asked him "what he wanted," he replied that he had come simply to call upon the General.

My father had already heard not a little about the "nihilist" son of the priest; he had not failed to notice his absence at his name-day, though, of course, he pretended to pay no attention to such an insignificant circumstance. But now he flew into a rage at the idea of the young upstart taking it into his head to present himself simply as a guest, as an equal, and he made up his mind to give him a good lesson; therefore he ordered the lackey to say to him, "The General receives people who come to him on business, and petitioners, in the morning only, before one o'clock."

Faithful Ilya, who always understood his master's faintest hints, executed his order in precisely the spirit in which it had been given to him. But the young *popóvitch*[1] was not in the least confused, and, as he took his departure, he remarked in a very free and easy way: "Tell your master that from this day forth I shall never set foot in his house again."

Ilya fulfilled this commission also, and it is not difficult to imagine what an uproar the prank of the

[1] The son of a priest.

priest's son created, not in our house alone, but in the whole district.

But the most startling thing was that Aniuta, when she heard what had happened, ran insubordinately into father's study, and, with crimson cheeks, and panting with excitement, exclaimed: "Why have you insulted Alexéi Philippovitch, papa? It is horrible, it is unworthy of you, thus to insult a well-bred man!"

Papa stared at her with astonished eyes. His amazement was so great that at first he could not tell what reply to make to his audacious little girl. Moreover, Aniuta's sudden fit of temerity had already evaporated, and she made haste to run away to her own room.

When he had recovered from his astonishment, and had thought the whole affair over thoroughly, my father decided that it was better not to attribute any great importance to his daughter's sally, but to treat the whole matter as a joke. At dinner, in Aniuta's presence, he related the story of a Tzar's daughter who had taken it into her head to champion a groom. Naturally, the Tzarevna and her protégé were represented in the most ridiculous light. My father was a master hand in the use of witticism, and we were terribly afraid of his ridicule. But to-day Aniuta listened to papa's story without being in the least troubled, but on the contrary, with an irritable and challenging aspect.

Aniuta expressed her protest against the insult to which the priest's son had been subjected, by seeking every occasion to meet him at our neighbors' or in her walks.

Stepán, the coachman, narrated one day at supper, in the servants' hall, how their dreadful young mistress had been walking alone in the forest with the *popóvitch.* "And it was fun to watch them! The young mistress walked along in silence, with downcast eyes, playing with the parasol which she held in her hands. But he strode along beside her, with his long legs, exactly like a long-legged stork; and he kept jabbering something all the time and waving his hands about. And all at once he pulls a towsled little book from his pocket and begins to read aloud, just as if he were reading her a lesson."

As a matter of fact, it must be confessed that the young priest's son bore very little resemblance to the fairy prince or the knight of the middle ages of whom Aniuta had been dreaming. His lank, awkward figure; his long, sinewy neck and pale face, framed in thin, reddish-sandy hair; his large, red hands, with flat and not always immaculately clean nails; and, worst of all, his unpleasant, vulgar pronunciation, smacking too much of the o,[1] which was an indubitable proof of his priestly extraction and his education in the free ecclesiastical seminary — all this did not make him a very fascinating hero in the eyes of a young girl with aristocratic habits and tastes. It was difficult to imagine that Aniuta's interest in the priest's son rested on a romantic basis. Evidently there was something else at the bottom of it.

And, in fact, the young man's chief attraction in Aniuta's eyes consisted in his having just come from

---

1 The church service is conducted not in modern Russian but in the ancient Slavonic language. The pronunciation of the Slavonic differs in divers respects from that of modern Russian, and the specially noticeable point is the full, round utterance of the letter o on all occasions. In the ordinary, cultivated language, the o gets its full sound only when it occurs in the accented syllable of a word, otherwise it sounds like a. From force of habit priests usually pronounce the o too distinctly in their ordinary language.—*Trans.*

7

Petersburg and brought thence the very newest ideas.
More than that, he had had the happiness to see with
his own eyes, only from a distance, it is true, many
of those great people whom all the young people of
the period adored. This was quite sufficient to render
him extremely interesting and attractive. But, in addition to this, Aniuta could, thanks to him, get possession of various books otherwise inaccessible to her.
Only the most stately and solid periodicals were taken in our house — the " Revue des Deux Mondes"
and the "Athenæum" among foreign journals, the
"Russian Messenger" among Russian journals. By
way of a great concession to the spirit of the times,
father had consented that year to subscribe to the
"Epoch," of Dostoévsky. But Aniuta began to get
journals of another stamp from the priest's son —
"The Contemporary," "The Russian Word," each
number of which was considered the event of the
day by the young people of the period. One day he
even brought her a copy of Hertzen's prohibited
"Kólokol" (The Bell).

I cannot say that Aniuta accepted all the new ideas
which her friend preached to her at once and without
criticism. Many of them disturbed her, seemed to her
exaggerated; she revolted against them and argued.
But in every instance, under the influence of her conversations with the priest's son, and of the perusal of
the books which he provided for her, she developed
very quickly, and changed, not day by day, but hour
by hour.

By the autumn the priest's son had succeeded in
quarreling so thoroughly with his father that the latter requested him to depart, and not to return on the
next holidays. But the seeds which he had sown in
Aniuta's brain continued to grow and develop.

Even her outward appearance was changed. She

began to dress simply in black gowns, with plain collars, and to comb her hair straight back into a net. She now spoke of balls and entertainments with scorn. In the mornings she collected the children of the house servants and taught them to read, and when she met the village women during her rambles, she stopped them, and held long conversations with them.

But the most noticeable thing was that Aniuta, who had hitherto hated study, now evinced a passion for it. Instead of, as hitherto, wasting all her pocket-money on toilettes and fripperies, she now ordered whole boxes of books from town; and not romances, either, but books with such wise titles as " The Physiology of Life," " The History of Civilization," and so forth.

One day Aniuta came to my father, and made a sudden and utterly unexpected demand — that he should allow her to go to Petersburg to study. At first father tried to turn her request into a jest, as he had done before, when Aniuta had announced that she would not live in the country. But this time Aniuta did not desist. Neither father's jests nor his witticisms had any effect on her. She hotly demonstrated that it did not follow, because father was obliged to live on the estate, that she must shut herself up in the country also, where she had neither occupations nor pleasures.

Father got angry at last, and shouted at her as if she had been a small child. " If you don't understand that it is the duty of every respectable girl to live with her parents until she marries, I won't argue with a stupid, bad little girl ! " he said.

Aniuta comprehended that it was useless to insist. But from that day forth the relations between her and father were very strained; each exhibited irritation against each other, and this irritation increased with every passing day. At dinner, the only time in the day when they met, they almost never addressed each other directly now, but a sting or a vicious hint was to be felt in every word which they uttered.

Altogether, unprecedented discord now began to reign in our family. There had been very few general interests hitherto; previous to this each member of the family had lived to suit himself, simply paying no attention to the others. But now two hostile camps seemed to have formed.

The governess had announced herself as the vigorous opponent of all new ideas, from the very beginning. She christened Aniuta the "nihilist," and the "progressive young lady." This last nickname had a particularly stinging sound on her lips. Feeling, by instinct, that Aniuta was plotting something, she began to suspect her of the most criminal designs — of running away from home on the sly, of marrying the priest's son, of entering the notorious community. So she became watchful, and distrustfully spied upon every step she took. But Aniuta, feeling that the governess was spying upon her, began deliberately, and for the purpose of irritating her, to surround herself with offensive mystery.

The warlike mood which now reigned in our house soon infected me. The governess, who had previously disapproved of my intimacy with Aniuta, now began to protect her pupil against the "progressive young lady," as if from the pest. As far as she was able she prevented my remaining alone with my sister, and every attempt to make my escape from the schoolroom, and run up-stairs to the world of the grown people, she began to regard as a crime.

I grew frightfully weary of the governess's watchful oversight. I also felt instinctively that Aniuta had acquired some new and hitherto unprecedented interests, and I had a passionate desire to understand precisely what it was all about. Almost every time that I happened to run unexpectedly into Aniuta's room, I found her at her writing-table engaged in writing. Several times I tried to make her tell me what she was writing, but as Aniuta had already received several scoldings from the governess for not only having deserted the right path herself, but for trying to corrupt her sister also, she was afraid of more reproaches, and always drove me away. "Ah, go away; do, please. Margarita Frantzovna will catch you here again. Then we shall both catch it," she said impatiently.

I returned to the school-room with a feeling of vexation and irritation against my governess, on whose account my sister would tell me nothing. The poor Englishwoman found it harder and harder to get on with her pupil. From the conversations which went on at dinner I gathered chiefly that it was no longer the fashion to heed one's elders. As a result the sentiment of subordination was considerably weakened in me. My quarrel with the governess now took place almost every day, and after one particularly stormy scene the latter announced that she would no longer stay with us.

As this threat had often been repeated before this I paid no great attention to it at first. This time, however, it turned out that she was in earnest. On the one hand the governess had gone too far, and could not honorably renounce her threat; on the other hand these continual scenes and rows had so wearied every one that my parents did not try to retain her, in the hope that the house would be more peaceful without her.

But, to the very end, I did not believe that the governess would go away until the very day of her departure dawned at last.

7*

IX

A LARGE, old-fashioned trunk, neatly covered with
a canvas case, and bound round with ropes,
had been standing in the antechamber since morning.
Over it rose a whole battery of little pasteboard boxes,
little baskets, little bags, and little packets, without
which no old spinster can set out on a journey. An
old tarantás, drawn by three horses in the plainest,
hardest used harness, which coachman Yákoff always
brings into play when a long journey is in prospect,
is already waiting at the door. The maids bustle to
and fro, bringing out and arranging divers small
articles and trifles, but papa's valet, Ilya, stands
motionless, lazily leaning against the door-post, and
expressing by his whole careless attitude that the
impending departure is of no great importance, and
that it is not worth while creating an uproar about it
in the house. All our family is assembled in the
dining-room. In accordance with the customary ceremony, papa invites all to seat themselves before the
journey is begun; the gentle-folk occupy the first
row, and the whole of the house-servants are collected
in a dense group a short distance away, sitting
respectfully on the edges of their chairs. Several
minutes pass in reverent silence, during which time
the sensation of nervous anguish inevitably evoked
by every departure and parting involuntarily takes

possession of the soul. But now father gives the signal to rise, crosses himself before the holy picture, the others follow his example, and then begin the tears and the embraces.

I glance now at my governess in her dark traveling gown, enveloped in a warm shawl of goat's down, and she suddenly appears to me in quite a different light from that in which I have been in the habit of regarding her. She seems suddenly to have grown old; her full, energetic figure seems to have fallen in; her eyes ("lightning flashes" as we called them in private to ridicule her), from which none of my misdeeds escaped, are now red, swollen, and filled with tears. The corners of her mouth quiver nervously. For the first time in my life I think that she is to be pitied. She embraces me long and convulsively, with such vehement affection as I never expected from her.

" Don't forget me: write. It is no jest to part from a child whom I have reared since her fifth year," she says sobbing. I also fall upon her neck, and begin to sob despairingly. A cruel sadness overwhelms me; the sense of irreparable loss, as if our whole family would fall to pieces with her departure. With this is mingled the consciousness of my own guilt. I am ashamed to the verge of pain when I remember that during all these last days, even as late as this very morning, a secret joy has seized upon me at the thought of her departure and my impending freedom.

Now I have got what I deserve. She is really going away, and we shall be deprived of her. At this moment I feel so sorry for her that God knows what I would not give to keep her. I cling to her; I seem unable to detach myself from her.

" It is time to start, that you may reach town by daylight," says some one. The luggage has already been placed in the carriage. The governess is put in also. One more long, tender embrace.

"Take care, miss, or you 'll get under the horses' feet!" some one cries, and the carriage moves off.

I run up-stairs to the corner room, from whose windows is visible the whole of the birch avenue, a verst in length, which leads from the house to the highway, and press my face to the pane. I cannot tear myself away from the window as long as the equipage is visible, and my feeling of personal guilt grows stronger and stronger. Heavens! How I regret at that moment the departing governess! All my skirmishes with her—and they have been especially numerous of late—now appear to me in quite another light than they have appeared previously.

"And she loved me. She would have remained had she known how I love her. But now no one, no one loves me," I say to myself, with tardy repentance, and my sobs grow louder and louder.

"Is it over Margarita that you are mourning so?" asks my brother Fedya as he runs past me. Surprise and mockery are audible in his voice.

"Let her alone, Fedya. It does her credit that she is so affectionate"—I hear behind me the hortatory voice of my old aunt, whom none of us children loves, because we consider her deceitful. My brother's mockery, and my aunt's sweetish praise, act upon me in an equally disagreeable, sobering manner. I never could bear from my childhood up to have people for whom I do not care comfort me in my heart-troubles. Consequently I angrily thrust aside the hand which my aunt lays on my shoulder by way of a caress, and muttering wrathfully, "I 'm not mourning at all, and I 'm not in the least affectionate," I rush off to my own room.

The sight of the deserted school-room comes near evoking another paroxysm of despair; only the thought that now there is no one who can hinder my being with my sister as much as I like comforted me a little. I decide to run to her at once, and see what she is doing.

Aniuta is pacing to and fro in the large hall. She always indulges in this exercise when she is engrossed or troubled by anything in particular. Her aspect at such times is very absent-minded, beaming; her green eyes become quite transparent, and see nothing that is going on around her. She keeps time as she walks with her thoughts, without being aware of it; if her thoughts are sad, her gait becomes weary, slow; when her thoughts grow more lively, and she begins to devise something, her pace quickens so that at last she no longer walks but runs about the room. Every one in the house is acquainted with this habit of hers, and laughs at her on account of it. I have often watched her on the sly as she walks, and wished to know what Aniuta was thinking about.

Although I know by experience that it is useless to approach her at such times, on this occasion I lose patience at last, and make an attempt to speak to her when I perceive that her promenade does not cease. "Aniuta, I am awfully bored. Give me one of your books to read," I say in a voice of entreaty. But Aniuta continues her walk, as if she does not hear me.

Several minutes more of silence elapse.

"What are you thinking about, Aniuta?" I make up my mind at last to inquire.

"Ah, leave me alone, please. You're still too young for me to tell you everything," is the scornful answer which I receive.

But I am thoroughly offended at last. "So that's

what you are like, and you won't talk to me. I thought that now Margarita had gone away that we were going to be very friendly, but you drive me off. Well, I 'll go, and I 'll never, never love you."

I am almost in tears, and am on the point of departing, but my sister calls me. In reality she is burning with the desire to tell some one about what interests her, and as she cannot talk to any member of the household about it, she contents herself with her twelve-year-old sister for lack of a better confidant.

"Listen," she says. "If you will promise that you will never tell any one, under any circumstances whatever, I will confide to you a great secret."

My tears vanish instantaneously; my wrath is as if it had never existed. Of course I swear that I will be as dumb as a fish, and I impatiently await her confidence.

"Come to my room," she says solemnly. "I will show you something which you certainly do not expect."

She takes me to her room, and leads me to an old bureau in which, as I am aware, she keeps her most precious secrets. Without haste, deliberately, in order to prolong my curiosity, she opens one of the drawers and takes from it a large envelop of business-like aspect, with a red seal on which is engraved, "The Epoch Magazine." The envelop bears the address, Dómna Nikítishna Kúzmin (this is the name of one of our housekeepers, who is heartily devoted to my sister, and would go through fire and water for her). From this envelop my sister draws another smaller envelop with the inscription, "For Anna Vasilievna Korvin-Krukovsky," and at last she hands me a letter in a large, masculine handwriting. I have not this letter by me at the present moment; but I read and re-read it so often in my childhood that it engraved itself on my memory so to speak, and I think I can give it almost word for word:

DEAR MADAM ANNA VASILIEVNA: Your letter, so filled with sincere and charming confidence in me, interested me to such a degree that I proceeded immediately to read the story you sent me.

I must confess that I began to read it not without secret trepidation. The sad duty so often falls to the lot of us editors of magazines, of destroying the illusions of young writers, just beginning, who send us their literary efforts for examination. In your case this would have been very painful to me. But as I read my trepidation vanished, and I yielded more and more to the spell of the youthful directness, the sincerity, and warmth of feeling with which your story is permeated. These qualities so predispose me in your favor that I fear I am still under their influence; therefore I dare not reply categorically and impartially as yet to the question which you ask me, "Will you develop into a great writer in the course of time?"

One thing I will say to you: I shall print your story (and with the greatest pleasure) in the next number of my journal. As for your question, I will advise you: write and work; time will show the rest.

I will not conceal from you that there is still much that is unfinished in your story, much that is too ingenuous; there are also, pardon my frankness, crimes against Russian grammar. But all these are petty defects which you will be able to conquer by diligent labor. The general impression is favorable.

Therefore, I repeat, write and write. I shall be sincerely glad if you find it possible to communicate to me more about yourself: how old you are, and what are the surroundings among which you live. It is important that I should know this, for a proper valuation of your talent.

Respectfully yours,

FEÓDOR DOSTOÉVSKY.

I read this letter and the lines swam before my eyes. Dostoévsky's name was familiar to me; he had often been mentioned of late at dinner during my sister's disputes with father. I knew that he was one of the most prominent Russian authors; but how came he to be writing to Aniuta, and what did it mean? For one moment it flashed across my mind that my sister might be fooling me in order afterward to laugh at my credulity.

When I had finished the letter I looked at my sister in silence, not knowing what to say. My sister was evidently enraptured by my amazement.

"Do you understand, do you understand?" said Aniuta at last, in a voice broken with joyful emotion. "I wrote a story, and, without saying a word to any one, I sent it to Dostoévsky. And, as you see, he considers it good, and will print it in his journal. And so my secret dream is fulfilled. Now I am a Russian authoress," she almost shouted, in a burst of irrepressible ecstasy.

In order to understand what that word "authoress" signified to us, it must be remembered that we lived in the depths of the country, far from any trace, even the slightest, of literary life. Our family read a great deal, and bought a great many new books. We and all those about us regarded every book, every printed word, as something that came to us from afar; from some unknown, strange world which had nothing in common with us. Strange as it may appear, it is nevertheless a fact that, up to this time, neither my sister or I had ever seen a single man who had written so much as a single line. There was, it is true, in our county town a teacher of whom it began suddenly to be rumored that he wrote letters to the newspapers about our county, and I remember with what respectful awe every one began to treat him until it was discovered at last that the letters had not been written

by him, but by a journalist who had come from
Petersburg.

And now all of a sudden my sister was a writer.
I found no words with which to express my rapture
and astonishment; I only flung myself on her neck,
and we hugged each other for a long time, and
laughed and talked all sorts of nonsense in our joy.

My sister could not make up her mind to tell any
other member of the household about her triumph;
she knew that all, even mother, would be alarmed,
and would tell father. In father's eyes her action in
writing to Dostoévsky without permission, and subject-
ing herself to his condemnation and laughter, would
have appeared a dreadful crime,

My poor father! He did so hate women writers,
and suspected every one of them of behavior which
had nothing to do with literature. And he was fated
to be the father of an authoress.

My father was personally acquainted with but one
authoress, the Countess Rostóptchin. He had seen
her in Moscow at the period when she was a brilliant
society beauty, with whom all the fashionable young
men of the day—my father among the number—had
been hopelessly in love. Then, many years afterward,
he had met her somewhere abroad, in Baden-Baden I
think, in the gambling hall.

" I looked, and I could not believe my eyes," my
father often related the story. " The countess entered,
followed by a whole string of sharpers, each more
vulgar than the other. They were all shouting, and
laughing, and gabbling, and treating her like a boon
companion. She went up to the gaming-table, and
began to fling one gold piece after another. Her eyes
shone, her face was red, her chignon was askew.
She lost everything, to her very last gold piece, and

screamed to her adjutants in French, 'Well, gentle-
men, I'm broke! The game's up!' Then in Russian,
'Let 's go and drown our grief in champagne!'
That 's what writing brings a woman to."
Naturally after this my sister was in no haste to
boast of her success. But this mystery in which she
was obliged to shroud her first appearance in the
literary career lent an added charm to it. I remember her raptures when a few weeks later the number
of "The Epoch" reached her, and we read in the table of contents, "The Dream," a novel by Yu. O——ff.
(Yúry Obryéloff was the pseudonym which Aniuta
had selected, because of course she could not publish
over her own name.)
Naturally Aniuta had already read me her story
from the rough copy which she had preserved. But
now in the pages of the journal the story seemed to
me entirely new and wonderfully beautiful.
The contents of the story were as follows: The heroine, Lílenka, lives among old people who have been
hardly used by life, and who have hidden themselves
in a quiet nook in order to seek rest and forgetfulness.
They endeavor to instil into Lílenka the same fear of
life and its turmoils. But that unknown life, of which
she hears only confused rumors, like the distant dashing of waves of the sea concealed behind mountains,
beckons her on and draws her to it. She believes
that there is a place

"Where people live more cheerfully,
   Alive with life ; and spin no spiders' webs."

But how is she to reach such people? Impercepti-
bly to herself Lílenka has become imbued with the
prejudices of the circle in which she lives. Almost
at every step the question unconsciously presents itself : Is it proper for a young lady to act thus or not?

She would like to tear herself away from that narrow world in which she lives, but everything which is "pas comme il faut" and vulgar alarms her. One day, during a festival in the city, she makes the acquaintance of a young student (of course, the hero of a novel of that day was bound to be a student). This young man makes a deep impression on her, but she behaves in a manner becoming to a proper, well-bred young lady, and shows no sign that he pleases her; and their acquaintance is confined to this one meeting.

After this Lílenka is bored, at first, but after a while she calms down. Only when some trifle that recalls this never-to-be-forgotten evening falls accidentally under her hand, among the various mementos of her colorless life with which her drawers are filled,—as is the case with most young ladies,—does she make haste to clap to the drawer; and then she goes about all day gloomy and dissatisfied.

But one day she has a dream — the student comes to her and begins to upbraid her for not having followed him. There passes before Lílenka, in her dream, a series of pictures, from an honest, industrious life with the man she loves, among clever companions, a life full of warm, bright happiness in the present, and of immeasurable store of hopes for the future. "Look and repent! Such was your life and mine!" the student says to her, and vanishes.

Lílenka awakes, and under the influence of her dream she makes up her mind to disregard the consideration of what is proper for a young girl. She, who has never hitherto left the house unaccompanied by either a maid or a lackey, now goes off secretly, hires the first public cab she encounters, and drives to the distant, wretched street where, as she is aware,

her dear student lives. After much searching and
many adventures, resulting from her inexperience and
awkwardness, she finds his lodging at last, but there
she learns from the comrade who shares it with him
that the poor fellow had died a few days before of ty-
phus fever. His comrade tells her what a hard life he
led, what want he suffered, and how, in his delirium,
he had several times mentioned a young lady. For
the comfort or the reproof of the weeping Lílenka he
repeats to her these verses of Dobroliúboff:

> I fear that even death hath played
> A scurvy trick upon me.
>
> .　.　.　.　.
>
> I fear that all I've craved in life,
> So warmly, eagerly,
> Will cheerily smile upon me, dead,
> As I lie in my coffin wearily.

Lílenka returns to her home, and none of the
household ever knows where she had spent that day.
But she always retains the conviction that she has
deliberately flung away her happiness. She does not
live long, and dies sorrowing over her wasted youth,
which has held nothing worth mentioning.

Aniuta's first success gave her so much courage
that she immediately set to work on another story,
which she finished in a few weeks. This time the
hero of her story was a young man, Mikháil by name,
reared apart from his family, in a monastery, by his
uncle, a monk. This story Dostoévsky approved more
highly than the first, and regarded it as more mature.
The portrait of Mikháil offers some resemblance to
that of Alyósha, in "The Karamázoff Brothers."[1]

When I read this romance several years later, as it
appeared, I was forcibly struck by this resemblance,

[1] A romance, by F. Dostoévsky.— *Trans.*

and commented on it to Dostoévsky, whom I then saw very often.

"Why, that is certainly true!" said Feódor Mikháilovitch, striking his brow; "but you must take my word for it, I had quite forgotten about Mikháil when I invented my Alyósha. However, perhaps he unconsciously recurred to my mind," he added, thoughtfully.

' But matters did not proceed so smoothly when this second romance was printed, as they had in the case of the first. A sad catastrophe occurred — Dostoévsky's letter fell into our father's hands and a dreadful row ensued.

This took place on the fifth of September, a memorable day in the annals of our family. A multitude of guests had assembled at our house as usual. That day we expected the post, which came to our estate only once a week. Generally the housekeeper, under cover of whose name Aniuta corresponded with Feódor Mikháilovitch, went out to meet the postman, and took from him her letters before she carried the mail to her master. But on this occasion she was busy with the guests. Unfortunately, the postboy who usually brought the mail had been taking a little too much liquor in honor of the mistress's name-day — that is to say, he was dead drunk, and in his place they sent a boy who knew nothing of the arrangements which they had made. Thus the post-bag arrived in papa's study without having been subjected to preliminary examination and weeding.

The registered letter addressed to our housekeeper, with the stamp of "The Epoch" magazine, immediately caught father's eye. What was the meaning of this? He ordered the housekeeper to be sent to him, and made her open the letter in his presence. It is

8

easy, or rather, it is not easy, to imagine the scene
that followed. The second misfortune was, that in
this letter Dostoévsky had sent to my sister the pay-
ment for her stories, something over three hundred
rubles, as I recall it. This circumstance, viz., that
my sister was receiving money from a strange man,
unknown to any one, seemed to father so disgraceful
and insulting that it made him ill. He had heart disease and gall stones. The doctor had said that any
emotion was injurious to him and might bring about
sudden death, and the possibility of such a catastrophe was a terror for the family in general. He
turned black in the face every time we children did
anything to displease him, and we were immediately
seized with fear that we had killed him. And here,
all of a sudden, what a blow! And the house was
full of guests, as if expressly!

Some regiment or other was stationed in our county
town that year. All the officers, and with them the
colonel, had come to us for mama's name-day, and had
brought the regimental band, by way of a surprise.

The festival dinner had ended about three hours
before this. All the chandeliers and candelabra in
the big hall up-stairs were lighted, and the guests,
who had had time to rest after dinner and dress for
the ball, had begun to assemble. The young officers,
panting and aching, were drawing on their white
gloves. Airy young ladies, in tarletan gowns and
huge crinolines, which were then in fashion, were
twisting about in front of the mirrors. My Aniuta
generally bore herself loftily toward all this company, but now the festive surroundings, the ball music, the flood of lights, the consciousness that she was
the handsomest and the most beautifully dressed woman at the ball, all these things intoxicated her.

Forgetting her new dignity as a Russian authoress, forgetting how little resemblance these red, perspiring young officers bore to the ideal men of whom she dreamed, she flitted about before them, smiling at each and all, and enjoying the conviction that she was turning the heads of all.

They were only waiting for my father's appearance to begin dancing. All at once a servant entered the room, and approaching mama, said to her: "His Excellency is ill. He begs you to come to his study."

Every one felt alarmed. Mama rose hastily, and holding up the train of her heavy silk gown with her hand, she left the hall.

The musicians, who were in the next room awaiting the signal agreed upon to begin a quadrille, were told to wait.

Half an hour elapsed. The guests began to feel uneasy. At last mama returned; her face was red and troubled, but she tried to appear composed, and smiled in a forced, constrained way. To the anxious inquiries of the guests, "What is the matter with the General?" she replied evasively: "Vasíly Vasilievitch does not feel quite well; he begs that you will excuse him and begin the dances without him."

Every one observed that something had gone wrong, but out of courtesy no one insisted further; moreover, every one wished to get to dancing as soon as possible, since they had assembled and dressed themselves for that purpose. So the dancing began.

As Aniuta passed mother in a figure of the quadrille, she looked into her eyes, and read in them that something disagreeable had taken place. Taking advantage of a pause between two dances, she took mama aside and pressed her with questions.

"What have you done? All is discovered! Papa

has read Dostoévsky's letter to you, and almost died
on the spot with shame and despair," said poor mama,
with difficulty restraining her tears.

Aniuta turned frightfully pale, but mama went on:
"Please to control yourself for the present, at least.
Remember that we have guests who would all be glad
of a chance to gossip about us. Go and dance as if
nothing had happened."

Thus my mother and sister continued to dance until nearly morning, both beside themselves with fear
at the thought of the thunderstorm which was ready
to break over their heads as soon as the guests were
gone.

And, in fact, a terrible thunderstorm did break.

Until every one was gone, papa admitted no one to
a sight of him, and sat locked up in his study. In
the pauses between the dances, my mother and sister
hastened from the room and listened at his door, but
dared not enter, and returned to their guests tor-
mented by the thought, "How is he now? Is he
ill?"

When all was quiet in the house he summoned
Aniuta to him, and what did he not say to her! One
phrase of his in particular engraved itself upon her
mind: "Anything may be expected from a girl who
is capable of entering into correspondence with a
strange man, unknown to her father and mother,
and receiving money from him. You sell your novels now, but the time will probably come when you
will sell yourself."

Poor Aniuta fairly turned to ice when she heard
these dreadful words. Assuming that she recognized
in her soul that this was nonsense, yet father spoke
so confidently, in a tone of such conviction,—his face
was so downcast, afflicted, and his authority, in her

eyes, was still so powerful,—that a torturing doubt assailed her, if only for a moment. Had she not made a mistake? Had she not, without knowing it, committed some terrible and improper act?

For several days thereafter, every one in the house went about as if they had been dipped in water, as was always the case after our family rows. The servants found out all about it at once. Papa's valet, Ilya, according to his praiseworthy custom, had listened to the whole of father's conversation with my sister, and explained it after his own fashion. The news of what had happened, in an exaggerated and distorted version, of course, made its way through the whole vicinity, and for a long time afterward the only topic of conversation among the neighbors was the "horrible" conduct of the young lady at Palibino.

Little by little the storm subsided. A phenomenon took place in our family which often happens in Russian families — the children reëducated the parents. This process of reëducation began with mother. At the first moment she took his part thoroughly, as she always did in all disputes between father and us children. She was afraid that he would fall ill, and she was angry. How could Aniuta grieve her father so? But when she saw that arguments were useless, and that Aniuta went about sad and hurt, she felt sorry for her. She soon developed a curiosity to read Aniuta's story, and then came a secret pride that her daughter was an authoress. Thus her sympathies passed over to Aniuta's side, and father felt that he was entirely alone.

In the first blush of his wrath, he had demanded from his daughter a promise that she would not write any more, and only on that condition would he consent to pardon her. Of course, Aniuta would not

8*

consent to give such a promise, and as a result, they did not speak to each other for days together, and my sister did not even appear at dinner. My mother ran from one to the other, reconciling and persuading. At last father yielded. This first step toward yielding consisted in his consenting to listen to Aniuta's novel.

The reading took place in a very solemn manner. All the family assembled. Fully conscious of the importance of this moment, Aniuta read in a voice which trembled with emotion. The situation of the heroine, her breaking away from the family under the persecution of the oppressions imposed upon her, all this so closely resembled the situation of the author herself, that it was patent to every one.

Father listened in silence, without uttering a word during the whole time of the reading. But when Aniuta reached the last pages, and hardly restraining her own sobs, began to read how Lílenka on her death-bed mourned for her wasted youth, large tears suddenly started to his eyes. He rose, without saying a word, and left the room. He did not speak to Aniuta about her story either that evening or on the following day; he only treated her with wonderful gentleness and tenderness, and all the family understood that her cause was won.

In fact, from that day an era of gentleness and concessions dawned in our house. The first manifestation of this new era was that the housekeeper, whom father had dismissed in his first burst of passion, received his gracious pardon and retained her place.

The second measure of gentleness was still more surprising. Father permitted Aniuta to write to Dostoévsky on condition only that she should show him the letters, and promised her to make Dostoévsky's personal acquaintance on his next visit to Petersburg.

As I have already said, mother and Aniuta went nearly every winter to Petersburg, where they had a whole colony of aunts, all spinsters. They occupied a whole house on Vasily Island, and when my mother and sister arrived they gave them two or three rooms. Father usually remained in the country. I also was left at home, in charge of the governess. But this year, as the Englishwoman was gone, and the newly-arrived Swiss governess did not yet enjoy their full confidence, mother decided, to my inexpressible delight, to take me with her.

We set out in January, taking advantage of the last good winter road. The journey to Petersburg was no easy matter. We had to travel for sixty versts on a road connecting two large villages, with our own horses; then two hundred on the highway, with post-horses; and at last, about twenty-four hours on the railway. We set out in the large covered carriage, or runners. Mama, Aniuta, and I rode in it, and it was drawn by six horses, while in front went a sledge containing the maid and the luggage, drawn by three horses with bells, and throughout the whole journey the ringing language of the bells, now near, now far, now quite dying away in the distance, then again suddenly resounding in our very ears, accompanied and sang a lullaby to us.

How many preparations were made for that journey! In the kitchen they cooked and roasted as many savory things as would have sufficed, I think, for a whole expedition. Our cook was renowned throughout the neighborhood for his puff-paste, and never did he make such efforts in that direction as when he prepared melting patties for his mistresses to eat on the journey.

And what a splendid journey it was! The first

sixty versts lay through a pine forest of thick pines, fit for ships' masts, broken only by a multitude of lakes and lakelets. In winter these lakes became huge, snowy fields, on which the dark pines surrounding them were sharply delineated.

Traveling was delightful by day, and still better by night. If you forgot yourself for a moment, you were awakened by a jolt, and for a minute you could not remember where you were. From the top of the carriage hangs a small traveling-lantern, illuminating two strange, sleeping figures, in big fur-cloaks and white traveling-hoods. I cannot at once recognize my mother and sister. Fantastic silver patterns start out on the windows of the carriage; the sleigh-bells jingle incessantly — all this is so strange, so unusual, that one understands nothing; only one feels a dull pain in one's limbs, caused by the uncomfortable attitude. All at once consciousness dawns on the mind with a bright gleam, — of where we are, whither we are going, and so much that is good and new which awaits us, — and all my soul is filled to overflowing with engrossing, dazzling happiness!

Yes, that was a splendid journey! And it remains almost the pleasantest memory of my childhood.

X

ON arriving in Petersburg Aniuta immediately wrote to Dostoévsky, and asked him to come to us. Feódor Mikháilovitch came on the day appointed. I remember with what a fever of expectation we awaited him; how we began to listen to every ring at the door for a whole hour before his appearance. But his first visit was not a success.

My father, as I have already said, bore himself with great distrust toward everything which proceeded from the world of literature. Although he had given my sister permission to make Dostoévsky's acquaintance, it was only with great reluctance, and not without secret alarm.

"Remember, Liza, that a great responsibility will rest upon you," were his last words to my mother, as he let us depart from the country. "Dostoévsky is not a man of our society. What do we know about him? Only that he is a journalist, and a former convict.[1] A fine recommendation! There 's no disputing it; you must be very, very cautious with him."

In view of these facts my father gave my mother strict orders that she was to be present at the meeting between Aniuta and Feódor Mikháilovitch, and not to leave them alone together for a single moment.

---

[1] Dostoévsky spent five years (1849–54) in Siberia for being implicated in a secret political society.—*Trans.*

I also begged permission to be present during his visit. Two elderly German aunts invented pretexts for making their appearance in the room from moment to moment, and stared curiously at the writer, as if he had been some sort of wild animal; and at last it ended in their seating themselves on the divan, and remaining there till the end of his visit.

Aniuta was furious that her first meeting with Dostoévsky, of which she had dreamed so much in advance, should take place under such petty conditions; assuming her angry mien, she maintained a persistent silence. It was awkward for Feódor Mikháilovitch also, and he was not himself in this constrained atmosphere. He grew confused among all these elderly ladies, and he got vexed. He seemed old and ill that day, as he always did when he was not in good spirits. The whole time he kept plucking nervously at his thin reddish beard, and biting his lips, which distorted his face.

Mama tried with all her might to start an interesting conversation. With the amiable society smile which was peculiar to her, she tried to find something agreeable and flattering to say to him, and something interesting to ask him, but it was evident that she felt timid.

Dostoévsky replied in monosyllables with premeditated discourtesy. At last, finding herself at the end of her resources, mama fell into silence also. After sitting with us for half an hour, Feódor Mikháilovitch took up his hat, and went away with a hasty awkward bow, and without having shaken hands with any one.

When he disappeared Aniuta ran off to her own room, and flinging herself on the bed she burst into tears. "They always, always ruin everything," she repeated, as she sobbed convulsively.

Poor mama felt herself in the wrong, yet innocent. She felt hurt that after all her efforts to please every one, every one should be angry precisely with her. She began to cry also. "You are always like that, dissatisfied with everything. Father did as you wished, allowed you to make the acquaintance of your ideal. I have listened to his rudeness for a whole hour, and now you blame us," she reproached her daughter, weeping like a child herself.

In a word every one felt wretched; and this visit, to which we had looked forward with such expectations, for which we had made such preparations, left behind it a very painful impression.

But five days later Dostoévsky came again, and this time his visit was the height of success. Neither mama nor my aunts were at home; my sister and I were alone, and the ice thawed immediately. Feódor Mikháilovitch took Aniuta by the hand, they sat down side by side on the divan, and immediately began to talk like old, intimate friends. The conversation no longer dragged as on the last occasion, limping painfully from one uninteresting subject to another. Now both Aniuta and Dostoévsky seemed to be in great haste to have their say, interrupted each other, jested and laughed.

I sat there, taking no part in the conversation, with my eyes fixed immovably on Feódor Mikháilovitch, eagerly drinking in all that he said. He seemed to me now quite another man, quite young and very simple, amiable, and clever. "He can't be forty-three already," I thought. "It is not possible that he is three and a half times older than I, and more than twice as old as my sister. And yet he is a great writer. One can treat him just like a comrade." And then I felt that he had become indescribably dear and near to me.

"What a splendid little sister you have!" said Dostoévsky all at once, quite unexpectedly, although a
minute previously he had been talking to Aniuta of
something entirely different, and seemed to be paying
no attention to me.

I flushed all over with joy, and my heart was filled
with gratitude to my sister when, in reply to this
remark, Aniuta began to relate to Feódor Mikháilovitch what a good, clever little girl I was; and how I
was the only member of the family who sympathized
with her. She grew very animated, praised me, and
invented unheard-of merits in me. In conclusion she
even confided to Dostoévsky that I wrote verses —
"Really, really, not bad at all for her age!" And
despite my feeble protest, she ran out and brought a
thick copy-book of my rhymes, of which Feódor Mikháilovitch immediately read two or three fragments,
smiling the while, and which he praised.

My sister beamed with satisfaction. Heavens! how
I loved her at that moment! It seemed to me that
I would give my life for those two dear people.

Three hours passed unperceived. All at once the bell
rang in the vestibule. It was mama returning from
the bazaar. Not knowing that Dostoévsky was with
us, she entered the room with her bonnet on, all la-
den down with packages, and excusing herself for being
a little late for dinner.

On seeing Feódor Mikháilovitch thus at his ease,
alone with us, she was dreadfully startled and even
alarmed at first. "What would Vasíly Vasilievitch
say to this?" was her first thought. But we threw
ourselves on her neck; and seeing us so happy and
beaming, she thawed also, and ended by inviting
Feódor Mikháilovitch to dine with us informally.

From that day forth he became an entirely different man when he was in our house; and in view of the fact that our stay in Petersburg was not to be long, he began to come to us very often — three or four times a week.

It was especially pleasant when he came in the evening, and when there were no other visitors. Then he brightened up, and became unusually agreeable and attractive. Feódor Mikháilovitch could not endure general conversation; he talked only in monologues, and that only on condition that all present were in sympathy with him, and listened to him with strained attention. On the other hand, if these conditions were fulfilled, he could talk better, more picturesquely, and more vividly, than any other person I ever heard.

Sometimes he related to us the contents of the romances he had conceived, sometimes scenes and episodes from his own life. I remember vividly for example how he described the moments when he was obliged to stand condemned to be shot, with bound eyes, before the file of soldiers, awaiting the fatal command, "Fire!"—when suddenly instead of that the drums began to beat, and the news of the commutation of his sentence arrived.

I remember still another of his stories. My sister and I knew that Feódor Mikháilovitch suffered from epilepsy; but that disease was surrounded in our eyes with such a magic terror that we could never make up our minds to touch the subject, even with the remotest hint. To our amazement he began himself to speak of it, and told us under what circumstances he had his first attack. Afterward I heard another totally different version of the affair — to the effect that Dostoévsky acquired epilepsy through the beatings with rods to which he was subjected in the Siberian

prison. These two versions are not in the least alike.
I do not know which is true, as many doctors have assured me that almost all persons who suffer from this
disease present one typical characteristic—that they
forget how it began with them, and are constantly
indulging in fancies on that subject.

At any rate, this is what Dostoévsky told us. He
said that the disease began with him when he was no
longer in prison, but among the colonists.[1] He grew
frightfully weary of the solitude, and for months at a
time he never saw a living soul with whom he could
exchange a rational word. All at once, quite unexpectedly, one of his old comrades came to him (I have
now forgotten the name which Dostoévsky mentioned).
This was on Easter Eve. But in the joy of seeing each
other again, they forgot what night it was, and sat
straight through it at home, engaged in conversation,
and paying no heed either to time or fatigue, but intoxicating themselves with words.

They were talking about what both valued most—
literature, art, and philosophy; of course, they touched
at last on religion.

His comrade was an atheist; Dostoévsky, a Christian; and both were hotly convinced, each of his own
position.

"There is a God; indeed there is!" shouted Dostoévsky, at last, beside himself with excitement. At
that moment the bells of the neighboring church began pealing for the Easter mass. The air hummed
and throbbed with them. "And I felt," said Feódor
Mikháilovitch, "that heaven had come down to earth
and swallowed me up. I positively attained to God,
and was permeated by him. 'Yes, there is a God!' I
shouted, and I remember nothing more."

[1] In Siberia, after release from prison.—*Trans.*

"All you healthy people," he continued, "have no conception of the bliss which we epileptics feel a second before the fit comes on. Mahomet asserts in the Koran that he had seen heaven and been there. All clever fools are convinced that he is simply a liar and a fraud. But no! he does not lie! He really was in paradise during a fit of epilepsy, from which he suffered, as I suffer. I do not know whether this bliss lasts seconds, or hours, or months, but you may take my word for it, I would not exchange it for all the joys which life can give!"

Dostoévsky uttered the last words in the passionate, broken whisper which was peculiar to him. We all sat as if we had been magnetized, wholly under the influence of his words. All at once the same thought occurred to all of us — is he going to have a fit now?

His mouth was twitching nervously; his whole face was distorted.

Dostoévsky probably read our alarm in our eyes. He suddenly broke off, drew his hand across his face, and smiled bitterly.

"Don't be afraid," he said; "I always know beforehand when it is coming on."

We felt awkward and conscience-stricken that he should have divined our thought, and we knew not what to say. Feódor Mikháilovitch took his departure soon after, and told us afterward that he really did have a severe attack that night.

Sometimes Dostoévsky was very realistic in his speech, quite forgetting that he was speaking in the presence of ladies. He sometimes horrified my mother. For example: One day he began to tell about a scene in a romance which he had invented while he was still very young. The hero, a middle-aged

landed proprietor, has been well and elegantly educated, and has been abroad, reads learned books, buys
pictures and engravings. He has been wild in his
youth, but has settled down later on; has become possessed of a wife and children, and enjoys universal
respect.

One morning he wakes early, and the rising sun is
peeping in at his window. Everything around him is
very clean, nice, and comfortable, and he feels himself
clean and respectable. His whole body is permeated
with a sensation of contentment and repose. Like a
genuine sybarite, he makes no haste to rouse himself wholly, in order that he may prolong, as much
as possible, this agreeable state of general, vegetating
well-being.

Halting on a sort of middle point between sleep and
waking, he mentally reviews the various best moments in his recent trip abroad. Again he sees the wonderful streak of light falling on the bare shoulders
of Saint Cecilia in the Munich gallery. Some very
clever passages also recur to his mind, from a book
which he has recently read, "about the beauty and
harmony of the world."

Suddenly, at the very height of these pleasant rev-
eries, and living over of the past, he feels uncomfortable — it is not exactly an internal pain, not exactly
uneasiness. It is the sort of thing which happens
with people who have old gunshot wounds, from
which the ball has not been extracted. A moment
ago there was no pain, and suddenly the old wound
begins to gnaw, and gnaw, and gnaw.

Our landed proprietor begins to think and to reflect:
what is the meaning of this ? He has no pain; he has
no grief; but it seems as if cats were clawing at his
heart, and it gets worse and worse. It begins to seem

to him that he must remember something, and he tries, and strains his memory in the effort. And suddenly he does remember, and very vividly, very realistically, the aversion which filled his being, as plainly as if it had happened the night before instead of twenty years ago. But for these twenty years past it has not troubled him a whit.

He remembers how, once, after a night of dissipation, and spurred on by his drunken companions, he injured a child.

My mother simply clasped her hands in horror when Dostoévsky said this.

"Feódor Mikháilovitch! For mercy's sake! The children are present!" she said, entreatingly, in a voice of desperation.

I did not understand, at the time, what Dostoévsky had said, but I guessed from mama's anger that it must be something dreadful.

However, mama and Feódor Mikháilovitch soon became excellent friends. My mother liked him very much, although she had to endure a good deal from him at times.

Toward the end of our stay in Petersburg, mama took it into her head to give a farewell party, and invite all her acquaintances. Of course she invited Dostoévsky. He refused, for a long time, but mama succeeded in persuading him, to her own undoing.

Our party turned out very stupid. As my parents had lived for ten years in the country, they had no real society "of their own" in Petersburg. There were various old friends and acquaintances whom life had long since dispersed in various directions.

Some of these acquaintances had succeeded in making for themselves very brilliant careers in those ten years, and in attaining to a very high

9

rung on the society ladder. Others, on the contrary, had become impoverished, and dragged out
a wretched existence in the distant streets of Vasíly
Island,[1] hardly managing to make both ends meet.
These people had nothing in common. Nearly all of
them, however, accepted mama's invitation, and came
to our party, out of old memory of "that poor, dear
Liza."

The company which assembled was rather large
and greatly mixed. Among the guests were the wife
and daughters of one Cabinet Minister (the Minister
himself promised to look in for a moment toward the
end of the evening, but did not keep his word). There
was also a very old, bald, and very pompous German
official personage, of whom I remember only that he
smacked the lips of his toothless mouth very ridicu-
lously, and kept kissing mama's hand and saying:
"She was fery britty, your mother. Neither of her
taughters is so britty!"

There was a ruined landed proprietor from the Bal-
tic Provinces, who lived in Petersburg in unsuccessful
search after a lucrative post. There were many respectable widows and elderly spinsters, and several
old academicians who had been friends of my grandfather. The prevailing element was German, stately,
airy, and colorless.

My aunts' apartment was very spacious, but consisted of a multitude of tiny cells, encumbered with a
mass of useless, ugly little trifles and stuff collected
during the whole long lives of two precise, active Germans. The large number of guests and the multitude

1 Vasfly Island, a suburb, situated across the Neva, much in
the same position as Brooklyn occupies to New York, but an integral part of the city, containing the University, Academy of
Fine Arts, and so forth.—*Trans.*

of candles rendered the atmosphere stifling. Two men-
servants, in tail-coats and white gloves, carried around
trays with tea, fruits, and sweets. My mother, who had
grown unused to city life, which she had formerly
loved so well, was in a state of inward trepidation
and excitement. Was everything as it should be?
Was n't it too old-fashioned, too countryfied? Would
not her former friends think that she had fallen behind their social circle?

The guests had nothing to do with each other. They
were all dreadfully bored, but, like well-bred people,
for whom wearisome parties constitute one of the
inevitable ingredients of life, they submitted unmur-
muringly to their fate, and bore all this dullness he-
roically.

But it is easy to imagine what happened to poor
Dostoévsky when he fell into this society! Both in
figure and appearance he presented a sharp contrast
to all the others. In a fit of self-sacrifice he had
deemed it requisite to don an evening suit, and this
dress, which set badly on him, enraged him during
the whole evening. He began to get angry from the
very moment when he set foot across the threshold of
the drawing-room. Like all nervous people, he felt
an irritating confusion when he got into a company
of strangers, and the more stupid, the more unsympathetic, the more insignificant this company was, the
more dire was his confusion. Excited by this feeling
of vexation, he was desirous of venting it on some one.

My mother made haste to present him to the guests;
but in place of a greeting he muttered something
unintelligible, resembling a growl, and turned his
back on them. But worst of all, he immediately
exhibited an intention to monopolize Aniuta. He
carried her off to a corner of the drawing-room, and

showed a decided resolve not to release her. This of course was in direct contravention of all the usages of society. Moreover his manner with her was anything but that demanded by society: he took her hand; when he spoke to her he bent down to her ear. Aniuta felt awkward, and my mother was beside herself. At first she tried "delicately" to give Dostoévsky to understand that his behavior was impolite. As she passed them, apparently by accident, she called my sister, and tried to send her off on an errand. Aniuta tried to rise, but Feódor Mikháilovitch detained her with the utmost coolness: "No, stay, Anna Vasilievna; I have not done talking with you."

At last my mother lost all patience and flared up.

"Excuse me, Feódor Mikháilovitch, but as the hostess she must busy herself with other guests also," she said very sharply, and led my sister away.

Feódor Mikháilovitch became thoroughly enraged, and settling himself in the corner he maintained an obstinate silence, glaring viciously at all present the while.

Among the guests was one for whom he conceived a special hatred at the very first minute. This was a distant relative of ours on the Schubert side; he was a young German, an officer in one of the regiments of the guards. He considered himself a very brilliant young man; he was handsome, and clever, and well-educated, and received in the best society —all this in proper measure, and not in excess. In his career he had also done what was proper, not with arrogant swiftness, but solidly, respectably; he had understood how to please the right people, but without openly seeking it, and without public toadying. By right of his relationship he courted his cousin, when he met her at their aunts'; but he did this also in proper measure, not that every one should observe it, but only in a way to make it understood that "he had views."

As is usual in such cases, all our family knew that he was a possible and a desirable match; but all pretended that they suspected no such possibility. Even my mother, when she remained alone with my aunts, could not make up her mind to touch upon this delicate question otherwise than by half words and hints.

It was enough for Dostoévsky to take one glance at this handsome, well-formed, self-satisfied person, to make him immediately hate him to madness.

The young cuirassier, picturesquely posed in an arm-chair, was displaying in all their beauty his fashionably made trousers, which fitted closely his long, shapely legs. Jingling his epaulets, and bending slightly over my sister, he related something amusing to her. Aniuta, still confused by the recent episode with Dostoévsky, listened to him with her rather stereotyped, drawing-room smile, "the smile of a tender angel," as the English governess viciously designated it.

Feódor Mikháilovitch looked at this group, and a whole romance immediately took form in his brain. Aniuta hated and despised this "horrid little German," this "conceited, impudent fellow," but her parents wished to marry her to him, and were throwing them together in every possible way. Of course the whole party had been arranged exclusively with that object. Having concocted this romance, Dostoévsky immediately put faith in it, and flew into a frightful rage.

The fashionable topic of conversation that winter was a little book published by some English clergyman or other—containing a comparison between the Russian State Church and Protestantism. In this

9*

Russo-High-German circle this was a topic which interested all, and when the conversation turned upon
it, it grew more animated. Mama, who was herself
a German, remarked that one of the advantages of
Protestantism over the Russian State Church was
that Protestants read the gospels more.

"But were the gospels written for society women?"
suddenly burst out Dostoévsky, who had hitherto preserved an obstinate silence. "It is written there, 'In
the beginning God created man and wife,' or again,
'The man shall leave his father and mother and
cleave to his wife.' That's the way Christ understood
marriage. But what would be said of it by the mamas
who think of nothing but of how to get their daughters off their hands in the most profitable manner."

Dostoévsky uttered this with unusual pathos. In
accordance with his habit when he was excited, he had
drawn himself into a heap, and fairly fired off his
words. They produced a wonderful effect. All the
well-bred Germans held their peace, and stared at
him. It was only after the lapse of several seconds
that they all comprehended the full awkwardness of
what had been said, and then all began to talk at
once in the endeavor to drown his voice.

Dostoévsky cast one more withering glance at all of
them, then retreated again into his corner, and never
uttered another word the whole evening.

The next time he made his appearance at our house,
mama tried to receive him coldly, to show him that
she felt insulted; but her wonderful kindness and
gentleness never allowed her to be angry long with
any one, least of all with a man like Feódor Mikháilovitch; so they soon became friends again, and everything went on as before with them.

On the other hand Aniuta's relations to Dostoévsky

seemed to have undergone a complete change after that evening—they seemed to have entered upon a new phase of existence. Dostoévsky entirely ceased to over-awe Aniuta; on the contrary she even manifested a desire to contradict him, to tease him. But he, on his side, began to display an unwonted nervousness and irritability toward her. He began to demand an account of how she had spent the day when he had not been at our house, and to bear himself with a hostile attitude toward all those people for whom she showed any enthusiasm. He did not come to us any less frequently; his visits were even more frequent than before, although he spent most of the time in quarrels with my sister.

In the beginning of the acquaintance my sister had been ready to give up every pleasure, to refuse every invitation on those days when she expected Dostoévsky; and if he were in the room, she had paid no attention to any one else. But now all this was changed. If he came when we had visitors, she remained calmly seated, and continued to entertain her guests. It even happened that she was invited somewhere on the evening when it had been arranged that he should come to see her, in which case she wrote to him and excused herself.

On the following day Feódor Mikháilovitch came, still in a rage. Aniuta pretended that she did not observe his bad humor, took her work, and began to embroider.

This enraged Dostoévsky more than ever; he sat down in the corner and remained persistently silent. My sister was silent also.

"Come, put away your embroidery," Feódor Mikháilovitch said at last, unable to restrain his temper, and took her embroidery out of her hands.

My sister folded her hands submissively on her lap, and remained silent.

"Where were you last night?" asks Feódor Mikháilovitch, wrathfully.

"At a ball," replies my sister, indifferently.

"And you danced?"

"Of course."

"With your second cousin?"

"With him and with others."

"And that amuses you?" Dostoévsky continues his catechism. Aniuta shrugs her shoulders.

"In the absence of something better, that is amusing," she replies, and takes up her embroidery again.

Dostoévsky glares at her in silence for a few moments.

"You are an empty-headed, silly, naughty little girl; that's what you are!" he says, decisively, at last.

That was the spirit in which conversation was now conducted at our house.

A constant and very burning subject of quarrels between them was nihilism. The disputes on this point often lasted until long after midnight, and the longer they both talked the warmer they grew, and in the heat of discussion they expressed far more extreme opinions than they really held.

"All the young people of the present day are dull and half educated!" Dostoévsky sometimes exclaimed. "They think more of soft-boiled boots [1] than they do of Púshkin!"

"Púshkin has, indeed, become old-fashioned for our day," my sister would remark calmly, knowing well

---

[1] This sentiment, expressed by a revolutionary writer, has become proverbial. The expression used declares that boots, cooked like soft-boiled eggs, were better than all Púshkin.— *Trans.*

that nothing so enraged him as disrespect toward Púshkin.

Dostoévsky, beside himself with wrath, sometimes snatched up his hat and departed, solemnly declaring that it was useless to argue with a little nihilist, and that he would never set foot in our house again. But he came again the next day, of course, just as if nothing had happened.

In proportion as Dostoévsky's relations with my sister became strained, my friendship for him increased. I was more enthusiastic over him every day, and completely subject to his influence. Naturally he noticed my boundless adoration of him, and it pleased him. He was always holding me up to my sister as an example.

It would happen that Dostoévsky related some profound or talented paradox, in contravention of accepted morality, and my sister would suddenly take it into her head to pretend that she did not understand. My eyes were beaming with rapture, but she, with the express purpose of angering him, would reply with some stale, threadbare truth.

" You have a worthless, insignificant little soul! " Feódor Mikháilovitch would then cry hotly. " It 's quite another matter with your sister! She is still a child, but she understands me, because she has a sensitive soul! "

I blushed all over with pleasure, and, had it been necessary, I would have allowed myself to be cut in pieces, to prove to him that I understood him. In the depths of my soul I was very content that Dostoévsky no longer exhibited for my sister such enthusiasm as in the beginning of their friendship. I was greatly ashamed of this feeling. I reproached myself for it, regarding it somewhat in the light of treason toward my sister; and entering into an unconscious compromise with my conscience, I tried to redeem my secret sin against her by particular obligingness and amiability toward her. But the pangs of conscience did not prevent my feeling a certain jubilation every time that Aniuta and Dostoévsky quarreled.

Feódor Mikháilovitch called me his friend, and I very ingenuously believed that I stood nearer to him than did my elder sister, and that I understood him better than she did. He even praised my personal appearance, to the disparagement of Aniuta's.

"You imagine that you are very handsome," he said to my sister; "but your little sister will be much handsomer than you in course of time. She has a more expressive face, and the eyes of a gipsy! But you are merely a tolerably comely little German, that 's what you are!"

Aniuta smiled disdainfully; but I drank in this unprecedented laudation of my beauty with rapture.

"But perhaps it is true," I said to myself, with sinking heart; and I began even to be seriously troubled with the thought—how was it that my sister was not annoyed by the preference which Dostoévsky exhibited for me?

I longed greatly to know for certain what Aniuta herself thought of all this, and whether it were true that I was destined to become beautiful when I should be fully grown up. This last thought interested me especially.

In Petersburg my sister and I slept in the same room, and at night, when we were undressing, our most intimate conferences took place.

Aniuta usually stood in front of the mirror brushing her long, golden hair, and plaiting it into two braids for the night. This operation required a good deal of time; her hair was very thick and silky, and

she enjoyed passing her comb through it. I sat on
the bed, already fully undressed, with my arms clasped
round my knees, and meditating how I could begin
the conversation which interested me.

"What ridiculous things Feódor Mikháilovitch said
to-day!" I began, at last, endeavoring to appear as
indifferent as possible. "What were they?" asked
my sister, in an absent-minded way, having evidently
quite forgotten the conversation which was so important to me. "About my having gipsy eyes, and being destined to become a beauty," I said, and felt
myself blushing up to the ears.

Aniuta dropped her hand which held the comb, and
turned her face toward me, with a picturesque bend
of the neck.

"And you believe that Feódor Mikháilovitch thinks
you handsome — handsomer than I am?" she asked,
gazing at me with a sly and mysterious look.

This cunning look, those gleaming, green eyes, and
the disheveled golden hair, made a perfect water-
nymph of her. Alongside her, in the big, full-length
mirror, which stood exactly opposite her bed, I beheld
my own small, swarthy face, and could make the comparison between us. I cannot say that that comparison was especially agreeable to me, but my sister's
cold, self-confident tone vexed me, and I would not
yield.

"Tastes differ!" I said, angrily.

"Yes; some people do have strange tastes!" remarked Aniuta, calmly, and went on brushing her
hair.

When the candle was extinguished, I lay with my
face buried in the pillow, and continued my reflections on the same subject.

"But perhaps Feódor Mikháilovitch has such a taste

that I please him more than my sister does," occurred to me, and I began to pray mentally: "Lord God, let every one, let the whole world, go into raptures over Aniuta, only make me seem pretty to Feódor Mikháilovitch!"

But my illusions on this point were destined to a speedy and cruel destruction.

Among the accomplishments which Dostoévsky encouraged was music. Up to that time I had learned to play on the piano as the majority of little girls learn, without feeling any particular liking or any particular hatred for it. My ear was only moderately good; but as, from the age of five years, I had been made to play scales and exercises for an hour and a half every day, a certain amount of execution had been developed in me now, at the age of thirteen — a tolerable touch, and a faculty of reading music at sight very readily.

It happened that once, at the very beginning of our acquaintance, I had played for Dostoévsky a piece in which I was remarkably successful—variations on the themes of Russian songs. Feódor Mikháilovitch was not a musician. He belonged to that class of people whose enjoyment of music depends on purely subjective conditions — on their mood at a given moment. Sometimes the most beautiful and artistically executed music only provokes a yawn in them; on other occasions, a hand-organ whining in the courtyard moves them to tears.

It chanced that, on the occasion when I played, Feódor Mikháilovitch was in just one of those sensitive, emotional states of mind, for he went into ecstasies over my playing, and allowing his feelings to run away with him, as usual, he began to lavish on me the most exaggerated praises—I had talent and feeling, and God knows what all!

Of course, from that day forth I became passionately fond of music. I begged my mother to get me a good teacher, and during the whole of our stay in Petersburg, I spent every leisure moment at the piano, so that in the course of three months I really did make a great deal of progress.

Now I prepared a surprise for Dostoévsky. One day he happened to say that of all musical compositions he loved most of all Beethoven's " Sonata Pathétique," and that this sonata always overwhelmed him with a whole world of forgotten sensations. Although the sonata was considerably more difficult than any of the pieces which I had hitherto played, I determined to learn it at any cost; and really, by expending a vast amount of labor on it, I got to the point where I could play it fairly well. All that I now waited for was a convenient opportunity when I might rejoice Dostoévsky. This opportunity soon presented itself.

Only five or six days remained before our departure. Mama and my aunts were invited to a grand dinner at the Swedish Embassy, the ambassador being an old friend of our family. Aniuta, who had already tired of balls and dinners, excused herself on the plea of a headache. We remained alone in the house. That evening Dostoévsky came to us.

Our approaching departure, the consciousness that none of the elders was at home, and that such an evening would not soon come again, put us in an agreeably excited frame of mind. Feódor Mikháilovitch, also, was in rather a strange, nervous mood — not irritable, as had often been the case with him of late, but, on the contrary, gentle, amiable.

This was a capital moment to play his favorite sonata to him. I had rejoiced in advance at the thought of the pleasure which it would cause him.

I began to play. The difficulty of the piece, the necessity of looking well at every note, the fear of making mistakes, soon absorbed all my attention to such
a degree that I was entirely taken out of my present
surroundings, and did not observe what was going on
around me. I finished with a self-satisfied consciousness that I had played well. I felt an agreeable
weariness in my hands. Still quite under the influence of the music, and of that pleasant emotion which
always lays hold of one after every bit of well-exe-
cuted work, I awaited the well-merited applause. But
silence reigned around me. I glanced around: there
was no one in the room.

My heart sank. Still suspecting nothing definite,
but with a dull presentiment of something evil, I entered the adjoining room. That was empty also! At
last, on raising the portière which masked the door
into the small, corner drawing-room, I beheld Aniuta
and Feódor Mikháilovitch there.

But heavens!—what did I behold?

They were sitting side by side on the little divan.
The room was dimly illuminated by a lamp with a
huge shade. The shadow fell directly on my sister,
so that I could not distinguish her face; but Dostoévsky's face I saw plainly; it was pale and troubled.
He was holding Aniuta's hand in his hands, and bending over her. He was talking in that passionate,
broken whisper, which I knew and loved so well.

"Anna Vasilievna, my darling, do you understand?
I loved you from the first moment that I beheld you;
and before that I had already had a presentiment of
it from your letters. And my love is not the affection of friendship, but passion—the passion of my
whole nature."

Everything swam before my eyes. A sensation of

bitter solitude, of deadly insult, suddenly took possession of me, and all the blood in my body seemed to
rush first to my heart, and then to pour, in a burning
flood, to my head.

I dropped the portière and fled from the room.   I
heard the crash of a chair which I had accidentally
overthrown.

" Is that you, Sónya ? " cried my sister's voice, in a
tone of alarm.   But I made no reply, and did not halt
until I had reached our bedroom, in the other extrem-
ity of the apartment, at the end of a long corridor.
When I stopped running, I immediately began to
undress in great haste, without lighting the candle,
fairly tearing off my clothes, and, still half-dressed,
I flung myself into the bed and hid my head under
the coverlet.   At that moment I feared but one thing
— that my sister would come and call me back to the
drawing-room.   I could not see them now.

A hitherto unknown sensation of bitterness, insult,
and shame filled my soul to overflowing, and especially the shame and insult.   Up to that moment I
had not, even in my most secret thoughts, accounted
to myself for the nature of my feelings toward Dostoévsky, and had never said to myself that I was in
love with him.

Although I was only thirteen years old, I had already heard and read a good deal about love, but for
some reason or other it had seemed to me that people
fell in love in books, but not in real life.   As for Dostoévsky, I had imagined that things would always go
on all our lives as they had been going on for the last
three months.

"And all at once, at one blow, all is ended!" I
kept repeating to myself in my despair; and only
now, when all seemed to me irretrievably lost, did

I clearly understand how happy I had been all those days — those evenings — to-day — a few moments ago. But now — good God — now!

Even now I did not tell myself plainly what had changed, what had come to an end. I only felt that everything had lost its bloom for me; that life was no longer worth living!

"And why did they make a fool of me; why did they make a secret of it; why did they dissemble?" I reproached them with unjust wrath.

"Well, let him love her, let him marry her, what business is it of mine?" I said to myself several seconds later; but my tears still continued to flow, and in my heart I felt the same pain, which was new to me.

Time passed. Now I would have liked to have Aniuta come to me. I was angry with her because she did not come. "I might be dead for all they care! Heavens! What if I were really to die!" And suddenly I felt inexpressibly sorry for myself, and tears flowed faster than ever.

"What are they doing now? How pleasant it must be for them," I thought; and at this thought there arose a fiendish desire to run to them, and say impudent things to them. I jumped out of bed; and, with hands quivering with excitement, I began to fumble for the matches, in order to find the candle, and dress myself. But I could not find the matches. As I had flung my clothes all over the room, I could not dress in the dark, and I was ashamed to summon the maid. Therefore I jumped into bed again, and again began to sob, with a feeling of helpless, hopeless solitude.

The first tears, before the organism is accustomed to suffering, soon exhaust one. My paroxysms of sharp despair passed into a dull torpor.

Not a single sound reached our bed-room from the drawing-room; but I could hear the servants prepar-ing their supper in the kitchen near by. They were rattling knives and plates; the maids were laughing and chattering. "Every one is merry, every one is happy, only I alone—"

At last, after the lapse of what seemed to me sev-eral eternities, a loud ring at the bell resounded. Mama and my aunts had returned from their dinner-party. I heard the hurried steps of the lackey, as he went to open the door; then loud, cheerful voices resounded, as they always did when our people re-turned from any entertainment.

"Probably Dostoévsky is not gone yet. Will Ani-uta tell mama what has happened now, or to-morrow," I said to myself. And then I distinguished his voice among the others. He was taking leave, making haste to depart. By straining my ears I could even hear him putting on his overshoes. Then the front door slammed again, and soon afterward Aniuta's resounding footsteps came down the corridor. She opened the door of the bed-room, and a bright stream of light fell full on my face.

This light hurt my tear-swollen eyes by its intoler-able brightness, and the feeling of physical enmity to my sister suddenly mounted to my throat.

"The disgusting thing, she is rejoicing," I said bit-terly to myself. I soon turned to the wall to pretend to be asleep. Aniuta deliberately placed the candle on the commode, and then approached my bed, and stood there for a few moments in silence.

I lay there motionless, holding my breath.

"I can see that you are not asleep," said Aniuta at last.

I still remained silent.

10

" Well, if you want to sulk, sulk away. It will be only the worse for you; you shall not know anything," cried my sister with determination at last, and began to undress as if nothing had happened.

I remember that I had a wonderful dream that night. This was strange altogether. Whenever during my life a great grief has overwhelmed me, I have always afterward, on the following night, had wonderfully beautiful, pleasant dreams. But how painful is the moment of awakening. The dreams are not yet quite dissipated; the whole body, exhausted with the tears of the preceding evening, experiences an agreeable languor after a few hours of vivifying sleep, a physical pleasure in the restoration of harmony. Suddenly, like the blow of a hammer, the memory of the terrible, irretrievable catastrophe which took place the night before beats upon the brain, and the soul is seized with the consciousness that it must begin again to live and suffer.

There is much that is evil in life. All views of suffering are repulsive. Painful is the paroxysm of the first wild despair, when the whole being rebels, and will not submit itself, when it cannot as yet understand to the full the seriousness of the loss. Almost worse are the long, long days which follow, when tears are all exhausted, and the excitement is allayed, and the man no longer beats his head against the wall; but only recognizes the fact that, under the stress of grief which has overwhelmed his soul, a slow process,— unseen by the rest of the world,—a process of destruction and of weakness, is in progress.

All this is very bad and torturing; but nevertheless the first moments of the return to the sad reality after a brief intermission of unconsciousness are almost the hardest of all to bear.

All the next day I passed in feverish expectation : "What will happen ? " I asked no questions of my sister. I continued to feel toward her, though in a weaker degree, the displeasure which I had felt the night before, and therefore I avoided her as much as possible.

Perceiving my unhappiness she made an attempt to approach me, and to caress me; but I roughly repulsed her in a sudden fit of wrath. Then she, too, got angry, and left me to my own gloomy reflections.

For some reason or other I confidently expected that Dostoévsky would come to us that day, and that then something terrible would happen; but he did not come. We had already sat down to dinner, but he had not made his appearance. In the evening, as I knew, we were to go to a concert.

As time passed, and he did not come, I felt rather relieved; and a sort of dim, undefined hope even began to penetrate my heart. Suddenly it occurred to me:

" My sister will certainly refuse go to the concert, and will remain at home; and Feódor Mikháilovitch will come when she is alone."

My heart contracted with jealousy at this thought. But Aniuta did not refuse the concert. She went with us, and was very cheerful and talkative all the evening.

On our return from the concert, when we had gone to bed, and Aniuta was preparing to blow out the candle, I could hold out no longer, and without looking at her, I asked:

" When will Feódor Mikháilovitch come to see you ? "

Aniuta smiled, " Why, you don't want to know anything about me, you don't want to speak to me, you are pleased to sulk."

Her voice was so soft and kind that my heart suddenly thawed, and she appeared to me dreadfully charming once more.

"Well, how can he help loving her when she is so splendid, but I am nasty and mean?" thought I, with a sudden burst of self-depreciation. I crept into her bed, nestled up to her, and began to cry. She stroked my head.

"Come, stop that, you little goose. Here's a silly child," she kept repeating in a caressing way. All at once she could control herself no longer, but broke into inextinguishable laughter. "Why, she has taken it into her head to fall in love, and with whom? With a man who is three and a half times as old as she is," she said.

These words, this laughter, suddenly aroused in my soul the senseless hope which utterly possessed me.

"So you do not love him?" I asked in a whisper, almost stifling with emotion.

Aniuta meditated.

"Well, you see," she began, evidently picking her words, and finding herself in difficulties, "of course I love him, and I have a frightful, frightful respect for him. He is so kind, so clever, such a genius!"

She grew very animated, but my heart contracted again. "But how can I explain it to you? I do not love him as he—well, in short, I don't love him in the way to marry him!" she said with sudden decision.

Heavens! How light dawned in my soul! I threw myself on my sister and began to kiss her hands and neck. Aniuta went on talking for a long time.

"You see, I am sometimes astonished myself that I cannot love him! He is such a fine man! At first I thought that perhaps I might come to love him; but he does not need such a wife as I, not in the least.

His wife ought to devote herself entirely, entirely to him; give up all her life to him, think only of him. And I cannot do that; I want to live myself. Moreover, he is so nervous and exacting. He seems to be constantly grasping me — sucking me into himself. I never was myself with him."

Aniuta said all this as if addressing me, but, in reality, in order to explain matters to herself. I pretended to understand and to sympathize, but in my innermost heart I was thinking: "Heavens! What happiness it must be to be always with him, and to submit one's self wholly to him! How can my sister repulse such happiness?"

At any rate, when I fell asleep that night I was far from being so unhappy as I had been the night before.

The day appointed for our departure was now close at hand. Feódor Mikháilovitch came to see us once more to bid us farewell. He did not remain long, but Aniuta bore herself in a simple, friendly manner, and they promised to write to each other. His farewell to me was very tender. He even kissed me at parting, but assuredly he was very far from suspecting the nature of my feelings for him, or the suffering which he had caused me.

Six months later my sister received from Feódor Mikháilovitch a letter, in which he informed her that he had met a wonderful young girl, with whom he had fallen in love, and who had consented to become his wife. This young girl was Anna Grigórevna, his second wife. "If any one had foretold this six months ago, I swear by my honor that I would not have believed it!" ingenuously remarked Dostoévsky, at the end of his letter.

My heart-wound also healed rapidly. During the few days which remained of our stay in Petersburg,

10*

I continually felt an unwonted burden on my heart, and went about more sadly and meekly than usual. But the homeward journey erased from my soul the last traces of the tempest through which I had recently passed.

We took our departure in April. In Petersburg the weather was still cold and disagreeable; but in Vitebsk real spring greeted us, having entered quite unexpectedly, in a space of two days, into all its rights. All the brooks and streamlets had overflowed their banks and flooded the adjacent land, forming perfect seas. The earth had thawed; the mud was indescribable.

The traveling on the highway was still tolerably good, but when we came to our district road we were forced to leave our traveling carriage at the posthouse and hire two wretched tarantásses. Mama and the coachman groaned and worried — how were we ever to get home? Mama's chief fear was that father would scold her for having stayed so long in Petersburg. However, in spite of all the groaning and sighing, we had a capital journey.

I remember how we passed through the pine forest late at night. Neither I nor my sister was asleep. We sat in silence, reviewing all the various impressions of the past three months, and eagerly inhaling the spicy odor of spring, with which the air was saturated. Both our hearts were aching with a sort of oppressive expectation.

Little by little complete darkness descended. We were proceeding at a foot-pace, on account of the bad road. The postilion seemed to be asleep on his box, and was not shouting at his horses; nothing was to be heard but the splashing of the horses' hoofs in the mud, and the faint, intermittent jingling of the bells.

The pine forest stretched out on both sides of the road, dark, mysterious, impenetrable. All at once, as we entered a glade, the moon seemed to swim out from behind the forest, and flooded us with silvery light so brilliant and unexpected that we were even startled.

After my explanation with my sister in Petersburg, we had not touched upon any private questions, and a sort of constraint still existed between us — some new sensation had taken possession of us. But at that moment, as if by mutual agreement, we pressed close to each other, exchanged an embrace, and felt that there was no longer any foreign element interposed between us, and that we were near to each other, as in the past. A feeling of reckless, unbounded joy in life overpowered us both. Heavens! how that life which lay before us attracted us, and beckoned us on; and how illimitable, how mysterious, and how beautiful, it seemed to us that night!

SÓNYA KOVALÉVSKY

A BIOGRAPHY

BY ANNA CARLOTTA LEFFLER
DUCHESS OF CAJANELLO

TRANSLATED FROM THE SWEDISH
BY A. M. CLIVE BAYLEY

NOTE

EXTRACTS FROM ELLEN KEY'S BIOGRAPHY
OF THE DUCHESS OF CAJANELLO

TRANSLATED BY I. F. HAPGOOD

BIOGRAPHICAL NOTE
BY LILY WOLFFSOHN

SÓNYA KOVALÉVSKY

IMMEDIATELY on receiving the news of Sónya
Kovalévsky's unexpected and sudden death, I felt
that it was a duty incumbent upon me to continue, in
one form or another, the reminiscences of her early
life which had been published in Swedish under the
title of " The Sisters Raevsky."

There were many reasons which made me consider
this my special duty; but the chief one was the fact
that Sónya had always entertained a feeling that she
would die young, and that I should outlive her; and
over and over again she made me promise to write
her biography.

Introspective and self-analysing as she was to an
extraordinary degree, she was accustomed to dissect
minutely her own actions, thoughts, and feelings;
both for her own benefit and, during the three or four
years in which we were together almost daily, for mine
also. She always tried to classify her ever-changing
moods and disposition according to a given psychological system. This habit of self-criticism was so
strong that she frequently recognized the truth. But
however keen, and at times unmerciful, her self-analy-
sis might be, there was blent with it the natural impulse
to self-idealization. She saw herself as she wished to
be seen; hence the picture she drew of herself was in

many details unlike what others found her to be. Sometimes she judged herself more harshly, sometimes more leniently, than others judged her.

Had she, as she intended, continued the reminiscences of her childhood by writing the whole history of her life, the picture would have been the one which she outlined and filled in for me in our many long, psychological conversations.

Unfortunately she cannot complete this work; which would undoubtedly have been the most remarkable autobiography in the world of literature.

It falls, then, to my lot to draw, in faint outline, the picture of Sónya's life, feeling that, limned by her own hand, it would have been deeply and intensely imbued with her own personality.

From the first I knew that the only way in which I could succeed in my task would be to write, so to speak, under her suggestion. I felt I must endeavor to identify myself with her as I used to do while she still lived. I must strive to be again what she so often called me, her "*second I.*" I must depict her, as far as possible, in the light in which she showed herself to me. Meanwhile I could not decide to publish the reminiscences which I began to write down shortly after Sónya's death, and I allowed a year to pass without doing so. During that year I conversed with many of her friends, both of former and of recent date. I corresponded with those who were absent in foreign lands whenever I could find them; and thus sought to supplement my own memory in all things concerning Sónya's external life. I have quoted from my correspondence all that seemed important as casting light upon her character, but always of course from the point of view I have indicated — that of elucidating her own interpretation of herself.

From an objective point of view the life-history I have sought to depict of my friend may perhaps be considered not real. But is the objective standpoint necessarily the true one when we deal with the interpretation of character?

Many may contest the justice of my estimate and interpretation; many may judge Sónya's actions and feelings in quite another light, but this in no way concerns me from my point of view.

The data which I have submitted are as accurate as I can make them. It is only when such data seem to have been slightly distorted by imagination that I have failed to adhere closely to Sónya's guidance.

When I met Henrik Ibsen last summer, and told him that I was writing a memoir of Sónya Kovalévsky, he exclaimed:

"Is it her biography in the ordinary meaning of the word which you intend to write, or is it not rather a poem about her?"

"Yes," I answered; "that is to say, it will be her own poem about herself as revealed to me."

"That is all right," he replied. "You must treat the subject romantically."

This remark strengthened and cheered me, encouraging me to follow out the plan which had presented itself to me.

Let others who can describe Sónya objectively. I cannot attempt anything but a subjective delineation of my own subjective conception of her, derived from the vividly subjective interpretation which she herself gave me.

ANNA CARLOTTA LEFFLER,
Duchess of Cajanello.

NAPLES.

I

SÓNYA was about seventeen years of age when her parents took her with them to pass a winter in Petersburg. Just at that time, in the year 1867, a strong movement was making itself felt among the thinking portion of the rising generation in Russia.

This movement especially affected the young girls of Russia, and may be described as an ardent desire for the freedom and progress of their fatherland, and the raising of its intellectual standard.

It was not a nihilistic, scarcely a political, movement. It was an eager striving after knowledge and mental development; and it had spread so far and wide that at this moment hundreds of young girls belonging to the best families abandoned their homes and betook themselves to foreign universities in order to study science.

But as parents, in the majority of cases, opposed such proceedings, their daughters had recourse to very strange tactics, characteristic of the times, to effect their purpose. They went through the form of marriage with young men devoted to the same ideas which they held sacred, and in this manner, as married women, they escaped from parental authority, and were enabled to go abroad at the first opportunity.

[1] Appendix A.

159

Many of the Russian women-students in Zürich, who were afterward recalled by an imperial ukase (being suspected of nihilistic tendencies, although they only thought of studying in peace), had entered into this sort of fictitious marriage with men who had accompanied them to the universities and by mutual agreement had then left them free to pursue their studies.

This kind of union, with its abstract and ulterior motive, was very popular at the time in the circles of Petersburg to which Sónya and her sister belonged. Indeed, it seemed to Sónya, and to most of her friends, a far higher conception of the marriage state than the low and commonplace idea of a union between two persons for the mere satisfaction of their passions, or the purely selfish happiness of what is generally termed a "love-match."

According to the ideal which these young people cherished, personal happiness was altogether a subordinate consideration. The sacrifice of self for unselfish purposes was their noble intention, and the development of intellect was the means by which these young people hoped to infuse new vigor into the fatherland they loved so dearly, and to assist its struggle from darkness and oppression into light and freedom.

This was the passionate longing which filled the hearts of the daughters of old aristocratic families, hitherto educated solely to be women of the world, future wives and mothers.

No wonder that their parents were unable to understand them, and were hostile to this sudden bursting into flame of the independence and determined rebellion which had long secretly smoldered, cherished by mysterious meetings and confabulations among the youth of Russia. "Oh, what a happy time it was!"

Sónya would often exclaim when talking of this period of her life. "We were so enthusiastic about the new ideas; so sure that the present social state could not continue long. We pictured to ourselves the glorious period of liberty and universal enlightenment of which we dreamed, and in which we firmly believed. Besides this, we had the sense of true union and coöperation. When three or four of us met in a drawing-room among older people,—where we had no right to advance our opinions,—a tone, a glance, even a sigh, were sufficient to show one another that we were one in thought and sympathy. And when we discovered this, how great was the inward delight at realizing that close to us was some young man or woman, whom we had never seen before, and with whom we had apparently only exchanged some commonplace remark, yet whom we found to be devoted to the same ideas and hopes, ready for self-sacrifice in the same cause!"

At that time no one noticed little Sónya in the circle which gradually gathered around her sister Aniuta, who was six years her senior, and the center of a group of friends. Sónya was still a child in outward appearance, and it was only through Aniuta's affection for her shy little sister with "the green-gooseberry eyes" that the girl was allowed to be present. How brightly those eyes sparkled at every warm and enthusiastic word which fell from the older members of the circle, though Sónya kept herself in the shadow of her more brilliant sister!

Sónya admired this sister above all things, and believed her to be her superior in beauty, charm, talent, and intelligence. But in her admiration lay a certain amount of jealousy; the jealousy which strives to emulate its object, not that which belittles and disparages it. This jealousy, of which Sónya speaks in her rem-
11

iniscences, was characteristic of her throughout her life. She was apt to overestimate the qualities she longed to possess, and the lack of which she deplored. She was also greatly impressed by beauty and charm of manner. These qualities her sister appears to have possessed in a far greater degree than herself, and her day-dream was to surpass that sister in other matters.

From her childhood, Sónya had always been praised for her intelligence. Her natural love of study, and her thirst for knowledge, were now seconded by her ambition, and by the encouragement she received from her master in mathematics. She showed such ex- traordinary keenness and quickness of perception, and such fertility of origination, that her scientific gifts were not to be mistaken. Her father had only per- mitted this unusual and "unfeminine" study through the influence of one of his oldest friends (himself somewhat given to mathematics), who had discovered Sónya's uncommon aptitude for this science. But at the first suspicion that his daughter intended to take up the study seriously, the father withdrew in concern. Her first shy hints that she wished to go to a foreign university were as unwelcome as had been, a few years previously, the discovery of Aniuta's authorship. It was regarded as a reprehensible tendency toward im- propriety. Young girls of good family who had already carried out similar plans were simply regarded as mere adventuresses, who had brought shame and sorrow upon their parents. Thus in the homes of the aris- tocracy there existed two opposing currents : first, the hidden, secret, and stifled, but rebellious and intense striving, which could not be resisted, and which found its own outlet like a natural force ; and, secondly, the open and genuine conviction, on the parents' side, of their right to stem and hold in check, to regulate and to discipline, this same unknown and mysterious natural force.

Aniuta and one of her friends, who was also full of the desire to study abroad, and likewise prevented from doing so by her parents, now came to a definite determination. Either of them—it mattered little which—was to make one of these ideal and platonic marriages before alluded to. They hoped that this arrangement would give both of them their liberty. They thought, if one of them were married, the other would obtain permission from her parents to accompany her friend abroad. Such a journey would no longer appear in an objectionable light, but might be regarded as a mere pleasure-trip.

Sónya was to accompany her sister. She was so entirely Aniuta's shadow that it was utterly impossible to imagine the one without the other. The plan once made, the first step was to find the right man to help them to carry it out.

Aniuta and her friend Inez reviewed their circle of acquaintance, and their choice fell on a young professor at the University, whom they knew only slightly, but of whose honesty and devotion to the common cause they were convinced. So, one fine day, the three girls— Sónya, as usual, bringing up the rear—went to see the professor in his own house. He was seated at his writing-table when the servant introduced the three young ladies, whose presence there somewhat astonished him, for they did not belong to the circle of his more intimate lady-friends. He rose politely and asked them to be seated.

Down they all three sat in a row on the sofa, and a moment's awkward pause followed.

The professor sat in his rocking-chair opposite them, and looked first at one and then at the other. At the fair Aniuta, tall, slim, with a peculiar charm in her *svelte* and graceful movements; whose large and lustrous eyes, dark and blue, were fixed upon him fearlessly, and yet with a certain indecision. At the dark Inez, stout and clumsy, with her eagle nose, and an intrepid look in her prominent eyes. At the fragile Sónya, with her abundant curls, her pure, correct features, childish, innocent forehead, and strange eyes, full of passionate inquiry, of wonder, and of attention.

Aniuta at last commenced the conversation as they had intended. Without the least sign of timidity she asked the professor if he were willing to "free" them by going through the marriage ceremony with one of them, accompanying them to a university either in Germany or Switzerland, and there leaving them. In another country, or under other circumstances, a young man could hardly listen to such a proposal from a handsome girl without, in his answer, showing some foolish gallantry, or expressing a touch of irony; but in this case the man was equal to the occasion. Aniuta had not been mistaken in her choice. The professor answered, quite seriously and coldly, that such a proposal he had not the least desire to accept. And the girls? One would suppose that they must have felt terribly humiliated by this flat refusal. Such, however, was not the case. Feminine vanity had nothing to do with the matter. The question of personally pleasing the young man had never entered into their project. They received his refusal as coolly as a young man might do whose friend had not accepted an invitation to travel abroad with him. So they all went off, shaking hands with the professor at the door, and did not meet with him again for many years. They felt sure he would not abuse the confidence they had placed in him, for he belonged to the secret brotherhood which, though it was not a society in the ordinary sense of the word, still united in one indissoluble bond the hearts of all those who were devoted to the same cause. Some fifteen years later, when Madame Kovalévsky was at the height of her celebrity, she met the professor in Petersburg society, and jested with him about the rejected offer of marriage.

Just at this time one of Aniuta's friends committed the crime of a love-marriage. How they despised her, and bewailed her lot! Sónya's heart swelled with anger at such a mean failure of her ideal. Even the newly married couple were as shamefaced before their young friends as though they had committed a veritable crime. They never dared to talk to them about their wedded bliss, and the wife even forbade her husband to show the least sign of affection in their presence.

Meanwhile an unexpected circumstance occurred in Sónya's life. Aniuta and Inez, who still kept to their original plan, not allowing themselves to be defeated by their first rebuff, had chosen another young man as their "liberator." He was only a student, but an exceptionally clever one, who also desired to go to Germany to complete his studies. He was of good family, and generally considered to be a "rising man." They therefore hoped that, if it came to pass, neither Inez's nor Aniuta's parents would have any serious objection to urge against the marriage. This time the proposal was made in a less formal manner. Once, when they met, as they often did, at the house of mutual friends, Aniuta took the opportunity of putting her proposal to the young man during the course of conversation. He replied, much to her astonishment, that he quite agreed to the suggestion, with, however, a slight variation in the program. He would like to

11*

marry Sónya. This declaration caused much anxiety to the three conspirators. How could they induce Sónya's father to allow her, hardly more than a child, to marry, while her elder sister, already twenty-three years of age, remained unmarried? They knew that if a moderately suitable match had been proposed for the latter, her father would not have been obdurate. In fact, Aniuta gave him much anxiety by her unaccountable and imaginative nature. She was, moreover, of an age at which she ought to have been married. Certainly the student Kovalévsky was young, but he had before him a promising future, and no doubt he would have been accepted willingly enough for the *eldest* daughter.

But with regard to Sónya it was altogether a different matter.

The proposal now made to the father was absolutely refused without appeal; and a return to the country-place of the family, Palibino, was immediately arranged.

The girls were in despair at returning to Palibino, for this meant the surrender of the hopes and interests which had been to them the very breath of life. It was a return to a prison, but without the charm of true martyrdom in a great cause. Indeed, a real imprisonment would have been easier for them to bear than the unpoetic banishment with which they were now threatened.

The timid Sónya took a bold resolution. The tender young girl, who could not bear an unkind glance or a word of disapproval from those she loved, at this critical moment became like steel. For though of a delicate, sympathetic, and affectionate nature, she had within her a vein of sternness and flint-like inflexibility, which came to the fore at any crisis. She who could,

like a little dog, creep up to and nestle in the arms
of any one who smiled kindly upon her, could, when
roused to battle, trample every feeling underfoot, and
wound in cold blood those on whom, a moment before,
she had lavished the warmest affection.

This arose from her intensity of will. For her will
was so strong that it became an overmastering force,
even when it had to do with a purpose entirely unconnected with feeling. What she desired, what she
wished, she desired with such intensity that she was
almost consumed by it. Now she wanted to leave her
parents' home, and continue her studies, cost what it
might.

One evening there was to be a family gathering at
her father's house. In the afternoon her mother had
gone out to choose flowers for her table and new music
for her pianoforte.

Her father was at his club, and the governess was
helping the maid to decorate the drawing-room with
plants.

The girls were alone in their room, and their pretty
new dresses were lying ready for dinner. They were
never allowed to go out of doors without being accompanied by the footman or the governess. But Sónya
seized upon this moment, when every one was occupied,
to slip out of the house. Aniuta, who was in the conspiracy, accompanied Sónya downstairs, and stood at
the door until she was out of sight. She then ran back
to her room with a beating heart, and began to put on
her light-blue dress.

It was already twilight, and the first gas-lamps were
just being lighted. Sónya had drawn down her veil
and pulled her Russian hood well over her face. She
hesitatingly went down the broad empty street, which
she had never before traversed alone. Her pulses were

beating high with the excitement which always accompanies and lends such a charm to great moments in the lives of romantic people. Sónya felt herself the heroine of the romance now opening — she, the little Sónya, who had hitherto been nothing but her sister's shadow!

But the romance was of quite a different kind to the love-tales of which literature is full, and which she herself despised.

For this was no lovers' tryst to which Sónya's light feet were speeding so rhythmically. It was no passionate love that made her heart beat, as, breathless with fright, she sped up the dark flight of steps of a dilapidated house in a miserable street. She rapped three nervous little taps on a certain door, which opened so quickly that it was clear the young man who presented himself had been on the watch and was expecting her. He immediately led her into a simple study, where books were piled up in every direction, and where a sofa had been evidently emptied of them to receive her.

The young man was not quite an ideal hero of romance. His large red beard and too prominent nose gave him, at first sight, an ugly aspect. But, once you met the clear glance of his deep-blue eyes, you found in them such a kindly, intelligent, and honest expression that they grew most attractive. His manner to this young girl, who showed such strange confidence in him, was quite that of an elder brother. The two young people sat down excitedly on the sofa, listening for heavy footsteps on the stairs. Sónya started up, turning red and white, each time she thought she heard a movement in the corridor.

Meanwhile her parents had returned home, but only just in time — as the girls had well calculated — to dress for dinner before their guests arrived. They therefore did not notice Sónya's absence until all the guests were assembled in the dining-room and were about to sit down to table.

"Where is Sónya?" they both asked in the same breath, turning to the pale Aniuta, who seemed more self-conscious than ever, with her defiant glance and nervous, expectant air.

"She is out," she answered, in a low voice, the trembling of which she could not conceal, and averting her eyes from her father.

"Gone out? What does she mean by it? And with whom?"

"Alone. There is a note for you on her dressing-table."

The footman was sent to fetch the note, and the company sat down to dinner amid a death-like silence.

Sónya had calculated her blow better than she perhaps knew. And it was more cruel than she could have dreamed. In her childish defiance, and with the selfishness of youth, which knows neither mercy nor consideration, understanding so little the pain inflicted, she had wounded her father in his most tender point. In the presence of so many relations of every degree the proud man was forced to swallow the humiliation of his daughter's wrong-doing.

The note contained only these words : "Father, I am with Vladímir, and beg you will no longer oppose our marriage."

General Krukovsky read these lines in silence. He rose immediately from the table, murmuring an excuse to those who sat near him. Ten minutes later Sónya and her companion, who had been listening more and more intently, heard the expected angry steps. The door, which had not been locked, sprang open without

any previous knock, and General Krukovsky stood
before his trembling daughter.

Just before the close of the dinner the General and
his daughter, accompanied by Vladímir Kovalévsky,
entered the dining-room.

"Allow me," said the General, in an agitated voice,
"to present to you my daughter Sónya's *fiancé.*"

II

IN the foregoing words Sónya used to relate to me the most dramatic incidents of her peculiar marriage. Her parents forgave her, and shortly after, in October, 1868, the marriage was celebrated at Palibino. The newly wedded couple went immediately to Petersburg, where Sónya was introduced by her husband to circles interested in political events; and thus one of her great desires was fulfilled.

A lady who afterward became her most intimate friend relates, in the following words, the impression which Sónya made on her new acquaintances:

" Among all the women, married and unmarried, of this circle interested in politics—women who were worn out and harassed by life—Sónya Kovalévsky made a peculiar impression. Her childish face procured her the name of 'the little sparrow.' She was just eighteen, but looked much younger. Small, slender, with a round face and short curly chestnut hair, she had very mobile features. Her eyes, especially, were exceedingly expressive; sometimes bright and dancing, sometimes dreamy and full of melancholy. Her whole expression was a mixture of childish innocence and deep thought. She attracted every one by the unconscious charm which was her principal characteristic at this period of her life. Old and young, men and women, all were fascinated by her. Natural in manner, she never seemed to notice the homage lavished upon her. She took no pains about her personal appearance or dress, the latter being as simple as possible, even showing a tendency to slovenliness—a trait which remained with her to the last."

In connection with this peculiarity the same friend relates the following characteristic little incident:

" I remember, shortly after our acquaintance began, how once, when I was talking enthusiastically to Sónya about something which interested us both,—in those days we never could talk otherwise than enthusiastically,—she occupied herself the whole time in pulling off the trimming of her left sleeve, which had become unsewn; and when at last she managed to tear it all off, she threw it on the ground as if it were of no value and she was only too glad to be rid of it."

After having lived during six months in Petersburg, the young couple left for Heidelberg in the spring of 1869; Sónya to study mathematics, and her husband to study geology. After they had matriculated there, they went to England, where Sónya had the opportunity of making acquaintance with the most celebrated persons of the day—George Eliot, Darwin, Spencer, Huxley, and others.

In George Eliot's diary, published in Mr. Cross's biography of his wife, we find the following remarks, dated October 6, 1869:

Last Sunday we had a visit from an interesting Russian couple, M. and Mme. Kovalévsky. She, a sweet, taking creature, with a shy voice and manner, who studies mathematics by special permission, which she procured with Kirchhoff's help in Heidelberg. He, amiable and intelligent, studying the natural sciences, especially geology, and on his way to Vienna, where he will stay for six months; he leaves his wife in Heidelberg.

This plan was not immediately realized, and Vladímir stayed for one term in Heidelberg with his wife. Their life at this period is described by the friend already quoted, who had, we may remark in passing, received through Sónya's intervention her parents' permission to study.

"A few days after my arrival in Heidelberg, in October, 1869, Sónya and her husband arrived from England. She seemed very happy and pleased with her journey. She was as fresh, rosy, and joyous as when I first saw her. But there was an increased fire and sparkle in her eyes. She felt within her the development of new vigor and energy in the pursuit of the studies she had barely begun. Her serious aspirations did not prevent her, however, from finding enjoyment even in the simplest things. I well remember our walk together the day after their arrival. We had wandered about in the neighborhood of the town, and when we came to a level road we two young girls began to run races like children. Oh, how fresh are those memories of the early days of our University life! Sónya seemed to me so very happy, and that in such a noble way; yet, when in after-years she spoke of her youth, it was always with a deep bitterness, as though she had wasted it. At such times I remembered those first happy months in Heidelberg; those enthusiastic discussions on every kind of topic, and her poetical relationship to her young husband, who in those days adored her with quite an ideal love, without any mixture of less noble feeling. She seemed to love him in the same way, and both were innocent of those lower passions which usually go by the name of love. When I think of all this, it seems to me that Sónya had no reason to complain. Her youth was really filled with noble feelings and aspirations, and she had at her side a man, with his feelings completely under control, who loved her tenderly. This was the only time I have known Sónya to be really happy. A little later—even a year later—it was no longer quite the same.

"Immediately after our arrival at Heidelberg, the lectures began. During the day we were all three at the University, and the evenings were also devoted to study. We had rarely time, during the week, to take walks, but on Sundays we always made long excursions outside Heidelberg, and sometimes we went to the theater at Mannheim.

"We had very few acquaintances, and very seldom called on any of the professors' families. From the first Sónya attracted the attention of her teachers by her extraordinary talent for mathematics. Professor Könisberg, and the celebrated scientist Kirchhoff, whose lectures on practical physics she attended, both spoke of her as something quite marvelous. Her fame spread so widely in the little town that people sometimes stopped in the streets to look at the wonderful Russian, and she came home and told me laughingly how a poor woman, with a child on her arm, had stopped and pointed to her, saying aloud to the child, 'Look! look! there is the girl who is so diligent at school!'

"Retiring and bashful, and almost awkward in her manner to her fellow-students and professors, Sónya always entered the University with downcast eyes; she never spoke to her companions, if she could avoid it, during the time of study. Her behavior enchanted the German professors, who always admire bashfulness in a woman, especially in one so charming and young, and, withal, one who was studying so abstract a science as mathematics. This bashfulness was not in the least put on, but entirely natural to Sónya at this time. I remember very well when she came home one day and told me how she had discovered an error in the demonstration which some pupil or the professor had made on the blackboard during the lesson. He got more and more confused and could not find out where the mistake lay. Sónya told me how her heart beat when at last she had the courage to rise and go up to the blackboard, pointing out where the error lay. "

"But our life à trois, so happy and so full,—for M. Kovalévsky was deeply interested in all subjects, even those which did not touch on science,—did not last long.

"Sónya's sister and her friend Inez arrived at the beginning of the winter. They were both many years our seniors. As we had not much room, Kovalévsky decided to move and give up his room to them. Sónya visited him very often, spending the whole day with him, and they often took walks together without us. It naturally was not pleasant for them to be surrounded by so many women, especially as the two recent arrivals were not always amiable toward Kovalévsky. They had their peculiar ideas, and thought that as the marriage, after all, was only a formal one, Kovalévsky ought not to try to give a more intimate aspect to his intercourse with his wife. This interference caused irritation, and spoiled the good understanding of our little circle.

"After a term spent thus, Kovalévsky decided to leave Heidelberg, where he no longer felt at ease. He went first to Jena, and then to Munich. There he lived for study alone. He was richly endowed by nature, exceedingly industrious, very simple in his habits, and with no desire for recreation. Sónya very often said that a book and a glass of tea were all that he needed to content him. This characteristic was not quite pleasing to Sónya. She began to be jealous of his studies when she found that they made up for the loss of her company. We sometimes went with her to pay him a visit, and in the holidays they always traveled together. These trips seemed to give Sónya great pleasure. But she could not accustom herself to live apart from her husband, and she began to worry him with continual demands. She would not travel alone, but he must come and fetch her and take her where she wanted to go. Just when he was most busy with his studies he had to undertake commissions for her, and help her in all those trifles which he had of his own accord very good-naturedly taken upon his shoulders, but which seemed to worry him now that he was absorbed by scientific study."

When Sónya, later on, recalled her past life, her complaint was always, "No one has ever loved me truly;" and if I pleaded, "But your husband loved you truly," she would reply, "He loved me only when he was with me, but he got on so well without me that he could quite well live apart from me."

It seemed to me a very simple explanation of the matter that he preferred, under the circumstances, and busy as he then was with study, not to spend too much time near her. But Sónya did not see it in this light. She had always, from childhood to her very last hour, a curious liking for ideal and exaggerated relationships; she wanted to *have* without giving aught in return.

I believe that in this particular lies the clue to her life's tragedy. I will again allow myself to quote further observations, made by the same friend and fellow-student, which show that even in her early youth this idiosyncrasy was already developed, and became the source of all Sónya's inner struggles and sufferings in after-life.

"Sónya valued success to a very great degree.

When she had once an aim, nothing could withhold her from its pursuit, and when her feelings were not in question she always compassed her end. When her heart was concerned, curiously enough, she lost her clear judgment; she required too much from those who loved her and whom she loved, and thought to gain by force what would have been given to her spontaneously had it not been demanded. She had a perfect craving for tenderness and intimate friendship. She also needed to have some one near her who would never leave her and was interested in all that interested herself; but she made life unbearable to all who lived with her. She was herself too restless, too ill balanced in temperament, to be satisfied with such loving companionship, although it was her ideal. Her own individuality was far too pronounced for her to live in harmony with others. Kovalévsky was also, in his way, restless by nature; always full of new ideas and plans. It is impossible to say whether these two, both so rarely endowed, could ever, under any circumstances whatsoever, have lived happily together for any length of time."

Sónya remained two years in Heidelberg, until the autumn of 1870, when she went to Berlin to continue her studies under Professor Weierstrass's direction. Her husband had meanwhile received his doctor's degree in Jena, and written a treatise which attracted much attention. He thus gained great celebrity and became a scientist of importance.

12

III

PROFESSOR WEIERSTRASS, much to his astonishment, one day found a young and beautiful
woman-student standing before him, asking him to
take her as a pupil in mathematics. The University
of Berlin was closed to female students then as now.
But Sónya's enthusiastic desire to be directed in her
studies by the man regarded as the father of modern
mathematical analysis induced her to entreat him to
give her private lessons. The professor looked at his
unknown visitor with a certain amount of incredulity.
He promised to try her, and gave her some of the
problems to solve which he had set for some of his
more advanced students in mathematics. He was convinced she would not succeed, and gave the matter no
further thought. Indeed, her appearance at the first
interview had made no impression on him whatever.
Badly dressed, as she always was at this period of her
life, she wore on this special occasion a bonnet which
quite hid her face and might have suited a woman
twice her age.

Professor Weierstrass himself told me later that he
had no idea at the time either of her extreme youth,
or of the highly intellectual expression of face which
usually predisposed every one in her favor.

A week later she came to him again, saying she had

178

solved all the problems. He would not believe her, and bade her sit down beside him and go through her solutions point by point. To his great astonishment, not only was everything quite right, but the solutions were eminently clear and original. In the eagerness of exposition she took off her bonnet, and her short curly hair fell over her brow. She blushed vividly with delight at the professor's approbation. He, no longer young, felt a sudden emotion of tenderness for this child-woman, who had evidently the gift of intuitive genius to a degree he had seldom found among even his older and more developed students.

From that hour the great mathematician was Sónya's friend for life, and the most faithful, tender counselor she could have desired. She was received in his family like a daughter and sister, and continued her studies under his guidance for four years — most important ones in the influence they exercised on her future scientific work, which was always pursued in the direction given to it by Weierstrass; applying to it, and developing, her master's premises.

Sónya's husband had followed her to Berlin, but left her to live alone there with her friend from Heidelberg, visiting her, however, very frequently. The relations between them continued peculiar and provoked some astonishment in the Weierstrass family, where her husband never showed himself, though his wife was on an intimate footing with all its members. Sónya never mentioned her husband, nor did she introduce him to the professor, but on Sunday evenings, when she went to Weierstrass (he coming to her once a week besides), her husband went to the door when the lesson was finished, rang the bell, and told the servant to inform Madame Kovalévsky that the carriage was waiting.

Sónya had always been shy about the unnatural
relations between her husband and herself. One of
the Heidelberg professors used to tell how, when
he happened to meet Kovalévsky at his wife's house,
she would introduce him in a vague way as a "relation."

Her oft-quoted friend says of their life in Berlin:
"Our life there was even more monotonous and lonely
than in Heidelberg. We lived all by ourselves. Sónya
was busy at her problems the whole day long, and was
at the laboratory till the evening, when, after partak-
ing together of a hasty repast, we again sat down to
work. Excepting Professor Weierstrass, who was a
constant visitor, we never saw any one within our
doors. Sónya was always in low spirits. Nothing
seemed to give her pleasure, and she was indifferent
to everything but study. Her husband's visits always
brightened her up; but the joy of meeting was clouded
by frequently recurring misunderstandings and reproaches, though they seemed to be very fond of each
other, and constantly took long walks together.

"When Sónya was alone with me she never wanted
to leave the house, not even for a walk, nor for the
most necessary shopping, far less to go to the theater
or any place of amusement. At Christmas-time we
were invited to the Weierstrasses', who had a Christmas
tree in our honor. Sónya was absolutely in need of a
dress, but could not be induced to go and buy one.
We nearly quarreled about this dress, for I would not
buy it alone. (Had her husband been there all would
have been well, for he always looked after her and
chose both the material and pattern of her dress.)
Finally she decided on allowing her hostess to choose
and order the dress, so that she need not stir out of
doors about it. Her powers of endurance when at the

most difficult mental work, sitting hour after hour im-
movable at her desk, were almost phenomenal. In the
evening, when she finally put up her papers, she would
be so absorbed in her own thoughts that she would
begin walking rapidly up and down the room, often
ending in a run; and she often talked aloud to herself,
and sometimes even burst into laughter. At such times
she seemed to be altogether beyond earthly things, and
to be carried away from the world on the wings of imagination. But she would never tell me what her day-
dreams were about. She did not sleep much at night,
and when asleep was always restless. Sometimes she
would wake suddenly, roused by some fantastic dream,
and then would frequently ask me to keep awake also.
She liked to relate her dreams, which were often interesting and peculiar. They were generally of the nature
of visions, and she believed them to be, to a certain
extent, prophetic; and certainly they did sometimes
prove true.

"On the whole Sónya had a highly nervous temperament. Never quiet, she was always setting some
greatly involved aim before her. She longed intensely
for success, yet never have I seen her more depressed
than just when she had attained some object for which
she had worked. The reality seemed so little to fulfil
her expectations. While striving to obtain her object
she was often far from agreeable to others, being intently absorbed in her work. But when one saw her
depressed and unhappy in the midst of success the
deepest pity was aroused. This continual variation
of light and shadow in her temperament rendered her
most interesting. But, on the whole, our life in Berlin,
spent in uncomfortable rooms, bad air, and amid in-
cessant, wearing mental labor, without any interval
of recreation, was so devoid of pleasure that I often

12*

looked back on our early Heidelberg days as on a lost paradise.

" When, in the autumn of 1874, Sónya had obtained her doctor's degree, she was so worn out, physically and mentally, that, on her return to Russia, she could not do any work for a long time."

The want of delight in her work above mentioned was peculiar to Sónya when she had any scientific labors in hand. She always overdid herself, and in no way could enjoy life or the work itself; and *thought,* instead of being her servant, was her tyrant. At such times she experienced none of the joys of creating. It was different later on, when she took up literary work. This always gave her delight and put her into good spirits.

Other causes besides Sónya's exaggerated manner of study contributed to make her stay in Berlin far from agreeable. To begin with, there was her position with regard to her husband. The sense of its strangeness had been aggravated by the interference of her parents. They had visited her several times, had even taken her back to Petersburg; had found out how matters stood, had reproached her for her behavior, and tried to drive husband and wife together. But Sónya would not hear of it. Secondly, Sónya was displeased with her isolated position. She had already that hunger for a fuller life which afterward consumed her. In her inmost heart she was as little as possible the female pedant which her manner of life suggested. But bashfulness, or a want of practical sense; the consciousness of the strangeness of her own circumstances; the fear of allowing herself to be compromised in her lonely position — all conduced to the isolation she so greatly regretted when speaking, in after-life, of her early youth.

The want of practical knowledge in her friend, too, contributed greatly to make their merely material life together unbearable. They always chanced on the most miserable lodgings, the worst servants, the worst food. Once they fell into the hands of a whole gang of thieves, who systematically plundered them. They had noticed that one of the maid-servants had been stealing their things for a long time. When they reproached her she grew impertinent, and they were obliged to dismiss her at a moment's notice. The same evening, as they sat alone, having no one to help them to make their beds for the night, some one knocked at the window, which was on the ground floor. Looking out, they saw a strange woman peering in. They called out anxiously to know what she wanted. She replied that she wanted to enter their service. She impressed them disagreeably, but such was their helplessness that, frightened though they were, they engaged her. This woman managed so to terrorize them, and plundered them so outrageously, that they had to call in the police before they could get rid of her.

Sónya was, however, very indifferent to the material side of life. She barely noticed whether her food was good or bad, whether her room was tidy, or her clothes in good order or torn. It was only when things got to be quite unbearable that she became conscious of them. But when she had no practical friend at hand, this happened pretty often.

In January, 1871, Sónya was obliged to break off her studies with Weierstrass to set forth on a most adventurous expedition.

Aniuta had wearied of her monotonous life at Heidelberg, and gone to Paris without her parents' permission. She wanted to educate herself as an authoress,

and naturally felt no interest in a circumscribed life
with Sónya in a student's chamber. She wished to
study the world and the theater, and live in literary
circles.

As soon, therefore, as she was free from parental
control, she definitely took her own way. It was impossible for her to write and tell her father that she
was living alone in Paris, so she gave full license to
her desire to live her own life independently, and de-
ceived him. She wrote to him through Sónya, so that
her letters always bore the same postmark as those
of her sister. She originally intended to make but a
short stay in Paris, and quieted her conscience by the
plea that she would explain her conduct by word of
mouth.

But she then entered into a relationship which fascinated her so entirely that it was impossible for her
to extricate herself. Every day she remained in Paris
it became more difficult to communicate honestly with
her parents. She entered into a *liaison* with a young
Frenchman, who later became one of the communist
leaders; and she thus found herself immured in Paris
during the whole of the siege.

Sónya was much disturbed as to the fate of her
sister, and deeply impressed with the responsibility
which rested on her own shoulders for having abetted
her secret journey. Immediately after the siege of
Paris was raised she and her husband sought to enter
that city in order to search for Aniuta.

Sónya could never speak of this journey in later
years without congratulating herself, and marveling at
their success in getting into the town right in the face
of the German troops. She and Vladímir wandered on
foot along the Seine till they came to a deserted boat,
drawn up upon the shore. Of this they at once took

possession and rowed off. But hardly were they at a little distance from the shore than a sentinel saw and challenged them. For reply they rowed away with all their might, and by good luck, owing to the carelessness and dilatoriness of the sentinel, they reached the opposite side, whence, unobserved, they slipped into Paris. They thus chanced to arrive there at the very commencement of the Commune.

Sónya had intended, later on, to publish her experiences during this epoch, but, alas! like so many other plans, this lies with her in the grave. Among other things she intended to write a novel to be entitled "The Sisters Raevsky under the Commune."[1] In it she meant to describe a night with the ambulance-corps, for she and Aniuta served in it. Here, too, they found other young girls who had formerly moved in their own circle in Petersburg.

While bombs were whizzing round them, and wounded men were being constantly brought in, the girls talked in whispers of their former experiences, so unlike their present surroundings that they seemed to them like a dream. And like a dream to Sónya, at least,—like a fairy tale,—were all the strange incidents which now pressed upon her. She was still at the age of intense fervor of feeling, and the events of world-wide historic interest that were taking place around her impressed her more than the most exciting romance. She watched the bursting bombs without the least trepidation; they only excited a not unpleasant fluttering of the heart and a secret delight that she was in the very midst of the drama.

For her sister she could at this moment do nothing. Aniuta took an active interest in the political disturbances, and asked for nothing better than to risk her

[1] Appendix B.

life for the man to whom she had indissolubly linked
her existence.

Shortly after, the Kovalévskys left Paris, and Sónya
resumed her studies in Berlin. But after the suppres-
sion of the Commune, Sónya was again called to Paris.
This time it was her sister who sent for her, entreating
her intervention with her father. Aniuta longed for
his forgiveness, and was anxious that he should use his
influence to extricate her from the exceeding distress
into which she had now fallen. The man for whom
she had forsaken all was a prisoner and doomed to
death.

When one recalls the picture which Sónya has given
of her father in the " Recollections of Childhood," one
can easily realize how terrible a blow it was to him
to learn the whole grim truth of the deception of his
children, and the fact that his eldest daughter had
taken her own course in a manner calculated to wound
most deeply all his instincts and principles.

Years before he had been almost out of his mind
with grief and deep annoyance on the discovery that
Aniuta had secretly written a novel and had received
money for it. He said to her at the time, " You sell
your work now, but I am not at all sure that the day
will not come when you will sell yourself." Strangely
enough, he was much more gentle on hearing the truth
now, when his daughter had given him a far more
terrible cause of grief. Both he and his wife, accompanied by Sónya and her husband, hastened at once to
Paris, and when Krukovsky met his erring daughter
he was most generous and forgiving. His daughters,
who knew that they deserved quite other treatment,
devoted themselves to him from that hour with a
tenderness they had never before evinced.

I cannot, alas ! give the whole story of this troublous

time. General Krukovsky was acquainted with Thiers; he therefore turned to him to procure a pardon for his future son-in-law. Thiers answered that no one could obtain this favor; but one day, in course of conversation, he mentioned, as if accidentally, that the band of prisoners among whom was Monsieur J—— would be moved the following day to another prison. They were to pass by a building in which there was an exhibition, and just at an hour when there would be a good many people about. Aniuta went to the spot and mixed with the crowd. The instant the prisoners appeared she slipped unnoticed among the soldiers who surrounded them, and, catching Monsieur J—— by the arm, disappeared with him through the crowd into the exhibition. From there they escaped by one of the other doors, and reached the railway-station in safety.

This tale sounds wild and improbable, but I have only been able to write it down as I, and many of Sónya's friends, remember it. When people we love are dead, how bitterly we regret that we have not stored up in memory their least word, noted down all the interesting things they have told us! In the present case I have all the greater cause for regret because Sónya often said to me that I must write her biography when she was dead. But who thinks at the moment of confidential talk that the day may come all too quickly when one will stand alone, with merely the memory of the living bond which united him to the departed? Who is not inclined to hope that the morrow will bring richer opportunities for supplying the gaps which so often occur in rapid conversation, when thoughts run on from point to point?

In 1874 Sónya received a doctor's degree from the University of Göttingen on account of three treatises which she had written under the guidance of Weier-

strass, and more especially on account of the one entitled " Zur Theorie der partiellen Differentialgleichun-
gen " (*Crelli's Journal*).   It is considered to be one of
the most remarkable works she ever published.   By
special dispensation she was exempted from the *viva
voce* examination.   The following letter to the Dean of
the Philosophical Faculty in Göttingen shows the
characteristic motive which led Sónya to crave this
favor, so rarely, and only in the most exceptional
cases, granted.

The very reverend Dean will graciously permit me to add
something to the letter in which I present myself for admission
to the degree of Doctor Phil. in the mathematical faculty.   It is
not lightly that I have decided on this step, which compels me
to forsake the retirement in which I have hitherto lived.   It is
only a wish to satisfy my dearest friends which causes me to
desire from my inmost heart to be fairly tested.   I wish to give
them an incontestable proof that, in devoting myself to the
study of mathematics, I am following the determined bent of my
nature, and that, moreover, this study is not without result.   It
is this which has made me overcome my scruples.   I have been
told that, as a foreigner, I can obtain the degree *in absentia* if I
can show works of sufficient importance, and produce recommen-
dations from competent authorities.

At the same time I hope the very reverend Dean will not mis-
construe me if I acknowledge openly that I do not know whether
I have sufficient *aplomb* to undergo an *examen rigorosum*, and I
fear that the unusual position, and having to answer, face to
face, men with whom I am altogether unacquainted, would confuse me, although I know the examiners would do all they could
for me.   In addition to this, I speak German very badly.   When
I try to speak it, it seems to escape me, though, when I am at
leisure, I can use it in all my mathematical work.   The cause of
my faulty German is that though I began to speak it five years
ago, I spent four of those years quite alone in Berlin, never having any occasion to speak or hear the language, except during the
few hours my honored master devoted to me.   For these reasons
I venture to request the very reverend Dean kindly to intervene
so that I may be exempted from the *examen rigorosum*.

This petition, but above all the great merit of her work and her excellent testimonials, enabled Sónya to gain the rare privilege of receiving a doctor's degree without appearing in person.

Shortly after, the whole family Krukovsky were once more united in their old ancestral home at Palibino.

IV

HOW that family had changed since the days of Sónya's childhood is described in her writings. The two young girls who had dwelt in the quiet home, dreaming of the strange world of which they were so ignorant, met there once more as grown-up women, tried and developed by the experiences which each had gone through alone.

Life, for them, had indeed been different from the life of which they had dreamed.

It had, however, been full and varied enough to give rise to long conversations round the fire during the long winter evenings spent in the large drawing-room, with its red-damask furniture, the samovár singing on the table, its home-like sound mingling with the dismal hunger-song of the wolves in the forest without.

The world beyond these precincts no longer seemed to the two girls so vast and immeasurable. They had seen it close at hand, and realized its proportions more fully.

Aniuta, on the one hand, had led a life full of excitement, and her craving for emotion had been more than gratified. She, at least, no longer indulged in such cravings. She was passionately in love with the husband who sat beside her, with a weary, satirical expression on his face. Nay, she was even jealously attached to him, and her life was still so full of excitement that no extra stimulus was needed.

Her younger sister had hithero lived entirely with her brain. She had so completely satisfied her thirst for knowledge that she was satiated, and mental work was now impossible. She spent most of her time reading novels and playing cards, and otherwise sharing in the social life of her neighbors, who had no higher or more intellectual pursuits.

Sónya's greatest joy at this period of her life was in the change which had come over her father. He belonged, as did Sónya herself, to the small class of individuals who are able by sheer force of purpose and will to modify and develop their own characters. The harshness and despotism which had been his chief characteristics were much subdued by the severe trials to which his daughters had subjected him. He had learned that no one being can really rule the destiny of others by force—not even in the case of a father with his children. He bore, with a tolerance marvelous in one of his nature, the socialistic and radical assertions of his communist son-in-law and the materialistic tendencies of the other son-in-law, the scientific professor. This was the most cherished memory Sónya kept of her father, and one which was the more deeply impressed on her mind because it was associated with the last winter of his life.

Her father died unexpectedly and without warning from an aneurism of the heart. The blow was terrible to Sónya. She had, during the last few months, been on terms of tender intimacy with her father, and had, indeed, always loved him more than she did her mother.

This mother had a bright and winning nature. Every one was kind to her, and she was kind to every one. But, just in consequence of this, Sónya was little in sympathy with her mother. She fancied herself less of a favorite with her than the other children. But her father had always preferred her to the others, and after his death she felt utterly sad and lonely.

Aniuta had her husband, on whose neck she could weep out all her grief. But Sónya had no one to turn to for comfort. She had always kept at a distance the man whose highest ambition was to be her comfort and support. But now this distance seemed to her painful and unnatural; and thus her desire for affection induced her to overcome her prejudices. During the silent hours of sorrow she glided into full relationship with her husband.

＊　　＊　　＊　　＊　　＊　　＊

During the next winter the whole family went to St. Petersburg. There Sónya soon found herself the center of an intellectual circle such as could be hardly found elsewhere — a circle alert and wide awake; mentally, so to speak, on the *qui vive.*

Enlightened and liberal-minded Russians are, it is generally agreed, far more many-sided, freer from prejudice, and broader in their views than any other nation.

This was the experience not only of Sónya, but of all who have moved in such circles. They are in the van of advanced thought in Europe, and are ever the first to discover the dawn of fresh light. They are also more enthusiastic, and have a greater faith in ideals, than the educated thinkers of other nations.

In such circles Sónya at last felt herself appreciated and understood.

After five long years spent in severe study, and utterly devoid of amusement, there was now to her, in the full prime of her youth, something captivating and enchanting in the sudden change. All her brilliant gifts developed as if by magic, and she threw herself heartily into the whirl of "society" gaiety, with its fêtes, theaters, lectures, receptions, picnics, and other pleasures.

The circle which now surrounded her was more literary than scientific in its interests. With the natural longing to be in full sympathy with her surroundings which was one of Sónya's strongest sentiments, she now threw herself into literary pursuits. She wrote newspaper articles, poetry, and theatrical criticisms. But her writings were always anonymous. She also wrote a novel entitled "The Privat-docent," a tale of a small German university town. It was considered to show great promise.

Aniuta, who, during these years, lived in St. Petersburg with her husband, now came definitely to the fore as an authoress, and with much success; while Vladímir Kovalévsky was busy translating and publishing popular scientific works, such as "The Birds" of Brehm.

The legacy left to Sónya by her father was small, for he left the bulk of his fortune to his wife. But the life into which Sónya had plunged demanded a certain amount of luxury and style. Perhaps it was this which first induced her to indulge in speculations. Her husband, who was personally utterly indifferent to luxury, allowed himself to be drawn into these transactions, for he was of a lively, imaginative, and also somewhat yielding nature.

Venture followed upon venture. The Kovalévskys built many-storied houses, baths, and extensive hothouses in St. Petersburg. They published newspapers, launched new inventions of every kind, and for a time it looked as though fortune would smile upon them. Their friends prophesied a brilliant future; and in 1878, when their first child, a daughter, was born, she was hailed as a future heiress.

13

But, as usual, Sónya had even then premonitions of coming evil. One of her friends recalls to mind that, on the day on which the foundation-stone of their first house was to be laid, Sónya remarked that the occasion was spoiled for her by a dream she had had on the previous night.

She dreamed that she was standing on the spot where the stone was to be laid, surrounded by the throng assembled to witness the ceremony. Suddenly the crowd parted, and she saw her husband in the midst, struggling with a diabolical being which strove to trample him beneath its feet, and which, on succeeding, laughed sardonically.

This dream affected Sónya so powerfully that she became depressed and low-spirited for some time; and truly it was a dream which, later on, was verified in a terrible manner.

When, one after another, these vast speculations failed, Sónya's fortitude and energy showed themselves in all their greatness.

She had for a while, it is true, permitted her imagination to be fired by the common temptation of using her intelligence and creative genius for the acquisition of a fortune; but her soul could not long be wedded to so paltry an aim. She was able to lose millions at one blow without suffering a sleepless night or acquiring a new wrinkle on her brow. She could behold all prospect of wealth vanish without one regret. She had desired to be rich because life, in all its forms, tempted her. Her passionate and imaginative nature made her wish for a full experience. But when she found that she could not succeed in this, she withdrew at once, and summoned up all her energy and fortitude in order to comfort her husband.

Strange to say, this simple-minded man, to whom

money for its own sake had never been a temptation, and who had never been attracted by the advantages it could offer, had thrown his whole soul into their undertakings, and it seemed as if, to his nature, defeat and failure were absolutely crushing. Sónya, on the other hand, with rare courage, not only bowed to the inevitable, but also threw herself with renewed zeal into fresh pursuits.

She succeeded in averting the impending crisis in their finances. She shunned neither effort nor humiliation. She went round to the friends who had been interested in their ventures, and offered terms which satisfied all parties. She thus earned her husband's intense gratitude and admiration. Again their fortunes seemed secured; but the diabolic being who had terrified Sónya in her dream now crossed their path in dread reality.

A kind of adventurer, with whom Kovalévsky had come into contact through his ventures, now tried to involve him in new and yet more dangerous speculations.

Sónya, who read character well at first sight, contracted such an immediate and strong aversion to this man that she could not endure his presence in her house. She entreated her husband to break with him and return to scientific pursuits. But in vain. Vladímir, in 1881, was made Professor of Paleontology at the University of Moscow, and there he settled with his family; but he could not tear himself away from speculation, which now took wilder flights than ever. Petroleum-springs in the interior of Russia attracted his attention. He hoped to gain millions for himself while increasing and developing Russian industries. He was so blinded by his coadjutor that he would not listen to his wife's warnings. As he could not induce her to adopt his view of the matter, he refused her his confidence, and carried out his ideas alone. This was most painful to Sónya, and quite unbearable to a person of her character.

After having once decided to enter into full union with her husband, she had done everything to deepen and intensify their relations to each other. It was her nature to give herself up with passionate devotion to that which, for the time being, was foremost in her life. She also drew marked lines between what was important and what was unimportant; and this trait in her character made her superior to others of her sex, for she never neglected primary for secondary duties, and never took a narrow view of life. She could not put up with half-heartedness where feelings were concerned. She would sacrifice everything to secure a deep, whole-hearted union. She strove to the utmost to rescue her husband from the danger she foresaw. One of her friends describes her struggles thus: "Sónya tried to interest Kovalévsky again in science. She studied geology, helped to prepare his lectures, and tried to make home life delightful to him, so that he might recover his mental balance. But it was of no avail. My notion is that Kovalévsky was at that time not in a normal state of mind. His nerves had been overwrought, and he could not recover himself."

The adventurer, of course, could wish for nothing better than to foster the misunderstanding that now arose between husband and wife. He made Sónya believe that Kovalévsky's reserve and inaccessibility were due to other causes, and that she had good cause for jealousy.

Through Sónya's own "Recollections of Childhood" we know that, as a child of ten, she already showed signs of being possessed by consuming jealousy. To touch that chord was to awaken the strongest passion of her violent nature.

Sónya now lost her critical judgment, and was not in a fit state to inquire whether this charge against her husband were true or not. Later on in life she became almost convinced that it had been a pure invention. But at the moment she felt a strong inclination to get away from the humiliation of feeling herself neglected, fearing lest her passion should make her condescend to the pettiness of spying upon her husband's movements, or lead to distressing scenes. She dreaded living with a man whose love and confidence she believed she had lost, or seeing him go to his ruin without being able to save him.

Such fears and dread were too much for a nature to which resignation was almost impossible. In matters of feeling she was as uncompromising and exacting as she was lenient and easy to satisfy in all material things. She had, without loving him, surrendered herself to her husband, and made his interests her own. She had striven to bind him to herself with all the exquisite tenderness which a nature like hers bestows upon, but also requires from, the man who was her husband and the father of her child.

When, despite all, she saw her husband turn from her, and believed he had put another in her place, the network of tenderness which she had purposely woven around him broke. Her heart contracted and shut out the picture of him whom she had determined to love, and once more she was alone.

She decided to make a future for herself and her little daughter entirely by her own endeavor, and she left husband, home, and country, to resume once more her student life abroad.

13*

V

WHEN the train had moved out of the station, and Sónya lost sight of the friends who had come to bid her farewell, she gave vent to the feelings she had hitherto suppressed, and broke into uncontrollable sobbing. She wept for the lost years of happiness, for the lost dream of full and perfect union with another soul; she trembled at the thought of the lonely student's room, which once had contained her whole life, but which could not satisfy her any longer, now that she had experienced the joy of being beloved in her own home, and by a circle of appreciative friends.

She tried to console herself by the thought of resuming her mathematical studies. She dreamed of writing a book which should make her celebrated and bring glory to her sex. But it was no good. These joys paled before the personal happiness which during the last few years had been the purpose and aim of her heart.

The paroxysms of tears became more and more violent, and she shook from head to foot.

She had not noticed that an elderly gentleman, sitting opposite to her in the carriage, was watching her with sympathy.

"I cannot see you cry in this way!" he exclaimed at last. "I suppose it is the first time you have gone out into the world alone. But you are not going into the midst of cannibals. A young girl like yourself will always find friends and help when she needs them."

She had allowed this stranger to witness her despair, though hitherto she had hidden her wounds from her nearest and dearest. It was a relief when she noticed that he had not the least idea who she was. During the conversation which now followed, it became evident that he took her for a little governess going abroad to earn her living in a strange family.

She kept up his illusion, only too happy to preserve her incognito, and even amused at playing a little comedy which served to distract her thoughts. It was not difficult for her to conceive her rôle so completely as to identify herself in imagination with the supposed poor little governess.

With downcast eyes she received advice and comfort from her good-natured traveling-companion. So strong was the fantastic element in her character that, despite her great sorrow, she began to enjoy the mystification.

When the gentleman proposed that they should stop in the town they were passing through, and see whatever it might afford that was interesting, she consented to do so. They spent a couple of days there, and then parted without having even learned each other's name or position.

This little episode is characteristic of Sónya's love of adventure. The stranger had been sympathetic to her. His kind interest in her sorrow touched her. She felt alone in the world; why not accept this bright gleam which chance had thrown in her way? Another woman might doubtless have compromised herself hopelessly in a man's eyes by such conduct. Two days' intercourse with a man from morning to

evening—a man who did not even know who she was!
But to Sónya, who had for so many years lived on
terms of *bonne camaraderie* with her husband, it seemed
quite simple. She knew well how to draw the line
whenever she chose. No man had ever misunderstood
her.

A few years later she entered into equally strange
and peculiar relations with a young man in Paris.

The keeper of the lodging-house in the suburbs of
that city where she lived must hardly have known
what to think. Time after time this woman saw a
young man leave the house at two in the morning, and
climb over the palings surrounding the garden. As
this young man spent all his days with Sónya, and
often stayed till late at night, and as, at this time,
she had no other friends, it certainly did seem a
rather doubtful proceeding. Nevertheless the friendship existing between these two was of the most ideal
kind imaginable.

The young man was a Pole, and a revolutionist;
moreover, a mathematician and a poet. His and
Sónya's souls were two fiery flames merged in one
glow. No one had ever understood her so well and
sympathized with her so much as he. No one had so
entered into every word, thought, and dream. They
were almost constantly together, and yet they em-
ployed the few moments during which they were
parted in pouring forth to each other, in writing,
their inmost thoughts. They composed poetry together, and began writing a long romance. They
indulged in the idea that every human being has its
twin soul, so that every individual man or woman is
but half a creature. The other half, which is to complete the soul, is always to be found somewhere on the
earth. But rarely in this life do they meet. It is

usually in a future state only that they find each
other. Where could one find any more full-blown
romance? In this life these two souls which had met
could never be united, for circumstances had destroyed
the possibility for them of true union. Even if Sónya
had still been free, yet she had been married; and he
had consecrated himself to one who was in future to
be his only love.

Neither did Sónya feel it right to belong to any one
but her husband, for the bond which united her to him
had not been entirely dissolved. They still wrote to
each other occasionally. There was a possibility of
their meeting again, and she was still fond of him in
the depths of her heart.

So the intercourse between her and the Pole was
only that of a responsive interchange of thought and
an abstract analyzing of feeling. They used to sit
opposite each other and talk on without stopping, intoxicating themselves with the increasing stream of
words so characteristic of the Slavonic race. But in
the midst of their visionary fervor, Sónya was crushed
by a great misfortune.

Her husband had not been able to survive the discovery that he had been shamefully cheated and had
ruined his family. This highly gifted scientist, so
simple and unostentatious, who had never desired the
delights which wealth can bestow, was the victim of
a swindle, in circumstances utterly opposed to his
character and the tendencies of his whole life.

The news of his death stretched Sónya on a sick-bed.
She lay for a long time suffering from a dangerous
nervous fever. She rose again broken in spirit, with
the feeling that an irremediable sorrow had drawn a
line across her life.

She reproached herself deeply for not having remained with her husband, even though by so doing she must have doomed herself to an almost unbearable struggle. She grieved bitterly, with the sense that now nothing could be helped.

During this illness she lost the freshness of youth. She lost her clear complexion, and a deep furrow, nevermore to be effaced, was drawn by care across her brow.

VI

DURING Sónya's stay in St. Petersburg in 1876, she had made an acquaintance which was to have a decisive influence on her future life. Mittag Leffler, a pupil of Weierstrass, had heard a great deal of Sónya's unusual talent from their mutual teacher, and came to see her.

On this occasion Sónya had no premonition of the influence he would afterward exert on her life. She only felt rather unwilling to receive her visitor when he was announced. She had at that time given up all studies, and did not even correspond with her former master.

During conversation, however, her former interests were aroused. She showed so much acuteness of judgment and quickness of perception in the most difficult mathematical problems that her visitor felt almost confounded when he looked at the girlish face before him. The impression she made on him as a woman-thinker was so strong that several years later, when he became Professor of Mathematics in the new University of Stockholm, one of his first steps was to induce the authorities to appoint " Fru " Kovalévsky as a privat-docent.

Sónya already, a few years before her husband's death, had expressed a wish to become a teacher at a university. Professor Mittag Leffler, who was greatly interested in the university recently established in his native town, and who also took a warm interest in the woman question, was eager to secure for his university the glory of attracting to it the first great woman-mathematician.

As early as 1881 Sónya wrote to Mittag Leffler, then at Helsingfors, the following letter:

BELLEVUESTRASSE, BERLIN, July 8, 1881.

I thank you none the less for the interest you take in my possible appointment to Stockholm, and for all the trouble you are giving yourself for this purpose. I can assure you that if it were offered to me, I should gratefully accept. I have never looked for any other appointment than this, and I will even admit that I should feel less bashful and shy if I were only allowed the possibility of applying my knowledge in the higher branches of education. I may in this way open the universities to women, which has hitherto only been possible by special favor — a favor which can be denied at any moment, as has recently happened in the German universities. Without being rich, I have still the means of living independently. The question of salary is, therefore, of no importance to me in coming to a decision. What I wish, above all, is to serve the cause in which I take so great an interest; and, at the same time, to be able to live for my work, surrounded by those who are occupied with the same questions — a piece of good fortune I have never enjoyed in Russia, but only in Berlin. These, dear professor, are my personal feelings on the subject, but I think I ought to tell you even more. Professor W—— believes that, as far as he can judge of Swedish matters, it is not possible for the Stockholm University to accept a woman even as a teacher. What is of still greater importance, he is afraid that if you insist on introducing such novelties, it may injure your own position. It would be selfish on my part if I did not let you know the opinion of our beloved teacher. And you can easily understand how unhappy I should be if, after all, I injured you, who have always shown so much interest in me, and helped me so greatly; you for whom I feel such sincere friendship. I believe it would be wiser, therefore, not to do anything at present, but to wait till I have finished the papers on which I am now engaged. If I succeed in completing them as well as I intend and hope, it would in every way help toward the aim I have in view.

It was after this that the dramatic episodes in Sónya's life occurred: the separation from her husband; the Polish romance; her husband's death, and her long illness. All this delayed the completion of the papers mentioned in her letter, so that it was not until August, 1883, that she could inform Mittag Leffler that the first thesis was completed. She writes to him from Odessa[1] on August 28, 1883:

I have at last succeeded in finishing one of the two works on which I have been busy during the last two years. My first wish, as soon as I found it satisfactory, was to let you know. But Mr. W——, with his usual kindness, has taken that trouble, letting you know the result of my researches. I have just received a letter from him, saying that he had told you about it, and that you have answered him with your usual kindness, asking me to go to Stockholm, and to begin there a course of private lessons. I cannot tell you how grateful I am to you for the friendship you have always shown me, and how happy I am to be able to enter a career which has ever been the cherished object of my desires. At the same time I feel I ought to tell you that in many respects I feel but little fitted for the duties of "docent," and at times I so much doubt my own capacity that I feel you, who have always judged me leniently, will be quite disillusioned when you find, on nearer inspection, how little I am really good for. I am truly grateful to Stockholm, which is the only European university that will open its doors to me, and I am already prepared to be in love with that city, and to attach myself to Sweden as though it were my native home. I hope that, if I do come there, it will be to find a new "foster-land." But just because of this, I think I should not care to go there before I feel prepared to deserve the good opinion you have of me, and to make a good impression. I have written to-day to W—— to ask whether he does not think it would be good for me to spend another two or three months with him, in order to grasp his ideas better, and to fill up the gaps which are still to be found in my mathematical knowledge. These few months in Berlin would also be useful to me, for I should then come into

[1] Appendix C.

contact with young mathematicians just beginning their career as tutors, and many of whom I knew pretty well during my last stay in Berlin. I could even arrange with them that we should correspond on mathematical subjects. I could then, no doubt, expound Abel's "Theory of Functions," which they do not know, and which I have studied deeply. This would give some opportunity of lecturing, which, up to this time, I have never had. Then I should arrive in Stockholm much more sure of myself.

This plan was not realized, and on November 11th of the same year Sónya left St. Petersburg and started for Stockholm *via* Hangö.

VII

AS is natural, now that Sónya is dead, my first meeting with her is vividly recalled to my mind, even in its most minute details. She arrived from Finland in the evening by boat, and came as a guest to my brother Leffler's house. I went there the day after her arrival. We were prepared to be friends, for we had heard much of each other, and were eager to become acquainted. Perhaps she had expected more from the meeting than I, for she felt a great interest in that which was my special aim and object. I, on the other hand, rather fancied that a woman-mathematician would prove too abstract for me.

She was standing in the window when I arrived, turning over the leaves of a book. Before she could turn, I had time to see a serious and marked profile, rich chestnut hair arranged in a negligent plait, and a spare figure with a certain graceful elegance in its pose, but not well proportioned, for the bust and upper part of the body were too small in comparison with the large head. Her mouth was large, her lips fresh and humid and most expressive. Her hands were small, almost like a child's; exquisitely modeled, but rather spoiled by prominent blue veins. Her eyes were the most remarkable feature of her face, and gave to her countenance the look of lofty intellect which so greatly impressed all who observed her. Their color was uncertain; they varied from gray to green and brown. Unusually large, prominent, and luminous, they had an intensity of expression which seemed to pierce the farthest corner of your soul when she fixed her eyes upon you. But though so piercing they were soft and loving, and full of responsive sympathy, which seemed to woo those on whom their magnetizing power rested to tell her their inmost secrets. So great was their charm that one scarcely noticed their defect— Sónya was so short-sighted that when she was very tired she often squinted.

She turned to me with a quick movement, and came across the room to greet me with outstretched hands. There was a certain shyness about her which made one at first feel rather formal.

Our first conversation turned on the bad toothache she had unfortunately suffered from during the voyage. I offered to take her to the dentist. A pleasant object, indeed, for her first walk in a new town! She was, however, the last person to bestow too much attention or time on so trivial an incident.

I was at that moment thinking out the plot of my play entitled "How to Do Good," but had not yet written it down. So great was Sónya's power of giving an impetus to one's inner thoughts that, before she had reached the dentist's, I had told her the whole play, worked out in far greater detail and breadth than I had ever been conscious of intending.

This was the commencement of the great influence she exercised on my writings afterward. Her power of understanding and sympathizing with the thoughts of others was so exceptional, her praise when she was pleased so warm and enthusiastic, her criticism so just, that, for a receptive nature like mine, it was impossible to work without her approbation.

If she criticized unfavorably anything I had written, I rewrote it until she was pleased. This was the commencement of our collaboration. She used to say that I should never have written "Ideal Women" if I had not done so before her arrival in Sweden. This work, and my novel, "At War with Society," were the only books of mine that she disliked. She disapproved of Bertha's struggle to try and secure the remnant of her mother's fortune, for she considered that when a woman has once given herself to a man, she must not for a moment hesitate to sacrifice her fortune to the very last farthing if he needs it. This criticism was so like her; she was always so subjective in her judgments of literary produce. If the thought and feeling in a book were in accordance with her own sympathies, she was prone to value it highly, even if it was only mediocre. If, on the other hand, it contained any opinion in which she did not share, she would not admit that the book had any merit at all.

In spite of this prejudice, she was as broad in her views as the most highly gifted individuals of her age. Of the prejudices and conventionalities of ordinary mortals she had not a trace. Her comprehensive genius and her high culture raised her far above the boundaries with which tradition limits most minds.

Limitations she found, but only in the strong individuality of her nature, the pronounced sympathies and antipathies of which withstood both logic and discussion.

On this first occasion we did not see much of each other, and our acquaintance did not deepen into friendship, for within a month of her arrival I went abroad for some time. Before that, however, she had learned enough Swedish to read my books. Immediately after her arrival she began to take lessons in that language,

14

and for the first week she really did nothing but study it from morning till night.

My brother, as soon as she arrived, told her that he wanted to give a *soirée* in order to introduce her to all his scientific friends. But she begged him to wait until she could speak Swedish. This seemed to us rather optimistic, but she kept her word. In a fortnight she could speak a little, and during the first winter she had mastered our literature, and had read the "Frithiof's Saga"[1] with delight.

This unusual talent for languages had its limitations. She used to say that she had no real talent that way, and had only learned several languages from necessity and ambition. It is quite true that, notwithstanding the quick results she obtained when she first learned a language, she never acquired it to perfection, and always forgot one language as soon as she learned another. Though she was in Germany when quite a young girl, she spoke the language very brokenly, and her German friends used to laugh at the ridiculous and often impossible words she coined. She never allowed herself to be stopped in the flow of her conversation by any such minor considerations as the correct choice of words. She always spoke fluently, always succeeded in expressing what she wanted to say, and in giving an individual stamp to her utterances, however imperfectly she spoke the language she was using. When she had learned Swedish she had nearly forgotten all her German, and when she had been away from Sweden a few months, she spoke Swedish very badly on her return. One of her characteristics was that when tired or depressed she had great difficulty in finding words; but when in good spirits she spoke rapidly and with great elegance. Language, like everything

[1] Appendix D.

else with her, was under the influence of her personal moods.

During the last autumn of her life, when she returned from Italy,—where she spent a couple of weeks, and fell in love with that country, as every one who goes there does,—she spoke Italian fairly; but, on the other hand, she spoke Swedish very badly, because she was out of harmony with Sweden.

French was the foreign language she spoke best, though she did not write it quite correctly. It was said that in Russian her style showed a certain foreign influence.

She often complained that she could not speak Russian with her intimate friends in Sweden. She used to say, "I can never quite express the delicate *nuances* of thought. I have always to content myself with the next best expression, or say what I want to say in a roundabout way. I never find the exact expressions. That is why, when I return to Russia, I feel released from the prison in which my best thoughts were in bondage. You cannot think what suffering it is to have to speak always a foreign language to your friends. You might as well wear a mask on your face."

In February, 1884, I went to London, and did not meet Sónya again till the following October. While in London I had only one letter from her. In it she describes her winter at Stockholm. The letter has no date, but it was evidently written in April, and, like the former letters quoted, was in French.

What shall I tell you about our life in Stockholm? [she says]. If it has not been very *inhaltsreich*, it has at least been very lively, and lately very tiring. Suppers, dinners, *soirées*, and receptions have succeeded one another, and it has been difficult to find time to go to all these parties, and also to prepare meantime my lectures, or to work. To-day we have suspended our lectures for the Easter fortnight, and I am as happy as a school-girl at the prospect of a holiday. The 1st of May is not far distant, and then I hope to go to Berlin *via* St. Petersburg. My plans for next winter are still undecided, as they do not depend upon me. As you can easily imagine, people talk constantly about you. Every one wants to hear about you. Your letters are read, commented upon, and make quite a sensation. The leading ladies of Stockholm seem to have very few subjects of conversation, and it is really a charity to give them something to talk about. I enjoy beforehand the effect of your play when it is put on the stage next autumn.

In April Sónya finished her course of lectures and left for Russia. She writes as follows to Mittag Leffler:

RUSSIA, April 29, 1884.

. . . It seems a century since I left Stockholm. I shall never be able to express or to show all the gratitude and friend-ship I feel for you. It is as if I had found in Sweden a new foster-land and family at the moment when I most needed them. . . .

The course of lectures Sónya had given that year in German at the University of Stockholm was quite private. The lectures had raised her greatly in public estimation, and Mittag Leffler was enabled to collect privately the funds necessary to give her an official appointment, which was to last, in the first instance, for five years. Several persons bound themselves to pay a lump sum of about £112 a year. The University gave about the same sum, so that Sónya had £225 a year. Her pecuniary position was such that she could no longer give her work gratis, as she had at first generously offered to do. But it was not only the pecuniary question which had raised difficulties in the way of her official appointment.

The conservative opposition which actually arose on many sides against the employment of a woman as a

university professor had to be overcome. No other
university had set the example. The funds might
possibly have been found to furnish a life-appointment, but the considerations urged against such an
appointment appearing to be insurmountable, Professor Leffler decided to postpone the attempt till a more
convenient season. At the end of the first five years he
succeeded in obtaining for Sónya a life-appointment,
which she enjoyed just one year.

On July 1, 1884, Mittag Leffler had the pleasure of
telegraphing to Sónya, who was then in Berlin, that
she had been appointed professor for five years. She
answered the same day in the following terms:

BERLIN, July 1, 1884.

. . . I need hardly tell you that your and Uggla's telegrams have filled my heart with joy. I may now confess that
up to the last moment I believed and feared that the matter
could not be carried through. I thought that at the critical
moment some unexpected difficulty would arise, and that all our
plans would come to nothing. I am also sure that it is only
owing to your perseverance and energy that we have been able
to attain our end. I now wish that I may now have the strength
and capacity requisite for my duties, and to help you in all your
undertakings. I firmly believe in my future, and shall be glad
to work with you. What joy and happiness it is that we
met! . . .

Further on she says:

W—— has spoken to several officials here about my wish to
attend lectures. It is possible that the thing may be arranged,
but not this summer, as the present Rector is a decided opponent of woman's rights. I hope, however, it may be arranged
by December, when I return to spend my Christmas holidays
here.

The University of Stockholm had already appointed
Fru Kovalévsky professor, while in Germany it was
still impossible for her, as a woman, to attend even
lectures.

14*

Another person might have been somewhat per-
turbed by the uncertainty of the appointment she now
accepted. But the future never harassed Sónya. If
the present were satisfactory, that was all she required.
She was ready at any moment to sacrifice a brilliant
future if by doing so she could secure a happier and
fuller present.

Before going to Berlin, Sónya had paid a visit to
her little daughter, who was living with the friend of
Sónya's youth in Moscow. Thence she wrote a letter
to Mittag Leffler, which may be taken as an exposition
of her ideas of a mother's duty, and which describes
the conflict between her duties as a mother and as an
official personage, as a woman and as a bread-winner :

> Moscow, June 3, 1884.
> I have had a long letter from J——, in which she expresses
> a warm wish that I should bring my little girl with me to Stock-
> holm. But, in spite of all the considerations which might in-
> cline me to have my little Sónya with me, I have almost decided
> to let her spend another winter in Moscow. I do not think it
> would be in the child's interest to take her away from this place,
> where she is well cared for, and to carry her back with me to
> Stockholm, where nothing is prepared for her, and where I shall
> have to devote my whole time and energy to my new duties.
> J—— says, among other things, that many people will accuse
> me of indifference to my child. I suppose that is quite possible,
> but I confess that I do not care in the least for that argument.
> I am quite willing to submit to the judgment of the Stockholm
> ladies in all that has to do with the minor details of life ; but in
> serious questions, especially when I do not act in my own inter-
> ests, but in those of my child, I consider it would be unpardon-
> able weakness on my part were I to let the shadow of a wish to
> play the part of a good mother in the eyes of Stockholm petti-
> coats influence me in the least.

On her return to Sweden, in September, Sónya went
to Södertelje for a few weeks, in order to finish in peace
the work commenced long before, " The Transmission

of Light through a Crystalline Medium." Mittag Leffler and a young German mathematician, whose acquaintance Sónya had made at Berlin during the summer, were with her at Södertelje, and the young mathematician assisted her by correcting her German.

On my first visit to her on my return from England, I was astonished to find her looking younger and handsomer. I at first thought it was the effect of her having left off her mourning, for black was very unbecoming to her, and she herself hated it. The light-blue summer dress she was now wearing made her complexion look brighter, and she also wore her rich chestnut hair in curls. But it was not only her outward appearance which was changed. I soon noticed that the melancholy which had enveloped her during her former sojourn in Stockholm had given place to sparkling gaiety, a side of her character which I now for the first time learned to know. She was in such a gay mood, sparkling with joy, dancing with life; a half satirical, half good-natured shower of wit surrounded her. One daring paradox followed another, and it was well for any one not quick at repartee to keep silence on such occasions, for she did not give people much chance of retort.

She was at this time occupied with preparing her lectures for the new term. These she read to the young German, saying jestingly that he must be her "pointer-dog," a rôle which had usually been filled by Mittag Leffler.

Sónya's bright mood lasted through the autumn. She led a social life, and was everywhere the center of a magic circle. The strong satirical vein in her character and the deep contempt she felt for mediocrity (she belonged to the aristocracy of the intellectual world, and worshiped genius) were, in her, wedded to a poet's ready sympathy with all human conflict and trouble, even the least important.

This caused her to take a lively interest in everything that concerned her friends. All the domestic worries of her married friends were confided to her, and young girls asked her advice about their dress. The usual verdict passed upon her by those who knew her was that she was as simple and unpretentious as a school-girl, and in no way thought herself above other women.

But, as I have already said, this was not a true estimate of her character, just as the impression of frankness and affability given by her manners was a delusion. She was in reality reserved, and she con-sidered few people her equals. But the mobility of her nature and intelligence, the wish to please, and the psychological interest she took in all human things, gave her the sympathetic manner which charmed all who saw her. She seldom displayed her sarcastic vein to her inferiors unless they were really uncongenial to her. But she used it freely among those whom she looked upon as her equals.

Meanwhile it did not take her long to exhaust the social interest in Stockholm. After a time she said she knew every one by heart, and longed for fresh stimulus for her intelligence. This was a great misfortune to her, and accounts for the fact that she could not be happy in Stockholm, or, perhaps, in any place in the world. She was continually in want of stimulus. She desired dramatic interests in life, and was ever hunger-ing for high-wrought mental delights. She hated with all her heart the gray monotony of every-day life.

Bohemian by nature, as she often called herself, she hated everything covered by the expression *bour-geois*. She herself attributed this trait in her char-acter to her descent from a gipsy woman who, I believe,

married her father's grandfather — a marriage by which
that gentleman forfeited his title of "prince," then
possessed by the family.[1]

All this was not only a peculiarity of temperament
in Sónya, but underlay her intellectual nature. Her
talents were of the productive order, and at the same
time she was very receptive by nature, and required
stimulus from the genius of others in order to do productive work herself.

This is the reason why her whole scientific career was
occupied solely with the development of the ideas of
her great teacher.

In literature she required intercourse with persons
similarly occupied.

With such a principle underlying her whole character and intelligence, it was only natural that life in
such a small town as Stockholm should be altogether
monotonous to her. She could only really *live* in the
great European capitals. There she found the mental
stimulus she needed.

She spent the Christmas of 1884 in Berlin. On her
return thence she made use, for the first time, of the
expression she afterward used every year, and which
so wounded and hurt her friends. "The road from
Stockholm to Malmö," she said, "is the most beautiful line I have ever seen; but the road from Malmö to
Stockholm is the ugliest, dullest, and most tiresome I
have ever known."

My heart bleeds when I think how often, with an
ever-growing bitterness in her heart, she had to take
that journey, which at last brought her to an early
grave.

A letter to my brother, written from Berlin during
that Christmas, shows how deeply melancholic her

[1] Appendix E.

mood really was, despite all outward show of cheerfulness. Her friends have told me how much happier
and full of the love of life she was during that Christmas—more so than ever before. She regretted that
during her real youth she had neglected youth's pleasures, and she now wanted to avenge herself, and began
to take lessons in dancing and skating. She did not
wish to expose her first awkward attempts at skating,
so one of her friends and admirers arranged a private
skating-ground for her in the garden of one of the
Berlin villas. Her lessons in dancing were also taken
in a similarly private fashion, with two admirers as
cavaliers.

She rushed from one entertainment to another, and
was much fêted—an experience she always enjoyed.

But this happy mood was short-lived. A month
later it had been chased away by the news of her
sister's illness, and by a love-affair, which, as usual
with her, took no happy turn. It caused her supreme
bliss, and also the melancholy which ensued.

She writes on December 27, 1884:

I feel in very low spirits. I have had very bad news from my
sister. Her illness makes terrible progress, and now it is her
sight which is affected. She can neither read nor write. This
is caused by the faulty action of her heart, which gives rise to
temporary stagnations of the blood and paralysis. I tremble at
the thought of the loss which awaits me in the near future.
How sad life is after all! and how dull it is to go on living! It
is my birthday,[1] and I am thirty-one to-day, and I may perhaps
have as many years still to live! How beautiful it is in operas
and dramas! As soon as any one has found out that life is not
worth living, some one or something comes on the scene and
helps to make the passage to the other world easy. Reality is
in this detail inferior to fiction. One speaks so much of the perfection of the organisms so fully developed by living creatures

[1] This is a fiction, for it was neither her birthday, nor was she
the age mentioned. (See Introduction.)

through the process of natural selection. I find that the highest perfection would be the power to die quickly and easily. From this standpoint humanity has decidedly retrograded. Insects and the lower animals can never choose to die. An articulated animal can suffer unheard-of tortures without ceasing to exist. But the higher you rise in the animal scale the easier is the transit. In a bird, a wild animal, a lion, or a tiger, almost every illness is fatal. They have either the full enjoyment of life — or else death, but no suffering. Man has reapproached the insect. Many of my acquaintances make me involuntarily think of insects with wings torn off, the different segments of their bodies crushed, or their legs and feet injured. Yet, poor things, they cannot decide to die. Forgive me for writing to you in such low spirits. I am really in a very gloomy mood. I feel no desire to work. I have not yet been able to settle down to prepare my lectures for the next term. But I have pondered much over the following problem. [And here a mathematical proposition is given.]

From the same letter I quote again:

I have received from your sister, as a Christmas present, an article by Strindberg, in which he proves, as decidedly as that two and two make four, what a monstrosity is a woman who is a professor of mathematics, and how unnecessary, injurious, and out of place she is. I think he is right *au fond*, only I wish he would prove clearly that there were plenty of mathematicians in Sweden better than I am, and that it was only *galanterie* which made them select me!

VIII

PASTIMES

AMONG the crowd of skaters who that winter frequented the Nybroviken and the royal skating-
ground at Skeppsholm, a little lady, clad in a tight-
fitting, fur-trimmed costume, her hands tucked into a
muff, might be daily seen trying, with small, uncertain
steps, to move along on her skates. She was accompanied by a tall gentleman wearing spectacles, and a
tall, slight lady, and none of them seemed very steady
on their feet.

While practising they kept up a lively conversation,
and sometimes the gentleman would draw a geometrical
figure on the ice; not, indeed, with his skates,—not
being dexterous enough for that,—but with his stick.
The little lady would then instantly pause and study
the figure intently. The two had come together from
the University to the skating-ground, and were generally engaged in hot discussion arising from a lecture
which one or the other had just given, a discussion
which was usually continued after reaching the ground.

Sometimes the little lady would cry mercy, and beg
to be excused from talking mathematics while skating,
as it made her lose her balance. At another time she
and the tall lady would engage in talk on psychological
topics, or communicate to each other some plot for a
novel or drama. They also argued and sparred about
their respective proficiency in the art of skating. In

any other occupation they willingly admitted each other's superiority, but not in this.

Any one who met Madame Kovalévsky in society that winter would have imagined she was a very proficient skater—one who might have carried off the prize in a tournament with the greatest ease. She spoke of the sport with great eagerness and interest, and was very proud of the smallest progress she made, though she had never shown any such vanity about the works which had brought her world-wide renown.

Even in the riding-school she and her tall companion might often be seen that winter, and it was evident they took great interest in each other's accomplishments. The celebrated Madame Kovalévsky was naturally much noticed wherever she made her appearance, but no little school-girl could have behaved more childishly than she did at such riding or skating lessons. Her taste for such sports was not supported by the least facility for them. She was scarcely in the saddle, for instance, when she was overcome with fear. She would scream if her horse made the least unexpected movement. She always begged for the quietest and soberest animal in the stables. But she would afterward explain why that day's riding-lesson had been a failure, alleging either that the horse had been fidgety or wild, or that the saddle had been uncomfortable. She never got beyond a ten-minutes' trot, and if the horse broke into a good pace, she would call to the riding-master in broken Swedish, " Please, good man, make the horse stop ! "

She bore with great amiability all the teasing of her friends on this account, but when she talked to other people about the matter, they easily went off with the idea that she was an accomplished horsewoman who could boldly ride the wildest animal at a gallop. All this was no boasting; she thoroughly believed in it. She always intended to do something wonderful each time she went to the riding-school, and was continually proposing riding-tours. Her explanation of her overwhelming fear when once mounted was that it was not really fright, only she was very nervous, which made her sensitive to every noise, so that the tramping of the other horses upset her composure. Her friends often could not resist asking her what kind of noise it was that, when out walking, made her jump over hedges and ditches to avoid a harmless cow, or run away from a dog that merely sniffed at her.

She describes this kind of cowardice very well in an otherwise great character in her posthumous novel, "Vera Vorontzoff":

> In the learned circle in which he lived no one would have dreamed of suspecting him of cowardice. On the contrary, all his colleagues dreaded lest his courage should lead him into difficulties. In his own heart he knew himself to be far from courageous. But in his day-dreams he loved to imagine himself among the most dangerous circumstances. More than once, in the silence of his quiet study, he had fancied himself defending a barricade. In spite of this, he kept at a respectful distance from village curs, and declined to make any near acquaintance with horned cattle.

Sónya perhaps exaggerated her fear out of coquetry. She possessed to a high degree that feminine grace so highly appreciated by men. She loved to be protected.

To a quite masculine energy and genius, and, in some ways, an inflexible character, she united a very feminine helplessness. She never learned her way about Stockholm. She only knew perfectly a few streets — those which led to the University or to the houses of her intimate friends. She could look neither after her money matters, her house, nor her child. The latter she was obliged to leave in the care of others. In fact, she was so impractical that all the minor details of life were a burden to her. When she was obliged to seek work that paid, to apply to an editor or get introductions, she was incapable of looking after her own interests. But she never failed to find some devoted friend who made her interest his own, and on whom she could throw all the burden of her affairs. At every railway-station where she stopped on her many journeys, some one was always waiting to receive her, to procure rooms for her, to show her the way, or to place his services at her disposal. It was such a delight to her to be thus assisted and cared for in trifles that, as I said before, she rather liked to exaggerate her fears and helplessness. Notwithstanding all this, there was never a woman who, in the deepest sense of the word, could be more independent of others than she.

In a letter written in German to the admirer who had taught her to dance and skate, Sónya describes her life in Stockholm during the winter of 1884–85 :

STOCKHOLM, April, 1885.

DEAR MR. H——: I am ashamed that I have not answered your kind letter sooner. My only excuse is the multifarious occupations which have filled up my time. I will tell you all I have been doing. To begin with, there are my lectures three times a week in *Swedish*. I read and study the algebraic introduction to Abel's "Functions," and in Germany these lectures are supposed to be the most difficult. I have a pretty large number of students, all of whom I retain, with the exception of, at most, two or three who have withdrawn. Secondly, I have been writing a short mathematical treatise, which I shall send to Weierstrass immediately, asking him to get it published in *Borchardt's Journal*. Thirdly, I and Mittag Leffler have begun a large mathematical work. We hope to get a great deal of pleasure and fame out of it—this is a secret at present, so do not yet mention it. Fourthly, I have made the acquaintance of a very pleasant man, who has recently returned to Stockholm

from America. He is the editor of the largest Swedish newspaper. He has made me promise to write something for his
paper, and, as you know,[1] *I can never see my friends at work
without wishing to do exactly what they are doing, so I have written*
a number of short articles[2] for him. For the moment I have
only one of these personal reminiscences ready, but I send it
to you, as you understand Swedish so well. Fifthly (last, not
least), can you really believe, unlikely as it sounds, that I have
developed into an accomplished skater! At the end of last
week I was on the ice every day. I am so sorry you cannot see
how well I managed in the end. Whenever I have gained a
little extra dexterity I have thought of you. And now I can
even skate a little backward!! But I can go forward with great
facility and assurance!! All my friends here are astonished
how quickly I have mastered the difficult art. In order to console myself a little, now that the ice has disappeared, I have
taken furiously to riding with my friends. In the few weeks of
the Easter holidays I intend to ride at least an hour every day.
I like riding very much. I really don't know which I like best,
skating or riding. But this is by no means the end of all my
frivolities. There is to be a great fête on April 15th. It is a
kind of fair or bazaar, and seems to be a very Swedish affair.
A hundred of us ladies will dress in costume and sell all sorts
of things for the benefit of the Public Museum. I am, of course,
going to be a gipsy, and equally of course a great guy. I have
asked five other young ladies to share my fate and help me.
We are to be a gipsy troupe, with tents, and our *marshalkar*,[3]
also in the costume of gipsy youths, to attend on us. We are
likewise to have a Russian samovár, and to serve tea from it.

Now what do you say to all this nonsense, dear Mr. H——?
This evening I am going to have a grand party in my own little
room, the first I have given since I have been in Stockholm.

In the spring of the year there was a suggestion
made that Sónya should lecture on mechanics during
the illness of Professor Holmgren.

---

[1] The italics have been added by the friend who sends the
letter.

[2] She had in reality written only *one* of the articles, but in her
vivid imagination what she *intended* doing was already done.

[3] Appendix F.

She wrote on this subject to Professor Mittag Leffler:

STOCKHOLM, June 3d.

I have been to Lindhagen, who told me that the authorities of the University are of opinion that I ought to be Professor Holmgren's substitute. But they do not wish this mentioned, as it might have a bad effect on Holmgren. He is really very ill, but does not yet seem to realize the fact. I replied to Lindhagen that I felt that this was quite fair, and that I am satisfied to know that the authorities think I should be Holmgren's *locum tenens* in case he is not able to give his autumn lectures. But if, contrary to present expectations, he should have recovered before then, I should be so pleased with the happy turn of events that I should not regret the work I should thus have missed. I am much pleased, my dear friend, that things have turned out so well, and I shall do my best to make my lectures as good as possible. Stories with a moral are always tiresome in books, but they are very encouraging and edifying when they occur in real life; so I am doubly pleased that my motto, *pas trop de zèle*, has been refuted in so brilliant and unexpected a manner. I do hope you will have no reason to reproach me with losing courage. You must never forget, dear friend, that I am Russian. When a Swedish woman is tired or in a bad humor she is silent and sulky. Of course the ill humor strikes inward and becomes a chronic complaint. A Russian bemoans and bewails herself so much that it affects her mentally as a catarrh affects her physically. For the rest I must say that I only bemoan and bewail when I am *slightly* unhappy. When I am in great distress, then I too am silent. No one can perceive my distress. I may sometimes have reproached you with being too optimistic, but I would not have you cure yourself of this on any account. The fault suits you to perfection, and, besides, the most striking proof of your optimism is the good opinion you have of me. You can easily understand that I should like you to be right in this detail.

Shortly after this Sónya went to Russia to spend the summer, partly in St. Petersburg with her invalid sister, and partly in the environs of Moscow with her friend and her little girl.

I here quote from a few letters written thence.

15

They are not very full of interest, as she was not fond
of writing. Our correspondence, therefore, was not
lively, but her letters always contained fragments of
her life-history. They are often, even in their brevity,
characteristic of the mood which possessed her while
writing them. They are thus of much value in depicting her character.

I was in Switzerland with my brother, and had invited her to meet us there, when I received the following letter:

MY DEAR ANNA CARLOTTA: I have just received your kind
letter. You cannot imagine how I should like to start at once
to meet you and your brother in Switzerland, and go on a walk-
ing-tour with you to the highest parts of the Alps. I have a
sufficiently lively imagination to picture to myself how charming
this would be. What happy weeks we would spend together!
Unfortunately I am kept here by a whole string of reasons, the
one more stupid and tiresome than the other. To begin with, I
have *promised* to stay here till August 1st; and though I am, in
principle, of the opinion that "man is master of his word," the
old prejudices are so strong in me that I always return to them
when I have a chance of realizing my theories. Instead of the
master, I also am the slave of my word. Besides, there are a
whole host of things which keep me here. Your brother (who
knows me *au fond* and judges me rightly—only you must not
tell him so, for fear of flattering his vanity too much) has often
said that I am very impressionable, and that it is always the
duties and impressions of the moment which determine my
actions. In Stockholm, where every one treats me as the
champion of the woman question, I begin to think it is my most
important obligation to develop and cultivate my "genius." But
I must humbly admit that *here* I am always introduced to new
acquaintances as *Foufi's Mama*,[1] and you cannot imagine what
an effect this has in diminishing my vanity. It calls forth in
me a perfect crop of genuine virtues, which spring up like mushrooms, and of which you would never suppose me capable. Add

[1] Sónya was staying at this time near Moscow with the friend
who had charge of her little girl.

to this the heat which softens my brain, and you can then picture what I am like at this moment. In a word, the result is that all the small influences and forces which dominate your poor friend are strong enough to keep me here till August 1st. The only thing I can hope for is to meet you in Normandy, and to go on with your brother to Aberdeen. Write soon to me, dear Anna Carlotta. How happy you are! You cannot imagine how I envy you. Do at least write to me. I shall do my best to join you in Normandy. *Bien à toi.*

SÓNYA.

As usual, there is no date to her letters, but at about the same time she wrote to my brother:

CHER MONSIEUR: I have received your kind letter, No. 8, and I hasten to answer though I have little or nothing to tell you; our life is monotonous to that degree that I lose the power, not only of working, but of caring for anything. I feel that if this lasts much longer I shall become a vegetable. It is really curious, the less you have to do the less you are able to work. Here I do *absolutely* nothing. I sit all day long with my embroidery in my hand, but without an idea in my head. The heat begins to be stifling. After the rain we had at first, the summer has set in quite hot — a regular Russian summer. You could boil eggs in the shade!

To her friend Mr. H——, in Berlin, she also writes an amusing account of her life that summer:

I am now staying with my friend Julia L——, on a small estate of hers in the neighborhood of Moscow. I have found my daughter bright and well. I do not know which of us has been the happiest in the reunion. We are not going to be separated any more, for I am going to take her back with me to Stockholm. She is nearly six, and is a very sensible child for her age. Every one thinks she is like me, and I really think she is like what I was in my childhood. My friend is very depressed; she has just lost her only sister, so it is rather dull and dismal just now in this house. Our circle of acquaintances consists entirely of old ladies. Four old maids live with us; and as they all go about in deep mourning, our house seems almost like a convent. We also eat a great deal, as people do in convents; and four times a day we drink tea, with all sorts of jams, sweetmeats, and cakes

—which helps us to get through the time nicely. I try to make a little diversion in other ways. For instance, one day I asked Julia to drive with me to the next village without the coachman, persuading her that I could drive beautifully. We arrived safely at our destination. But coming home the horses shied, came in collision with a tree, and we were thrown into a ditch! Poor Julia injured her foot, but I, the criminal, escaped unhurt from the adventure.

A little later Sónya wrote to the same friend:

Our life here continues to be so monotonous that I have nothing to say beyond thanking you for your letter. I have not even thrown any one out of a carriage lately, and life flows tranquilly as the water in the pond which adorns our garden, while my brain seems to stand still. I sit with my work in my hand and absolutely think of nothing.

In connection with this, it is worth while referring to the extraordinary power Sónya had of being completely idle when not engaged in her special work. She often said she was never half so happy as during these periods of entire laziness, when it was an effort to rise from the chair into which she had sunk. At such times the most trivial novel, the most mechanical needlework, a few cigarettes, and some tea, were all she required. It was probably very lucky for her that she had this capacity for reaction against excessive brain-work and the increasing mental excitement to which she surrendered herself between whiles. Perhaps it was the result of her Russo-German lineage, each race by turns getting the upper hand and causing these sudden changes. Nothing came of all her projected travels. Sónya spent that whole summer in Russia, and it was not until September that we met in Stockholm.

IX

CHANGING MOODS

D URING the following winter the sentimental element began to play a great part in Sónya's life.
She found nothing to satisfy and interest her in her
social surroundings. She was not engaged on any
special literary work. Her lectures failed to interest
her much. Under these circumstances she was very
often apt to become too retrospective, brooded over
her destiny, and felt bitterly that life had not afforded
her what she most desired.

She no longer preached of "twin souls," or of a
single love which would rule her whole life, but, instead, dreamed of a union between man and wife in
which the intelligence of the one was to complement
that of the other, so that together only could they
realize the full development of their genius.

"Laboring together in love" was now her ideal, and
she dreamed of finding a man who could, in this sense,
become her second self. The certainty that she could
never find that man in Sweden was the real origin of
the dislike which she now took to this country—the
land to which she had come with such hope and expectation. This idea of collaboration was based on her
secret craving to be in spiritual partnership with another human being, and on the real suffering caused by
her intellectual isolation. Scarcely could she endure

15*   229

to work without having close to her some one who
breathed the same mental atmosphere as herself.

Work in itself—the absolute search after scientific
truth—did not satisfy her. She longed to be understood, met half-way, admired and encouraged at every
step she took. As each new idea sprang up in her
brain, she longed to convey it to some one else, to en-
rich with it another human being. It was not only
humanity in the abstract, but some definite human
being, that she required—some one who in return
would share with her a creation of his own.

Mathematician as she was, abstractions were not for
her, for she was intensely personal in all her thoughts
and judgments.

Mittag Leffler often told her that her love of and
desire for sympathy was a feminine weakness. Men
of great genius had never been dependent in this way
on others. But she asserted the contrary, enumerating
a number of instances in which men had found their
best inspiration in their love for a woman. Most of
these were poets, and among scientists it was more
difficult to prove her statement; but Sónya was never
short of arguments to demonstrate her propositions.
When she had no real facts to go upon, she would,
with great facility, construct suppositions. It is true
that she succeeded in quoting several instances going
to prove that a feeling of great isolation had been the
cause of intense suffering to all profound minds. She
pointed out how great was the curse of feeling deeply;
how hurtful the loneliness of isolation to man, whose
highest happiness it is to merge his own in another's
welfare.

I remember that the spring of 1886 was a specially
trying one for Sónya. The awakening of nature—the
restlessness and growth which she has depicted so

vividly in "Væ Victis," and later in "Vera Vorontzoff"[1]—exercised a strong influence upon her, and
made her restless and nervous, full of longing and
impatience.

The light summer nights, so dear to me, only en-
ervated Sónya. "The everlasting sunshine seems to
promise so much," she would say, "but fails to fulfil
the promise. Earth remains cold—development is
retarded just when it has commenced. The summer
seems like a mirage—a will-o'-the-wisp which you cannot overtake. The fact that the long days and light
nights begin so long before full summer comes is all
the more irritable because they seem to promise a joy
they can never fulfil."

Sónya could not work, but she maintained with more
and more eagerness that work—especially scientific
work—was no good; it could neither afford pleasure
nor cause humanity to progress. It was folly to waste
one's youth on work, and especially was it unfortunate
for a woman to be scientifically gifted, for she was
thus drawn into a sphere which could never afford her
happiness.

As soon as the term ended that year, Sónya hastened
on "the short and beautiful journey *from* Stockholm"
to Malmö, and thence to the Continent. She went to
Paris, and wrote thence only one letter to me. Contrary to her custom, it is dated.

142 BOULEVARD D'ENFER, June 26, 1886.

DEAR ANNA CARLOTTA : I have just received your letter. I
reproach myself very much that I have not written to you before.
I am ready to admit that I was a little jealous, and thought you
no longer cared for me. I have only time for a few lines—if my
letter is to be in time for to-day's post—to tell you that you
are quite wrong in reproaching me for forgetting you when I

[1] Appendix G.

am away. I have never felt so much how I love you and your brother. Every time I am pleased I unconsciously think of you. I enjoy myself very much in Paris. Mathematicians and others make much of me [*font grand cas de moi*], but I long intensely to see a truant brother and sister who are quite indispensable to my life. I cannot leave this before July 5th, and cannot get to Christiania in time for the National Science Congress.[1] Can you meet me [in Christiania] so that we may go home together? Please reply at once. I have taken your book[2] to Jonas Lie. He speaks of you very kindly. He has returned my call, but had not yet read your book. He also thinks you have more talent for novel-writing than for the drama. I hope to see Jonas Lie once more before I leave. I send you my love and long to see you again, my dear Anna Carlotta. *Tout à toi.*

SÓNYA.

As usual, Sónya could not tear herself away from Paris till the last minute. She arrived at Copenhagen on the last day of the Congress. I was accustomed to her sudden changes of mood, but this time the contrast was amazing between the mood she was now in and that which had ruled her during the whole of the spring, when she was in Stockholm.

She had been in Paris together with Poincaré and other mathematicians. While in conversation with them she had felt a desire awaken within her to occupy herself with problems the solution of which was to bring her the highest fame, and to gain for her the highest prize of the French Academy of Science.

It now seemed to her that nothing was worth living for but science. Everything else—personal happiness, love, and love of nature, day-dreaming—all was vain. The search after scientific truth was now to her the highest and most desirable of things. Interchange of

---

[1] We had intended to meet in Norway and spend the rest of the summer together.

[2] "A Summer Saga."

ideas with her intellectual peers, apart from any personal tie, was the loftiest of all intercourse. The joy
of creation was upon her, and now she entered into
one of those brilliant periods of hers, when she was
handsome, full of genius, sparkling with wit and
humor.

She arrived at Christiania at night, after three days'
voyage from Havre. She had been very seasick all
the time, but this did not prevent her—indefatigable
as she always was when in good spirits—from joining
the next day in a fête and picnic which lasted far into
the night. All the most distinguished men present
thronged around her, and she was always on such
occasions most amiable and unassuming; so girlishly
soft in her manner that she took every one by storm.

We afterward made a trip together through Telemark, where we visited Ullman's Peasant High School,
in which Sónya became warmly interested. It was
this visit that gave rise to the article on "Peasant High
Schools" which she published in a Russian magazine.
The success of the article was so great that there followed a large increase in the number of subscribers to
the journal.

From Siljord we climbed a mountain on foot, and
it was certainly the first time that Sónya had ever
performed such a feat. She was very brisk and indefatigable in climbing, and delighted in the beauty of
nature. She was full of joy and energy, her pleasure
being only now and then marred by fear of a cow near
one of the cheese-dairies, or by having to surmount
a heap of stones which rattled down under our feet,
when she uttered little childish shrieks and exclama-
tions which much amused the rest of the party. She
had a great appreciation of nature in so far as her
imagination and feelings were stirred by its poetry, by

the spirit of the scenery, and its light and shadow.
But as she was very near-sighted, and objected, out of
feminine vanity, to wearing spectacles, the traditional
mark of the student, she never could see any details of
the landscape, and certainly would not have been able
to tell what sort of trees were growing, or of what
material the houses she passed were built, etc. Notwithstanding this, in some of her works already mentioned she succeeds not only in giving the spirit of
the scenery,—its *soul*, so to say,—but also exact and
delicate descriptions of purely material details. This
arose, not from her own observation, but from purely
theoretical knowledge. She had a very sound knowledge of natural history. She had helped her husband to translate Brehm's "Birds," and, as already
mentioned, had studied paleontology and geology
with him, and had been personally acquainted with
the most eminent natural scientists of our time.

But she was not a very minute observer when it concerned the small, commonplace phenomena of nature.
She had no love of detail, and did not possess a finely
cultivated sense of beauty. The most unattractive
landscape might be beautiful in her eyes if it suited
her mood, and she could be indifferent to the most
exquisite outlines and colors if she were personally out
of sympathy with the scene.

It was the same with the personal appearance of
people. She was utterly devoid of all appreciation of
purity of outline, harmony, proportion, complexion,
and other outward expressions of beauty. People with
whom she was in sympathy, and who possessed some
of the external qualities she admired—these she considered beautiful, and all others plain. A fair person,
man or woman, she could easily admire, but not a
dark person.

In this connection I cannot help mentioning the absence of all artistic appreciation in a nature otherwise so richly gifted. She had spent years of her life in Paris, but had never visited the Louvre. Neither pictures, sculptures, nor architecture ever attracted her attention.

In spite of this, she was much pleased with Norway, and liked the people we met. We had intended to continue our trip in a *carriole* through the whole of Telemark, over Haukeli Fjäll, and thence down to the west coast, where we meant to visit Alexander Kielland on the Jäderen. But although Sónya had long dreamed about this journey, pleased with the idea, and though she had for some time desired to make Kielland's acquaintance, another voice was now so strong within her that she could not resist it. So while we were on a steamer in one of the long, narrow lakes which run up into Telemark, and which resemble fiords cut off from the sea, she suddenly decided to go back to Christiania and Sweden, and settle down quietly in the country to work. She left me, stepped into another steamer, and was taken by it back to Christiania by way of Skien.

I could not remonstrate with her, nor did I blame her. I knew well that when once the spirit of creation makes itself heard, its dictates *must* be obeyed. Everything else, however otherwise attractive, becomes indifferent and unimportant. One is deaf and blind to one's surroundings, and one listens only to the inner voice — which calls more loudly than the roaring waterfall, or the hurricane at sea. Sónya's departure was, of course, a great disappointment to me. I continued the journey with a chance companion; visited Kielland; returned *via* Östland, and took part in a fête at a peasant high school which would certainly have pleased Sónya as much as it did me, had she had spiritual freedom to join in it.

I had several times noticed the following trait in her: she might be engaged in the most lively conversation at a picnic or party, and apparently be entirely occupied by her surroundings, when suddenly a silence would fall upon her. Her look at such times became distant, and her replies, when addressed, wandering. She would suddenly say farewell, and no persuasions, no previous plans or arrangements, no consideration for other people, could detain her. Go home and work she must. I have a note from her, written in the spring of the year, which is characteristic of her in this connection.

We had arranged a driving-expedition in the neighborhood of Stockholm with a few other friends, when she repented at the last moment, and sent me the following note:[1]

DEAR ANNA CARLOTTA: This morning I awoke with the desire to amuse myself, when suddenly my mother's father, the German pedant (that is to say, the *astronomer*), appeared before me. He pointed menacingly at all the learned treatises and dissertations which I had intended studying in the Easter holidays, and reproached me most seriously with my unworthy waste of time. His severe words have also at other times put to flight in me my grandmother the gipsy. Now I sit at my writing-table in dressing-gown and slippers, deeply immersed in mathematical speculations, and I have not the slightest desire to join your picnic. You are so merry that you can amuse yourselves just as well without me, so I hope you will enjoy yourselves and pardon my ignoble desertion.

Yours affectionately,
SÓNYA.

There had been an arrangement that we should meet again in Jämtland later in the summer, where

[1] This note is written in Swedish, as are all the other letters which follow and are not otherwise indicated.

Sónya was staying with my brother's family. But scarcely had I arrived there before Sónya had to leave. She was called away by a telegram from her sister in Russia, who had a new and serious attack of illness.

When Sónya returned again in September, she brought her little daughter, now eight years old, with her. For the first time she now lived in an apartment of her own in Stockholm. She was tired of boarding-houses. She was certainly most indifferent to any kind of comfort and domestic conveniences, and did not care what furniture she had, nor what food she ate. But, at the same time, she greatly wanted to be independent and master of her own time. She could no longer put up with the many ties which living with others always entails. So she got her friends to help her to choose a house and a housekeeper, who would also look after the child. She bought some furniture in the town, and ordered the remainder from Russia. She thus made a home for herself, which, however, retained the appearance of a temporary arrangement that might be upset at any moment.

The furniture sent from Russia was very characteristic. It came from her parents' home, and had the old aristocratic look about it. It had occupied a large drawing-room, and consisted in a long sofa, which took up a whole wall; a corner sofa of the old pattern, with floral decorations; and a deep arm-chair. It was all of rich carved mahogany, upholstered in bright-red silk damask, now old and tattered. The stuffing was also spoiled, and many of the springs broken. It was always Sónya's intention to have this furniture repaired, newly polished, and newly upholstered; but this was never done, partly because, with Sónya's bringing up, tattered furniture in a drawing-room was nothing

astonishing,[1] and partly because she never felt sufficient interest in Stockholm to have things put to
rights, feeling sure that her home there was but a
half-way house, and she need not therefore trouble to
spend money on it.

Sometimes, when she was in good spirits, a sudden
frenzy would seize her, and she would amuse herself
by ornamenting her small rooms with her own needle-
work.

One day she sent me the following note:

ANNA CARLOTTA! Yesterday evening I had a pleasant proof
that the critics are right who maintain that you have eyes for the
bad and ugly, but not for the good and beautiful. Each stain,
each scratch, on one of my old venerable chairs, even if hidden
by ten antimacassars, is very certain to be discovered and de-
nounced by you. But my really lovely new rocking-chair *cushion*,
which was in evidence the whole evening, and which endeavored
to draw your attention to itself, was not honored by you with
even a single glance!

Your SÓNYA.

[1] It may be remembered that in her childhood's home the
nursery was papered with newspapers.

X

SCARCELY had Sónya got her possessions into some kind of order in her quaint ramshackle lodgings than she was again summoned to Russia. She had to go in midwinter by sea to Helsingfors, and thence by rail to St. Petersburg, in order to reach her ailing sister, who continued to hover betwixt life and death. On such occasions Sónya was never frightened, nor was she to be deterred by any difficulty. She was tenderly devoted to her sister, and always ready to sacrifice herself for her sake. She now left her little girl in my care during her absence of two winter months. In that time I only received one letter from her, which is of no interest beyond the fact that it shows how sad her Christmas holidays were that year.

ST. PETERSBURG, December 18, 1886.

DEAR ANNA CARLOTTA: I arrived here yesterday evening. To-day I can scarcely write these few words to you. My sister is fearfully ill, though the doctor thinks her better than she was some days ago. A long, wearing illness like this is truly one of the most terrible trials possible. She suffers untold agonies, and can hardly sleep or even breathe. . . . I do not know how long I shall remain here. I long so much for Fouzi [her child], and also for my work. My journey was very trying and wearisome. Loving messages to you all.

Your affectionate friend,

SÓNYA.

During the long days and nights that Sónya passed by her sister's sick-bed, many thoughts and fantasies

naturally filled her mind. Then it was that she began
to ponder on the difference of "how it was, and how
it might have been." She remembered with what
dreams, what infatuations, she and her sister had
commenced life, young, handsome, and richly endowed as they both were. She realized how little
had been given of all that they had pictured to themselves in their day-dreams. Life had, indeed, been to
them rich and varied, but in the depths of both their
hearts was a bitter feeling of disappointment.

Ah, how utterly different, would Sónya say to herself, might it not have been had they not both of them
committed mistakes! From these thoughts was bred
the idea of writing two parallel romances which should
depict the history of a human being in two different
ways. Early youth, with all its possibilities, should be
described, and a series of pictures followed up to some
important event. The one romance was to show the
consequence of the choice made at the critical moment,
and the other romance was to figure " what might have
been " had that choice been different. " Who is there
who has not some false step to regret," soliloquized
Sónya, "and who has not often wished to begin life
anew ? "

She wished, in this work, to give the reality of life
in a literary form, if only she had talent enough to
produce it. She did not then know that she possessed
the power of writing. So when she returned to Stockholm she tried to persuade me to undertake the
romance. At that time I had begun a book called
"Utomkringäktenskap," which was to be the history of
old maids; of those who, for one reason or another,
had never been called upon to become the head of a
family. Their thoughts, their ideas of love and marriage, the interests and struggles of their lives, were

to be described. In a word, it was to be the romance of women who are commonly believed to have no romance at all—a sort of counterpart to "Mandvolk" ("Men"), in which Garborg tells how bachelors live. I wished to describe the life of the lonely women of my time. I had collected materials and types, and was much interested in my design.

Then Sónya appeared with her idea, and so great was her influence upon me, so great her power of persuasion, that I forsook my own child in order to adopt hers. A few letters I wrote to a mutual friend at this time will best describe the hot enthusiasm with which this new project had inspired both Sónya and myself.

February 2, 1887.

I am now writing a new novel, entitled "Utomkringäktenskap" ("Unmarried"). Only fancy! I am so deep in it that the outside world, the world which is unconnected with my work, no longer exists for me. The state, physical and mental, in which one finds one's self when writing something new is wonderful. A thousand doubts as to its merits, and as to your own value, assail you. And in the depths of your heart there is the joy of possessing a secret world of your very own, in which you are at home, and the outer world becomes a shadow. . . . In the midst of all this I have a new idea. Sónya and I have got an inspiration. We are going to write a drama of two parts, which will occupy two evenings. That is to say, the idea is hers, and I am to carry it out and fill up the plot. I think the idea very original. The first portion will show "How it was," and the second "How it might have been." In the first every one is unhappy, because, in real life, people generally hinder rather than further one another's happiness. In the second the same personages assist one another, form a little ideal commune, and are happy. Do not mention this to any one. I really do not know more of Sónya's idea than this mere sketch. To-morrow she is going to tell me her plot, and I shall be able to judge whether there be any dramatic possibilities in it. You will laugh at me for always anticipating the *finale* as soon as I have seen the *start*. I already see Sónya and myself collaborating in a work which will have a

16

world-wide success, at least in the present, and perhaps also in the future. We are quite foolish about it. If we can only do it, it would reconcile us to everything. Sónya would forget that Sweden is the greatest *Philistia* on earth, and would no longer complain that she is wasting the best years of her life here. And I—well, I should forget all that I am brooding over. You will of course exclaim : What children you are ! But fortunately there exists a realm better than all the kingdoms of earth, a kingdom of which we have the key—the realm of the imagination, where he who will may rule, and where everything is precisely as you wish it to be. But perhaps Sónya's plot, which was at first intended for a novel, will not do for a drama, and I could not write a *novel* upon some one else's plan, for in a novel you are in much closer relation to your production than in a drama.

February 10th.

Sónya is overjoyed at this new project, and the fresh possibility in her life. She says she now understands how a man grows more and more deeply in love with the mother of his children. Of course *I* am the mother, because I am to bring this mental offspring into the world ; and she is so devoted to me that it makes me happy to see her beaming eyes. We enjoy ourselves immensely. I do not think two women-friends have ever enjoyed each other's society so much as we do—and we shall be the first example in literature of two women-collaborators. I have never been so kindled by an idea as by this one. As soon as Sónya told me of it, it shot through me like a thunderbolt. It was a real explosion. She told me her plot on the 3d, but it was made for a novel in Russian surroundings. When she left me I sat up half the night in the dark in my rocking-chair, and when I went to bed the whole plot lay clear before me. On Friday I talked it over with Sónya, and on Saturday I began to write. Now the whole first portion, a prologue and five acts, is sketched out. That is to say, I did it in five days, working only two hours a day, for when working at high pressure one cannot sustain it long. I have never done anything so quickly. Generally I contemplate an idea for months, even for years, before I begin to write.

April 21st.

The most pleasant thing about this work is, as you will have noticed, that I admire it so much. This is the result of collaboration. I believe in it because it is Sónya's idea, for naturally it is much easier for me to believe that she is inspired, than to believe such a thing of myself. She, on the other hand, admires my work, the spirit and artistic form which I give to the design. It would be impossible to have a better arrangement. It is delightful to be able to admire one's own work without conceit. I have never felt so much confidence or such little misgiving. If we fail, I think we must commit suicide! . . . You wish to know Madame Kovalévsky's share in the work. It is quite true that she has not written a single sentence. But she has not only originated the whole, but has also thought out the contents of each act. She has given me besides several psychological traits for the building up of the characters. We read daily what I have done, and she makes remarks and offers suggestions. She asks to hear it over and over again, as children ask for their favorite tales. She thinks nothing in all the world could be more interesting.

On March 9th we read the play aloud for the first time to our intimate friends. Up to that moment our illusion and joy had been continually rising higher and higher. Sónya had such overwhelming fits of exultation that she was obliged to go out into the forest to shout out her delight under the open sky. Every day, when we had finished our work, we took long walks in *Lill Jans'* wood, close to our houses in town. There Sónya jumped over stones and hillocks, took me in her arms and danced about, shouting that life was beautiful, the future fascinating and full of promise. She cherished the most exaggerated hopes of the success of our drama. She fancied it would march in triumph from capital to capital in Europe. Such a new and original idea could not but prove a triumph in literature. "This is how it might have been." It is a dream actually experienced by every one; and seen in the objective light lent by the stage, it could not fail to prove entrancing. The very essence of the plot was the glorification of love as the only important thing in life; and the social community of the future lay in the vista it opened up, a community in which each man should live for others, even as now two live for each other. In all this lay very much of Sónya's deepest feeling and ideal of happiness.

The motto of the first part was to be, "What shall it profit a man if he gain the whole world and lose his own soul?" and of the second part, "He who loses his life shall save it."

But after the first reading to our friends the work entered into a new phase. Up to then we had seen it *as it might have been* rather than as it was. Now all the faults and shortcomings of the work, which had been written in such feverish haste, became apparent. And then began the tedious process of revision.

During the whole of that winter Sónya could not bring herself to think of her great mathematical work, though the date of the competition for the *Prix Bordin* was already fixed.[1] She ought to have been working for it with the utmost diligence. Mittag Leffler, who always felt a kind of responsibility for her, and knew that it was of the greatest importance for her to gain the prize, was in despair when, each time that he called upon her, he found her embroidering in her drawing-room. She had, just then, a perfect mania for needle-work. Like the Ingeborg of ancient romance, weaving the deeds of her heroes, so she embroidered in silk and wool the drama she could not indite with pen and ink. While her needle mechanically went in and out, her imagination was at work, and one scene after the other was pictured in her mind.

I, for my part, worked with the pen, and when we found that needle and pen had arrived at the same re-sult, our joy was great. It certainly reconciled us

[1] Appendix H.

to the differences of opinion to which we were often led, as our imaginations worked in opposite directions. But this more frequently took place during revision than in the first draft of our play. Many were the crises through which the drama passed at this period. The following little note from Sónya is in answer to some communication from me on one of these occasions:

My poor child! how often it has hovered between life and death! What has happened now? Have you been inspired, or the reverse? I am inclined to think that you have written as you did to me out of pure wickedness, so that I might lecture badly to-day! How can you imagine that I can think about my lecture when I know that my poor little bantling is going through such a dangerous crisis! I am glad I have played the part of father, so that I can feel what poor men must suffer from this miserable necessity of revision. I wish I could see Strindberg, and shake hands with him for once! . . .

I wrote about our drama on the 1st of April to a friend:

I have tried to introduce a little change into the method of our work. To Sónya's great despair I have forbidden her my study until I have furbished up the whole of the second part of the play. I was too much interrupted and worried by the unceasing collaboration while writing the first part. I lost both the survey of the whole, and all interest and intimate sympathy with my characters. The desire for solitude which is so strong in me has been denied me. My personality has been merged in Sónya's by her powerful influence, and still her individuality has not had full expression. The whole strength of my working power lies in solitude, and this is a chief objection to collaboration even with such a sympathetic nature as Sónya's. She is the complement of my nature. She is Alice in the "Struggle for Happiness," who cannot create anything nor embrace anything with her whole heart unless she can share it with another. Everything she has produced in mathematical work has been influenced by some one else, and even her lectures are only successful when Gösta is present.

16*

Sónya often jestingly acknowledged this dependence
on her surroundings, and once wrote a note to my
brother, saying:

DEAR PROFESSOR: Shall you come to my lecture to-morrow?
Do not, if you are tired.   I will try to lecture as well as if you
were there.

Once, when I had sent her some birthday wishes in
rhyme, she replied in the following verses, characteristic of herself, in which, as often before, she terms
herself a chameleon:

> The changeful chameleon, you always knew,
>   So soon as he sits alone in his nook,
>   Is dull and ugly and gray in his look;
> But in a bright light he is lovely to view.
>
> No beauty has he, but he always reflects
>   What around him exists of beautiful hue;
>   He can shimmer alike in gold, green, or blue,
> And of all his friends' hues there is none he rejects.
>
> In this creature, meseems, my likeness I see;
>   For, dearest of friends, wherever you go
>   I go in your steps; for it is ay so
> That I can't stay behind, nor be turned back from thee.
>
> To a friend such as you all my reverence is due;
>   You write and you paint and you draw and what not.
>   These things are to me but rubbish and rot,
> But, mercy upon me! you *poetize* too!

In the character of Alice, Sónya, as I have already
remarked, thought to reproduce herself. Indeed, some
of the sentences in the book are so characteristic of her
that they are almost reproductions of words that she
actually spoke. In the great scene of Hjalmar (1st
part, act iii., sc. 2) she has tried to give expression to
her own ardent desire for tenderness, and union with

another; to her despairing feeling of loneliness, and
the peculiar want of self-confidence which was always
aroused when she felt herself less beloved than she
desired.

Alice says: "I am well accustomed to see others
beloved more than myself. At school it was always
said that I was the most gifted of pupils; but I felt
the irony of fate in bestowing upon me so many
gifts only to make me feel what I might have been to
others. But no one cared for my affection. I do not
ask for much — very little — just sufficient to prevent
any one from intervening betwixt me and the one I
love. I have all my life wished to be first with some
one. . . . Let me only show you what I can be when
I am loved! I am not, after all, a soul utterly without resource. Look at me! Am I handsome ? Yes,
if I am loved! Then I become beautiful, not otherwise! Am I good? Yes, if any one is fond of me
I am goodness itself! Am I unselfish? I can be so
utterly unselfish that my every thought is bound up
in another!"

Thus touchingly and passionately could the admired
and celebrated Sónya Kovalévsky entreat for a devotion which she never received. Not once was she the
first nor the only one with any person, though she
longed so passionately for this boon, and though one
would have imagined she possessed all the gifts which
could win and preserve such love.

Alice desires to participate in all Karl's interests.
She grows bitter when, for various reasons, he draws
back from her. She will not listen to reason. She
tries to force him to put aside all other considerations
and be true both to himself and his calling, and to his
love. This is Sónya through and through.

When, in the second part of the drama, Alice breaks

violently with her past life, and sacrifices riches and
position to live and work with Karl in a garret, it is
again Sónya as she pictured to herself what she would
have been had she had the good luck of such a choice.
I do not doubt that if she had written the scene
in which Karl's happiness is depicted, it would have
been stronger, and have received a more personal and
warmer coloring than is now the case.

Alice's dreams about the People's Palace at Herr-
hamra, and about the great Labor Association; her
remark, "How different it would have all been had we
received the same education and had the same social
traditions, so as to form a band of comrades," describe
also Sónya's dreams, and are her own identical words.

Sónya idealized the socialism of the future, and
often described, in glowing and eloquent words, a
happy commonwealth in which every one felt bound
to every other by identity of fate—a commonwealth
in which there were no opposing interests; where the
happiness of one would be the happiness of all, the
sufferings of one the sufferings of all.

After her death a friend of hers told me that once,
when her husband telegraphed to Sónya that he believed one of his speculations had resulted in a vast
fortune, she had immediately planned a socialistic community. It was her favorite dream, and she sought to
give expression to it in the second part of the drama,
"A Struggle for Happiness." Her dream was of both
personal happiness and the happiness of mankind in
general.

It is a pleasure to me to quote some sympathetic
words of Hermann Bang, in a short sketch which he
wrote of her whom we have lost, and published in a
Danish review. Speaking of the above-mentioned
drama, he says:

I admit that I love this strange play, which, with mathematical exactness, depicts the almighty power of love, and proves that love, and love alone, is everything in life, and alone decides growth or decay. In love alone lie development and strength, and alone through love can duty be fulfilled.

No one could have better formulated than in the above words the essence of the dramas which were the " confession " of Sónya's life. It only grieves me that they were written too late for her to feel the joy of being so fully understood.

With her characteristic wish to explain scientifically all the phenomena of life, Sónya had also invented a whole theory to account for the idea of this double drama. She wrote the outline of an unfinished prologue, which, even now, and in spite of its fragmentary form, will be read with interest, as is everything which fell from her pen. She sent it to me accompanied by the following lines:

DEAR CARLOTTA: I cannot help it. I cannot make it any better. But if you can link my stray thoughts together, it is well. If you cannot, we must let the book appear without a prologue. If any one attacks us we can explain later.

Your SÓNYA.

The prologue ran thus:

Every one, perhaps, has at one time or another given his imagination play, and pictured how different his life would have been had he acted differently at some decisive moment. In every-day life one often realizes that he is the slave of outward circumstance. The even tenor of the days binds one with a thousand invisible links. Every one fills a given sphere in life. Every one has certain definite duties which are fulfilled almost automatically, without straining the energies to the utmost. It matters little whether to-morrow one is a little better or a little worse, a little stronger or a little weaker, or a little more or less gifted, than to-day. One cannot divert the stream of his life from the channel it has taken, without, at the same time, presupposing the possession of qualities so unlike those which he

really has that it is impossible, except in a dream, to imagine
being possessed of them without losing the feeling of identity.
But when remembering certain moments in one's life, the case
is altogether different. At those moments the illusions of free
will become strangely intense. One fancies that if he could
have tried a little harder, had been cleverer or more decided, he
might have turned his destiny into another channel. On much
the same ground stands our belief in miracles. None but a mad
person can think of asking the Creator to change the great laws
of nature; for instance, to awaken the dead. But I should like
to put a test-question to orthodox people. Have they never, at
any time, asked for a small change in the course of events, such,
for instance, as recovery from sickness? Often a small miracle
seems so much easier than a great one, and it requires quite an
effort of the mind to realize that both are precisely alike. So it
is with our thoughts about ourselves. It is almost impossible
for me to realize what I should feel if I woke one morning with
a voice like Jenny Lind's, with a body supple and strong as ——,
or with a ——; but I can easily imagine that my complexion is
——.   It is just such a critical moment which the authors
attempt to describe in these dramas. Karl, according to their
idea, is one and the same person in either play, only gifted
with such slight differences of character as one can easily imagine without losing the sense of individuality. In ordinary life
such differences would scarcely be noticeable. Under most
circumstances they would have no influence on the decision
between two actions. Suppose, for instance, that all had gone
well with our hero and heroine; that the father had lived a couple of years longer; in that case Karl, as described in either
drama, would have had no different fate. The divergence of
life under such circumstances would have been so small that it
would not have affected the main current of events. But, as
it was, a decisive moment arrived at a time that two different
duties seemed to call in two different directions, and it was the
slight difference in character above alluded to that decided the
choice of opposite ways, and, once made, caused their fates to
diverge without ever meeting again. Or let us choose an example from mechanics. Think for a moment of a common pendu-
lum, or, if you prefer it, a small ball hanging, by a very slight
but supple string, from a nail. If you give the ball a little
touch, it will swing to one side, describe a given circle, rise to
a given height, and return again, but not to stop at the same

point; it swings to about the same height on the opposite side, and continues to oscillate for some time. Had the original impulse been a little stronger, the ball would have swung higher, and the rest of the movement would have been on the same scale. But if the original impulse had been so strong as to cause the ball to pass the highest point which the length of string permitted, the ball would not swing back, but would continue its course on the other side of the periphery, and in this case the movement would be utterly changed in character.·

Two similar impulses, one of which, however, is weaker and the other stronger than a certain average force, always produce two entirely different results. In mechanics one is accustomed to study just the extreme and critical moments, and it is evident that, if you wish to gain a clear idea about phenomena, it is all-important to study them when near the critical point of balance. The authors of the double drama have deemed it might be interesting to depict the effect of such a critical moment on two individuals, similar but not identical. In order to understand the play perfectly, Karl in the two parts must not be imagined as one and the same person. But the difference in the two characters, though the one is rather more ideal than the other, and better able to distinguish between important and unimportant things, is so small that in every-day life it would be almost impossible to distinguish one Karl from the other. Had all gone well, had his father lived till his son had an established position, no doubt the destiny of the two Karls would have been almost identical. They would have become celebrated as scientists, married at the same age, and made the same choice. But trial comes at the critical moment, and the almost imperceptible advantage which the one has over the other enables him to surmount the critical point, while the other falls heavily back.

The revision of the work took much longer than the original composition, and when Sónya and I separated for the summer it was not yet concluded.

XI

SÓNYA and I had intended to spend the summer (1878) together. The new literary partners, "Korvin-Leffler" (Sónya and her biographer), intended to go to Berlin and Paris in order to make acquaintances in the literary and theatrical world, which would prove useful to them later on when the offspring of their genius was ready to make its triumphal progress through the world.

But all these dreams fell to the ground.

It had been decided that we should start in the middle of May. We were as happy in the prospect as though the whole world of success and interest lay safely before us, when once more sad news from Russia frustrated all our plans. Sónya's sister was again dangerously ill. Her husband had been forced to return unexpectedly to Paris. There was no help for it; Sónya was obliged to take a sorrowful journey to a painful sick-bed. Any thought of pleasure was out of the question, and all her letters of that summer show that she was in very bad spirits. She writes:

My sister continues in the same state as last winter. She suffers much, and looks desperately ill. She has not strength enough to turn from side to side, but yet I think she is not quite without hope of recovery. She is so glad I am with her. She always says she would have died if I had refused to come. . . .

I feel so depressed that I cannot write more to-day. The only thing that is pleasant is to think of our "fairy dream" and of "Væ Victis."

This alludes to the plan we had formed in the spring of uniting the works together. The "fairy dream" was mine, and was to be called "When Death Shall Be No More." When I mentioned the idea to Sónya she seized upon it so vehemently, and worked it out in her imagination so fully, that she was a partner in its production. "Væ Victis" was *her* creation, and was to be a novel. Its idea and plot were very characteristic of her, but she did not think she could write it alone. She wrote to me:

You tell me I am of some importance in your life — and yet you have so much more than ever I had. Think, then, what you must be to me, who am so lonely, and who feel myself poor in affection and friendship.

Still later she wrote:

Have you never noticed that there are periods when everything in life, both for one's self and one's friends, seems to be covered as with a black veil? One hardly recognizes one's dearest and nearest. The sweetest strawberries turn to dust in your mouth. The wood-fairy says that this always happens to little children who pay him for truant visits to his haunts. Perhaps we two had no permission to spend this summer together —and yet we had worked so hard during last winter! I try, however, to make use of every moment I can spare. I think out my mathematical problem, and muse deeply upon Poincaré's treatises, which are full of genius. I am too depressed, and have no energy to do literary work. Everything seems so faded and uninteresting. At such moments mathematics are a relief. It is such a comfort to feel that there is another world outside one's self. One really does want to talk of something besides one's self; only you, my dear and precious friend, are always the same — and always dear. I can scarcely express in words how much I long for you. You are the dearest thing I possess, and our friendship must at least last all my life. I do not know what I should do without it.

Later on she wrote in French:

My brother-in-law has decided to remain in St. Petersburg till my sister is able to accompany him to Paris. I have thus sacrificed myself quite uselessly. If I knew you were free, I would join you in Paris, though I must say all this has quite taken away any wish to enjoy myself. I feel rather anxious to stay somewhere where I could write in peace. I have such a strong desire for some kind of work, either literary or mathematical. I want to lose myself in work, so as to forget myself and every one else. If you wanted to meet me as much as I want to meet you, I would go anywhere to join you. But if your summer is already, as is probable, planned out, I shall stay here, most likely, a couple of weeks, and then return with Fouzi to Stockholm, where I intend to live on the islands and to work with all my might. I do not wish to make any arrangements for pleasure-trips. You know what a fatalist I am. I fancy I see in the stars that I must expect no happiness this summer. It is better, therefore, to be resigned, and use no more vain endeavors. . . . Yesterday I wrote the beginning of "Væ Victis." *I shall most likely never finish it.*[1] Perhaps what I have written to-day may nevertheless be useful to you as material. In order to write about mathematics one must feel more at home than I do at this moment.

In a letter written later on, when Sónya had settled down in the islands near Stockholm, she writes:

I enjoyed the last few weeks in Russia very much. I made some rather interesting acquaintances. But a conservative old mathematical pedant like me cannot write well away from home. So I returned to old Sweden with my books and my papers.

Later, from the same place:

I have been thinking a great deal about our first-born. But, to tell the truth, I find *awfully many* faults in the poor little creature, especially in the composition. As though in ridicule, fate has brought me into contact with three "explorers" this year, all very interesting in different ways. One of them, in my opinion the least gifted, has already been successful. The other, who is full of genius in some ways and in others very

_____
[1] The italics are her own.

limited, has just begun to struggle for fame. What the result will be I cannot say. The third, an interesting type, is already helplessly broken, mentally and physically, but most interesting for an author to study. The history of these three "explorers" —in all its simplicity—seems to me much fuller than all we have written about Karl and Alice. In accordance with your brother's wish, I have brought a volume of Runeberg's poems to study here ("Hanna," "Nadeschda," etc.), and I am now reading them. But I do not care for them much. They have all the same fault as Haydn's "Creation." The *devil* is missing, and without some touch of this high power there is no harmony in this world.

During this summer I also received a jesting letter from Sónya, which I quote because it gives a fair sample of her satirical mood. As she did not shine in the habit of order in the keeping of her papers and other matters, she often received from me, in confidential letters, some sharp admonitions to be careful not to let such letters lie about. She consequently wrote me the following note:

POOR ANNA CARLOTTA! It seems to me that it is getting to be a regular malady with you to think that your letters are going to fall into other hands than those for whom they were meant. The symptoms are getting more and more serious each time! I think any one who writes such an unintelligible hand as yours ought not to be uneasy about this matter. I assure you that, with the exception of the few people personally interested in what you write, you would hardly find any one who would have the patience to decipher your scrawl. As to your last letter, it was, of course, lost in the post. When I finally did get it from the Dead Letter Office, I hastened to leave it open on the table for the benefit of maids and the whole G—— family. They all thought the letter rather well written, and that it contained rather interesting things.—To-day I intend to call on Professor Montan, in order to ask about translations from the Polish. I shall take your letter with me, and try my best to lose it in his reception-room. I can do nothing better to make you a celebrity.

Your devoted
SÓNYA.

When we met in the autumn we began the final revision of our double drama. But the work was purely
mechanical; all the joy, the illusion, the enthusiasm,
had already vanished. By November the printing had
begun, and we offered the work to the Dramatic Theater.
The correction of the proofs occupied us till winter.
At Christmas the drama was published, and received
the approbation of Wirsén and the Stockholm *Dagblatt;*
but shortly afterward it was refused by the Dramatic
Theater. A note from Sónya on receiving the news
of this check shows that she took it lightly:

What are you going to do now, you faithless, cruel mother?
Divide the Siamese twins, and put asunder what nature has
joined? You make me shudder. Strindberg was right in his
opinion about woman; but in spite of this I will come to you
this evening, you horrid creature!

The fact was that we were rather indifferent as to
the fate of the work now that we had done with it.
We were so far alike that we only cared about "gen-
erations yet unborn," and we were already dreaming
of productions that were to have far greater success.
The difference between us was, that Sónya still clung
with all her heart to the idea of collaboration, while
in mine the idea was already dead, though I did not
dare to acknowledge this to her. Who knows if it
were not a secret craving to be once more mistress of
my own thoughts and words which unconsciously contributed to the decision I now arrived at, namely, to go
to Italy for the winter? This journey had been often
discussed, but Sónya had always been against it as
a treachery to our friendship. But that friendship,
though in one way so precious to me and fecund in
delight, now began to oppress me by its exactions. I
mention the fact in order to throw light on the later
tragedy of Sónya's love. Her idealistic nature sought

for a completeness which life seldom gives. The perfect union of two souls could not be realized either in friendship or in love. Her friendship, as afterward also her love, was tyrannical, in the sense that she would not allow to any one she loved a feeling, an affection, or a thought, of which she was not the object. She wished to have such full possession of the person of whom she was fond that it almost excluded the possibility of individual life in that other person. Even in love this is almost impossible, at least as regards two highly developed personalities; and naturally it is still more difficult in friendship. The very foundation of friendship must be the individual liberty of each friend.

To this peculiarity in Sónya is perhaps owing the fact that maternal love did not satisfy her craving for tenderness. A child does not love in the same way in which it is loved. It does not enter into the interests of its parent. It takes more than it gives. Sónya desired and demanded self-sacrificing devotion.

I do not mean that she exacted more than she gave in her relations with those of whom she was fond. On the contrary, she gave full meed of sympathy, and was prepared to sacrifice herself to any amount. But she expected to get back as much as she gave. She wished to be met half-way, and she considered herself to be of the same importance to her friend as he or she was to her.

During the autumn before alluded to, besides literary disappointment, Sónya was called upon to bear a great and bitter sorrow. The sister to whose sick-bed she had so often hurried over land and sea, often sacrificing her own plans and wishes to the desire of being with her at the last, had been taken to Paris for an operation.

Sónya was at the time kept fast in the University

17

by her lectures, but, had her sister sent for her, she
would have gone even if it had cost her her professor-
ship and livelihood. But she was told that there was
no danger in the operation, and every hope of full
recovery. She had already received news that the
operation had been successful, when a telegram suddenly announced her sister's death. Inflammation of
the lungs had supervened, and the weak state of the
patient had caused her to sink almost immediately.

Sónya, as we learn in her " Recollections of Childhood," had always loved this sister most dearly. To
the sorrow of having lost her forever, and of not
being with her at the last, was added her grief at the
sad tragedy of Aniuta's life. She who had once been so
brilliant, so greatly admired, had been consumed by a
most painful illness. Disappointed in everything she
had hoped for, unhappy in all personal circumstances,
hampered in her career as an author, she was now cut
off by inexorable death in the very flower of her age!
To such a brooding nature as Sónya's all sufferings
were magnified because she generalized them. Any
misfortune which befell herself or those she loved became the misfortune of humanity. She not only bore
her own sorrows, but those of the world at large.

It pained her much to think that with her sister's
death the last link was broken which united her to the
home of her childhood.

"There is no one now who remembers me as the
little Sónya," she said. "To all of you I am Madame
Kovalévsky, the celebrated scientist. To no one am I
any longer the little, shy, reserved, *negligée* Sónya."

But the great self-command she possessed, and her
power of concealing her feelings, enabled her to appear, in society, much the same as before. She did
not even wear mourning. Her sister, like herself, had

had a great aversion to crape, and Sónya considered it would be a false conventionality to mourn for her in that manner. But the inner anguish showed itself in intense irritability. She would cry at the least annoyance—for instance, if any one happened to tread on her foot, or if she tore her dress. She would burst into a flood of angry tears at the least contradiction. In analyzing herself, as she always did, she said:

"My great sorrow, which I try to control, shows itself in such petty irritability. It is the tendency of life in general to turn everything into pettiness, and one never has the consolation of a great and complete suffering."

Sónya hoped that her sister might somehow appear to her, either in dreams or in an apparition. She had all her life maintained that she believed in dreams as portents, as we have already learned from the friend of her youth, and she believed also in forebodings and revelations of other kinds.

She knew long beforehand whether a year was to be lucky or unlucky. She knew that the year 1887 would bring her both a great sorrow and a great joy. She had already foretold that the year 1888 would be one of the happiest of her life, and that 1890 would be the saddest. 1891 was to bring her the Dawn of Light—this dawn was that of death.

Sónya always had troubled dreams when any one whom she loved was suffering, or when something had happened which would bring her sorrow. The last night before her sister's death she had very bad dreams—to her great astonishment, for she had just had good news. But when the telegram arrived announcing Aniuta's death, Sónya said she ought to have been prepared for it.

But the vision or apparition of her sister, which she expected and hoped for after death, never came.

XII

I LEFT Sónya in January, 1888, and we did not meet again till September, 1889. Two years had not passed, yet both our lives during those months had gone through their most decisive crises. We met again like changed beings. We could not be as intimate as formerly, for each of us was engrossed in her own life's drama, and neither could speak to the other of the conflicts through which she had passed.

As it is chiefly the object of this Memoir to relate what Sónya said about herself, I shall, with regard to this last tragedy of her life, narrate only what she herself told me. It will naturally be imperfect and indefinite in detail, because she no longer allowed me to read her inmost heart.

Shortly after my departure she had made the acquaintance of a man who she said was, in her opinion, more full of genius than any one she had ever known. She had from the first been attracted to him by the strongest sympathy and admiration, which, little by little, had developed into passionate love. He, on his side, had admired her warmly, and had asked her to be his wife. But she felt that he was drawn to her more by admiration than by love, and naturally refused to marry him. She now threw her whole soul into the endeavor to win him completely and awaken in his soul the same devotion which she felt for him.

In this struggle we have the story of her life during the long period in which we were separated. She worried herself and the man she loved with exactions. She made "scenes"; was jealous and irritable. They parted several times in anger and bitterness, and then Sónya was torn to pieces by despair. They met again, forgave each other, and parted once more as violently as ever.

Her letters to me at this time show very little of her inner life. She was reserved by nature where her deepest feelings were concerned, and more especially when touched by sorrow. It was only under the influence of personal intercourse that she melted into confidence. It was only on my return to Sweden that I learned what I know of this portion of her life.

Shortly after my departure from Stockholm in 1888 she wrote:

This story about E—— [referring to an incident in her circle in Stockholm] inclines me to take up again, directly I regain my freedom, my first-born, "The Privat-docent." I believe, if I worked it over, I could make something good of it. I really feel quite proud that when still so young I understood certain sides of human life. When I now analyze E——'s feelings to G——, I feel I have depicted the relations between my "Privat-docent" and his professor marvelously well. What an admirable opportunity I shall have for preaching socialism! or at least for developing the theory that the democratic but *not* socialistic state is the greatest horror possible.

Shortly after this she writes:

Thanks for your letter from Dresden. I am always so glad when I get a few lines from you, though your letter on the whole gave me a melancholy impression. What is to be done? Life is sad. One never gets what one likes, or what one thinks one needs — everything else, but not just that one th'ng. Some one else will get the happiness I desire, and get it altogether unwished for. The service in Life's Banquet is badly managed. All the guests seem to get the portions destined for others.

17*

Nansen, at least, seems to have got the position he desired. He is so kindled with enthusiasm about his voyage to Greenland that no "sweetheart" could, in his eyes, be of any importance compared with it. So you must refrain from writing to him the brilliant idea which occurred to you. For I am afraid you do not know that not even the knowledge that —— would keep him from visiting the souls of dead heroes which the Lapland Saga says hover above the ice-fields of Greenland. For my part, I am working as hard as ever I can at my prize-treatise, but without any special enthusiasm or pleasure.

Sónya had shortly before made the acquaintance of Frithiof Nansen, while he had been in Stockholm. His whole personality and his bold enterprise had made a great impression on her. They had met only once, but they were so delighted with each other during that one meeting that later on they both thought it would have been possible, had nothing else intervened to dim the impression, for it to deepen into something more decided and lifelong.

In Sónya's next letter, in January, 1888, she writes again on the same subject:

I am at this moment under the influence of the most exciting book I have ever read. I got to-day from Nansen a little pamphlet with a short outline of his projected wanderings through the ice-fields of Greenland. I got quite depressed by it. He has just received a subscription of five thousand kroner [about three hundred pounds] from a Danish merchant named Gamel, and I suppose no power on earth could now keep him back. The sketch is so interesting that I shall send it to you as soon as you forward me a definite address, but only on the understanding that I get it back immediately. When you have read it you will have a very fair idea of the man himself. To-day I had a talk with B—— about him. B—— thinks his works full of genius. He also thinks him much too good to risk his life in Greenland.

In her next letter appears the first sign of the crisis now impending in her life. The letter is not dated, but was written in March of that year. She had now made the acquaintance of the man who was to exercise such a powerful influence on the rest of her career. She writes:

You also ask me other questions, which I do not even wish to answer to myself—so you must excuse me if I do not answer them to you. I am afraid of making plans for the future. The only thing that unfortunately is certain is that I must spend two months and a half at Stockholm. But perhaps it is just as well for me to realize how really I am alone in life.

I had written to Sónya that I had heard from some Scandinavians in Rome that Nansen had been already engaged for several years. In answer to this I received the following merry letter:

DEAR ANNA CARLOTTA: *Souvent femme varie, bien fol est qui s'y fie.* If I had received your letter with its awful news a few weeks ago, it would no doubt have broken my heart. But now I confess, to my shame, that when I read your deeply sympathetic lines yesterday, I could not help bursting out into laughter. It was a hard day for me, for stout M—— was leaving that evening. I hope some of the family have already told you of the change in our plans, so that I need not mention that subject to-day. On the whole, I think this change of plan good for me personally. For if stout M—— had stayed longer, I do not know how I should have got on with my work. He is so great, so *grossgeschlagen,*—according to R——'s happy expression,—that he really takes up too much room on the sofa and in one's mind. It is simply impossible for me, in his presence, to think of any one or anything else but him. During the ten days he spent in Stockholm we were constantly together, generally *tête-à-tête,* and spoke of scarcely anything but ourselves, and that with a frankness which would have amazed you. Still I cannot, in spite of all this, analyze my feelings for him. I think I could best give my impressions of him in music set to De Musset's incomparable words:

> "Il est très joyeux, et pourtant très maussade—
> Détestable voisin, excellent camarade—
> Extrêmement futil, et pourtant très posé—
> Indignement naif, et pourtant très blasé—
> Horriblement sincère, et pourtant très rusé."

A real Russian he is into the bargain. He has more genius and originality in one of his little fingers than you could squeeze out of both yours put together, even if you put them under a hydraulic press.

The rest of the letter only contains the outlines of Sónya's plans for the summer's trip, which were not realized, so I only quote the most important facts:

I cannot believe I shall go to Bologna [to the Jubilee, at which she had always intended to be present], partly because such a journey, including dresses and everything, would be too expensive, and partly because all such celebrations are tedious and not at all to my taste. It is also very important that I should be in Paris for a short time. I intend to stay there from May 15th to June 15th. After that we shall come with fat Mr. M——— to meet you in Italy, and, as far as I can see, shall certainly spend ten months there *with you*. That is the chief thing, but *where* is a matter of detail which affects me less. I, for my part, propose the Italian lakes or Tyrol. But M——— would prefer to make us accompany him to the Caucasus *via* Constantinople. I admit that this is very tempting, especially as he assures me that it would not be very expensive. But on that point I have my doubts, and I think it would be more suitable for us to keep to well-known and civilized countries. There is another reason which, to my mind, is in favor of the first plan. I should like, during the summer, to write down some of my dreams and fancies, and you must also begin to work after three months' rest. This is only possible if we settle down in some quiet place and lead a regular idyllic life. I have never been so tempted to write romance as when with fat M———. Despite his vast proportions—which, by the by, are quite in keeping with the character of a Russian *boyár*—he is still the most perfect hero for a novel (a realistic novel, of course) that I have ever met with. I believe that he is also a good critic, with a touch of the sacred fire.

Nothing came of our plans for meeting that summer. Sónya joined her new Russian friend in London at the end of May, and later in the summer she went to the Harz Mountains, and looked up Weierstrass in order to get his advice on the final editing of her work.

She had sent it in the spring to the Academy in a half-finished condition, with a request to be allowed to send in a fuller definition of the problem before the awarding of the prize. The short letters which I received at this time show how feverishly she was at work during the whole spring. A note from Stockholm was addressed jointly to my brother and myself, as we were then together in Italy.

MY DEAR FRIENDS: I have no time to write long letters. I am working as hard as I can, and indeed as hard as any one could. I do not yet know whether I shall have time to finish my treatise or not. I have come to a difficulty which I cannot yet get over.

Toward the close of May, while on the way to London, she writes the following:

BELOVED ANNA CARLOTTA: Here I sit in Hamburg, waiting for the train which is to take me to Flushing, and thence I go to London. You can hardly imagine what a delight it is to me to be mistress of myself and my thoughts once more, and not be obliged to concentrate myself forcibly on one subject, as was the case during the last few weeks.

During her visit to the Harz Mountains she often complained of the restriction her work exercised on her thoughts. There a group of younger mathematicians had gathered round the old veteran Weierstrass—Mittag Leffler, Hurwitz, Hettner, and others. Of course, among so many representatives of the same science, much interesting conversation took place, and Sónya grumbled that she was obliged to sit over her work instead of enjoying this interchange of thought. She was jealous of those who had more time at their disposal to receive the inspiration imparted by the ideas of their honored and beloved teacher, full as they were of new light on the subject then occupying her mind.

Shortly after she returned to Stockholm, and during the autumn months, she lived in a perpetual state of overexcitement and exertion, which broke down her health for a time.

This year (1888) was, she had long been forewarned, to bring her to the summit of success and happiness. It bore within it, also, the germ of all the sorrows and misfortunes which were to break upon her with the new year. But that Christmas, at the solemn session of the French Academy of Science, she received in person the *Prix Bordin*, the greatest scientific honor which any woman has ever gained; one of the greatest honors, indeed, to which any one can aspire.

The man in whom she had found such "full satisfaction," as she declared; in whom she found all that her soul thirsted for, all that her heart desired, was present on that occasion. At that supreme moment all she had dreamed of as the highest joy of life became hers. Hers was the highest acknowledgment of her genius; hers the object of her truest devotion.

But she was the princess in whose cradle the fairies had placed all good gifts, which were always fated to be neutralized by the baneful gift of the single jealous fairy. She indeed gained all that she most desired, but it came at the wrong moment, and under circumstances which embittered it to her. In the midst of her intense striving for the prize which her scientific friends knew was a matter of honor for her to win, there had come into her life this new element—an element for which she had often longed.

During the last few months before the essay was despatched to Paris she had lived in a frightful state of excitement, torn by two conflicting claims—she was at once a woman and a scientist. Physically she nearly killed herself by working exclusively at night;

spiritually she was racked by the two great claims now
pressing upon her—the one requiring her to finish an
intellectual problem, the other demanding her surrender to the new and powerful passion which possessed
her. It is a conflict which every one must undergo in
some degree who gives himself up to creative work.
This is one of the strongest objections that can be
made to intellectual talent in woman, because the exercise of it prevents her from throwing herself entirely
into matters of affection, such as every man demands
of his wife.

For Sónya it was in any case a terrible trial to feel
that her work stood in the way between her and the
man to whom she would fain have devoted her every
thought. She felt dimly, though she never gave it expression in words, that *his* love was chilled by seeing
her, just when they were most closely drawn together,
engrossed by a scheme which perhaps seemed to him
a mere ambitious striving for honor and distinction,
arising from pure vanity.

Such an honor naturally does not increase a woman's
value in men's eyes. A singer or an actress, covered
with laurels, will often find the way to a man's heart
in spite of her celebrity, as Sónya often remarked. A
beautiful woman is admired for her superior beauty;
but the woman who studies seriously until her eyes are
red and her brow wrinkled, in order to win an academic
prize—what is there in *that* to catch a man's fancy ?
Sónya said to herself, with bitterness and irony, that
she had acted unwarrantably ! She ought, she thought,
to have sacrificed her ambition and vanity for that
which was so much more to her than worldly success.
But still she could not do it. To withdraw at the very
verge of success would have been to give the world a
striking proof of woman's incompetence. The force of

circumstances and her own nature carried her forward to the goal she had set before her. Had she known what the delay which had taken place in finishing her treatise was to cost her, she would never have wasted precious time in writing "A Struggle for Happiness," the composing of which made her own struggle for happiness so much more difficult than it might otherwise have been.

However, she arrived in Paris and received the prize.[1] She was the heroine of the hour. Speeches were made in her honor, which she was obliged to acknowledge in like manner. She was interviewed and received visits all day long, and had scarcely a moment to give to the man who had come thither in order to be present at her triumph. In this way both the happiness of her love and the triumph of her ambition were spoiled. Separately they would have given her great joy. Her tragic destiny gave her all she desired in life, but under such circumstances that, as she herself complained, the sweetness was turned to gall.

But perhaps this was also due to the peculiarity of her nature, divided always between the world of thought and that of feeling; between her need of yielding herself to another and her need of having herself in her own keeping. This eternal dualism enters of necessity into the life of every woman of genius, as soon as love arrives and makes itself felt as a force.

To this were joined the complications engendered by Sónya's jealous, tyrannical temperament. She exacted from her lover such absolute devotion and self-abnegation as must have surpassed the powers of all but a few very exceptional men. On the other hand, she could not decide to cut her life in two at one blow, surrender her work, and become merely a wife.

[1] Appendix I.

On the rocks of the impossibility of reconciling such different claims, their love suffered its final shipwreck.

About this time Sónya met in Paris a cousin whom she had not seen since she was a girl. He was a rich proprietor in the interior of Russia, where he led a happy life with a beloved wife and large family. In his youth he had had certain artistic inclinations, which he had afterward abandoned. He and Sónya now talked much about their early aspirations. He beheld her in her full triumph, surrounded and fêted as the heroine of the day, and that in Paris, where any personal triumph becomes more intoxicating than elsewhere. No wonder a faint feeling of bitterness came over Sónya's cousin when he thought of his own life. She had won all of which they had dreamed. But he! He had sunk into a mere insignificant country gentleman, and the happy father of a family.

Sónya looked at his handsome, well-preserved face, with its calm and restful expression; she heard him speak of his wife and children, and thought that he at least had found happiness. He did not wear himself out with complicated questions; he took life simply as he found it.

She wished to found a story on this meeting and this mood. She told me so, and I regret deeply that she found no time to write it when full of her personal philosophy.

The following is a letter of this period addressed to my brother:

DEAR GÖSTAV: I have just this minute received your kind letter. I am so grateful for your friendship. Yes, I believe it is the only good thing life has really given me! How ashamed I am to have done so little to prove to you how much I value it! But forgive me. I am not at this moment mistress of myself. I receive so many letters of congratulation, and, by a strange irony of fate, I have never felt so miserable in my life. Unhappy as a dog; but—I hope, for the dog's sake, it is *not* so unhappy as human beings can be. *Comme les hommes, surtout comme les femmes peuvent l'être.* But perhaps I shall grow more sensible by and by. I shall at least try. I will attempt to begin a new work and interest myself in practical things. I shall, of course, be led entirely by your advice, and do whatever you wish. At this moment all I can manage is to keep my sorrows to myself. I take care to make no mistakes in society, nor give people any opportunity of talking about me. I have been a great deal this week to Bertrand and Menabrea; and afterward to Count Lewenhaupt and Prince Eugène, etc. But to-day I feel too low to be able to describe all these dinner-parties to you. I will do so another time.

When I return to my rooms I do nothing but walk up and down. I have no appetite, neither can I sleep. I do not know whether I should care to go away. I shall decide that next week. Good-by for to-day, dear Göstav. Keep your friendship for me. I am in sore want of it; that much I may say. Kiss Foufi for me, and thanks for all your care of her.

Yours most affectionately,
SÓNYA.

She decided to leave Paris in the spring, and wrote to me from there in French:

Let me first congratulate you on the joy which has come to you. What a happy "child of the sun" you are to have found so great, so deep a love at your age! That is really a fate worthy of such a lucky soul as yours. But it has always been so. You *were* "*happiness*," and I am, and most likely shall always be, "*struggle.*" It is strange, but the longer I live the more I am governed by the feeling of fatalism, or rather predestination. The feeling of free will, said to be innate in man, fails me more and more. I feel so deeply that, however much I may struggle, I cannot change my fate one jot. I am now almost resigned. I work because I feel I am at the worst. I can neither wish nor hope for anything. You have no idea how indifferent I am to everything.

But enough about me! Let us talk of something else. I am glad you like my Polish story.[1] I need not tell you how delighted

---

[1] A memory of her youth, written in French, and translated later on in the *Nordistidschrift*.

I should be if you would translate it into Swedish. But I should reproach myself with taking up your time, which you might employ to so much better purpose. I have also written a long story about my sister's childhood, her youth, and her first steps in a literary career; and about our connection with Dostoévsky. Just now I am busy at "Væ Victis," which, perhaps, you remember. I have also another story in hand, "Les Revenants" ("Ghosts"), which also takes up much time. I should much like you to give me full powers to dispose of our "child," "When Death Shall Be No More." It is *my* favorite of all our children, and lately I have often thought of it. I have found an admirable frame for it — Pasteur's Institute. I have lately got, quite accidentally, to know all about the departments of that Institute; and it seems to me that all this might be put together dramatically. I have for some weeks been turning over in my mind a plan for making our "child" happy. But it is so bold and fantastic that I do not like to carry it out without full powers from you.

In August she wrote again from Sèvres, where she stayed, during the summer months, with her little daughter and some Russian friends:

I have just received a letter from Göstav, telling me that I shall perhaps meet you on my return to Sweden. I must say I am selfish enough to rejoice with all my heart. I am so impatient to know what you are now writing. On my part, I have a great deal I should like to show you and tell you. Up to now, thank God, I have never been at a loss for a subject for a novel. And at this moment my head is in a ferment with plots. I have finished "Recollections of Childhood" ("The Raevsky Sisters"); I have written the preface to "Væ Victis," and I have commenced two stories — who knows when I shall have time to finish them!

XIII

IN the middle of September, 1889, when Sónya returned to Stockholm, we met again after a separation of nearly two years. I found her very much changed. Her brilliant wit and playfulness had disappeared. The wrinkle between her eyebrows had deepened; her expression was gloomy and abstracted. Even her eyes had lost the marvelous luster which was their chief charm. They were now dull and sometimes squinted slightly.

Sónya succeeded in hiding from her less intimate friends her real feelings, and, to them, appeared much the same as before. She even said that when she had felt more depressed than usual in society, people would remark of her that Madame Kovalévsky had been really quite brilliant. But to us, who knew her well, the change was only too apparent. She had lost all wish for society, not only of strangers, but even of her friends. She could not remain idle for a moment, and only found peace in hard work. She recommenced her lectures from a sense of duty, but had no longer any real interest in them.

It was in literary composition that she now sought an outlet for the increasing restlessness which consumed her. This was partly because such work had points of contact with her own inner life, and partly because she had not yet recovered from the overstrain she had

272

undergone, which prevented her from resuming her scientific studies. She now began again to revise her " Væ Victis," and write the preface. The book had been translated from the Russian MS., and published in the literary calendar *Normann* for that year. In it there is a short passage depicting the struggle of nature, the awakening from the long winter sleep in spring. But it is not, as usual in such compositions, written in praise of Spring. On the contrary, it is the calm restful *Winter* which is here idealized. Spring is depicted as a brutal, sensual being, which awakens great hopes only to disappoint them.

Sónya intended this novel to be part of her own inner history. Few women have become more celebrated, or been so surrounded by outer success. Yet in this novel she depicts the story of defeat, because she felt herself defeated, in spite of her triumphs, in her struggle for happiness ; and her sympathies were rather with those who succumb than with those who conquer.

This deep feeling for suffering was very characteristic of her. It was not the ordinary " charity " of the Christian. It was that she made the sufferings of others her own, not with the superiority which strives to console, but with the sympathy that is the outcome of despair — despair at the cruelty of life. Sónya always said that what she most loved in the Greek religion, in which she had been educated, and for which she never quite lost her veneration, was its sympathy for suffering, which is much more emphasized in this than in any other form of religion. In literature she was always most touched by this note in any writer, and it is in Russian literature that the feeling has found its most beautiful expression.

Sónya now began to put the finishing touches to the

18

books which contained the memories of her childhood, and which Fröken (Miss) Hedberg had translated from the Russian.

In the evenings, in our own family circle, these books were read aloud, chapter after chapter, as soon as they were translated. In spite of the melancholy mood which had overcome both Sónya and myself, that autumn was still full of interest in consequence of her great eagerness for work—an eagerness felt by both, though we were no longer in collaboration.

During October and November I wrote five new tales, which, together with Sónya's, were read aloud in the family circle. We were very happy in each other's work. We went together to the publishers, and our books—Sónya's "Raevsky Sisters" ("Recollections of Childhood") and my "From Life : No. III."—appeared simultaneously. It was a faint reflection of our work together in earlier days.

Sónya had intended to publish her memoirs in a defi- nite autobiographical form, and it was in that style that she wrote them in Russian. But as soon as we had read the first chapter we dissuaded her from the attempt. We considered that, in a small community such as ours, it would shock people if a still unknown writer sat down and wrote, without disguise, all the most intimate details of her family life for the benefit of the public.

The whole was written in Russian, and several chap- ters already translated, when she turned the autobi- ography into a novel called "Tánya."[1] From that moment we had little or nothing to object to, and could only express our astonishment on finding that, at one stroke, our friend had become an artist in lit- erature.

[1] Appendix J.

While our books were going through the press we once more attempted a work in collaboration.

Sónya, during her last visit to Russia, had found in her sister's desk the MS. of a drama which Aniuta had written many years previously. It had met with warm approval from some of the best literary critics in Russia, but it was not ready for the stage. It contained scenes full of inspiration. The delineation of character was admirable, and throughout there lay in it a wonderfully deep, melancholy spirit. It had, besides, a very strong Russian local coloring.

When Sónya read it to me in full translation I at once felt that it was worth revising in order to offer it to the Swedish stage. Sónya, moreover, ever since her sister's death, had felt a keen desire to make some of her works known. It pained her to remember how Aniuta's rich gifts had been repressed in their development, and she found a kind of consolation in the thought of obtaining for her sister at least a posthumous fame. We set to work. We discussed scene after scene, act after act, and agreed as to what alterations were necessary. Sónya sketched the drama in Russian, and added nearly a whole act, thus making her first attempt in dramatic dialogue. She then dictated it to me in her broken Swedish, and I put it into shape as I wrote it down.

But it seemed as though no form of collaboration could succeed. We read the new drama to a select circle of literary and artistic friends in Sónya's red drawing-room. It had, after much deliberation, received the somewhat clumsy title of " Till and After Death." The opinion of our friends was not very encouraging. They found the drama too monotonously gloomy. They did not think it would be successful on the stage.

Meanwhile Sónya and I had each many personal
cares, and now that Christmas was approaching we
had to consider where we should spend that holiday.
Neither of us had the heart to spend it at home. Stockholm was hateful to us both, but for different reasons.
So we finally decided to try and realize our old plan
of traveling together, as we had never yet managed to
do. After many suggestions of places, we decided on
going to Paris. There, we thought, we could, more
easily than anywhere, come into contact with literary
and theatrical people. And we hoped to divert our
thoughts from our own personal worries. We left
Stockholm in the beginning of December.

But how different was this journey from what we
had been used to plan ! We neither of us expected to
enjoy this journey. It was only intended as a kind of
morphine—to deaden our thoughts. We sat silent and
sad, staring at each other, and feeling that our individual melancholy was increased by that which each
saw in the face of the other. We spent a couple of
days at Copenhagen, and called on some friends and
acquaintances. They were all astonished at the change
in Sónya. She had grown much thinner. Her face
was much wrinkled, her cheeks were hollow, and she
had, besides, a bad cough, caught during the influenza
epidemic which had raged in Stockholm. She took no
care of herself, and it was a wonder that she recovered
at all. One day, when she had received a letter which
excited her, she got out of bed, when she lay in a high
fever, and, half dressed and in thin shoes, went out into
the cold, wet snow. She came back drenched to the
skin, and sat without changing her clothes till night-
fall. "You see," she said to me when I entreated her
to take more care, "I am not even lucky enough to
take a serious illness. Do not be frightened. Life will

spare me. I should only be too lucky to have done with it, but such happiness will not fall to my lot."

While, as we traveled through from Copenhagen to Paris, we sat together motionless in the railway-carriage, Sónya said, over and over again:

"Just think if the train which is passing should run off the line and crush us! Railway accidents happen so often. Why cannot one happen now? Why cannot fate take pity on me?"

During the long days and nights she spoke unceasingly of her own life, her own fate. She talked more to herself than to me. She went through a kind of self-examination, as though seeking the reason why she must be always suffering and unhappy; why could she never get what she wanted—illimitable love? "Why, why can no one love me?" she cried, again and again. "I could be more to a man than most women—and why are the most insignificant women loved while I remain unloved?"

I tried to explain. She asked too much. She was not one to be content with the kind of love that may fall to any woman's lot. She was too introspective. She brooded too much about herself, and had not the kind of devotion which forgets itself. Her devotion demanded as much as it gave, and unceasingly worried itself and its object by considering and weighing all that it received.

How melancholy was our arrival at Paris! We had often pictured it as so bright! We drove straight from the station to Nilsson's Library, in order to ask for letters which we were expecting with impatience. They had arrived, and gave us sufficient food for thought. I had only been once before in Paris, and then only for a short time on my return from London in 1884. I asked Sónya about the palaces and squares which

18*

we drove past on our way to the hotel near the Place
de l'Étoile, but she answered impatiently, "I do not
know. I know nothing about these places. I cannot
tell which is which."

The Tuileries, the Place de la Concorde, the Palais
de l'Industrie, awakened no recollections in her, nor
made any impression. Paris, great and gay, which
had always been her favorite city, the place she would
have chosen to live in had she had the choice, was to
her at this moment a dead mass of dull buildings.
She had not received a letter from *him*, and only one
from a friend, whose news was anything but satisfactory—that was why Paris was dull.

We spent some feverish, strangely restless weeks in
the place where, the year before, Sónya had received
so much adulation and honorable distinction. But
now scientific Paris seemed to have forgotten her.
She had had her "quarter of an hour."

We looked up our friends, made new acquaintances,
and ran about from morning to night, but not as tour-
ists. Of the city and its sights I saw nothing—not
even the Eiffel Tower. We were only interested in
studying people and theaters, trying to get into the
whirlpool, and to find the necessary stimulus for our
intended literary work.

The circle of our acquaintance was varied, and on
some days curiously mixed. All nations and all types
were represented in our rooms. A Russo-Jewish family
and a French banker's family lived in the palaces of
former aristocrats. Their footmen wore knee-breeches
and silk stockings, and the whole turnout was in a
high style of luxury. Among our friends, besides,
were Swedish and Russian scientists, some of the latter being ladies; Polish emigrants and conspirators;
French literary men and women; and several Scandi-

navians—Jonas Lie, Walter Runeberg, Knut Wicksell, Ida Erikson, and other scientists and authors.

Sónya, of course, called on some of the leading mathematicians in Paris, and received invitations from them. But at the moment her head was full of anything but science, and consequently she was less interested than usual in such society. Among the interesting figures in our circle I must specially mention the afterward famous Padlevsky. He was a sickly young man, about whom still lingered the air of a prison. He spoke French badly. He at once interested us by the vehemence and enthusiasm with which he had embraced revolutionary principles. He seemed to us to be boiling with impatience to be once more in danger. He evidently loved martyrdom; and imprisonment, in which state he had passed so much of his youth, had no horrors for him. His father had been executed during the Polish revolution; his brother had died a horrible death in the Peter-Paul Fortress of terrible fame. In order to save her youngest son from a like fate, and get him away from the influence which had seduced his father and brother, his aged mother took him to Germany. But all in vain. Revolution was in his blood, and before he was twenty he was a political prisoner. He escaped, and passed through countless adventures. Just now it seemed that he had nothing in prospect. But he did not conceal his readiness to fling himself again into the furnace of revolt at the very first opportunity. These facts of his life I relate as told to me by Sónya. As a private individual, Padlevsky was most sweet and winning, gentle and charming in his ways. He was absolutely without means of livelihood. I believe conspiracy was his only profession. But he was constantly the guest of the richer members of his party.

It was of deep interest to me to make acquaintance
with the strange group of enthusiastic patriots who
lost themselves so entirely in the love of their country; who sorrowed so deeply over its misfortunes;
who so longed to save it that what the ordinary community called crime was to them a sacred duty.

Just at this time a great English newspaper published a horrible account of the cruelties which Siberian
prisoners, and among them some highly educated English ladies, had had to undergo.

There was something deeply touching in the sorrow
which the intelligence aroused in the Polo-Russian
clique in Paris. It seemed as though its members
had suffered personally. The sympathy of the clique
with the Russian martyrs of the Tzar's cruelty was so
strong that to all intents and purposes they were but
one family.

The center of that clique was one of Sónya's most
intimate friends—a woman whom she admired more
than any other, and who impressed her so greatly that
she lost all her critical judgment in regarding her.
Sónya admired this woman with the jealous adoration
characteristic of her. This friend possessed several of
the qualities which Sónya herself desired and envied
—beauty, a rare power of fascination, and an equally
rare talent for dressing in perfect taste. While in Paris,
Sónya used to get this friend to choose her dresses for
her, but they never looked so well on her as on the
charming Pole.

The latter had a gift for attracting a small court of
admirers, who vied with one another in winning a smile
from her. But Sónya admired in this friend least what
the others admired most—her genius, intelligence, and
courage. A genius not creative in its nature had no
attractions for Sónya.

As to courage,— that is, moral courage,— Sónya considered that, if tried as her friend had been, she would prove to have just as great an amount of it.

The life this friend, Madame J——, now lived — when all the storms and the trouble of her past life were over for the moment—seemed to Sónya the ideal of happiness. Recently married to a man who adored her; surrounded by a sympathizing and admiring circle of friends in whose sight she was a queen; the mistress of a hospitable mansion open to all friends; living in Paris in the very midst of the intellectual movement of the time, and inspired by a mission in which she intensely believed, Madame J—— was, in Sónya's opinion, in a position of supreme and ideal happiness.

In this circle, so sympathetic to her feelings, Sónya became open-hearted. I had never seen her so communicative, except when in private conversation. She spoke openly of her dissatisfaction with life; of her sterile triumphs in science. She said she would willingly exchange all the celebrity she had won, all the triumphs of her intellect, for the lot of the most insignificant woman who lived in her proper circle—a circle of which she was the center, and in which she was beloved.

But Sónya noticed with some bitterness that no one believed her statement. All her friends thought her more ambitious than affectionate or sensitive, and they laughed at her words as though she were but indulging in one of her paradoxes.

The Norwegian author, Jonas Lie, was the only person who understood Sónya fully. Once, in a little speech he made, he showed his comprehension of her so plainly that she was moved to tears. It was on one of the pleasantest of our Paris days. We were

dining with Jonas Lie; and Grieg and his wife, who
were just then enjoying their triumph at Paris, were
present. There was about this little dinner the indescribable festive feeling which sometimes springs up
in a small circle when each person present is pleased
to see the other, and all feel themselves to be fully
understood and appreciated. Jonas Lie was in high
spirits. He made one speech after the other, bright
and sparkling, and full of imagination, and yet withal
— as was his wont — somewhat involved and obscure.
The spontaneity and poetic fervor inherent in all his
utterances gave to his cordiality a special charm. He
spoke of Sónya, not as the great mathematician, nor
even as the successful author, but as the little "Tánya
Raevsky," whom he said he had learned to love so truly,
and for whom he felt so great a sympathy. He said
he was so sorry for the poor little misunderstood child
who so longed for tenderness. He doubted, he said,
whether she had ever been understood. Life, he had
heard, had lavished on her every gift upon which she
set no value; had given her honors, distinction, and
success. But it had denied her what she most wanted.
She still remained standing there with great, wide-open
eyes, yearning for a touch of tenderness. There she
stood, with her empty outstretched hands. What did
she want? Only an orange. " Thank you, Mr. Lie,"
Sónya murmured, in accents deeply moved and choked
with tears. " I have had many speeches made about
me in my life, but never one so beautiful." She could
say no more. She sat down — for she had risen in the
impulse of the moment — and tried to conquer her emotion by drinking a glass of water.

When we left Lie's house, Sónya was in a brighter
mood than she had been for many a day. She felt
that there existed at least one person who understood

her, though he had seen her but a few times, and knew
nothing of her private circumstances. He had penetrated further into her inmost soul by merely reading
her book than her most intimate friends had done,
though they had known her for years. Now, after all,
she felt that there was some pleasure in writing, and,
after all, life was worth living.

We had intended to go straight from Lie's house
to another friend, and not run home between whiles.
But Sónya was always expecting letters, and was never
happy if away from the hotel for many hours at a time.
So we returned home, taking a circuitous road to the
hotel in order to ask the eternal question, Are there
any letters? The next moment Sónya had clutched
the letter which lay close to the key of our rooms, and
rushed up the flight of stairs.

I followed her slowly, and went straight to my own
room, for I did not want to disturb her.

Almost immediately she came to me, threw her arms
around my neck, laughed, danced round me, and then
flung herself down on the sofa, almost shouting with
delight.

" Oh, what happiness ! " she exclaimed. " I cannot
bear it ! I shall die of joy ! "

The letter explained and did away with an unfortunate misunderstanding—one which had worried her
for months, and had worn her to a shadow. The very
next evening she left Paris in order to meet the man
on whom her whole existence depended.

XIV

A COUPLE of days after Sónya's departure I received a few lines from her. Already the spark of happiness, which had flamed up so brightly and inspired most extravagant hopes, had died out. I have not kept her letter, but I remember the main contents:

I see [she wrote] that he and I will never understand each other. I shall return to my work at Stockholm. In future my only consolation will be work.

That was all. During the remainder of that winter, and all next spring, I had not a line from her, except a few heartfelt words of congratulation on my marriage in May.

She suffered, and avoided showing me her sorrows, not wishing to disturb my happiness. She could never make up her mind to write on indifferent matters. Therefore she kept silence. But this reticence, after our recent intimacy, wounded me deeply. Afterward I well understood that she *could not* have acted otherwise.

In the April of that year (1890) Sónya went to Russia. She had rather expected to be elected a member of the Academy of Sciences at St. Petersburg, the most advantageous position which she could have acquired. It would have yielded her a large salary, and no duties beyond a two-months' yearly residence in St. Petersburg. To be a member of the Academy is the greatest honor to which any Russian scientist can attain. Sónya had built her hopes on obtaining it. She would have then been delivered from the insufferable yoke of Stockholm life, and her wish to settle in Paris could have been realized.

During our stay in that city she had often said to me, "If you cannot have the best in life, namely, true heart-happiness, life may be bearable if you get the next best thing—an intellectual atmosphere in which you can breathe and flourish. But to have neither is insufferable."

She now fancied that if she were elected a member of the Academy she might be reconciled to life. I could not guess whether her plans would prosper, nor did I ever know where she was going after leaving St. Petersburg. She was very mysterious about her plans for that spring, mentioning them to no one. I met her by chance, however, in Berlin in the middle of June. I was then *en route* for Sweden, whither I was returning with my husband shortly after our marriage. Sónya had arrived the same day from St. Petersburg.

I found her in an unnaturally excitable state of mind—a mood which a stranger might easily have mistaken for light-heartedness. I knew her too well not to realize that sorrow crouched behind it. She had been fêted at Helsingfors and St. Petersburg; she had been hurried from place to place; had met the most interesting people, and had made a speech before a thousand listeners. She assured me that she had enjoyed herself immensely, and had good expectations; but she continued to be mysterious and to shun all intimacy, carefully avoiding remaining alone with me, for fear of being searchingly questioned.

We spent, however, some cheerful days together, filled with jesting and small talk. Still she impressed

me painfully, for I saw how nervous and overexcited
she really was, and how utterly out of tune. The only
thing she said to me about her personal concerns was
that she never intended to marry again; that she
would not be so commonplace; she would not do as
other women did—forsake her work and mission in
order to marry as soon as she had a chance. She did
not want to leave her post at Stockholm until she had
won such a sure position as an author that she could
support herself by her writings. She did not deny
that she wished to meet and travel with M——, who
was to her the best of friends and comrades.

A few months later we again met at Stockholm,
where she had resumed her lectures in September.
Once more her forced gaiety had vanished. She was
still more out of sorts, and troubled with an increasing
restlessness. I had no opportunity of seeing deeper
into her heart. She hid her feelings from me. She
continued to shun a *tête-à-tête*, and, on the whole, showed
herself more or less indifferent to all who formerly had
been her most intimate friends. It was evident that
her heart was elsewhere, and that she felt these months
at Stockholm as a kind of banishment. She counted
the days that must pass before the Christmas holidays,
when she meant to travel. She was in a desperate condition. She could neither manage to live without or
with M——. Thus her life had lost its balance. She
was like an uprooted plant—could not strike root
again, and seemed to wither away.

When my brother removed to Djursholm, in the villa
quarter of Stockholm, he tried to persuade Sónya to
come to the same neighborhood. She had always liked
to live near him, so that they might meet as often as
possible. But though my brother's removal to new
quarters was a great trial to her, and she felt more

lonely than ever, she could not make up her mind to move.

"Who knows how long I shall stay in Stockholm? This cannot last forever!" she often exclaimed. "And if I am in Stockholm next winter I shall be in such bad spirits that you will not care to see much of me."

She could not be induced to go and see Mittag Leffler's new villa when it was being built. She took no interest in it, and did not wish to enter the new home of one of her most intimate friends in such a spirit of indifference. And when others in her company went to see the rooms, she insisted on waiting without at the door.

A feeling of the fleeting, evanescent nature of her sojourn in Stockholm was growing upon her. She began to let drop all the ties that bound her to the place. She neglected her friends, withdrew from society, and was more than ever indifferent to her house and dress. All the inspiration and soul had even died out of her conversation. The former heartfelt interest she had taken in all spheres of human life and human thought had faded. She was entirely engrossed by the tragedy of her life.

XV

THE last time I saw Sónya alive was in the same year (1890). She had come to say good-by to us at Djursholm before she went to Nice. No forebodings told us that this was to be the last farewell.

My husband, Sónya, and I had agreed to meet at Genoa directly after Christmas, so we said but short farewells. But the plan was not carried out, in consequence of a misdirected telegram, which was intended to meet us on our return to Italy. While Sónya and her companion were waiting for us, we passed through the town in which they were staying without knowing they were there.

New-Year's Day—which we had hoped to spend together—was passed by Sónya and her friend in going to the lovely marble dwelling of the dead at Genoa. While there a sudden shadow flitted across Sónya's face, and she said, with prophetic emphasis: "One of us will not survive this year, for we have spent its first day in a burial-ground!"

A few weeks later Sónya was on her. way back to Stockholm. The voyage she so hated was this time not only to be a trying, but also a fatal one.

With a heart wounded once more by the pain of separation, feeling that the torture was almost killing her, Sónya sat in the railway-carriage lost in despair. These bitter-cold winter days differed so cruelly from the mild and fragrant air she had left behind in Italy. The contrast between the Mediterranean and the northern cold had now become symbolic to her. She began to hate the cold and darkness as intensely as she loved sunshine and flowers.

Her journey was also physically more than usually disagreeable to her. A strange contrariety of fate made her fail to take the shortest and most convenient route from Berlin, where she had spent a few days. An epidemic of smallpox had broken out at Copenhagen, and as she was mortally afraid of this disease, she would not risk a single night in that town.

She therefore took the long and troublesome route across the Danish islands. The never-ending change of trains in bad weather was very likely one of the causes of the severe chill which she caught.

At Fredericia, where she arrived late at night in pelting rain and storm, she had no Danish coin by her, and therefore could not hire a porter; so she carried her luggage herself, dead-tired and frozen as she was, and so dispirited that she was ready to faint. When she arrived at Stockholm on the morning of February 4th she felt very ill. Nevertheless she worked the whole of the next day (Thursday), and gave her lecture on Friday, February 6th. She was always very plucky, and never missed a lecture if it were possible for her to stand. That evening she went to a party at the Observatory. There she began to feel feverish and went away alone, but could not get a cab. Unpractical as she always was in such matters, and never knowing her way about Stockholm, she got into the wrong omnibus, and in consequence had to go a long way about on that cold, raw evening. When she reached home—alone, helpless, trembling with fever, with mortal sorrow in her heart—she sat down in the

19

cold night, feeling the violence of the illness which had attacked her. That very morning she had told my brother, who was Rector of the University, that she must have leave of absence during the following April, on whatever terms she could obtain it.[1]

Each time she had returned to Stockholm her only consolation in the midst of her despair had been to make plans for the future. Between times she tried to numb her sorrow and restlessness by working hard. She had thought of several new plans, as concerned both mathematics and literature, and spoke of them with much interest. To my brother she divulged an idea of a mathematical work, which he thought would be the greatest she had yet written. To her friend Ellen Key, with whom she spent most of these last days, she spoke of several new novels which she had worked out in her head. One she had already commenced, and in it she meant to give a character-sketch of her father. She had also written two thirds of another, which was to be a *pendant* to " Vera Vorontzoff." She meant to call it " A Nihilist," and it was to describe an episode in Tschernyschévsky's life. The last chapter, which she had not yet written, she described to Ellen Key, who noted it down in the following words:

T——, from obscurity, has suddenly risen to celebrity among the young generation by his social revolutionary novel entitled "What to Do." At a fête he has been hailed as the hope and leader of the rising generation. He has returned to his garret, where he lives with his beautiful young wife. She is asleep when he arrives. He goes to the window and looks down on sleeping St. Petersburg, where lights still glimmer. He talks, in imagination, to the terrible silent city. There it lies — still the home of violence, poverty, injustice, and oppression. But he will conquer; he will breathe his spirit into it. What *he*

---

[1] Appendix K.

thinks, *they all* shall gradually come to think; even as the rising generation does now. He remembers especially a deep-souled girl whose sympathy has gone out to him. He begins to dream, but rouses himself to go and kiss his wife and tell her of his triumphs, when, at that moment, he hears a sharp knock at the door. He opens it, and there stand the gendarmes who have come to arrest him.

Eagerly as Sónya had often invoked death, she had at this moment no wish to die. But those friends who were near her at the last thought her more resigned than she had been formerly. She no longer yearned for that complete happiness the ideal of which had ever consumed her soul with its burning flame. But she now longed, with ardent, clinging love, for the broken gleams of the happiness which had of late cast a light upon her path.

In her innermost heart she was afraid of the *great unknown*. She often said that it was the possibility of punishment in the other world which alone kept her back from leaving this one. She had no definite religious belief, but she believed in the eternal life of each individual soul. She believed, and she trembled.

She was especially afraid of the awful moment at which earthly life ends. She often quoted Hamlet's words:

> For in that sleep of death what dreams may come,
> When we have shuffled off this mortal coil,
> Must give us pause.

With her vivid imagination she pictured those awful moments which perhaps may occur when the body, physically speaking, is dead, but the nervous system still lives and suffers — suffers a nameless martyrdom, known by none but by those who have taken the dread leap into the great darkness.

Sónya was anxious to be cremated, because she had also a fear of being buried alive. She pictured to herself how it would feel to awaken in her coffin. She described it in such words as to make all who heard her shudder.

Her illness was so short and violent that probably she had no time or power to recall at the last moment all these sad forebodings. The only thing she said which suggested that she had any idea of her approaching end she uttered on Monday morning, the 9th of February, barely twenty hours before she died. "I shall never get over this illness," she said. And on the evening of the same day she remarked, "I feel as if a great change had come over me."

But as to the rest, her fear was chiefly that her illness might be a long one. She had not strength to speak much, for she had severe pleurisy, high fever, and asthma. She suffered cruel pain, and could not bear to be alone for a moment.

The last night but one she said to Ellen Key, who scarcely ever left her: "If you hear me moan in my sleep, wake me, and help me to change my position; otherwise I fear it may go ill with me. My mother died in just such an access of pain."

She had hereditary disease of the heart, and had in consequence often expressed a hope that she might die young. This disease, however, was found at the post-mortem to have been of no importance, though it may have increased the asthma caused by the pleurisy.

The friends who were near her during her short illness cannot say enough about her goodness, gentleness, and patience; or how unselfish she was, fearing to give trouble; and how touching was her gratitude for every little service rendered.

On Tuesday her little girl was to go to a children's

party, and Sónya interested herself in it to the last, wishing that her child should not miss this pleasure. She begged her friends to help her to get what was required, and when, on Monday evening, the child came to her mother dressed in a gipsy costume, Sónya smiled kindly on her little daughter, and hoped she would enjoy herself. Only a few hours later the child was roused from her sleep to receive her mother's dying look, which was full of tenderness.

On the Monday evening both the friends who had nursed her during the last few days had left her, and a St. Elizabeth's sister took their place. The doctors did not apprehend any immediate danger. They seemed rather to believe the illness would last some time. The friends, therefore, considered it wiser to forego the night-nursing and spare their strength.

At Sónya's own desire they were to rest that night, as there seemed no special need for their presence. Precisely on that night the great crisis came.

Sónya lay in deep sleep when her friends left her. But at two o'clock she awoke. The terrible death-agony had begun. She showed no sign of consciousness. She could neither speak nor move, nor even swallow. This lasted for two hours. Only at the last moment did one of her friends, summoned tardily by the nurse, arrive.

Alone—alone with a hired stranger, a nurse who did not even speak her language—she had to struggle through the last and bitter battle. Who knows what consolation a beloved voice, the touch of a loving hand, might have been to Sónya during those two terrible hours?

I wish even that a Russian priest could have read the parting prayers to her during that time. With the veneration in which she still held the Orthodox religion,

19*

and, indeed, all memories of her childhood, the familiar words would have been sweet and calming in her ears if she had been able to catch them. Could her hands, in their wandering, have clasped the cross, it might have consoled her, as it has so often consoled other dying mortals. To her it was ever a much-loved symbol—the symbol of the sufferings of mankind.

But there was nothing—not a word of consolation; no help; not even a loving hand to place its cool pressure on her burning brow. Alone in a strange country, with a broken heart and shattered hopes, trembling, perhaps, at what she was about to meet! Thus she closed her earthly life, "this soul of fire, this soul of thought."

Out of the hopeless darkness which seemed to enshroud this death-bed, little by little some gleams of hope have arisen before me. It matters not whether life be long or short; all depends on what it has contained for one's self and for others; and, from this point of view, Sónya's life had been longer than most. She had lived intensely; she had drained the cup both of sorrow and of joy. She had quenched the thirst of her spirit at the wells of wisdom. She had risen to the heights to which genius and imagination alone can carry the soul. To others she had given instinctively of her knowledge, experience, fantasy, and feeling. She had spoken with the inspiring voice which genius alone possesses when it does not isolate itself in selfish retirement. No one who knew her could remain unmoved by the influence ever exercised by the keen intellect and glowing feeling which spread sunshine and growth around. Her mind was fertile because her intellect was unselfish. Her highest aspiration was to live in mental union with another.

If there was much that was fantastic and superstitious in her forebodings and dreams, it is nevertheless true that there was much in her of the "seer." When her luminous eyes, full of genius, were fastened on the person to whom she spoke, one felt that they penetrated the very soul. How often did she, with a look, pierce through the mask beneath which less sagacious glances had failed to discover the real countenance! How often would she divine the secret motives that were hidden from others, and even unrevealed to their very owner! It was her poet-soul which thus became in her the seer. A chance word, a single insignificant episode which she came across, could reveal to her the whole connection between cause and effect, and enable her to develop them into the story of a whole life. It was this *connection* for which her soul was always searching—the connection in thoughtful works, and between the varied phenomena of life. She even sought for the unknown connection between these phenomena and the laws of thought. She sought for unity in the world of thought, and longed for it also in the world of feeling.

Just as her intellect craved absolute clearness of thought and absolute truth, so her heart craved that perfect love and union which the limitations of life, and more especially the limitations of her own nature, rendered impossible.

It was a never-ending source of grief to her that in this world "we can only see in part, and only know in part." Thus it was that she loved to dream about another and a higher life, of which the Apostle so beautifully says, "Now we see through a glass darkly, but then face to face." To perceive unity in the manifold was the aim of her scientific and poetic mind. But ah! did she ever attain to this? The possibility of such attainment, dim and uncertain as it is, makes the brain reel; but one breathes more freely, and the heart beats with a fluttering hope that takes away the sting of death.

Sónya had always wished to die young. In spite of the inexhaustible freshness of mind which made her ever ready to receive new impressions, to drink from fresh sources of pleasure and find enjoyment in trifles, there was still in her mind and soul a longing which life could never satisfy.

It was the impossibility of harmonizing and fulfilling all the desires of such a nature as hers that wrecked her life. And in this light we can look upon her death with less sadness.

Starting from her own belief in a deep relationship between the different phenomena of life, one cannot fail to understand that death was, as it were, the natural outcome of it all. It was not merely that destructive and fatal microbes had settled on her lungs; and not even because life could never give her the joys for which she craved. But also the necessary organic relationship between her inner and outer being was wanting; the link between the worlds of thought and feeling, between her temperament and disposition, was lacking. She *saw*, as it were, " as when that which is perfect is come," but she *acted* only " in part."

If there be a world in which these contrasts are harmonized, truly she must be happy now. If not—then she has gained the desired harmony in another way, because in complete rest there is also harmony.

Few deaths have awakened such great and such general regret as did that of Sónya. From nearly all quarters of the civilized world telegrams of condolence reached the Stockholm University. From the highly conservative University of St. Petersburg, of which she had been made a corresponding member during the

last year of her life, down to the Sunday-school[1] in
Tiflis and the *kindergarten* in Kharkoff, all joined in
showing honor to her memory.

The women of Russia decided to raise a monument
on her grave in Stockholm. At her burial, carriage-
loads of flowers covered the dark, newly turned earth
among the snow-drifts in the Stockholm cemetery.
All the papers[2] and reviews contained honorable mention of the unique woman who had brought honor on
her sex.[3]

But one picture stands out by itself from among
all these signs of homage, these tributes of esteem.
Sónya will be for posterity what she least wished to
be—a marvel of mental development and beautiful
womanhood; or, if you will, a kind of giantess of such
extraordinary proportions that you regard her with
wonder and admiration.

I have, perhaps, in describing her life, in unveiling
its mistakes and weaknesses, its sorrows and humilia-
tions, as well as its greatness and its triumph, reduced
too much its true dimensions. What I had in mind
was to depict Sónya as I knew her, and as she wished
to be known and understood. I have, above all,
sought to emphasize the *human* traits in the picture,
and in this way place its subject nearer to the level of
other women; to make her one of them—not an exception to, but a proof of, the rule that the *life of the heart*
is the most important, not only for women, but for the
whole of the human race. At this central focus of all
humanity the most and the least gifted may ever meet.

[1] Appendix L.   [2] Appendix M.   [3] Appendix N.

NOTE

EXTRACTS FROM ELLEN KEY'S BIOGRAPHY OF THE
DUCHESS OF CAJANELLO

TRANSLATED BY ISABEL F. HAPGOOD

WHEREVER Anna Carlotta Leffler went, her personal appearance attracted general attention, but she was never
such a brilliant conversationalist in society as, for example,
Sophia Kovalévsky. When the two friends passed the
evening in any company, a circle of listeners almost always
formed around Sophia, while Anna Carlotta, on the contrary, liked to play the part of a listener herself in the
circle which gathered round her. Her conversation did not
shine by any particular originality of thought, or witty
sallies, but it was distinguished by its wealth of material.
When she related anything, analyzed any psychological
problem, expounded the contents of a book, one always got
the actual delineation of the person or situation in question,
a delineation set forth in a clear and definite manner; she
hewed out the block of marble, so to speak, and presented
it to her hearers in its natural state. But when the same
block of marble fell into Sophia's hands, she, the Michael
Angelo of conversation, flung herself upon it with stormy
energy, and very soon, where there had been only material
before, the contour of a figure was revealed. Everything
had taken place thus always, as Anna Carlotta Leffler narrated it; everything might take place thus, as Sophia
narrated it, and then everything would have been much
more interesting than it was in reality. When she lacked
material, Sophia worked over what she had at hand. Thus,

for example, she one day read somewhere that if a man possessed, in proportion to his size, the same capacity for jumping which is possessed by some insects, he would be able, with one leap, to reach the moon. Thereupon she began, with all the force of her eloquence, to demonstrate, on the basis of astronomical, physical, and mechanical facts, that the problem of future civilization and culture, to which she, among others, wished to devote her life, consisted in developing in the human race the capacity to jump, and thus to render them capable of leaping to another planet, when it should prove impossible to live any longer on the earth; by the aid of such a leap, people would save themselves and the memory of culture, which has attained to such a high degree of development on our earth. And she developed this jest with such a serious mien, that the comic impression was irresistible. It not infrequently happened, during conversation, that Anna Carlotta expressed some thought which Sophia afterward took up. Thus, the former once made the following quotation from a Danish author: " Genius is needed in order to love," an expression which several young poets who were present would not accept in its real sense, but interpreted to signify that " only geniuses can love." Sophia strove, for a long time, to explain the real meaning, but in vain. But when these men took their departure, she exclaimed: " Really, it is incredible how stupid even the most gifted people can be, when love is in question ! Here are these nice young men discussing and writing books on this subject, and yet they do not understand that some people possess a talent for love, just as others possess talent for music or mechanics, and that for these geniuses of love, love is converted into a vital matter, while for all the rest of mankind it constitutes only one of the episodes of life. And it is generally the case — according to Darwin's theory it is perfectly natural — that the genius of love should fall in love with the idiot of love; precisely this constitutes one of the most puzzling problems of life, and our young men have not even observed that. But if there exists a realm in which the most stupid woman is wiser than the cleverest man, that realm is love. When I was six years old, and fell in love,— my first love,— with a student who visited at our house, and loved him with a strong, silent love which I confided to no one except to a stone lion which adorned my grandfather's garden, I understood more about the meaning of this matter than these young men do."

A. C. Leffler listened in smiling silence to the flood of eloquence, which rang out for a good while longer, until, at last, it descended with full force upon her, upon " sly Anna Carlotta," who had thrown down the glove, and then beaten a retreat, leaving Sophia to extricate herself from the scrape. The fact was, that Anna Carlotta, like many others, disliked to interrupt Sophia when the latter got excited ; there was so much depth of thought, brilliant wit, humor, lyrism, imagery, and vividness in her speech, that every one preferred to listen to her. A. C. Leffler, with the good nature which constituted one of her most attractive qualities, often took Sophia's jests in earnest, which not infrequently provoked fresh sallies of wit and laughter.

Sophia took great delight in profiting by the psychological perspicacity which was peculiar to her, to delineate the character of a given person — to imagine for herself his distant future on the foundation of some gesture of his, some intonation of his voice, and so forth. None of Sophia's brilliant qualities aroused such a degree of wonder and admiration in A. C. Leffler as this. In order to explain what we mean by this quality of Sophia, we will cite the following fact. One day Sophia Kovalévsky chanced to be traveling in the same carriage with a woman who is now doing much work in the interest of her native land. Mme. Kovalévsky entered into conversation with her, and began to inquire her plans. When the woman stated them, Sophia said : " You will certainly be successful. There comes a decisive moment in the life of every person, when his whole future fate depends upon whether he chooses the path on which he should go, or not. He who lets that moment slip ruins his whole future life. You belong to the class of

people who understand how to choose the right road."
"But how can you know all this about me?" asked the astonished woman. "I saw the way in which you took leave
of your mother at the station," replied Sophia. "You
laughed as you bade her farewell, and then, when the train
started, you began to cry. I immediately perceived that
you have a heart and courage; such people always understand how to choose the right road at the proper moment."

Sophia Kovalévsky loved argument for the sake of argument; she often retorted on herself, and then triumphantly
refuted her own arguments. A. C. Leffler was much more
interested in the matter of the conversation than in argument, and when she was called upon to defend any idea,
she did it with a remarkable calmness, which impressed her
friend greatly, because she admired nothing so much as
she did calmness. She often said that there were people
who, by their mere presence in the room where she was,
shed abroad peace, brought harmony into her inner world,
producing on her "the freshness and repose of marble, or
the softness of velvet." In Anna Carlotta she found not
only calmness of temperament, but also a breadth of view
and thought which acted upon her like a charm. The
love for psychological problems and clearness of thought
these women had in common, though their gifts presented
such a wide difference in many other respects. Sophia was
most fond of music and lyrics, and often thought in images;
she possessed that peculiar comprehension of nature which
seeks in it, first of all, that which most nearly corresponds
to a given mind or personifies it; at the same time she was
distinguished by a wonderful capacity for conveying these
impressions in a remarkably vivid, artistic, and poetical
form. Anna Carlotta, on the contrary, loved nature most
of all; and, next to it, the arts which reproduced it— paint-
ing and sculpture. She never expressed her thoughts in
images, but always in separate sentences; but she greatly
admired Sophia's wealth of imagination and imagery, and her
lyrical qualities, just as the latter admired Anna Carlotta's
power of setting forth her thoughts in a clear, simple form.

The difference in character between the two friends was also expressed, among other things, in such trifles as those by the aid of which Sophia was sometimes fond of building up a delineation of certain persons, attributing to these trifles great significance. When Sophia was well, for instance, she put out her hand with a sharp, brisk movement, and her thin, nervous fingers instantly slipped out of the hand of the person who met her, like the wings of a captured bird. This manner of shaking hands indicated a nervous, impressionable nature; bespoke a person who always acted under the influence of impulse. On the contrary, Anna Carlotta's manner of moving her beautiful hands expressed calm grace. She extended her elegant, white hand, with its slender fingers, with a sort of reserve, but left it for a while in the hand of her interlocutor, calmly awaiting a responsive pressure. As in trifles, so in more serious things, she always produced the impression of a solid, well-poised, reserved personality. She seemed unsympathetic to some men, thanks to the fact that she was as daring as she was independent; but one had only to get better acquainted with her, and this unpleasant feeling gave way to the warmest sympathy, so that more than one man regretted that he had met her too late. Women admired in her the authoress who worked seriously; who was distinguished for such masculine impartiality, and such wonderful clearness of thought.

BIOGRAPHICAL NOTE[1]

BY LILY WOLFFSOHN

"THE life of a woman by a woman" might be the sub-title of the book now presented for the first time to the British public; and the adjectives, "eminent and remark-able," might with justice be added to both nouns. For Anna Carlotta Leffler, the author of "Sónya Kova-lévsky," was no less gifted than the subject of the biog-raphy, and it is for this reason that, by way of introduction, we here give a sketch of her life founded on the following works: an inedited autobiography, kindly lent by the Duke of Cajanello, her second husband; a biography in the Swe-dish language, by Ellen Key, published by E. Bonnier, Stockholm; an article in the "Vie Contemporaine," entitled "Femmes du Nord," by Count Prozor; a biography, by Gegjerstam, in "Ord ô Bild"; and an introduction to the novels of Anna Carlotta Leffler, by the Duchess of Andrea (Italian edition, Loescher and Co.).

Anna Carlotta was the only daughter of J. A. Leffler, a Swedish rector, and was born on October 1, 1849. From her mother, the daughter of a minister named Mittag, she

---

[1] Since this biographical introduction was written, we have become acquainted with a biography of Anna Carlotta Leffler, written by Madame Laura Marholm in her "Buch der Frauen," which contains many erroneous facts and data, and judgments which prove that the writer has never really known Anna Car-lotta Leffler, but has gathered her information from impure sources.

inherited the literary tendencies which showed themselves so early, that, when only six years old, she dictated a little tale to her brother Fritz, which the lad wrote down.

The little girl grew up in an atmosphere of tender affection, equally beloved by her parents and by her three brothers — Göesta Mittag-Leffler, who afterward became an eminent mathematical professor in his own country, and also obtained a doctor's degree at Oxford; Arthur, who became an architect, and Fritz.

The latter was nearest to her in age, and was her constant playfellow, in whose company she enjoyed summer trips to Folglelos on the Vettern Lake, which were repeated yearly up to 1858, and looked forward to by the children, during the long winters spent in Stockholm, with longing and delight.

During these sojourns in the beautiful scenery of Vettern Lake, Anna Carlotta imbibed the love of Sweden, its lakes and mountains, which remained true and strong even when she was transplanted to the fairer regions of the South.

Her intimate companionship with her brothers, and participation in their studies, were of great influence on Anna Carlotta's character. She became a frank, intrepid girl, free from all feminine caprice, capable of simple, loyal friendship, looking at life with a wider charity.

As a young girl, she was of a placid and amiable disposition, and became a favorite with all the pupils of the Wallenska school, which she attended for some years. Her masters praised her for several compositions in Swedish, but offended her by hinting that her brothers must have helped her. Even during her school years she indulged in writing fiction, and the strong religious impression she received at her confirmation found expression in a never-published romance, which she was busy writing from her fifteenth to her seventeenth year.

Very wisely her brothers would not allow her to publish her first attempts; they rather encouraged her to study earnestly the language, history, and literature of her native land, and thus saved her from the peril of dilettantism.

20

But both they and her parents never denied her that admiring sympathy which is so welcome to all young writers.

In autumn, 1869, under the pseudonym of "Carlot," she
published a collection of tales entitled "By Chance," which
were well received by the public. In 1872 she married,
under peculiar circumstances, Mr. G. Edgren, with whom
she lived like an affectionate and tenderly-loved sister.
She reserved full liberty to dedicate herself to a literary
life, but never neglected the duties of the mistress of a
household.

The excellent financial conditions in which she lived, and
the high position she held, not only enabled her to pursue
the vocation to which she felt herself called, but also gave
her abundant opportunity of frequenting society, without,
however, wasting her strength on mere frivolities.

She grew in experience, her imagination became more
fecund, and her literary development made great progress.
Yet some deeper aspirations of her soul remained unsatis-
fied, and the traces of this want may be found in the thirst
for independence, for a personal life freer from conventionality, depicted in her drama, "The Actress," and in
"Elfvan," now that their true authorship is known. But
at the time of their appearance this of course was unnoticed, except by her intimate friends.

"The Actress" was represented on the stage in 1873;
"Henpecked" and "The Curate" in 1876; "Elfvan" in
1880.

"The Actress," though it was played at the Stockholm
during a whole winter, was never suspected to be the work
of a woman, and no one would have believed it possible
that a girl only twenty-three years of age, who had never
been in a theater above two or three times in her life, could
have produced such a drama. Her parents, during their
daughter's early youth, considered theater-going a luxury,
and her own religious convictions forbade her to indulge
in such a pleasure often.

In this first work Anna Carlotta expressed the idea which
dominated her life; an idea set forth by her long before

Ibsen wrote " The Doll's House." It was that love, in a
woman, must be subordinated to duty, not in the limited
sense of conjugal duty, but in the wide sense of duty to
oneself and to mankind.

Contemporaneously with her dramatic works, the young
author wrote short stories, descriptions of travel, essays,
etc., principally for the " New Illustrated Journal," of
Stockholm.

Her works had already excited attention when, in 1882,
she first published a collection of tales under her own name.
The book was entitled " From Life " (a title that was added
to all her later works), and made an immense impression.
At one stroke Anna Carlotta Leffler acquired an eminent
place in northern literature — due, no doubt, partly to the
fact that she had never habituated the public to associate
her name with the miniature literary attempts of a beginner.

By translation into Danish, Russian, German, and other
languages, her name became famous abroad as one of the
best Swedish writers of the time. Many of her dramas
were represented on different Northern stages, and even in
Germany.

Not long ago her comedy, " A Charity Fair," was translated into Italian. Benedetto Croce, a distinguished Nea-
politan critic, wrote an introduction to this publication.
It is owing to the purely Swedish character of her first
works that the social life of Sweden began to excite interest in Europe.[1]

In 1883, the second volume of " From Life " was published. It was written in a freer manner, with fine sar-
casm, and greater knowledge, but the public cried out
against the tendency of some of the stories. " At Strife
with Society" and "Aurora Bunge," the two most full of
genius, were called " scandalous."

But the adverse critics laid down their arms on the appearance of the novel " Gustav, the Pastor," which was rich
in true Swedish humor.

[1] The writer seems to have forgotten Frederika Bremer and
Emilie Flygare-Carlén.—I. F. H.

Anna Carlotta possessed a very sensitive literary conscience, and if she sometimes disobeyed its behests, it was only out of consideration for her family, who were wounded by the criticism to which she was exposed. But when she felt that the criticism was just, she was always modestly willing to revise her work.

Gradually the young author grew more courageous in representing real life, and began to touch on the problems of modern life.

But she never sympathized with "party," nor became the center of a fanatic literary circle such as she has been falsely represented to have been. As her literary works became more important, and her fame increased, criticism grew more virulent, and even among her greatest admirers discussion arose as to her real meaning. Some said that her entire personality was to be found in her writings, while the fact is that those produced later, and the change in her own being, have shown the error of this opinion. Others, and they were the most numerous, saw in all her novels and romances nothing but a struggle for the emancipation of woman, thus trying to limit within the narrow sphere of a single aim the large and liberal ideas of a writer who, though displaying quite a special individuality, was thoroughly objective.

The most common opinion was indeed that Anna Carlotta Leffler fought for the emancipation of woman with more courage and energy than any other writer, and this opinion was confirmed by the fact that around her gathered all the pioneers of the new school, all the most illustrious champions of the woman question, and precisely at that epoch the emancipation of woman was passionately discussed in Sweden. Anna Carlotta's house was the rendezvous for all the adherents of the new literature, who rendered her homage, not only and not so much as a writer, but principally as a woman who had raised her voice, and obtained a hearing, among the most famous men in Sweden. She was certainly impelled toward the promulgators of the rights of woman by her lively sympathy with the cause in its moral and social aspects, but she kept herself free from any party spirit, and her literary sphere belonged to a larger and more serene field of thought.

But there was another thing that seemed to prove those to be right who, at all costs, sought to imprison Anna Carlotta within the strict limits of the woman question, and this was her manner of regarding and understanding love in the abstract, a manner to which she was led by all the woman movement.

Love, at this time, seemed to her only an episode of life, *not* life's essence, or, so to speak, the life of life. Her works seemed to be wanting in something indefinable, and this something was the intimate and complete conception of the sentiment only obtained by the absolute abandonment of the soul to love. In the story " Doubt," and another one, " At Strife with Society," very much is said, and well said, *about* love ; but love itself is only seen by glimpses, as if the author deliberately wanted to deny to her own soul the knowledge of an invading power that she almost feared. And, in fact, it was only later in life that she possessed the entire and perfect knowledge of the power of love.

The famous representatives of Northern literature, who met at Anna Carlotta's house to discuss all things under the sun, were put at their ease by the sympathizing amiability of their hostess, who gave the impress of her personality to the conversation, yet was as ready to listen as to speak. She often displayed, however, a coldness and pride of manner due to a shyness which she never entirely overcame, but these soon vanished on more intimate acquaintance.

In 1884 the young writer began to travel, taking with her a dear friend, Julia Kjellberg, now Madame von Vollmar. She obtained many introductions to different circles in foreign lands partly through Madame Sónya Kovalévsky, who had come to Stockholm in 1883, and with whom she had become most intimate.

Thus Anna Carlotta became acquainted, especially in England, with some of the most noted personages, and acquired new ideas.

20*

The new impulse given to her literary talent is shown in her description of travel in " From Modern London "; in the above-mentioned drama, " A Charity Fair," and in " True Women," published in English by S. French, London.

This drama, which seemed to have been written in favor of the emancipation of married women, was really the outcome of the author's pity for the domestic troubles of one very dear to her. After its publication many regarded her as a despiser of men, an amazon thirsting for battle ; but they would have become aware of their mistake had they seen the tears in the author's eyes when she received the thanks of her friend for her expressions of noble indignation, a feeling which was a force in her writings, and was not the cold indignation proper to persons who only regard fictitious life from within their four walls, but the warm resentment against the wrongs of actual sufferers.

In 1886 our author published a romance entitled " A Summer Story," which has quite lately been translated and published in German, and which, more than any other of her productions, contains the personal feelings of the writer.

In this tale love already begins to appear as an actual force in human existence, as a thing that has tyrannous rights able to balance all other intellectual exigencies. Here still these intellectual exigencies triumph, and love is enslaved, but in all the life of Ulla, the heroine of the romance, there is a lament and homesickness for the very love which she would conquer and trample upon, but which destroys the balance of her existence, and condemns her to a continual and sterile struggle between her old self and the new spirit born within her, because the latter is not so fully incorporated with love as to give it the victory over the former state of feeling. This story shows that a woman who sacrifices love to personal dignity — a sacrifice of which the writer nevertheless approves — can never be happy.

In the biography of Sónya Kovalévsky, now before the reader, Anna Carlotta Leffler relates the circumstances of her intimacy with that gifted woman, and therefore we need not touch on the subject here.

At the beginning of 1888 she went to Africa with her brother, Professor Mittag-Leffler, and his wife, Signe, to attend the Mathematical Congress in Algiers. During this journey, while returning through Italy, she met, for the first time, with a mathematician, professor at the Naples University, who had long been in correspondence with her brother.

This was Signor Pasquale del Pezzo, the Duke of Caja-nello. Their acquaintance ripened into a true and tender love, which, after the divorce of Anna Carlotta, and the overcoming of many difficulties made by the Duke's family, who objected to his future wife as a Protestant, was finally crowned by a happy marriage, which was celebrated in Rome, in May, 1890.

Previously to this, in 1889, Anna Carlotta published a new collection of tales also under the common title of "From Life." The Duke and Duchess of Cajanello, after their marriage, spent a large portion of the year at Djurs-holm, near Stockholm.

The now happy woman shortly published a romance, "Womanliness and Erotics," inspired by the new senti-ments and sensations which crowded upon her, and also a comedy called "This Love!"

This romance was much talked of, and was criticized with more than usual acrimony. The author herself considered it the most complete and vivid manifestation of her own personality. The first part had been written seven years previously, and, at one point of the heroine's destiny, there arose a question to which the writer at that time knew no answer. She felt that there was missing the real explana-tion of all the psychological evolutions in her heroine — that Alie who was awaiting the full development of her per-sonality from the love that must finally awaken and subju-gate her. But how, and under what circumstances, would Alie love? — she "who was so much convinced that the reality could never afford her anything but delusions that

she shrank back from all opportunities of executing what
she had dreamed of."

The author herself did not yet know; but then came
that crisis in her own life which rejuvenized and trans-
formed her, giving her the power to reply to the question
that had arisen in the life of her heroine. Alie *loves*, because Anna Carlotta at last understood what love was —
the love that rids life of all disharmony and all hesitation,
and, from the perfect balance and fusion of the feelings,
evolves the still intact but renovated and completed individual. " Womanliness and Erotics " indeed reveals the
bliss derived by its author from an affection for the first
time felt and requited.

After this, the Duchess wrote a drama in three acts, entitled " Domestic Happiness "; some character sketches ; and
a fantastic dramatic poem, " The Search after Truth,"
which, under the influence of the rich Southern imagination
of her husband, displays a force of artistic representation
not found in her early productions.

When Sónya Kovalévsky died in 1891, Anna Carlotta forsook all other work in order to write the biography of her
friend. It was her own *last* work, and was generally considered to be one of the most exact and perfect psychological studies to be found in contemporary literature, and, at
the same time, a delightful and genial work of art.

The newly married Duchess of Cajanello felt quite at
home in Italy, and was never afflicted by home-sickness.
She was already perfectly acquainted with the Italian language, and surrounded herself with a select circle of scientific and literary men, old and new friends of her husband.

One of those who frequented the Duke's house in Naples
describes it as full of sunshine and happiness. The Duchess, tall and fair, had the charm of simple dignity, and at
the same time the grace of cordiality. The Duke, on the
other hand, had the ease and unconventionality of manner
proper to a man of science, and one who had broken with
the prejudices of his aristocratic class.

Much as Anna Carlotta had been beloved by her early

friends in Sweden, she was now even more attractive in her new-found happiness.

The bliss of the husband and wife was completed by the birth of a son in June, 1892, and the letters written by the young mother during the summer of that year are proof that she had attained a height of human felicity which almost made her tremble. And indeed the last years of her life were a luminous progress to ever intenser joys. First the expectation of maternity, then maternity itself, beautified and consecrated by the love which shone forth in her eyes and her smile — by the complete happiness that caused her mature nature to bud and blossom anew, as if it had never before enjoyed a springtime. With the cradle of her child close beside her, she wrote with ever-increasing delight, interrupting herself every now and then to attend to her infant, and again resuming her work without the least impatience. There also stood one who awaited the result of her work with intense sympathy, ready to hear her read the freshly-written pages, which she communicated with the calmness induced by the certainty of being comprehended. She had trembled at all this happiness, and she was snatched away just as she had tasted its full sweetness.

She had been in *villeggiatura* on the island of Capri, had returned home and set her house in order for the winter, and was preparing for a long period of peace and quiet, during which she would devote herself to literature, and commence a new romance which she was meditating, to be entitled "Narrow Horizons."

For the first time for many years she felt at perfect rest within and without, enriched by new experiences, viewing the things of life with clearer eyes and able, as she remarked to a friend, "to write a great book on a broad basis."

On Sunday, the 16th of October, she wrote a happy letter to her mother and brother, expressing her delight in her work, her hope for continued good health.

The very next day her husband was forced to insist on

her giving up all work; on laying down her pen in the middle of a sentence in order to nurse herself, for she had confessed to a rapidly increasing indisposition. In vain she exclaimed, " Oh, no! I have still so much to write!" She was obliged to yield to her husband's entreaties, and laid down her pen — never to take it up again. That pen had just corrected the last proofs of " Sónya Kovalévsky."

Anna Carlotta had been seized with acute peritonitis, and, in spite of all efforts on the part of physicians, and the most tender nursing, succumbed to the terrible malady five days later, on the 21st of October, 1893, at the age of only forty-one years.

Anna Carlotta Leffler, Duchess of Cajanello, was more than a distinguished writer. She was a woman void of vanity and pretense, utterly sincere; strong, but not violent; possessed of great moral courage; of a calm, cheerful, sanguine disposition ; of perfect sanity of mind and of body; regarding the problems of human life in such a simple manner as excited the admiration of her friends. She knew nothing of the hysterics and vagaries of the " new woman," and, more than all else, she possessed a thoroughly kind heart, and was so sweet and loving that those who knew her well forgot the genius in the perfect woman. Her ideal of happiness in this world had been realized. She had arrived at the summit of her desires, — husband, child, a happy home, a true sphere of work, — and ceased to be.

APPENDICES

APPENDIX A

The date of Madame Kovalévsky's birth is differently given by different persons as 1850, 1851, 1853. Her intimate friend Julia V. Lermontoff, who is frequently mentioned in these pages, fixes it in 1853. Her tutor, F. F. Malevitch, on the contrary, speaks of beginning to teach her in 1858, "when she was eight years old." The marriage in 1868 would seem to confirm M. Malevitch's date.— I. F. H.

APPENDIX B

Madame Kovalévsky's "Recollections of Childhood" were published in Swedish under the title of "The Raevsky Sisters." —I. F. H.

APPENDIX C

She was in Odessa for the purpose of reading a paper before the Congress of Naturalists.—I. F. H.

APPENDIX D

By Tegnér.—I. F. H.

APPENDIX E

I think the Duchess of Cajanello is mistaken on this point. Marriage with a gipsy would not entail the loss of title. The omission of this statement from the Russian translation of the duchess's biography confirms me in my view.—I. F. H.

APPENDIX F

Aides-de-camp. — I. F. H.

APPENDIX G

While yet a mere child, but already an acute observer, she had witnessed the great crisis of the liberation of the Russian serfs. In her romance, "The Vorontzoff Family," she tells the impression produced on the noble proprietors by this crisis. The daughter of one of these proprietors becomes a nihilist, and is taken a prisoner to Siberia. The author read this book aloud to a scientific circle in Stockholm shortly before her death, and produced great enthusiasm. Fortunately the manuscript was found complete, and will be published.

Of the other romance, the "Væ Victis," only one chapter was published. Its fundamental conception reveals, more than any other work, its author's nature.

APPENDIX H

Madame Kovalévsky very accurately described this fluttering to and fro between mathematics and literature in a letter to Madame Schabelskoy. "I understand," she says, "your surprise at my being able to busy myself simultaneously with literature and mathematics. Many who have never had an opportunity of knowing any more about mathematics confound it with arithmetic, and consider it an arid science. In reality, however, it is a science which requires a great amount of imagination, and one of the leading mathematicians of our century states the case quite correctly when he says that it is impossible to be a mathematician without being a poet in soul. Only, of course, in order to comprehend the accuracy of this definition, one must renounce the ancient prejudice that a poet must invent something which does not exist, that imagination and invention are identical. It seems to me that the poet has only to perceive that which others do not perceive, to look deeper than others look. And the mathematician must do the same thing. As for myself, all my life I have been unable to decide for which I had the greater inclination, mathematics or literature. As soon as my brain grows wearied of purely abstract speculations it immediately begins to incline to observations on life, to narrative; and, *vice versa*, everything in life begins to appear insignificant and uninteresting, and only the eternal, immutable laws of science attract me. It is very possible that I might have accomplished more in either of these lines if I had devoted myself exclusively to it; nevertheless I cannot give up either of them completely." (From Ellen Key's "Biography of the Duchess di Cajanello.")—I. F. H.

APPENDIX I

Her work was entitled "On a Particular Case of the Problem of Rotation of a Heavy Body around a Fixed Point." The prize was doubled (to five thousand francs), on account of the "quite extraordinary service rendered to mathematical physics by this work," which the Academy of Sciences pronounced "a remarkable work." The competing dissertations were signed by mottoes, not with names, and the jury of the Academy made the award in utter ignorance that the winner was a woman. Her dissertation was printed, by order of the Academy, in the "Mémoires des Savants Étrangers." In the following year Madame Kovalévsky received a prize of fifteen hundred kroner from the Stockholm Academy, for two works connected with the foregoing. ("S. V. Kovalévsky," published by the Mathematical Society of the University of Moscow.)—I. F. H.

APPENDIX J

Madame Kovalévsky calls herself "Tánya Raevsky" in the Swedish translation of her "Recollections of Childhood."— I. F. H.

APPENDIX K

According to what Mittag Leffler says, Sónya had not thought of abandoning scientific study entirely. In the last conversation she had with him, the day before she was taken with her short and fatal illness, she told him of a plan for a new mathematical work, which she believed would be the most important she had ever written. According to her usual manner, considering herself gifted with *second sight* in all intellectual things, she said she had divined the solution of certain profound enigmas, which would open out a new path in the field of thought.

APPENDIX L

Russian Sunday-schools are far from being identical in character with American Sunday-schools. They are schools where working-men who are occupied during the week can obtain instruction in the elementary and other branches of *secular* learning. Religion is taught in all schools on week-days—I. F. H.

APPENDIX M

The newspapers mentioned her under the name by which she was known in Sweden—" *our* Professor Sónya."—I. F. H.

APPENDIX N

In the commemoration made by Mittag Leffler, as Rector of the Stockholm University, after the death of Sónya, he thus speaks of her influence on her students:

"She came to us from the center of modern science full of faith and enthusiasm for the ideas of her great master of Berlin, the venerable old man who has outlived his favorite pupil. Her works, which all belong to the same order of ideas, have shown, by new discoveries, the power of Weierstrass's system. We know with what inspiriting zeal she explained these ideas, what importance she attributed to them in resolving the most difficult problems. And how willingly she gave the riches of her knowledge, the genial divinations of her mind, to each student who had the will and the power to receive them! Her simple personality, free from any trace of scientific affectation, and the eagerness with which she sought to comprehend the individuality of every man, induced all her students to confide to her, almost at the first meeting, their own most hidden thoughts and sentiments; their scientific doubts and hopes; their hesitancies before new systems; their sorrows, disillusions, and dreams of happiness. With such qualities she entered on her teaching, and on such bases she founded her relations to her scholars."